STRANDS

IN THE

FATE OF THE DEHMI: BOOK ONE

— K.T. HOST —

K.T. Host

k.t.hostauthor@gmail.com

Cover Design by Getcovers

Contents

Content Warnings

This book is written for adults ages 18+. It is not suitable for children.

This novel contains the following situations that may be uncomfortable for some readers: domestic violence, sexual assault, vulgar language, stalking, explicit sexual content, derogatory language (specifically towards women and gay men), detailed descriptions of gory violence, and death. I understand that these situations and terms are upsetting to some readers. However, there are events in this book that exist to serve as a glimpse into some of the more horrible realities people face every day. Sensitivity readers familiar with these circumstances have been consulted, but you as the reader reserve the final judgment on what you are comfortable with. This list is not exhaustive and other triggering circumstances or topics may be present within the work without any further warning beyond this point.

Please prioritize your own mental health and read at your own risk.

Thank you and take care.

To anyone whose brain is their own worst enemy.

I see you, I feel you, I am you.

You are not alone.

Prologue

- Conall -

A bone-shattering cold arrests the air in my lungs. It's my first indication that I'm on my way to meet with the Paragons of Death, deep in the bowels of the Haven. The pair of deities ruling over the Underworld are my most frequent patrons, but they are not the only ones to ever visit me. As my breath fogs in front of me and my feet crunch on a light layer of frigid hoarfrost, I'm wishing death was associated with more pleasant conditions. The steps into the Sacrarium are treacherous enough in the dim lighting without being slick with the ice melting and reforming beneath my boots.

I reach the landing and the iron doors part in front of me to reveal a spartan, yet comfortable room. The spicy scent of incense weaves tantalizingly out of the open entrance. The round walls of the Sacrarium are the same bare gray stone as the steps I slipped and slid down. They are adorned with ten ornate banners depicting the crests of the nine lower members of The Council and the joint crest of the Underworld. Three plush armchairs are currently situated in the center of the room beneath a crystal chandelier that glows with the purest moonlight despite being deep underground. This room never ceases to make me awestruck, but tonight my awe is overshadowed by a strange sense of foreboding.

Esraa and Amon, the queen and king of the Underworld and the two most powerful beings in all the worlds, have already taken their seats across from the one remaining chair in the center of the room. Initially, the two seem to be pillars of opposite virtues—Esraa with her willowy frame and skin made of the pastel shades of evening clouds, her face the epitome of serenity; Amon with his imposing brawn and deep, midnight complexion accentuating the scowl of a soldier on the warpath. The truth, however, is they are both two halves of the same whole. The duo exist in perfect harmony with one another, overseeing their domain with a hand both comforting and condemning in equal measure.

As I pass through the doorway, the Paragons look at me with eyes that hold small flames and twin smiles promising an eternity of peace and security. Despite what others may say, the Underworld rulers have always felt comforting to me. Esraa and Amon work to ensure the Underworld is a place of rest for souls to spend their eternities. Because of them, those who would prey on the innocent pass into the fires of the Pit and are consumed with pain forever, while the rest of their realm is blanketed with peace and security. That's admirable, not frightening.

I bow low before taking a seat in the open chair. "Evening, Esraa, Amon," I say quietly, nodding at both of them in turn. "I hope you're well."

Amon relaxes back in his chair, but Esraa reaches out and touches my hand with her long fingers. "Yes, my child," she replies in a soft voice reminiscent of smoke and starlight, "we are well. Thank you for meeting us so late—we apologize for waking you. Time is hard to keep track of between the worlds."

"I understand," I say, keeping my worries about this meeting to myself. It is not uncommon for the deities to show up at odd hours; this alone is no reason to be concerned.

Then why am I so uneasy?

I take a subtle breath, ensuring my face remains composed. It wouldn't do to embarrass myself by getting flustered. I'm no newly assigned dehmi receiving their first mission.

"How are your tasks going? I trust things aren't too overwhelming here?" Amon leans forward, resting his elbows on his knees as he speaks to me.

Through the wispy shadows surrounding his face, I can make out his twinkling gaze and the pleasant smile. Others see the Underworld duo as a force close to terrifying, but I've always found comfort in their soft voices and warm gazes. On this night, however, the strange sense of calm they bring me isn't enough to banish this uncomfortable sinking feeling deep within my gut.

"No, Amon," I reply. "Tasks have been fairly straightforward recently, and the Haven has been as welcoming as always. Domenic and Marguerite make sure of that."

The dual heads of our Haven have much in common with Esraa and Amon. At first glance, Dom's stern visage and Margie's welcoming arms are also complete opposites. Spend a few days with our family, however, and any guest soon sees their outward differences are nothing compared to the matching golden hearts they both carry within.

Esraa clears her throat, the delicate sound resembling piano chords. "My dear, as much as I would like to continue to talk about life until the moon sinks below the horizon here on Earth, we unfortunately have a bit of a unique situation on our hands." She shifts uncomfortably as her companion grips the arms of his chair with pale knuckles.

A tense pause fills the room. Esraa sighs, her face taking on an oddly melancholic shadow as she waves her hand. The chill in the air grows ever colder, causing our breaths to twine in puffs of vapor in front of us. An oval of air the size of a large dinner plate thickens at her eye height. The ethereal lighting of the magic chandelier overhead dims as the space solidifies, turning a milky white.

I stiffen, clasping my hands in front of me while I await my newest task. The Avalleans are bathed in the glow of the clouded portal, their faces mirrored portraits of tight lips and creased brows. They look as uncomfortable as I am.

My heart begins to pound in my chest. I rub my sweaty palms on my pants. I've had several official meetings with Paragons, and none of them have ever looked uncomfortable when delivering a task. Esraa and Amon have more power than all the other members of the Avallean governing body. What could possibly be going on to make these two so upset?

Esraa twists her right hand as if she were turning a doorknob, and an image begins to form through the pale fog of the plate. I lean forward, elbows on knees, taking in the soundless vision.

A girl, roughly my age, sits at a stone table surrounded by colorful flowers. My breath catches slightly as she comes into focus. She has a strange sort of beauty, as though she's the otherworldly creature brought to this mundane planet, rather than me. Her heart-shaped face is adorned by huge, slate gray eyes, a delicate nose and a full mouth, all haloed with a wild mane of onyx curls. The girl tips her head back towards a robin's egg sky, laughing at something beyond my view, her rose-colored lips stretched into a wide, convincing smile.

At first glance, the pleasant scene unfolding in the vision confuses me, but as the girl leans forward and brushes her unruly black hair away from her face, I catch a glimpse of the storm clouds inside her eyes. A man's hand, slim and unwrinkled, reaches into view and cups her chin. The gesture could be mistaken as loving if not for the faint red marks forming beneath his fingertips. She turns in his direction and her captivating stare is once again hidden behind dark locks, but not before I glimpse the panic hidden in its depths. The visions always feel so real, I swear I can almost smell those flowers surrounding her.

The scene gently fades out into a swirl of gray smoke and begins to replay itself.

I am perplexed, but my heart aches for the strange woman. Her sadness is so potent, it hits me through space, time, and the magical barrier separating us. My powers are drawn to her pain, a magnetic tug that is equal parts irritating and exhilarating. I'm ready to get to work.

Shaking off the fugue I fell into while watching the vision, my gaze lifts towards the Paragons. Esraa's pastel skin is ashen, with Amon a wall of tense muscle beside her. I am used to maintaining a calm facade for my missions, but they spend most of their time sequestered in the Underworld or their Council chambers. I can read their pained faces like a book; they want to save the girl.

This is what we're here for: helping the mortal worlds, the organisms inhabiting them, and their struggling planets until we are called home. Until my day comes, I'm focused on completing as many tasks from The Council as possible. I want to leave this world better than it has ever been when I return to Avallea. And something involving this girl is my next assignment.

I ask the all-important question: "So, who is she?"

I'm itching to gain any information possible. The sad-eyed girl deserves more than whatever she's being subjected to at the hands of that man. His possessive grip, secure enough in his power over her to be leaving marks in broad daylight, is vivid in my mind's eye.

"Her name is Valorie Vargas. She is twenty years old." Amon murmurs. Esraa exhales a shuddering breath. Both Paragons look to be on the verge of tears, and my heart stutters out a staccato beat as I battle with the unwelcome dread crawling its way along my spine, threatening to overwhelm me.

There is no reason for this unease. The girl is fine, or she will be once I get to her. That's how this process works. It's seamless. Find the person, provide the necessary help, move on. Occasionally I provide covert assistance to a medical agency instead, but the steps are the same no matter the target.

I rock back and forth in my chair slightly as I speak, my pent up energy making me itch. I'm always impatient when I am receiving a new task, but this strange churning in my gut is making me more anxious to set off than usual. "She's clearly caught in some type of domestic situation, based on her proximity to the male in the vision and her reaction to his presence. So, I'm guessing my task is to help her start over somewhere. Am I supplying her with information to escape? Finding an inconspicuous way to heal her wounds? Tipping off the local authorities?"

"No, sweet boy, it's none of those." A single tear finally escapes the edge of Esraa's eye as she meets my bewildered stare. Her desolation is so forceful, the whole world seems to dim. "Your task is to kill her."

Chapter 1

Beginnings

- Valorie -

Two and a Half Months Later

Some day, one of my idiotic decisions is going to get me killed, I think to myself as I trip over a loose stone hidden in the gloom of one of the dimly lit pathways through campus. Someone—an engineer, or focus group member, or one of my parents—should have told the dean they needed more lamp posts along these smaller side routes when they did the latest landscaping redesign. I can barely see my hand in front of me. But then again, how would they have known? Who else is dumb enough to be walking around here at five in the morning?

When I offered to help my mom move her equipment before my first class, I didn't think she would want me up before sunrise. I figured I would run over to the Biological and Biomedical Sciences building after breakfast, grab a couple boxes for her, and walk her to her new office and faculty lab on the other side of the building. But apparently, that's not what she envisioned happening. Now I'm up before dawn, tripping over my feet in the almost-dark. I hope she at least bought a box of doughnuts from the twenty-four hour shop down the street she knows I love.

I rub my gritty eyes and shove my hands back into my jacket pockets, looking around at the tree-lined cobblestones and manicured green spaces of Sycamore University. In the lush darkness, lit by the light of the occasional antique street-lamp peeking through the trees, the campus looks like something out of a fairy tale. The soft lighting sparkles off the steel and glass that make up the buildings of the Science Quarter. This section of the campus is the newest one, and it looks radically different from the mixture of historic marble and brick buildings found in the other areas of the school. The older buildings are beautiful and majestic, but I have to admit the sleek, modern style of these new behemoths is amazing to behold.

Especially when you're running on about four hours of broken sleep.

As I approach the front of my mother's laboratory building, I slow to a stop, flop onto one of the wrought-iron benches surrounded by flowers that flank the entrance, and release an exhausted huff. The gathered dew soaks into the blue cotton of my skater dress, the cold droplets cutting straight through to my skin like icicles. The dress will dry, but I can't muster the energy to open my eyes and walk the last few steps to the door without a little break.

David kept me up until midnight last night sending memes to our group chat from some Netflix dating show he's always trying to get me to watch. He only stopped when I threatened to wake his boyfriend and the third member of our "Best Friends Forever" group chat, Charlie. Char is almost as much of a bear when he's woken up early as I am. Bringing him into the equation finally made David shut up so I could attempt to fight my brain and get a few hours of sleep before having to wake up at this ungodly hour to be a good daughter.

Despite living in their house, I rarely see Mom and Dad off-campus. Having two senior professors as parents means their days are filled with lecture, school events and conferences. When I was younger, they made an effort to be home by dinner and planned family vacations for every school holiday. Now that I'm an adult, however, they spend their time together on the road or in one of their offices most evenings.

The steady tapping of footsteps along the cement cuts through the quiet stillness. A low chuckle has me cracking one eye open to find Johnathan Sanderson in front of me, running a hand through his thinning sandy hair while he rifles through his black backpack with the other one.

"Hey, Professor Sanderson." I smile blearily as I stand up from my damp seat on the bench and yawn. Resting will have to wait. "How's my favorite Director of Biological Studies this morning?"

"Hello Valorie," he replies with a bashful smile. I've known Professor Sanderson since I was in diapers. He used to hold me for my mom and we would wander the halls while she graded papers her first year as a junior professor here at Sycamore. The man is practically a second father to me. "I'd be doing better if I could find my keys. I know they're in one of these pockets, but it's so hard to find them in the dark. You don't happen to have a spare on you, do you?"

"As a matter of fact, I do. But, we don't need it. Mom is inside already; it's lab moving day. Hence why I'm here at the ass crack of dawn instead of sleeping like a sane person." I throw him a wink and open the door closest to him with a bow and a flourish. I affect my most over-the-top, theater-hawker flair and intone, "After you, kind sir!"

"Why thank you, my dear! Whatever would I do without you?" he quips back as we walk together into the brightly lit entryway. My gaze drifts up through the hole cutting straight through the center of all fifteen floors of the building. A massive skylight in the center offers a beautiful, uninterrupted view of the early morning sky. The view never gets old, no matter how many times I see it.

We make our way into the elevator and tap the button for the thirteenth floor. The mirrored doors close with a soft hiss and we whoosh upwards towards the floor of laboratories reserved for senior faculty. After a few seconds of comfortable silence, the elevator gives a soft ping, and Sanderson and I part ways. He kisses me lightly on the forehead, ruffles my neck-length black curls, and turns left towards his lab, likely to spend his morning grading papers.

I stifle another yawn and turn down the opposite hall towards my mother's new room in the right wing. Through the large plate glass windows making up the interior wall of the lab, I can already spy her directing a small army of teacher's assistants like a mass of terrified worker drones. My mother is a very sweet person, but heaven help the poor soul that messes with the organization in her lab space. Those poor assistants are probably close to tears by now and certainly walking on eggshells.

I fling open the door and several of the lab-coated juniors prove my point by audibly sighing in relief. My laugh echoes through the partially-decorated room as I head towards my mom and her charges gathered around the machinery at the rear of the lab.

"What are you doing?" Mom asks the blond-haired boy in front of her in a soft, firm voice. The tone may seem unassuming, but it means she's serious as a heart attack.

My mother never yells, ever. I can count on one hand the number of times I've heard her raise her voice. You'd think this would make her less scary than a normal parent, but it's quite the opposite. When my mom is mad, anyone who values their life should run for the hills. She always says lesser people shout because they have something to prove, because they want to be the biggest presence in the room. Mom is frequently the smallest person in the room, with her diminutive frame barely passing five feet, but she's always a formidable presence. I've seen her put a room full of men in their place more than once without ever having to raise her voice. My dad is a giant mammoth of a man who is the world's biggest goof, despite his intimidating visage. Mom, however, she's power, a firecracker in a travel-sized package. I'm here to save her unlucky crew from the force that is Justine Vargas.

"Mommy," I singsong from across the room, smiling from ear to ear, "are you terrorizing the townsfolk again? I can't afford for you to scare them away before they can help us move. I'm not carrying your centrifuge." The last time mom moved labs, I got stuck hauling her heavy centrifuge up four flights of stairs while she reminded me to keep it level. Repeatedly. From two inches behind me.

Never again. That's what the underlings are for.

My mom laughs, shooing the flock of assistants towards the elevator with instructions to get more boxes from her old lab downstairs. "Where is your father?" she calls to me without turning around. "He's supposed to be here by now. You and I have classes to get to at half past seven; he said he would oversee the moving while I was gone since he only has afternoon lectures today."

As if he was summoned, the familiar smell of eucalyptus aftershave and old parchment surrounds me seconds before I'm enveloped in a crushing bear hug. "I think I found him!" I laugh. Wrapping my arms around my father, I pull in a deep breath. He picks me up and swings me around the same way he's done with every hug for as long as I can remember. Dad puts me back on my feet and kisses my forehead like Sanderson did not long ago, his smile creasing his entire face.

Of course, my anxiety chooses this time to rear its horrific head, despite there being no catalyst for it here. An uncomfortable acid roils in my gut and sweat beads on my palms. I cringe inward, wishing there was some way for me to hide from the devil in my own mind. If my dad notices my sudden change, he doesn't say. He's used to it by now; years of therapy can only help so much.

Something feels...off about today. I wish I could stay here, nestled safely in the love emanating from my parents. If I could, I'd pretend I'm still a child and avoid the stress of the rest of the world for a while.

"Kenneth," mom calls, "come over here so I can explain how I want things laid out before Valorie and I have to leave."

"Yes dear," my father sighs dramatically with a conspiratorial wink in my direction. He crosses the room and sticks himself to Mom's side like glue. They do everything together—companies know to book accommodations for two when they secure one of them as a speaker—and never seem any less in love than they were the day they met on this very campus over two and a half decades ago. Having a love as deep as my parents' is the dream for most people, myself included.

The next two hours are a blur of shuffling boxes up from my mother's old lab in the basement and getting them put away in the exact places she has envisioned for them. My parents and I pass the time sharing stories about our summer vacations and our plans for the year with the student volunteers. Several of the assistants are in the Organic Chemistry course I took the previous semester, and I offer up my phone number in case they need help with the material. It's the least I can do after they've suffered through mom's regime this morning.

Before I know it, an alarm is blaring from the phone in mom's front pocket. I sigh tiredly as I set down my final load of boxes and rub my sore shoulders. I would have dropped them the second her phone went off if she wouldn't have killed me for it.

"All right, time for my two brilliant ladies to head off to class! This dumb brute will take over and make sure all your fancy science doodads get safely placed in what I'm sure will be all the wrong places," Dad jokes, chuckling to himself. In his mind, he's the funniest man in the world, no matter how many times we groan and heckle at his jokes.

Dad towers over my mother and I, his gray eyes glimmering with mirth as he shuts the door behind us. I may have gotten my stature from mom—although thankfully I'm not quite as tiny as she is, but my looks are almost all dad.

The door clicks behind us and she tugs on a lock of my hair. I look over at her, falling into step with her as we move towards the elevator, and catch her smiling as I let out a huge, jaw-cracking yawn.

I desperately need to find a quiet corner to nap in for a bit later.

"Your father has a late lecture tonight and I'll be at the biomedicine mixer to celebrate the new labs. You'll be alright for dinner?" She pushes the call button for the elevator as we reach the end of the hall.

"Yeah, mom," I reply, entering the steel box and thumbing the button for the ground floor. "I'll probably hang with David and Charlie tonight. Maybe play some video games, order out, the usual."

"No plans with Xavier?" The sound of his name makes me jerk.

Mom is trying to be nonchalant but her sideways glance gives away her true motive. She's fishing for details. She always blames her "thirst for information" on being a scientist, but I know the truth. She's nosier than an old woman in church.

We walk out of the elevator and through the pristine lobby, now lit with the glow of early daylight through the glass ceiling. Overachieving students are already beginning to file through the front entrance in preparation for the morning's first lectures, several of them calling greetings to my mother and I as we pass through the doors and out into the morning. Science students are always showing up early to catch up on some project or check in on an experiment before classes begin for the day. We're an insular community, since many of us don't have much time for social lives outside of lectures and labs. I'm one of the lucky ones that manages to make time for friends after work and classes are finished, but I vividly remember those frazzled days as an underclassman.

"I'd rather hang out with my friends," I mumble my overdue response under my breath.

"What was that honey?" my mother asks as she fumbles around in her enormous purse to find her sunglasses. I slip my own pair of aviators off the collar of my dress and shield my eyes from the glare.

"Oh nothing, Mom, I just said I think he's busy." My nonexistent relationship with my ex-boyfriend is a subject I don't want to broach with my mother at a quarter past seven on a Monday. The simple possibility of dealing with one of her talks about Xavier is enough to turn my stomach and make me sweat buckets, but my mom doesn't understand that. I'll need a full serving of caffeine and a real meal in me if she's going to start prying for answers again. After the last time, I barely managed to leave the room before I started shaking harder than a sapling in a hurricane. If I get my way, she'll never know the truth of why Xavier and I split up. Or why he keeps coming around when he's not wanted.

Even if the reasons might finally make her shut up about him.

I peck her on the cheek and wave goodbye, catching sight of a familiar turquoise shock of hair coming towards me through the crowd that's crisscrossing between buildings like threads in a spider's web.

"David, if you brought me caffeine you'll be my best friend," I call out to him as he emerges from the throng. I look up into his warm, honey gaze and prop a hand on my hip as I pretend to contemplate the status of our friendship.

"I've been your best friend for fourteen years, and I'm dating your other best friend, so I think you'll love me either way or you'll be one lonely girl on this lovely summer morning! But, fear not, I have taken pity on you because I love you." He throws a carefree arm around me without breaking stride and holds out a yellow Styrofoam cup from the campus coffee shop. Steam rises in curls from the opening in the lid and "Vally" is written on the side with a little heart in David's impeccable handwriting. How he gets the baristas to let him wield their Sharpie is beyond me, but David is self-assured to the point of hubris. He spins his confidence into a magical disposition that's impossible to resist.

"If you weren't already my favorite person you'd definitely be at the top of the list now, weirdo," I say, taking the drink before he can hold it above my head and taunt me with it.

I inhale the warm, nutty scent of my favorite latte order and sigh happily, not knowing how I would survive without my best friend. The first scalding sip hits the back of my throat. Though the coffee is hot enough to blister, I'm too impatient to wait until it's a less dangerous temperature. Caffeine doesn't usually do much for me, but on a morning like this I need all the help I can get.

"I've got to keep my position secure!" he jokes, linking his arm through mine. "Lets go over my highlight reel, to be on the safe side.

Remember when I saved you from those creepy guys outside of the Fall Out Boy concert a few years ago?"

"Yeah, well remember when *I* saved *you* from being bullied on the playground over and over again in elementary school? You were such a scrawny little dork, where would you be without me taking you under my wing?" He scruffs his knuckles through my hair, frizzing the top of my head faster than I can push him away.

"Plus, Charlie brought me a bagel with extra cream cheese last week, so your position might be on thin ice. Make sure to keep the gifts coming, just in case!" Our laughs intertwine, his loud bark and my tired chuckle. Another yawn plagues me, and I savor a deep drag of my coffee as we walk into the lecture hall for our first class of what promises to be an incredibly long day.

Chapter 2
Blending In

- Conall -

If there's one thing I cannot stand, it's forced complication. If something can be simple, let it be simple. Humans think simplicity is for children, but it's a mark of maturity to have the ability to cut the unnecessary extras out of a plan or process, leaving behind only the cogs needed for functionality. A simple system is a refined system. A simple plan is a safe one.

The American collegiate system has not received that memo.

I never thought I would be signing myself up for courses at another university—especially not one in North America—but when I received my task from Esraa and Amon in June, they mandated it be done as smoothly and painlessly as possible. Ending the life of an innocent is something only done under extreme circumstances. We're helpers, not assassins. Agents of the fate the Web weaves. And apparently the Web has decided Valorie Vargas' time is coming to an end.

This whole plan was Esraa's idea. Usually, members of The Council don't involve themselves in the planning; they lay out their end goal, head back to Avallea, and leave the logistics to the dehmi in charge. However, this is no ordinary mission. Esraa was nearly distraught at the thought of sending me out with this weight on my shoulders alone. The Paragons of the Underworld have always had a soft spot for me, though I don't know why. I may not like this job, but that has no bearing on my ability. I will get this done.

It was decided I will insert myself into the fringes of Valorie Vargas' life, become her acquaintance, and learn enough minutiae about her existence to pick a time to peacefully terminate it without any undue hardship to her, all before a full year passes. Which gives me a little over ten months to get this over with.

Simple enough...except all I can focus on is how taking a life is my least favorite part of this position.

I shake my head in an attempt to clear my mind as I make my way out of the early morning light and into the Administration building at Sycamore University, my booted footsteps soft against the shining black-and-white checkered floors. My goal is the admissions office, which the plaque next to the brushed steel elevator doors tells me is on the fifth floor of the large, brick building.

My reflection warbles and warps on the interior walls of the metal box as it glides upwards. It seems as though every surface in this building is polished, mirroring my hardened expression wherever I turn.

The gentle whirring of the elevator transitions into a faint chorus of some pop rock song coming from a speaker behind an office door as I emerge onto the fifth floor. Another helpful plaque sends me along a hall so heavily papered in fliers and staged alumni photographs that the cream paint beneath is nearly invisible.

"How can I help you?" the bottle-blond receptionist asks, swinging her feet off of the long front counter at the end of the corridor as I approach. The *Vogue* issue in front of her is already touting the so-called "hottest holiday trends" despite the fact that it is not quite September.

If I wanted predictions, I'd ask my sister. Gabrielle is much more reliable than some fashion rag.

The girl looks me up and down and not-so-subtly leans over the counter towards me, causing the vee of her collar to gape open. Typical, and annoying. I don't know if she's attracted to me or merely bored and looking for fun. Either way, I'm not interested.

I pointedly make eye contact with her, forgoing a smile. "Here for a welcome packet." I spell my name for her and she grins like a fox. The receptionist slowly turns, walking to the filing cabinet behind her with entirely too much hip movement.

If my eyes rolled any harder they would fall out and roll away like errant marbles. Her nonexistent ass is the least of my concerns at this point; I'm simply trying to get out of here as quickly as possible.

The welcome packet isn't necessary. I already have all the information I need to begin my assignment, but this is part of the role I need to play. Every new student at Sycamore is given a large packet complete with map, campus store vouchers, and a laminated copy of their schedule, among other detritus. The odds of a professor asking about the leaflets is low, but a non-zero possibility is still a possibility.

I see her scribble something on a Post-It and slip it into my packet before bringing it over to me, and I sigh. Reaching into the folder printed with a bright picture of the campus' main gates, I slide the pink note back to her, her phone number in plain view. "Not interested, thanks."

Her outraged scoff follows me back to the elevator.

It's not that I want to offend the girl, but I don't have time to be falsely kind to someone right now. It's taking everything in me to focus on getting through the rest of the day with an attitude landing north of caustic.

This assignment saps my patience, reducing me to a terse shell filled with reluctant determination. It simply isn't in my nature to end lives. I was put here to help save them. But sometimes, sacrifices are necessary to help the world at large. In the receptionist's case, it is merely her pride that takes a hit.

Valorie won't be so lucky.

The large clock tower over the door of the Administration building chimes the hour: ten o'clock. Three whole hours until my first class with Valorie, but I have a morning class in the building next door starting in fifteen minutes. Ideally, I would've mirrored Valorie's schedule exactly, but Esraa and Amon claimed this option could draw too much attention to me. So, I'm stuck taking Foundations of Art History and pretending to learn a subject I likely know more about than the professor—a middle-aged man currently setting his briefcase on the desk in the front of the lecture hall.

This folding stadium-style seat creaks beneath me, the sound loud as a gunshot in the nearly empty room. How did I get through an entire decade of study with the other dehmi, and yet I'm driven mad by a simple in-person lecture? My fingers itch for something more to do than tap a simple tune against the veneer of my tiny desk.

Students filter in around me in a riot of color and sound, but the stark white walls and gray carpet in the room perfectly match my emotions today: bleak.

By the time the class ends at eleven thirty, the professor has thoroughly reviewed the syllabus, and I am certain of two things:

One, there will be nothing covered in this course I haven't already mastered.

Two, I have yet to come up with even the barest beginnings of a plan to go about earning Valorie's trust. Simply bumping into her in a crowd doesn't guarantee she will take the time to talk to me. Engaging her in a random conversation could easily backfire if I come on too strong. My dossier says both of her parents are professors and she is an only child after her mother had three miscarriages, but none of that is fit for an introductory chat. Pertinent information that could lead to a somewhat lasting connection between us is limited.

The best course of action at this point? Pause for lunch and resume my brainstorming after a mental break.

The picturesque walkway radiates heat as I move towards the large dining hall, but a light breeze keeps it from being uncomfortably hot. A man in a tweed suit holds the door open for me and I nod my thanks, the transition to the cool darkness of the entryway momentarily blinding me until my enhanced eyesight adjusts. My senses are more honed than a human, but even I have limits.

A massive two-story cafeteria stretches out ahead of me, neon signs pointing towards quick-service restaurants catering to every dietary preference imaginable. Speckled tiles underfoot are somehow spotless despite nearly one-hundred students congregating at tables scattered near a wall of east-facing windows. The smells of dozens of freshly cooking foods wind through my nostrils. My growling stomach reminds me I haven't eaten since before training this morning. It's not our kitchen back at the Haven, but the cafeteria is impressive. As much as I loathe my reason for being stuck at Sycamore University, I can admit they have amenities most college students couldn't begin to dream of.

Tucked into a corner on the second floor of the complex is an Asian restaurant that looks promising. The quality seems much higher than the swill you find at a mall food court. A line of ready-to-order hot items is on display along the counter in large woks, and a duo of chefs are preparing fresh sushi for the cold case by the registers. Nothing compares to the meal I'll receive tonight when I pay my weekly visit to the Huangs, but there's always room in my stomach for a spicy tuna maki and egg rolls.

Despite its somewhat hidden location, there's already a substantial line. I clench my jaw in frustration. Seven other students stand guard between me and my lunch. As my vision wanders mindlessly, reflexively searching for clues on how to blend into campus life, I see a guy roughly my age with a shock of bright blue hair, and next to him...

It can't be.

A wild, onyx halo brushes against the man's shoulder as a distinctly feminine hand reaches to grab a plate from one of the workers behind the glass. I've seen those curls through the rippling pane of magic Esraa conjured in the Sacrarium almost three months ago.

Valorie.

At first glance, she looks like any other happy twenty-something in this school, merrily talking to her brightly colored friend and his more demure companion about whatever or whomever is important to the public these days. I wonder if her friends notice the way her hands are trembling slightly as she picks up her meal and turns to find a table. To me, it's as obvious as a seizure. Her head faces away from me, leaving me unable to see whether or not her stare still holds the film of despair from the vision. I'd bet my brother's prized roses it's still there, hiding beneath her carefree facade.

I pay for my lunch and head in the same direction, choosing a table close enough to pick up snippets of their conversation yet far enough away that the average person would not be suspicious. They're discussing Valorie's relationship with someone called Xavier. Her friends seem to disapprove.

I frown, confused. My briefing didn't mention a significant other. Could he be the wielder of the hand from the vision?

Their conversation is interrupted by Valorie's gasping and wet coughs. Her obvious choking has me out of my seat and halfway to their table before I stop short.

What the hell? I scold myself, pivoting towards the garbage cans. *Her death would make this easy on me, so why am I trying to save her?*

I attribute my actions to reflex; a combination of my predisposition towards helping and my innate healing ability. My empty plate slides into the trash bin and I continue out of the building. I don't want my spying to create any suspicion. It's unlikely, but I can't risk Valorie or her friends having a reason to suspect anything is amiss this early into my task. This mission must be executed perfectly.

Sunlight blazes in stripes through the manicured trees as I roam aimlessly until my first class with her this afternoon, dodging varying groups of students sprawled on any available piece of grass. The beauty of the day is wasted on me. My face is schooled into an unfeeling mask, thanks to years of practice, but inside I'm restless, jittery, like a small animal sensing an unseen predator is near.

One couple catches my eye as I round the corner near their wrought-iron bench, situated in a small garden between two of the university's famous architectural quarters. He is a behemoth, almost as large as Finnegan, his massive physique seeming all the larger by the diminutive woman sitting next to him. His partner—for they must be close with how a single meal is split between them on the bench—can barely be above five feet in height. Her cornflower hair blows in the wind and tangles with his messy black curls while she laughs quietly at something a student says in front of her. The man's guffaw assaults my ears, and I am struck by how familiar they seem, despite never having met either of them.

"See you later, Mr. and Mrs. Vargas!" The student's lighthearted goodbye sends a stab of pain through me. *Of course.* Out of a campus teeming with people, I would run into her parents, happy and oblivious. As I hurry towards the building where their daughter will unwittingly share space with her killer, my uncontrollable brain picks out pieces of Valorie's appearance in her parents. Her father's untamable hair and her mother's pert nose with a slight bump in the bridge are both present in the image that has haunted me since the vision.

Will I see their blissful expressions in my mind's eye as I end her life?

The large, brick structure in front of me is plain in comparison to the marble, steel and daubed plaster I've seen in the other parts of the campus, but it does sport one central tower with an arched doorway. A green, copper plaque reading "Mathematics" is positioned over the center of the entryway, leaving a faint whiff of oxidized metal on the warm breeze. Judging by the weathered patina it sports, I'd guess the metal is as old as the campus itself.

I join the queue of students filing into the classroom and pick a seat across the room from the full table Valorie and her friends occupy. Finally, I can make some progress. A quick glance at my schedule reminds me this is a statistics course, another subject I'm familiar with. This should make it easy to quickly complete the assignments and get back to devoting most of the period to figuring out how to approach my quarry.

A put-together woman in business casual khakis and a white blouse heads in my direction. "Hello," she says with a welcoming smile, "I'm Amanda Simmons, statistics professor and the track-and-field coach. I hear it's your first day?"

"Yes ma'am." I didn't expect the faculty to know of a new student in a school this large. They must be more organized than I expected.

"Well, welcome! I hope you enjoy your time studying here with us. If you need any help acclimating yourself to campus life, our new student center offers peer liaisons that can help you settle in and offer tours or guidance." She looks around, her demeanor brightening further when she lands on Valorie's table. "As a matter of fact, Valorie Vargas is over there, in the blue dress. She practically grew up on campus—kid has two professor parents—and she's known to be a liaison in her spare time. I don't know if she's technically working at the help center this semester, but tell her I sent you and I'm sure she'll help you out. She's a great kid, and that's a good group for a newbie to hang out with."

She gives me a cursory once-over and continues her speech. Professor Simmons is a talkative one, but she's helped me more than she knows this afternoon. Though, not in a way I think she would approve of if she knew my motive. "You seem like the athletic sort. If you're looking for a sport once you settle in, feel free to check out our rolling track-and-field tryouts. They're posted on-line, but Valorie happens to be friends with Charlie, our team captain. He's gearing up for another big win this year, I can feel it. Like I said, they're a well-connected bunch." She winks and walks back to her desk, chatting animatedly with a few students along the way.

Thank you, Professor, for your unknowing contribution to my cause. It seems the Web weaves in my favor today.

Chapter 3
Exhaustion

- Valorie -

I swear the swinging lecture hall door aims directly for my face as David and I leave our Economics 200 class. A rapid side-step lets me avoid spending the rest of the day covered in blood and getting my nose set at the campus clinic, but it's a close call. I'm a walking disaster, a danger to myself and others due to my rapidly dwindling ability to stay awake. It's only eleven, but I'm beat.

"*Chica*, what the hell?" David yells.

"Sorry, sorry," I yawn and flap a hand in his direction as we exit the building into the clear blue of a late August afternoon. I'm usually all for these glorious days full of sweet-scented breezes and the soothing green hues of the trees and plants across campus. Today, everything is too bright for my sleep deprived brain to handle. "I've been up since five helping mom after *someone* kept me up half the night spamming texts, and I desperately need a break or I'm going to keel over and face plant into the pavement."

"Come on," he urges, "let's grab some loungers on the quad. You can use my backpack as a pillow and catch some *z*'s while we wait for Charlie. We don't have another class until Simmons' lecture, so we have time for you to take a little *siesta* before lunch."

"You're a brilliant man, David. Oh, hey, before I forget, do you and Charlie want to hang out tonight? Mom and Dad have some faculty thing and I'm all free."

Please say yes. Being alone makes the devil come out to play. I'm too tired to fight my own brain tonight.

David happily agrees to come over and picks out a pair of padded chaise lounges bathed in the warm of the summer. My skin would prefer the shade, but there isn't any to be found today.

I flop onto the closest chair with a grunt. Exhaustion is making my bag weigh a ton, and my eyelids could be made of sandpaper with the way they're dragging against my corneas with every blink. I could barely keep them open during our last lecture; there were a few close calls where David had to elbow me to keep me from dozing off. He's right—I desperately need to rest for a bit ahead of our afternoon class.

Kicking off my shoes, I close my eyes and curl up on my chaise like a cat that's found a sunbeam through a window pane, murmuring something about him waking me up in twenty minutes. As I drift off, I hear David chuckle and mutter something about how he'll wake me in an hour instead.

It feels like only minutes later, however, when I'm awoken by the tinny sound of Hugh Jackman belting out "The Greatest Show" from my pocket. I groan, throwing one hand over my face while I use the other to fish my phone out so I can see who I have to thank for waking me up. The sound fades and the call goes to voice-mail, saving the caller from what would have been a very cranky conversation.

I unlock my phone, grinning at the photo of Charlie, David, and me at the beach this summer, our arms full of cheap stuffed animals we won from boardwalk games. We spent an entire week at Ocean City this past July, just the three of us in a condo we rented by the water. Seven fun-filled days of sandcastles, cheap fried foods and partying until we crashed in the early hours of every morning. At the end of it all, we swore this would be our new annual tradition. I hope it sticks, because every time I see this goofy picture my heart practically bursts.

All pleasant memories of our beach-time adventures are thrust from my head the instant I swipe down to see whose call I missed. I gasp, scrubbing my hand across my face as I struggle not to panic. The screen may say "unknown caller", but I know exactly who those ten digits belong to. *Shit, shit, shit.*

"Vally? What's wrong?" David asks, startling me out of my spiral. "Who rang? Whoever it was, call them back later. You barely slept, and you're bitchy when you're tired."

"Xavier," I breathe. *Shit.*

"Oh, great," he drawls with an eye roll. "Like I said, let it go. You're sleeping."

But I'm already typing out a response as fast as my fingers will move. I've kept the dirtiest details of my horrific high school relationship away from more than just Mom and Dad. Charlie and David think they know what happened to make me leave Xavier, but they don't. I only told them I ended things because he got a bit too overbearing.

It doesn't matter Xavier and I haven't been together for two years, or that *I* broke up with *him*. He still finds ways to terrorize me whenever possible. Showing up outside of my classes, asking professors to give him my ever-changing number under the guise of needing tutoring, cornering me in public so I'll look crazy if I ignore him. Or, worst of all, finding me when I'm alone and he doesn't have to keep up appearances. Xavier is a ticking time bomb, one I haven't found the code to defuse.

"It's fine, I've got it handled," I tell David absentmindedly, still furiously typing my response. "He probably wants to meet up for lunch. Let me shoot him a text and tell him no before he shows up here."

In truth, he probably wants me to do another easy assignment he claims he can't figure out on his own while he sits there and makes snide comments.

My sweaty fingers slip as I recall the last time Xavier found my number. I pretended I had no clue who he was, which worked for a few days, until he paid some computer science whiz his friend knew to confirm it was, in fact, my cell phone he was texting. A half-hour of screaming showed me how much he appreciated the wild goose chase.

Angering Xavier is never a good idea. To keep his rage to a minimum, I usually try to avoid him as much as I can, but that isn't always possible when we go to the same school.

"Don't make it some nice text, Val. Tell him to go to hell in a hand-basket."

"You know I can't do that," I whisper, hating the tears that are already welling up. Fighting with David makes me sick.

His hands clasp around mine. "Vally, I'm not mad at you, I'm worried about you. And, yeah, maybe a little mad. Seeing you dragged around behind him like some puppy on a leash infuriates me. You're nobody's bitch. Mom says you've got more Latin fire than I do, and it's the damn truth!" He reaches out and tips my chin up, wiping away the single tear that escaped during his speech. "I hate to see him scaring you like this. You were supposed to be free of him years ago. I don't know what I would do if he hurt you."

I scoff lightly, flashing a wobbly grin in his direction. My issues with Xavier aren't his burden to bear. "There's no fear, David, only irritation.

Don't you think if he was going to hit me I would've seen some signs by now? Calm yourself." The half-truth burns my throat as it comes out, as if I'm being punished for voicing it. Xavier has never beaten me, but there's an entire realm of violence he has made me intimately familiar with.

Of course I'm afraid. I'm scared of so many things, I can't keep track of them most days. Therapy didn't make the fear dissipate, it simply made me better at hiding it and keeping the panic to a minimum so I don't spread my problems to other people.

David sighs, reaching out to grab my hand. "All right. If you want me to stop, I'll stop. I still think you're making a mistake, but you've always been too polite. Promise me, if something goes too far you'll tell him off. And take one of us with you whenever you have to be around that idiot. Charlie and I will always be here for you."

I cross my heart and pull him into a hug. It smells of the mix of chocolate and spice that's uniquely David. True to form, he flails dramatically and pretends to die. His "dead" weight crushes me into the chaise. I wheeze out a laugh into the summer sky and manage a bit of peace before life drags me back down.

I take my phone out and turn my back to David, hiding my trembling hands while I check for a response. A tremor runs through my chest, mocking me for my lies.

I'm absolutely terrified of Xavier. But I can't find a way to cut the cord he has wrapped around my neck. My only hope is time will fade his obsession. I'll remain meek and uninteresting, but I won't give him the satisfaction of seeing me sweat.

David throws his arm around my shoulders. "Block his number, because here comes Charlie and I'm starving."

I look over my shoulder. A tall, wiry figure with a mop of honey brown curls almost as unruly as mine strolls towards us. Charlie cracks a smile, his blue eyes shining when he notices us staring at him. He throws us a small finger wave and rolls his bothersome left shoulder, stretching out the kinks in his lean muscles. Judging by the lumpy bag thrown over one arm and the light sheen of sweat left on his brow, he's nearly as exhausted as I am. He likely came straight from his morning run to meet us.

"Hey Charlie," I call. "Get in a good run this time around?"

He collapses onto the edge of my chair and blows me a kiss. I pretend to catch it and smack it against David's cheek. "Yeah, I found a new route, almost entirely uphill. Gonna win this next track meet for sure. I'm beat from all the running, and I could eat a horse, so who wants lunch?"

"Me!" David and I shout in unison, and the three of us collapse into giggles like children. One quick three-way rock-paper-scissors match later and we're heading to my personal favorite campus lunch spot for some cheap Asian fusion. Lo mein and crispy shrimp rolls are singing a siren song I am all too happy to answer. I swing open the door to the dining complex and inhale, assaulted by the combined scent of twenty different food stalls all corralled into the shining two-level building; everything from Italian to Mexican to vegan barbecue melding together into a perfume that sets my stomach growling loudly enough to make the boys laugh. I can't help it; on a day like today, carbs are the closest thing to heaven.

David steers us towards the stairs that will take us to Dim-Sumthing. "Come on Val, let's find you something to put in your black hole or it'll suck up the entire campus." He hands me a tray and I proceed to pile on my favorites, crowning my masterpiece with an egg roll and a Coke on the side. If I can't catch a decent nap before class, I'm going to stuff my face and hope the sugars can keep me awake long enough to get home. It may not be perfect science, but I'm not looking for an award right now—I only need a few hours of semi-alertness ahead of the inevitable crash.

"So, what's been going on this morning? You guys seemed a bit tense when I walked up." Charlie shoves a spoonful of miso soup into his mouth and waves the now-empty spoon between David and me. I'm chewing as fast as I can to try and beat David to the punch, but unfortunately David's mouth is empty while mine is full of General Tso's chicken.

"Xavier is up to his usual bullshit. Val refuses to tell him where to shove it and insists on being seventeen times nicer than the guy deserves."

I choke on my food and glare at him through streaming eyes. David reaches over to thump me on the back, unafraid. If I could breathe, I'd tell *him* where to shove it.

Out of the corner of my watery vision, I glimpse someone from a neighboring table bolt in our direction. But, when I finally stop coughing and look over, there's no one to be seen.

"I'm not being nice, I'm trying not to make things more annoying than they already are. Kill him with kindness, right? If he gets bored of me, maybe he'll finally find someone else to piss off." My argument would sound more convincing if my throat wasn't raspy from my brief brush with chicken-induced asphyxiation. At least David and Charlie can't feel my sweaty palms.

"Sorry, Vally, I'm with Dee on this one. It's been two years and Xavier still gets his rocks off on making you squirm. I don't like him anywhere near you." Charlie's eyes are filled with a cocktail of love and concern that keeps me from blowing up at him. I know the boys are looking out for me, though it occasionally gets on my nerves. And honestly, I know what they mean. If I was in their shoes and saw them going through this, I'd be begging them to do something excessive too.

"We'll try it my way for now, but if anything escalates I'll give your methods a shot. Deal?" I look down at my hands. The guys don't get my situation, mostly because I've kept secret the extent of what went on at the end of mine and Xavier's relationship. It's the only secret I have from them. I don't want to talk about it, ever. What would people think? What would my parents think, knowing I let someone walk all over me? Xavier will get bored of bothering me if I keep my head down, I'm sure of it. Until then, I have no choice but to weather the storm.

Charlie gets up, gathers our trays, and pats my head on his way to the trash station, leaving me alone with David. I look towards my best friend, silently pleading for him to understand. More tears find their way to the surface as he wraps his arms around me and crushes me against his chest. I hate that I'm an easy crier, especially when I'm stressed. And thanks to a certain intimidating blond who doesn't understand the word "no", I'm always stressed.

"Whatever you choose, we'll always be here for you. We're the three *caballeros*, remember?" He nudges my forehead with his chin until I look up at his quirky grin. I flash him a watery smile and Charlie throws his long arms around both of us. They squeeze me so hard that, for a brief moment, there's nowhere left for the worries to creep in.

David, Charlie, and I settle ourselves into our seats in Mrs. Simmons' Applied Statistics lecture ten minutes before class is due to begin. We spread our things out, covering the surface of the large, wooden table. Professor Simmons loves group discussion in her classes, and I love the extra space compared to other lecture halls, even if David uses the communal design as an excuse to take up half the available leg room by himself. Students file in behind us, laughing and chatting about their adventures over the weekend or who is sleeping with whom.

David sits up a bit straighter, tugging on my arm. "New guy, three o'clock," he whispers to us. "Who shows up two weeks into the semester? And in their senior year, too. Wonder what his deal is. I hope he's hot."

My chin drifts over my shoulder enough to catch a glimpse of the man in question, but all I see is the back of a head. It's draped in chin length onyx waves almost as dark as my own curls. How David realized there's a new student without seeing their face is beyond my comprehension, but he has a diabolical gift for ferreting out any bit of gossip within a five mile radius.

"You don't know he's a senior, and you have a man," I mumble back as Simmons heads to the front of the room to begin her lecture.

David scoffs loud enough that a few nearby heads turn towards us. I send a swift kick into his shin under the table.

He rubs his leg and replies, "Please, Val. There's literally one person in this entire class that isn't a senior, and she's only one year below us. Don't insult my fabulous statistical reasoning skills in the very class where they belong. And *you* don't have a man." The last sentence is punctuated with a pointed look at the empty chair next to me.

After an hour and a half of puzzling out complicated statistical assignments with the Panchito and Jose to my Donald Duck, these three *caballeros* are ready to head out and relax before a long night of takeout food and video games. If I don't finish the shut eye that was rudely interrupted this morning, the chances of me collapsing into our pizza later tonight are near absolute.

As we gather up our things at the end of the class, Mrs. Simmons calls out to Charlie, asking him to stay behind for a quick chat. They usually have some sort of track-and-field strategy to discuss after class, and I'd bet Charlie wants to tell her about his new running route.

We gesture to Charlie to meet us at the table out front once he's done. David and I always show up to cheer for the team, but the actual ins and outs of the sport are a mystery to both of us.

I collapse into one of the wrought-iron chairs and melt onto the sun-warmed garden table, pulling a chuckle from David. I fold my arms around my backpack to make myself a pillow and snuggle in. The heady mix of chrysanthemums and black-eyed Susans on the hot breeze is a lullaby to my exhausted brain.

"Vally, you have to be part cat, I swear. If you don't get your nap you turn feral." His chuckle turns into full blown laughter at my unintelligible, growled response. He's not wrong; I do require several daily *siestas* to function at peak performance. And today, I haven't finished a single one.

I barely manage to nestle into my arm cocoon when a low, melodic voice drifts to my ear from beside me. "Valorie Vargas?"

My head tilts enough to peek one bleary eye out from the blissful darkness of my crossed forearms. I quickly sit up and crane my neck back to take in the bronzed, green-eyed man in front of me, his full lips pursed into a shy, concerned pout. A head of somewhat-familiar unruly black waves tells me we've cracked the code on the face of the new student. And what a face it is.

David is going to have a coronary.

Chapter 4
Breaking Point

- Valorie -

Mr. Mystery cocks his head. I realize I've been staring blankly at him for the past thirty seconds while he waits for a response. I clear my throat, blood rushing to my face and tinting my cheeks pink. "That would be me. Can I help you with something?"

His hand scrapes through his wavy hair as he replies, his low, clear voice rolling straight through me, "I'm new. Got here today, actually, and I haven't a clue where most things are on campus. My advisor, Mrs. Simmons, recommended you specifically as a good person to talk to about the ins-and-outs of the school. So I am here to beg for assistance."

I barely catch the gist of what's he's saying. My attention keeps getting snagged by the strange accent dripping off his tongue. Part Scottish brogue, part Irish lilt, with a hint of Australian drawl on a few words. I find myself trying in vain to puzzle out where on Earth he could possibly be from. His beautiful features seem more Egyptian, or possibly Greek, but his voice places him in a completely different set of locales.

Mr. Mystery indeed.

I realize he's waiting for an answer while I'm once again staring at him like this is my first day in public. David snickers behind me—I shoot him a glare and smile up at the newcomer. "Sorry, I haven't had much sleep today. My parents both work for the school, I was practically raised here," I explain. "Plus I occasionally volunteer as a liaison. Teachers have a habit of offering me up to new students, or even new faculty members."

"If it's too much trouble, I can just follow a map. I didn't mean to impose."

"Oh, no, it's fine!" I gesture to the empty chair across from me, motioning for him to take a seat. A strange sense of ease fills me, like I've known him for years instead of two minutes. Weird. "I have no problem showing you around, seriously. Sit down, if you want. We're waiting on the third member of our group, then we're heading out."

I scrawl my number on an old receipt I fish out of my bag and slide it across the table to him. He slips into the chair and takes the crumpled paper. "Here you go. That's my cell, in case you have a question and can't easily ambush me during my nap time." I flash him a cheesy grin to make sure he knows I'm joking. Sometimes people don't grasp sarcasm, which should be a crime. I hope new guy isn't one of them, because I can't have a friend who doesn't understand humor.

Get it together, Val, I chide myself. I've known the guy for less time than a commercial break, and already I'm planning out our friendship.

He ducks his head, but not quickly enough to hide the hint of color flitting across his cheeks. Is he *blushing?* "Thanks, this is more than I deserve from you," he mutters, slipping the paper into a pristine leather wallet.

I cock my head to one side, stare narrowing slightly in confusion as I ponder his strange turn of phrase. I offered him simple human kindness, but he's acting like he's some sort of pariah. My heart constricts at the thought of someone being so unaccustomed to receiving a simple nicety, they'd think themselves undeserving. Even *I'm* not that insecure.

Something in me aches to keep this strange boy close, while the rest of me balks in fear of drawing Xavier's attention further by becoming friends with another man.

Screw it, I'll take the risk.

My arms refold and I flop my head down, leaning sideways to affix one eye on my new charge. "Well, the first thing you should know about Sycamore is this place is huge. The days are long, and it's a lot more fun spending all day in lectures if you've got a friend or two to keep you awake. And since I'm in the business of being unbelievably generous," I lift my head enough to crack another goofy grin in his direction before collapsing back onto my arms with a yawn. "I'm going to offer you the once in a lifetime opportunity to hang out with me and my two favorite losers. The pretty one with a head like a blue highlighter is David." I hike an unnecessary thumb in his direction and Charlie appears in the corner of my eye. "The much less obnoxious hunk over there is his boyfriend Charlie. Charlie, this is..." I trail off, realizing I've been sitting here talking to this guy for ten minutes and never caught his name.

Mystery man holds out a hand to David and Charlie in turn. "Conall. Conall Raoult. It's a pleasure." He pauses, as if searching for the right words to say. "You are all so welcoming, I can see why Mrs. Simmons pointed me in your direction." He smiles, but it doesn't reach his eyes.

A strange sort of melancholy I can't quite place lurks under his generic platitudes. The look in his shadowed eyes is not quite sadness, more like...resignation? Whatever it is, his slightly clenched fists aren't hiding it very well.

Conall finally extends his hand in my direction. I lean over to shake it, but he shocks me by flipping them over and brushing a faint kiss onto the back.

"Well, well, well, what do we have here?" a familiar voice drawls from directly behind me.

I snatch my hand back as if burned, my skin breaking out into a cold sweat despite my best effort to remain unaffected.

"A Rami Malek look-alike putting his mouth on my girl? How scandalous." Xavier flashes a smile, but his gaze is ice-cold when it lands on me.

The world dims a bit as I shut down, reflexively becoming small and unimportant.

Suddenly, David's words from earlier screech through my head. I straighten my spine, and for a few minutes, I forget to be afraid. I plaster my falsest smile onto my face as I turn my body towards Xavier, glare filled with cold flame. "Funny, I didn't realize you had a girl, Xavier. How good for you. Conall, meet Xavier. He hangs around a lot."

I'm dripping with all the saccharine sweetness of a toothache, my anxiety shoved behind a solid wall of rage. David and Charlie are posted up on either side of me like the most unconventional bodyguards in the world, matching masks of pure loathing on their faces. If looks could kill, this entire table would be a crime scene.

Xavier moves to sit with me, and I don't miss the way his fists ball when I refuse to make room for him. He gives up and drapes himself into the chair he drags beside mine as if it was his intention all along.

Note to self: don't leave open seats nearby in the future.

I sit stiff as a board on the edge of my chair, watching Xavier's focus moves from me to Conall. He looks almost as furious as Xavier. The tension between the two of them is palpable, which is strange considering Conall doesn't know Xavier and he only met me a few minutes ago. He seems awfully protective, or maybe he simply doesn't appreciate the way Xavier is looking at him like he's lower than dirt.

"Hello, Conrad," Xavier sneers.

What a petty asshole.

A firm pinch on the inside of my thigh shocks me back into reality. I hiss as the pain blazes through me and jerk away, looking under the table for the source of the ache.

Xavier's fingers dig mercilessly into my skin while his other hand nonchalantly scratches at his close-cropped blond hair. He isn't looking at me, but his small smirk says he felt my reaction.

What the hell?

I wrench at Xavier's hand in a vain attempt to get him to let go of the now swollen skin between his fingers. The radiating pain eclipses the conversation. I barely hear Conall introduce himself.

Xavier finally releases his vise grip and I nearly sigh in relief, only to jump again when he captures another sensitive spot higher on my inner thigh. My eyes start to water and I give up, lurching to my feet so quickly I knock into the table in my haste to escape.

Xavier's been an overbearing piece of shit for years, but he's always preferred wielding emotional damage over physical. Or so I thought.

"Well, look at the time." The wrist I bring to my face is conspicuously watch-free. "I'd say it's been great to see you, Xavier, but I hate lying. We're going to go now." Between my anger, my exhaustion and the throbbing in my leg, I don't have the energy to be cordial. I only want to escape.

"Of course, dear. You kids have fun now, be safe," Xavier responds in a patronizing tone, waving a bored hand in my direction. Everything in me wants to slap that smirk to smithereens. I don't believe for a second he isn't absolutely furious at my blatant disregard for his self-ordained superiority, but this is all part of the fun for him.

My head tilts and whirls, a carnival ride of emotions I cannot climb off of.

I'm so tired of this game. I want my life back.

I turn and take the step that will free me from the table that has become claustrophobic in the wake of Xavier's appearance, but my left foot doesn't follow through.

I topple over in slow motion, everything crawling by at a glacial pace. The small, beige stones pressed into cream colored cement move almost lazily into view, yet I'm unable to do more than raise my hands before slamming into the pavement with a bone-jarring thud. Dirt and dust grinds itself into my skin, making a new home where my blood once was.

In the split second of silence that follows, I look up and lock onto Xavier's cold sneer. He casually removes his loafer from underneath my sneaker.

Then, the world restarts.

"Valorie!" he chides from his wrought-iron throne, making no moves to help me up. "You really should watch your step. What if you had gotten hurt?" As if my raw hands and the bleeding cut on my face are invisible to him. He just sits there, a cocky grin on his face while I bleed onto the concrete in the arms of my friends, Conall standing sentry behind us.

It's not a question, it's a warning. A threat.

His smug sneer the look of a man secure in his power, a king lording over his peasant plaything. It's the face that made me flee two years ago. This isn't some misguided joke, it's a calculated attack designed to break me apart so he can own me again.

And I'm all out of ideas on how to save myself.

Chapter 5
Revelations

- Valorie -

A record of the darker years of my life plays through my head, a film running in fast forward. I'm barely aware of the three boys hustling me away from Xavier. I sit inside the theater of my mind, a captive audience. The fall tore through more than skin; it shredded the paper-thin walls I built up to keep these memories at bay—and now they're back with a vengeance.

Reels of small events I've buried in the dusty corners of my nightmares amass and crash over me in a tidal wave, pulling me under. My body quakes as I remember one-sided arguments punctuated with that same cruel grin; snide remarks about my weight paired with haughty laughter like sour wine; rules, which slowly suffocated me under his thumb; and angry, unwanted touches foisted upon me day after day drip through my consciousness like the blood congealing on my mangled palms.

One of the guys mentions something about a concussion, but I don't catch any other words. Everything is jumbled, past and present mixed up inside of the roaring sea in my head. My breathing races, and I'm back in high school, flickering fluorescents illuminating me as I cry in the dirty basement bathroom after Xavier screamed at me in front of the entire sophomore fitness class. I choke on a scream, and we're standing under a shade tree on the sidewalk in front of my house, avoiding the hot pavement.

David grabs the spare key from under a rock in our tidy flowerbed. Charlie ushers me through the doorway. I waver in the cool, dim foyer—a marionette with cut strings—while they fuss over me.

The sting of antiseptic briefly cuts through the haze as David dabs at my face with an astringent-scented cotton ball. Charlie and David are almost as at home in my house as I am; they know where to find anything they could need. Tonight, I guess they're raiding the entire first aid cabinet. I can't find it in myself to care whether my wounds are treated or not.

Can someone bleed out if their entire body is made of lead? I weigh a million pounds, my body so burdened with exhaustion and hopelessness I'm surprised I don't sink straight through the polished hardwood beneath my socks.

Socks? I was wearing white Vans, the ones with tiny daisies on the sides. David and I drew them on with Sharpies in our Mythology lecture last year. What happened to my shoes?

I'm dimly aware of Charlie and David guiding me to the overstuffed leather couch Dad bought during Mom's modern design phase. Charlie tucks a blanket around me as David makes garbled sounds into the telephone, meaningless syllables that make no sense. Charlie looks at me with wide eyes, fear etched into his face. He and David babble back and forth like infants learning to speak.

I have no hope of comprehension. I can only shake my head at their mystery, which seems to disturb them.

There's a strange, near-violent trembling in my back and shoulders. Before I can worry about the earthquake, the fog creeps across my view yet again and I sink back into the depths.

The world briefly smells of tomatoes and spices, and the scent draws me out of my current nightmare—a memory of Xavier cornering me in a dark bathroom at prom four years ago, saying he needed me to "prove" I didn't find anyone else attractive. As if I would be interested in the groups of gangling boys in poorly fitted tuxedos grinding on random girls in the hotel ballroom. I did as he asked that night, then vomited into a dumpster on the walk to my car.

My stomach roils with the images. The cloying stench of cheap cologne and sweat threaten to pull me back under, but the strange shaking prevents me from fading away.

"Valorie, come on, honey, snap out of it." The voice is muddled yet close, like my head is underwater and they're waiting just above the surface.

I swim up towards the comforting sound and emerge into the familiar coziness of my living room with a barely audible gasp.

David and Charlie hover over me, frantically searching my face. Charlie holds both my hands in his tight grip, while David's fingers are clamped around my shoulders. As details begin to filter through to my brain I notice the source of the delicious smell that had pierced through my panic earlier: two pizza boxes lying untouched on the glass coffee table behind them. The black Venetian blinds are shut tight, keeping the room cool and dim.

I stir, and the boys freeze.

"What time is it?" I croak and cough to clear my painfully dry throat. Coughing does little to alleviate the feeling of having gargled broken glass, but it'll have to do. I'm too exhausted to trek to the kitchen for a glass of water. The fifteen-foot journey might as well be a cross-country hike.

Two sets of sagging shoulders accompany their relieved smiles when I speak, evidence that my friends have been scared to death while I was trapped in the confines of my horrific ride down memory lane. A pang of guilt shoots through me. I haven't had a breakdown like that since freshman year of college.

Xavier was the cause of that one, too.

Charlie's soft answer cuts through my musing, "It's seven thirty. You've been...out for a while."

Seven thirty. I've been out of it for four hours, stuck inside my head, watching the procession of five wasted years spent under the thumb of a man whose only true love is himself. Followed by two years of freedom that haven't been free at all.

"Want to tell us what happened?" David gets straight to the point; subtlety is an art in a museum he never visits.

A plate of pizza is nudged into my injured hands. My reflection in the mirror over the mantle snags my attention and I'm briefly lost to the view. Shell-shocked, vacant stare, and translucent skin—a picture of the lost girl adrift inside of me. The soft glow of the brass side-table lamps throws the bandage across my cheek into sharp shadow, making me look battered and worn.

I won't let him win. It's time to put on my armor and gather the troops. We have work to do.

I straighten my spine and lock eyes with David. "You were right."

"Honey, I'm right about every—"

Charlie cuts in, glaring daggers at his boyfriend. "Right about what, Val?"

"Xavier."

They blanch.

David chokes on his pizza, spluttering as he croaks, "You said what now?"

"You were right. About Xavier...and the..." — *come on* — "abuse." A shuddering breath escapes. I wipe my sweaty palms on my dress and they come away covered with a fine layer of grit. "I never told you guys half of the things he's done. I didn't want to upset you." My voice cracks. I swallow hard and force out, "And I was ashamed. I didn't want people to think I was some stupid girl who was too lovestruck and spineless to stand up for herself. But that's exactly what I was. And when I finally left him, I was too much of a wuss to do anything. I spend my days avoiding him, always watching my back instead of enjoying the things I love. And, when he inevitably finds me again, I go right back to doing his assignments to try and get him to go away again when I should be telling him to shove his overdue papers up his ass. It's pathetic." By the time my air runs out, I'm staring at my hands, embarrassment coloring my wet cheeks. I can't bear to look at their faces—I can already picture the disgust.

My fingers trace the buttery leather under my legs. A sock-clad toe snags on a small whorl in the hardwood beneath my foot. The couch creaks, two sets of warm arms wrap around me, and I find myself sandwiched between my favorite people. I scrub at my cheeks, sniffling in a vain attempt to keep myself from breaking down completely.

The battle is lost when Charlie pats my head and whispers, "We are *so* proud of you, Valorie." His voice is a lifeline, a ladder up and out of the guilt I've been wallowing in.

David claps his hands, pure joy shining from him as he grins from ear to ear. "Everything is going to be okay," he says, and I believe him.

With my newfound calm, I'm suddenly ravenous. My pizza has sat cold and forgotten in my lap this entire time, my mind too frantic to begin to think about eating. I lurch towards the kitchen, steps faltering on the cool wood planks. Charlie and David mutter to each other as my pizza spins in the microwave.

I burn my mouth scarfing down an entire gooey slice on my way back to the living room. They'll eat theirs cold, but I can't stand cold food. My friends and family love to make fun of me for being picky, but they won't change my mind. If it's supposed to be hot, it better be hot, or it's not going in my mouth.

"Okay, so what's the plan?" David rubs his hands together like a cartoon villain. "Are we going to go full out? Leave a flaming bag of dog shit on his step? Make a video bashing him and go viral online? Call the morning radio show and blast him on the air?"

"Slow down there, clown," I chuckle. "We aren't going to do any of those things."

David crosses his arms and huffs like a three-year-old in time-out. I laugh, flicking a grease-stained paper packet of Parmesan cheese from the pizzeria at his forehead. It narrowly misses its mark. He swipes the packet in midair and upends the whole thing onto his pizza.

"Val is right," Charlie interjects. "The most important thing right now isn't revenge, it's freedom. We need to figure out some way to get it through his thick skull she's never coming back. And keep him from bothering her."

"Which won't be easy, since I'm not switching schools or moving any time soon. Honestly, I'm thinking about texting him and being done with it. No niceness, no beating around the bush." What I don't tell them is I'm petrified of what will happen if I tell him to his face.

I doubt this will work, but it's my best shot at getting him to back off, short of calling the cops, and I simply don't have enough evidence for that route. Xavier has connections I don't, thanks to his father's political influence. Paul Schmitt was the lieutenant governor for four years, and a sheriff's deputy for two years before donning his gubernatorial hat. He isn't politically active anymore, but he has enough friends in high places to keep Xavier's name out of the mud.

My phone suddenly vibrates on the table. David snatches it up quicker than I can and grimaces at the screen. "Speak of the devil and he shall appear," he mutters.

I usually don't let them see what Xavier sends to me, but I'm not keeping secrets about him anymore. David's gaze roves over my phone and his grimace turns into a snarl. Charlie leans in to read the incoming message and hisses a breath through gritted teeth. Whatever is on that screen, it can't be good.

I stand behind them and my cheeks flame.

Xavier

I thought we had a good thing going, baby. You follow my rules, and I leave you alone. You screwed up today, embarrassing me like that. Clumsy whore.

And he has the gall to add a smiley face at the end. Bastard.

"You didn't need to see that," I say, sliding my phone out of David's hand. With his current mood, he's liable to crush it.

"What does he mean, Val?" Charlie asks gently. "You don't have to tell us anything you don't want to, but it might make you feel better to talk it out. And I have to admit, there are a few questions I'd like answered about this asshole." When I don't object, he asks, "Does he force you to do things for him?"

No more secrets. My throat closes around the words I'm too mortified to say, so I nod slowly.

"Fuck," he hisses. "And if you don't? Valorie, has he hurt you?"

I give another small nod and hang my head in shame.

Charlie turns over my hands with gentle fingers, tracing the long bandages that hide where my skin had been sloughed off during my fall. He places a soft hand against the congealed gash above my left eye.

"How did this happen, Val? We were all there, but things went too fast. One minute you were fine, and the next you were on the ground with him glaring at you like a worm. Tell me," he urges.

I lift the hem of my dress slightly, baring the purple, mutilated marks where Xavier gripped my skin.

Charlie's usually our calm bastion, but the sight of the bruised welts fills his brown eyes with enough lava to burn the room to ashes.

"He was pinching me under the table. I tried to get him to let go, but he wasn't stopping. It hurt so badly I couldn't take it anymore." I take a deep breath before continuing. "When I fell, I thought I had tripped at first. I was moving quickly, and accidents happen, y'know? But, when I looked up at him, he smirked at me and pulled his foot out from under mine so nonchalantly, like making someone face-plant onto concrete was normal."

I barrel on, worried that I'll never continue if I stop now, "That's when it clicked. Xavier's been doing these things for years and I always wrote it off, accepted his excuses and half-assed apologies. I was so used to dealing with his nonsense it became normal. I left him two freaking years ago, and he's *still* treating me like I'm going to come crawling back. Probably because I haven't had the guts to tell him to fuck off like David's been saying this whole time. I keep making nice, doing whatever the fuck he demands, and dealing with his insane stalking in hopes he'll get bored eventually. But I'm done with his bullshit. I can finally *see* now, guys. And I don't ever want to go back." A large inhale punctuates the end of my rant. A huge weight lifts off my shoulders now that the truth is finally out into the open.

David and Charlie stare at me, wide-eyed and shocked silent. Our heads whip in unison as phone buzzes once again.

Xavier

You don't have the balls to ignore me, bitch. I have a paper due for Poly Sci next week, and you're gonna do it. Meet me tomorrow. Don't be late, I have a party. Don't make me come find you.

I turn my phone towards the guys. They both look one second away from fighting over who gets to crush it beneath their shoe.

This has gone on long enough, and it's time to bite the bullet. I flip the phone back around. My fingers fly across the screen and I stab the send button with vitriol before I can lose my nerve.

My sigh of nervous relief is followed by two victorious whoops from my best friends, who sneaked up behind me to read my response.

Me

No. Lose my number, I'm done. Fuck you, Xavier.

I slide my phone onto the table and take my first free breath in years.

Chapter 6
Close Encounter

- Valorie -

"So you still haven't heard anything from Xavier?"

David and I head towards the gym to meet up with Charlie. We're basking in one of those perfect days where summer drifts into fall, when the sun gilds everything from within a clear cerulean sky and the world is still blanketed in the last vestiges of vibrant green. There's only a few short weeks left to go until the trees begin changing colors.

We've barely seen Charlie during daylight hours this week. He's been spending extra hours at the gym every day, working to make sure he's ready for the huge track meet he's competing in tomorrow. It's one of his last events before he retires. We've been trying to meet up afterwards and spend the evenings together to keep his mind off of the run.

David and I scoped out the best seats two weeks ago—two rows up, perfectly shaded while still offering an unobstructed view of the entire arena. You won't catch either of us running unless it's a life-or-death situation, but we aren't going to complain about showing up to cheer for our boy. The added possibility of catching a glimpse of any mouth-watering displays of athleticism from the stands is a nice bonus.

"No, I haven't heard from him or seen him around campus lately. It's strange. It's been over a week—I would've expected a full-on meltdown by now, since his favorite punching bag is gone." For a split second, I get lost in memories of exactly what used to happen when Xavier lost his tenuous grip on his temper. My skull pounds and my palms moisten.

No, Val. Don't think about the past. It's over.

I tear myself back to the present with a shake of my head.

Most days I've been doing well with keeping the flashbacks at bay, though I did have to resort to sleepovers with Charlie and David twice this week. It was the only way I could sleep without my nightmares waking me up every hour. I'm a work in progress, but there's no giving up this time.

"If he comes near you, go right for the groin, 'kay? You're no MMA fighter, but anyone can manage one swift kick. And scream. We all know you're loud as hell." David punctuates his last quip with a wink and shoulder checks me as we enter the hulking gymnasium building.

Sycamore University boasts a state-of-the-art gym touted by three news outlets as "The Best University Fitness Complex in the Eastern United States." We exit the lobby into the first level of the four-tiered open equipment room. Rows and rows of exercise machines stand sentinel atop pristine, white-tiled floors. Through the glass doors across the room, I see my favorite part of the center—the indoor pool, with its matching outdoor twin through another set of doors.

Unfortunately, we're here on a search-and-rescue mission, so I push thoughts of spending a few blissful hours swimming laps out of my mind until another day.

David looks over the lines of athletes sweating away under the bright lights. He's long past the point of searching for Charlie. It's time for David's favorite hobby: people-watching.

I reach over and pull his baseball cap over his face, laughing. "Aren't you practically married to your man at this point? What are you looking at?"

"*Chica*, I'm looking to find *you* a man. I've got my hands full with Charlie, but you, you're single. That means it's your duty to check out all the meat on the market." He flings his arm out to encompass the room full of sweaty people like he's presenting a new, life-changing invention.

"David, I don't even know how to date. I'm stuck in relationship stasis—I think I've had coffee dates with three guys since the breakup. Nobody ever clicks. Relationship Val is like sixteen." That's honestly a bit sad when I say it out loud. It's hard to date when you're constantly looking over your shoulder for a five-foot-nine lurker with an attitude problem.

"Exactly. It's time for Relationship Val to grow up and glow up, honey. So let's take a look around while we wait, shall we?"

David posts up and lounges against the wall next to the men's locker room door while we wait for Charlie. He scans the room, looking for someone to latch onto like a shark. I huff out a resigned chuckle and settle in beside him. When David gets an idea in his head—especially one he believes will help someone—it's next to impossible to stop him. He's a battering ram, demolishing everything and anything in the way of his plan. In short, he's the best friend a girl could ever ask for, even if he's currently scoping out the crowded gym harder than a 19th-century mother at a ball.

I play along, letting my stare roam around the lanes of machines whirring and beeping out the music of human exertion. I try to envision myself with one of the various guys scattered around the room, for David's sake and my own, but the sea of faces never quite manages to come into focus. A pair of baby blues here, a mop of sandy hair there, plenty of sets of toned muscles gleaming under the harsh white LEDs, but nobody manages to hold onto my attention long enough to make an impression.

That is, until I see someone working on one of the machines on the far side of the room, facing the windows opposite our stake-out point. Dark, wavy hair brushing the nape of his neck; sweaty, bronzed skin that gleams in the stark lighting. I can hardly take my eyes off the way his back muscles bunch and relax with each rep. Something about him feels familiar, but I'd know if any of my friends looked like *that*.

"*Oooh*, you've got a look in your eye." David is practically vibrating with glee. He follows the arc of my gaze and lets out a low whistle. "*Damn*. That's one juicy prime rib. Who is he?"

"David, would you please wipe your drool and stop objectifying innocent people in the gym? Your boyfriend needs to hurry up, or else I'm going to go in there and drag him out to shut you up." My threat would carry more weight if I wasn't staring across the room as intently as he is.

On cue, the door opens into my shoulder and I jump halfway out of my skin.

"Hey, guys." Charlie says as he walks out of the locker room, towel-drying his damp hair. "Hope you haven't been waiting long."

"Long enough for Vally to spy a hot guy across the way. Take a look over there!" David extends his entire arm in the direction we had been looking, as if a finger wouldn't have been sufficient.

Classic David. As subtle as a hurricane and twice as loud. I frantically shove his arm back down before someone can see him.

Charlie looks around. "Who? I don't see anyone. All those machines are empty."

"Aw, man," David whines. "He must've left while we weren't looking."

Truthfully, I'm just as bummed as he is, though I'll never tell him. I'll keep my salivating to myself.

"Oh, well," I chuckle. "Guess you'll never get to invite him to be your third wheel."

My stomach chooses this time to loudly remind me I haven't eaten a real meal since breakfast. I studied my way through lunch, barely finding the time to finish a granola bar between flashcards, and now my body is pissed.

I tell David and Charlie to go ahead to the track-and-field office to get Charlie's school bag while I grab a snack from the closest dining hall. Promising to meet up with them at the edge of campus in half an hour, I head out to satiate the monster currently trying to devour my insides.

The balmy air caresses my skin as I emerge into the warmth of a Mid-Atlantic September day. A shaft of buttery light falls over my face and I inhale the heady scent of the chrysanthemums in the planters by the fitness center entrance. I'm going to miss this weather when everything is cold and gray in a few months. I love Christmas, but I could do without the frigid temperatures that accompany it.

I meander my way towards an alley that gives me a direct route to the cafeteria. My skin aches to soak in the last vestiges of warmth, so I slough off my thin jacket and bundle it up in my arms, exposing my arms and shoulders with the black tank I have on underneath. The shade of the alleyway can't quite pierce the hazy heat of the day. This season is a fighter, clinging valiantly to the remnants of the year, but fall is coming to take her place.

Halfway through the alleyway, I hear a set of footsteps rapidly approaching from behind me. A shadow eclipses mine, black against the gray concrete at my feet. Probably a runner or some poor kid late to class. I move closer to the wall on my left to make room for the other person to rush by me. Instead, a shoulder smashes into mine, crunching me into the rough bricks with enough force to make my arm go numb for a second. Pain explodes through my side.

"Hey baby, long time no see. Did you miss me?"

The voice in my ear sends chills through me. It's instantly recognizable, because it's the one that haunts my nightmares.

Xavier.

A hand drifts down my back, far too low for comfort. Not that any of his touches could ever be comfortable. My whole body convulses in disgust despite my best efforts to remain composed.

I shove myself away, ignoring the sickening grinding of bones in my injured shoulder. "Leave me alone, Xavier. I'm not your baby."

"No can do, *baby*, it's not over unless I say it's over. So, you're going to shut up and come over here. Give me what I want, or you'll make me cause a scene." His hand darts out before I can run and his fingers hook through the belt loops on the rear of my jeans.

I struggle as he grinds himself against me with a dark laugh. It's no use; trying to escape seems to only excite him further, but I'm not giving up.

He tangles my hair into his fist and shoves my face against the wall, mashing my mouth and nose into the bricks and muffling my cries for help. Mortar dust invades my lungs, but I scream until my throat feels like I've swallowed knives.

I'm a feral animal, flipping and thrashing against the hands keeping me in place. My mind flashes through a dozen memories of being pinned down and "taught a lesson" by the demon looming over me.

Never again.

He *rips* his hand out of my hair and slides it along my neck in a perverted caress, squeezing my throat until I'm gasping for air. Several mangled, mutilated strands are twisted around his fingers as if they're trying to restrain him. Blood and dust forms a paste, obscuring my view—one of the bricks must have cut me at some point during the attack.

My flailing legs finally meet resistance and Xavier grunts. I manage to gulp the soupy summer air, but his hand doesn't loosen enough for me to make my escape. My struggling isn't quiet, yet the sound of a zipper rolling cuts through the noise like a blade.

My blood turns icy. No, no, *no!* He flattens me against the wall, using his chest to pin me to the bricks while he works at my fly with both hands. Bloody nails snap and shatter in the flesh of his forearms, and I'm rewarded with a pained hiss that flutters the hair above my ear. I redouble my efforts to free myself, determined to make him let go or die trying. This will not happen to me, not again.

He'll have to kill me first.

CHAPTER 7
Rescued

- VALORIE -

The sudden absence of Xavier's body makes me stumble. Fresh air rushes in to fill the space he occupied. Whipping around with raised fists, I come to a screeching halt when I see Xavier on the ground, cowering as someone rains punches and kicks with cold precision. It takes a few seconds to recognize my rescuer through the haze of adrenaline and blood.

As my stunned mind begins to restart itself, I rasp out, "Conall?"

The instant Conall turns to face me, Xavier seizes the opportunity to run away. Coward.

Conall is at my side in a flash, but something seems off compared to the last time I saw him.

"Hey, did you grow? You're huge. I mean, you were probably, what? Six feet? Six-one? But now you're humongous." My head is level with his knees as if I was speaking to a giant from a children's book. I giggle at the mental image of a benevolent Conall towering over the townsfolk in some rural village, letting children climb his tree-trunk legs like a jungle gym.

His brief, low chuckle sets butterflies loose in my stomach, but his icy expression nearly convinces me I imagined that hint of laughter. He folds himself in half at the knees and suddenly his emerald gaze is level with my own. "You're on the ground, wildcat. I think the shock is setting in. Can you stand?" His voice is a gentle murmur that washes away the last of my terror.

"Your eyes are green like the trees," I breathe, a goofy grin plastered on my face. As soon as the words are out, my stupid, frozen brain kicks into high gear and embarrassment paints itself across my cheeks. "Shit. I mean, yeah I can stand. It's my arm that's fucked up, and my face. Does this mean you aren't a giant after all?" *Shit, Val, stop rambling.* Maybe I am in shock. "My brain feels like it's churning its way through molasses, and I can't feel my face. Wait, did I say that out loud?" I pause, trying and failing to collect my thoughts. One piece of this bizarre conversation niggles at the back of my head. "What did you call me?"

A warm smile lights up his face, a brighter sun than the one I was basking in not long ago, in a happier time. "Wildcat. You fought like one back there." As quickly as it came, his joy is gone once again, replaced by dark clouds of fury.

Conall can't seem to hold onto a smile for more than three seconds.

"I was coming from the gym and heard you struggling. I was almost too late. I'm so sorry." A strange, torn look passes over his features.

I can't begin to decipher that one, not when I feel like I've been through a blender.

"But, you weren't too late. Without you, I'd have been..." I choke on the last word. It sticks in my throat, a burr I can't force out. *Raped.* "Xavier has never been angry enough to attack me like that in broad daylight; he's usually too worried about his appearance. He wants to be a politician, so everything has always been about his image." Until today, I guess.

"Do you want to talk about it?" A gentle, hesitant question from the man with a glare sharp enough to shred diamonds.

"I told him no. He doesn't like being told no." The bitterness in my voice is palpable.

"Is he going to bother you again?" An edge to his tone makes the question sound rhetorical, like he's asking out of courtesy but already knows the answer.

My answer is as final as death, a nail in a coffin that should have been buried long ago. "Not if I can help it."

A nod. "Good."

The fog in my head is beginning to clear, and with it, the pain in my arm and face is increasing by the second. I think I'm doing a good job of hiding it, but Conall's stare narrows and he gently takes hold of my arm, turning it around with a feather-light touch that still manages to make my shoulder bark. I grit my teeth to hold in a scream, but of course, he notices.

Stupid, beautiful eyes that see everything and look like my favorite weeping willow in the forest behind our house.

I'm sinking into a horrific combination of adrenaline withdrawal and the mind-numbing pain of a dislocated shoulder; my arm is bleeding and torn and my face feels as though it's been scrubbed with sandpaper. My best efforts to hold myself together in front of this kind man I barely know aren't enough to stop my resolve from crumbling. The brave facade slips and a single tear cuts its way through the grime plastered to my skin.

Conall brushes his hand along my arm and the feeling of cool water spreads over my body. I expect to see him washing my wounds, but my flesh under his palm is still dry and chalky with dust.

"What just happened?" I mumble, raising my uninjured hand to my cheek.

"Nothing, wildcat. Your body is acclimating to the pain. It happens as a survival mechanism." He runs an assessing gaze over my injuries. His voice is so calm and reassuring, I can't help but believe him.

It doesn't make sense, but my brain isn't in the best position to judge right now. Fear can make things seem larger than they are, like when David tries to tell me a tiny house spider is big enough to eat him.

"Okay." I finally haul myself up on trembling legs and check my watch. "Crap, I was supposed to meet up with Charlie and David by the campus exit five minutes ago. They're going to freak." I don't mention my missing meal; eating is the last thing on my mind right now.

"Which exit?" Conall asks.

"We live in The Heights, so east."

Sycamore Heights is the closest suburban neighborhood to campus, basically butting up against the east end of University property. Living there means I can walk to and from school every day. It also means Charlie, David, and I have lived five minutes apart our entire lives. The neighborhood is peaceful, with single-family homes, fenced backyards, and tree-lined streets filled with basketball hoops and rowdy kids every summer. It also, unfortunately, is the furthest exit from where Conall and I are currently located.

"I know the one; I live in The Palisades. We're practically neighbors." Another ghost of a smile flits across his features as we begin walking eastward.

"Damn, rich boy," I joke.

Where Sycamore Heights is firmly middle- to upper-middle-class, The Palisades is filled with palatial homes most people could only dream of owning. At least three celebrities, four current members of Congress, and one former Presidential candidate own homes within its fences.

Xavier's family bought a house in The Palisades three years ago. It took him a solid year to stop bragging about it. Their house is smaller than most in The Heights, but he only cares that he lives within the coveted iron gates.

"What do your parents do?" I ask.

Conall is suddenly closed off, retreating behind the wall I thought was slowly lowering while we chatted. I instantly regret asking.

"Uhm, I don't live with my parents. I live with some family friends. The house is more of a joint effort, we all pitch in." His voice is firm.

No further questions, got it.

"That's cool, lots of people don't live with their parents in college. Pretty normal around here, unless your parents live right next door to the school like mine." I flash a sunny smile in an attempt to reassure him. It seems to work.

His answering grin is hesitant but real, and the butterflies from earlier make a sudden reappearance.

I hurry to squash them. *Bad brain, calm it down.* Just because the guy is built like a young god and happened to rescue me doesn't mean we're going to live happily ever after or anything.

My hobbling gait makes our journey across campus twice as long as usual. Most of my injuries are confined to my face and arm where Xavier crushed me against the bricks, but my legs are sore and bruised from my struggle. Every step sends small jolts of pain from the soles of my feet to the top of my head, compounding slowly into a full-body experience. The sensation has me longing for a hot bath to soothe my muscles and scrub the evidence of this afternoon from my lacerated skin.

Conall and I spend the journey swapping small pieces of our pasts. He tells me about how he was homeschooled and went to an online college for a while. He transferred to Sycamore so he could focus on his work as a private contractor—whatever that means. I trade him stories of my childhood with David and Charlie and my work at the campus animal conservatory in the summers. At his look of confusion, I explain Sycamore University has a facility affiliated with the College of Natural Sciences that houses injured or otherwise incapacitated animals which would not be able to survive in the wild.

The conservatory is my baby; I spend every summer and parts of the school year working there amongst the mini manufactured biomes, SCUBA-diving with rehabilitated turtles and fishes, feeding small mammals and reptiles, and caring for any infant animals that have been born throughout the year. Charlie and David frequently catch me hiding in there amongst the trees, reading a novel or singing the tracks of a musical with a cacophony of animal sounds as my accompaniment. The conservatory is my sanctuary as much as it is the animals'.

The frantic pounding of two sets of feet and raised voices causes me to flinch into Conall's side. He stiffens, and I quickly pull back with a muttered apology. He shoots me a pained half-smile that vanishes almost as quickly as it appeared as David and Charlie descend upon us.

Good to see he's not anywhere close to breaking his three-second smile limit. His sudden return to the aloof, detached state from earlier is confusing and a bit hurtful. I was hoping we were on our way to friendship, but maybe it's simply a one-sided trauma bond.

David begins yelling at Conall, hands waving wildly in front of him. Charlie yanks me away by my injured arm and I hiss as pain blazes its way through my nerve endings.

Someone growls behind me. I turn my head to find Conall completely ignoring David's tirade, glaring daggers at the hand Charlie has wrapped around my left bicep. My best friends mean well, but all I can focus on are Charlie's long fingers currently crushing the fresh abrasions hidden beneath the paper-thin sleeve of my jacket. The pain radiates through my limbs and weakens my knees.

"Are you listening to me, man?! What the hell happened to her? She left the gym an hour ago and here you come dragging her along with her face looking like Carrie at the prom! *Hello?*" David's voice reaches an embarrassingly loud volume as he realizes Conall is paying him absolutely zero attention, continuing to give Charlie's hand a look that could melt steel.

"Let. Her. Go." His voice is thunder rumbling; lightning flashes in his glare.

"Char," I plead. "My arm..." Tears burn and dribble through my cuts. My body threatens to crumble from the sheer amount of agony I've been in this week, both mentally and physically.

Charlie's hand springs open, releasing my arm as if electrocuted. I heave a sigh of relief. The sleeves of my jacket stick to my bloody and battered skin as I slowly peel it away, revealing the full extent of my injuries.

The boys suck in harsh inhales before rounding on Conall with renewed vigor.

Of course, they don't wait for an explanation.

"Guys." My voice is barely audible, a rasp of air whispering out of my lungs. I rally my final wave of energy and try again, "Guys! Leave him alone. Conall *saved* me. He didn't do this."

"Then who did?" Charlie asks.

Utterly spent, I flutter my hand dismissively, focusing on trying to stay upright.

Understanding surfaces in their faces, but it's Conall who answers, "Her ass of an ex-boyfriend." His vision bores into mine with some unreadable emotion shrouding the forested depths. Is it guilt? Sadness? Fear? I can't decipher their puzzle, but I could spend my life trying.

I can see David itching to find Xavier and drag him from whatever hole he's hiding in, so I say the one thing that will placate him for now, "Conall kicked his ass, Dee. And I'm okay, honest."

I might not have been without Conall, but I don't want to think about that. I definitely don't plan on voicing it around David. He's been itching to fight Xavier for years, and now he has nothing holding him back.

Conall pours gasoline on the dumpster fire that is this conversation. "He was trying to rape her in broad daylight."

"Technically it was in the shade," I can't help but add.

His voice could cut glass. "*Not* funny."

I glare at Conall from where I've seated myself on the grass at their feet while he recounts his side of my encounter with Xavier. So much for not telling Charlie and David the details. They spend the next five minutes attempting to get me to call the police, but I tell them I only want to go home, take a bath, and continue with our dinner plans. There's no forensic evidence on my body, thankfully, and I worry any police report will implicate Conall if Xavier starts whining about his injuries. And he will because he's a slimy coward.

"Conall, do you want to come with us?" I ask. We've finally reached a tentative truce on the no-police front, and I'm itching to get home, literally. The dried blood crusting my arm and face is worse than ants crawling on my skin. “We’re heading to my house for…obvious reasons.” I gesture to my macabre appearance. “And then we’re heading to Slice of Heaven for dinner and games.”

David’s cousin Tomas opened the gourmet-pizza-restaurant-slash-craft-beer-brewery three years ago, and it’s a huge hit with Sycamore’s crowd. There’s always a group of chairs at the bar for us, no matter how packed they are. Perks of being in with the owner. I would kill for a barbecue chicken pizza right now, but if I walk in there like this, someone *will* call the cops.

He shakes his head, shaggy black waves rustling around. “No thanks, I have plans tonight with some of the guys at home.” His hand darts into his pocket and comes back with a piece of paper and a black ballpoint pen. In a flash, he turns to the lamppost behind him. Conall scrawls something on the paper, folds it back up, and presses it into my hand. “My number. In case you ever want to give me that tour you promised.”

I’m graced with another of those fleeting smiles that come and go like stars winking in and out of view on a clear night. As quickly as it appears, it’s replaced by a grim scowl juxtaposed with a strangely yearning, gentle look. “Or if you need to talk about what happened today. Your secrets are safe with me.”

With that final cryptic line, he strides away.

David and Charlie bracket me and we move towards the sidewalk leading to our neighborhood. While the two of them bicker jovially about pizza toppings they’re going to try tonight, I take the time to pull out my phone to add Conall’s number to my contacts list. Unfolding the note he gave me, I pause and my heart fills to the brim with emotion. The simple line written underneath his phone number brings a trembling smile to my face:

I'm proud of you, wildcat.

Chapter 8
Consequences

- Conall -

"Wait, you did *what*? Does Dom know?"

I nod. Of course Domenic knows. I paid a visit to his office as soon as I returned home from campus. He wasn't particularly pleased with the events of this afternoon, but he claims to understand the reasoning behind my actions. It probably helped that I spent over an hour detailing all of the small pieces of Valorie's life I have already collected, and how I think each one could eventually be used to help me complete my mission.

The small black notebook full of her life—distilled to mere strokes of pen on paper—still weighs heavily in my front pocket.

"Okay, why don't you run everything by me again, but in detail this time." Finnegan lounges against the massive marble island, his cropped honey-brown hair matching the loaves of bread beside him on the counter.

The kitchen is filled with the warm scent of cinnamon and bananas wafting around us like the dust motes in the shaft of light through the little window over the sink. It's bread-making day, and my adopted brother dragged me in here an hour ago in hopes Marguerite would take pity on him and let him swipe some fresh from the oven before the others had a chance to get here.

Unfortunately for Finn, she wasn't swayed by his pout or his pleading blue eyes. Margie isn't fooled by any of our tactics; she sees right through every one of us, a product of over a decade of watching us grow up here. Undeterred, Finn's resorted to waiting as close to her as possible until the second she deems the bread cool enough to cut.

I close my eyes and launch into yet another recap of the fight between me and the human I found attacking Valorie two hours ago. My blood boils as I recount how I emerged from the gym after my workout and began heading towards a shortcut I knew would cut my trek through campus in half. I was preoccupied with thoughts of home and finally being able to relax at the end of another long day of reluctantly brainstorming ways to maintain my fragile connection with Valorie. I saw her in the equipment room with that friend she's always with—David, the loud one with the blue hair—but I don't think she noticed me.

For some reason, that doesn't give me the relief it should. The idea of us being in the same room and her not even noticing makes me...uneasy.

Seven days ago, she offered to give me a tour of the school and I accepted, feigning a lack of knowledge about a campus I've already thoroughly canvassed. I saw how shattered she looked when her imbecile ex-boyfriend tripped her in broad daylight. The asshole had the audacity to blame her for it in front of her friends and myself, a veritable stranger who could have easily called the authorities. It took everything I had to get up and follow her and her friends that afternoon when what I wanted to do was bash Xavier's smug face into the table. She hadn't reached out since then, though, and I was beginning to become concerned that I would have to use the number she gave me to contact her and try not to seem too suspicious.

My mind was churning with indecision, fragmented plans, and my family's repeated justifications for my task when I heard the telltale grunts and scrapes of a fight up ahead. I had initially turned to go a different way and avoid what I assumed were two idiots brawling in the alley when Valorie's muffled screams reached my ears. I squinted through the blinding afternoon sunlight to see her valiantly attempting to force Xavier off of her a scant fifteen feet in front of me, hidden within the shadowy mouth of an alley.

I reacted without a thought. Instantly, I was roaring into the gloom of the alleyway, ripping Xavier off of her and throwing him to the ground. The imbecile lay there with his cock out while my foot drove into his ribs in a fit of blind rage over and over, tears streaming down his idiotic face.

I told Finnegan I was so far gone I might have killed him right there, ended his pathetic life quickly and easily if it weren't for the tiny, pained whimper behind me.

Valorie was a beautiful wreck on the dirty stones, and my heart broke for her. I had seen firsthand how Xavier treated her in front of others, but something told me this was the first time he had tried something to this extent in public. I didn't know if this new level of boldness had something to do with how she had left things the other day or if he had always assumed nobody would ever dare to challenge him.

Valorie sported the glassy, far-off stare that told me shock was setting in fast. I'd seen it countless times in the past, both in previous missions and during those rare cases when injured dehmi came here to rest. Her face and arms were a pulpy mess of flesh and blood where Xavier had driven her into the brick wall she was slumped against. She didn't seem to notice her left arm's incorrect angle, or the blood coursing down her cheek. Her stare remained curiously focused on mine in a way that made something inside of me twist.

I gloss over her ramblings in my recollection—amusing though they were—and completely skip the message I wrote beneath my number on that scrap of paper. Finn doesn't need to know about those details. Still, I'm not vague enough to avoid his sigh when I mention I healed her.

I am prepared for the ramifications. Technically I didn't break any rules, because there's no proof I did anything. She had no doctor's notes detailing her injuries, there were no witnesses, and I doubt Xavier stopped to catalog the gruesome results of his sick power play. He was too busy running off with his tail between his legs. I even made sure to leave enough evidence of her assault that her well-meaning but overzealous friends somehow thought *I* was the one to hurt her.

If they only knew what is to come for her in the near future.

My story finally complete, I open my lids and discover I've gained a larger audience. Gaius and Gabrielle entered the kitchen at some point during my retelling. The tall, wraith-like twins that complete our quartet are now staring at me from where they're stationed at the counter next to Finn, unmistakably siblings despite the polarity of their appearances. Gaius' floppy, oil-spill hair is closely cropped atop his snowy skin, where Gabrielle's bone-white tresses reach past the slight dip of her waist, her midnight flesh a color so pure and deep, no human complexion can quite compare. Matching rose-colored gazes meet mine over the chilled marble, assessing my every move.

"That's one hell of a tale." Finn says, breaking the tense silence. "I can see why you came in here all riled up. Is the girl okay now?"

"As okay as someone could be with what happened. She was pretty shaken up, but no permanent damage. Her friends are taking her out to eat at some pizza place close to the college. Not exactly a quiet evening, but the food should help her recover, and those guys seem like they would murder anyone who looks at her the wrong way. They were half a second away from coming after me." I smirk, thinking of the rude awakening they would've experienced if they had decided to fight me.

Combat training has been a daily occurrence for all of us since we got here at age thirteen. Even wispy Gabrielle is more than a match for a couple of college kids. Charlie may be able to run, but that's not much help in a skirmish, and David's mouth would earn him a giant target on his chest.

"Well, I think it's great you saved her. Probably earned yourself a whole bucket of bonus points in the friendship department, too," Finn says with a wink.

I never once thought about how my actions could shift Valorie's opinion of me in a favorable direction. This should make me relieved—it's a step in the right direction—but instead, my gut roils with a sour, churning feeling.

I shut it down immediately. There's no place for guilt or remorse on a mission.

"Wouldn't it have been easier to...not, though?" Gaius asks. He shifts uncomfortably on his stool at the island countertop, avoiding my pointed glare. "If the guy would've killed her, you wouldn't have to deal with this anymore."

"Yes, Conall," Gabrielle's airy voice wafts through the tension in the room, thickening it into something palpable. "We all know you loathe the idea of kill—" At my flinch, she amends, "completing your mission, but you've been given a task. It has to be done. So, wouldn't it be best to get it over with so everyone can begin to heal?"

"*Does* it have to happen, Gabs?" Finn skirts around the subject I cannot bring myself to broach.

I'm grateful he is able to voice the question that chokes me. I'm fully committed to my cause, of course, but this doesn't mean I wouldn't appreciate another way out of this. None of us are comfortable with the idea of murdering an innocent.

Gabrielle's weary sigh slices my minuscule scrap of hope into ribbons. "I haven't been able to See a way out of this. The Web is too tangled, and if Esraa and Amon have brought this to you, there must be no other choice, Con. At least, not a reliable one..." She trails off.

My tiny shreds of hope begin to stitch themselves back together. *Is there an option that* isn't *reliable? What does that mean?*

I'm too afraid to ask. Gabby will tell me if she Sees something concrete. Until that happens, I have to keep to my current course. I steel myself for the possibility that whatever ephemeral twist of fate she has Seen will never come to pass. This is my job, simple as that. It's the way of the dehmi. For the good of this planet and the others we are called to steward.

"Gaius, I couldn't let her go in such a horrible way. She was terrified and in pain. My instructions were clear—Esraa and Amon want the girl finished peacefully. Besides, there was no guarantee it would have ended in murder, anyway."

Gaius scoffs, "Healers. You're all too compassionate for your own good. Gotta make the rabbit happy before the slaughter."

I can tell there's more he is going to say.

Sure enough, he takes a quick drink of water, ignores my pointed glare and bared teeth, and continues. "Don't get too attached. Her days are numbered, after all."

"Yes, Gaius," Gabrielle huffs. "We all see your point. You're as subtle as a knife to the gut."

I wince at the mental image, tracing a vein in the marble under my fingertips.

Finn interjects, "Why *do* Esraa and Amon need her gone, anyway? This is so unlike them."

"They said her mom is poised to make some huge biomedical discovery that will lead to a cure for a handful of major diseases, but The Web shows she will never devote herself enough to her research while she has Valorie around. Her love for her child is too great for her to realize her 'full scientific potential'." My voice is bitter by this point, but I don't care. Part of me irrationally hates Justine Vargas for unknowingly putting her daughter, and by extension, myself, in this position.

I lurch to my feet, suddenly unable to take this conversation any longer. Ignoring the calls of my adoptive siblings, I rush through the soaring archways of the foyer and out the side entrance of the Haven into the small thatch of forest that borders the west wall. I need to be alone. Hopefully, some fresh air and open space will help fix my thoughts and reorient myself towards my goal.

Because the problem is, it's too late.

I've already become too attached to Valorie Vargas, and I hate it. I've barely spent any time with her, but something about her calls to me like a kindred spirit. I've seen the darkness hiding within her, the bleak hopelessness lurking beneath those slate eyes. It sings to my own, tugs on my innate desire to heal, to protect.

But I can't protect her when I'm the villain in her story. I need to get over this. I can't risk jeopardizing this mission and my progress towards going home.

A rustling through the brush behind me announces someone's arrival.

Gabrielle weaves her way through the tangled undergrowth towards the flat-topped rock I'm seated on. She doesn't say a word as she settles next to me on the warm stone and leans her head against my shoulder.

I'm momentarily shocked by the casual contact. Gabrielle isn't like Finnegan, who shows affection as easily as breathing. Her gift leaves her prone to being aloof and subdued, almost as if erecting a barrier between herself and others will protect her from Seeing their fates in the often unpredictable flashes of The Web bestowed upon her. She's become better at showing her emotions over the last few years, but is still by far the most reserved of our group.

"You're all tangled up, Con." Her voice reminds me of a breeze, quiet but firm.

"What do you See, Gabby? Am I choosing the right path?"

I'm embarrassed by the questions, the vulnerability they portray. I've never been one to shirk my duties or question The Council, but this is different. Valorie is no serial killer eluding the human authorities or cult leader masquerading as a friendly face. She's merely an innocent girl in an unfortunate position.

"I can't See much, and believe me I've tried." She sighs. "But I can See one thing. Stay on your current course, and you'll make it out of this intact. I can't tell how or when, but this trajectory eventually leads you through all of this turbulence. But..."

"But?"

Her gaze drifts as she analyzes the twisted threads of time only she can view.

I once asked Gabby what it was like to See. She said it was like having the past, present, and future all stretched out around her in a tangled mess. Sometimes, things flash in front of her—fragments of some time or another—and she barely catches a coherent image or a passing emotion before they're gone. If she concentrates, however, she can sometimes drag portions of that snarled Web in front of her and sort through them. She can See how an action from the past led to now, and from there, how the actions taken in the near future could have ramifications that affect the span of time. It's exhausting work and often leaves her frustrated over the vague answers she receives. We try not to ask her for help unless it's important.

"I See...changes. The way things are now is not the way things will end. There's light and darkness...and pain." Her voice fades to a whisper on the last word.

Of course there will be pain. Valorie's, her friends', her family's. Mine. Pain is the one thing I can guarantee without Gabrielle's help. What I need is a method. A plan of action. A way to save her.

A way to save me.

"There's something you're not telling me, isn't there?"

Another sigh. "If I give you any more information, everything goes bad. I can't risk it. I won't risk you on this."

I lean over and rest my cheek against the top of her opalescent hair. "Thanks, Gab. Guess I'll have to figure this one out on my own."

"I'll keep looking. None of us like this mission. Not even Gaius, despite his comments."

"I know." Gaius may not have any tact, but he's as committed to our cause as the rest of us. "If you can find something, you'll be my favorite sibling."

She chuckles and musses up my hair. "I should already be your favorite sibling."

We sit in silence for a while, and then, "Oh, Con, I forgot. Finn and Domenic want you to go meet up with them in the games room. Something about darts again?"

A mischievous smile spreads across my face. The third round of our ongoing darts tournament between my gargantuan brother and father figure is exactly what I need to take my mind off of all this. And maybe getting my head into this game will prepare me for the subterfuge yet to come.

Domenic finally calls an end to our antics after four solid hours of dart-throwing. The score remains locked in our three-way tie, one that has not been broken in months of playing. I think we're all enjoying ourselves too much to allow the tournament to end. Somehow, Dom only ever seems to call it a night when the scores are once again evenly matched. Gabrielle and Gaius joined in for a few rounds, although their form of gamesmanship is less actual throwing and more heckling whoever is up at the time.

By the end of the night, we're all full of laughter and Marguerite's famous cinnamon banana bread. Finnegan ate a whole loaf by himself, hidden in the corner like a drug addict getting his fix. He hissed at Gabrielle when she tried to sneak an extra piece from his stash.

Sometimes I swear I live with a bunch of children.

An image races through my head as I climb the stairs to my room, too fast for me to stop. Valorie, laughing and comfortable with my family as we lounge in the game room. A glance over her shoulder turns into a broad smile when she finds me, and she reaches out to brush her hand along my arm. Then, reality rushes back in.

Furious, I shove open the door to my small suite of rooms and head straight to the en-suite bathroom, ready for a hot shower. My shoulders and back are throbbing from a combination of four hours throwing darts, an afternoon spent exercising, and beating the shit out of Xavier. My clothes settle into the wicker hamper in a pool of dark blue denim and white cotton, and I allow the shower to wash away the pain of the day, both mental and physical. The scalding water continues to paint the planes of my chest and back long after I've finished scrubbing myself clean. I watch the droplets cling to the clean white tiles and will my mind to go blank for a while.

Eventually, I emerge from the flow, wreathed in steam and wrapped in a fluffy cobalt towel Marguerite must have picked out during one of her shopping trips. My bare feet leave damp marks on the warm oak flooring and dark blue area rug in my bedroom as I pad my way towards my closet.

A pair of black pajama pants quickly replaces the towel around my waist. I collapse into my bed against the far wall. The moonlight through my open window provides the only light I need, casting stark stripes of light and darkness throughout the room. Things seem less ominous, less pressing in the quiet of the night. My lids drift shut, lulled towards a peaceful slumber by the calm sounds of the evening carried on the breeze.

Bling.

I shove my head under the pillow, but it does little to muffle the shrill noise.

Bling.

I roll as close to the wall as possible. Maybe distance will cause the sound to go away.

Bling.

Cursing, I flip over and swipe the phone from my nightstand. I jab at the screen to unlock it, hoping to find the setting that stops my recurring alarm for unread messages. My fingers pause when I see the alert displayed across my screen.

My night has suddenly become much more interesting.

Chapter 9

A Slice of Heaven

- Valorie -

My third slice of pizza melts in my mouth with an explosion of flavors. Rich, peppery sauce, a hint of lime, and freshly grilled chicken combine with the crisp crust in a perfect, decadent bite. I could happily eat this every day for the rest of my life without getting tired of it.

Four hours, two scalding showers, and a change of clothes later, I finally feel a little more like myself—the delicious food and pleasant cacophony of tonight's dinner crowd are helping. Sitting on my favorite bar stool in Slice of Heaven, sharing Tomas' new prototype chili lime chipotle chicken pizza with David and Charlie, I can almost pretend this afternoon's events never happened.

Almost.

I close my eyes and let the sounds of the pizza bar press into me—the hoots and cackles of a rowdy bachelor party pre-gaming in a dimly lit corner booth, the rapid-fire Spanish spoken by the kitchen staff as they prepare custom pizzas at a breakneck pace, the clinks and clangs of glasses and shakers at the bar. A heady mix of acidic tomatoes, vibrant spices, and effervescent spirits combines into Slice of Heaven's unique perfume. The simple magic of a night out is a balm to my tired soul.

Slender fingers tap against the back of my right hand and my lids drift open.

"Everything okay there, Val?" Charlie asks, barely loud enough to be heard over the din of the bar. "You look like you're falling asleep. Do you need to go home?" His concerned stare bores into mine as if he can yank the truth out of me without needing to wait for a response.

David is equally as intense on my opposite side. That's the thing about David and Charlie; at first glance, people wonder what could have possibly brought them together. David, with his constantly rotating rainbow of hair colors matched by his loud voice and vibrant, unapologetic spirit, seems out of place beside Charlie's carefully polished appearance and quiet athleticism. Below the surface, however, they both radiate confidence and are fiercely protective of the ones they love, almost to a fault.

"No way. I'm fine guys. I was...soaking it all in, I guess."

Going home is the absolute last thing that will help me. The idea of sitting in my dark bedroom makes me shudder. Being left alone with my brain all night is a terrifying concept, especially following today's chaos. Having the guys stay over again would mean I get a full night's sleep, but my pride prevents me from asking them to spend another night crammed in my bed. Queen mattresses aren't made for three fully grown adults.

My desperation must bleed out into my stare, because David nonchalantly throws over his shoulder as he returns to his half-eaten pizza slice, "Hope you changed the sheets because we're having a slumber party again, Vally. I need some snuggles!" His tomato-coated lips stretch into a huge grin that pulls a giggle out from the place deep inside of me where my happiness is hiding.

"A slumber party? Hey, is there room for one more?" Tomas' voice booms over us as his broad frame slides in behind the pristine, polished bar.

A mix of hefting huge sacks of flour and bushels of produce combined with a healthy penchant for sampling his own recipes results in Tomas' physique matching his large-than-life personality, despite only standing a few inches taller than me. David and his cousin may not share much in terms of appearances, but in a darkened room you wouldn't be able to tell the two apart. Add David's mother into the mix and you'll find boisterousness is a Curbelo family requirement.

"Not for you, *gordito.* I need my wiggle room," David asserts. All four of us burst into laughter.

"I doubt Karina would be very happy with me staying over anyway," Tomas says. His wife, Karina, is six months pregnant and as much of a firecracker as her husband.

"She'd have your balls in a soup if you weren't home to rub her feet tonight," I laugh, already feeling lighter than I have in days. This is the kind of therapy I desperately needed. A night out filled with my best friends and amazing food can cure almost anything.

Tomas fixes his chocolate browns on the scabs and raw flesh covering one side of my face. His expression hardens, fingers clenching the smooth lacquered wood of the bar-top. "David told me you had a problem today. The pizza oven is always yours if you need to...dispose of something." He smiles, but the joke doesn't touch the anger on his face. "I've gotta say, though, you don't look as busted up as I expected. You must've put up one hell of a fight. I'm proud of you."

I'm proud of you, wildcat.

I look up into the reflection of my face in the mirror above the bar. An impressionist painting looks back, transforming me into a piece from the art history course I took freshman year. The artist brushed over my ivory skin with broad slashes of crimson. Daubs of deep blues and purples bracket my brows and cover the planes of my cheekbones, with my mouth a delicately crafted bow below the carnage, only faintly marred by shadows and swelling. The colors are muted, however, as if the painter depicted his muse a few days post-upheaval instead of a mere handful of hours. Tomas is right, I don't look nearly as horrifying as I had expected.

"So, Val," David purrs. His tone can mean nothing good for me. "What exactly happened between you and your knight in shining armor today? We didn't hear much at school except for the fact that he beat Xavier's ass, which automatically makes him my new best friend. But you know I won't be able to sleep without *allllll* the details."

A large bite of pizza grants me a reprieve to compose a response. Three sets of eyes bore into me with rapt attention and barely concealed impatience. When it comes to gossip, my friends are insatiable. They're a bunch of vultures, searching for whatever scraps they can find.

Guess I'm their latest meal.

I explain the turn of events that led from me enjoying the afternoon to becoming intimately acquainted with the alley wall, then launch into a detailed description of Conall coming to my rescue—conveniently leaving out the weird sensations and butterflies fluttering in my stomach and only briefly glossing over our walk across campus.

"And then you accosted the poor guy and accused *him* of being the one to fuck up my face," I finish with a pointed look at my two best friends, who at least have the decency to look ashamed of themselves.

"How were we supposed to know what happened?" David's voice is caught between bashful and indignant, his volume steadily rising. "He showed up half carrying you, with you looking like you'd been shoved through a meat grinder. And, to top it off, your arm was hanging half off under your jacket and hero boy practically bit Char's head off for touching you!" He punctuates his speech with a fist against the wooden bar top, sloshing his drink.

Charlie swoops in to save the day, reaching around me to rub a soothing thumb over David's knuckles. "Easy there, tiger. I think it's sweet that Conall cared enough to make sure Val got to us safely. She was practically asleep on her feet by the time she got to her house, imagine what could have happened if he had left her alone after chasing Xavier off. Plus, I *was* hurting Val's arm, even if I didn't know it."

Tomas leans his elbows onto the bar, his eyebrows nearly reaching his hairline at this point. "So, this Conall guy. Are you and him..." He takes the first two fingers of his right hand and taps them together a few times, as if I need the visual aid. "Together?"

David chokes on his soda, thumping himself on the chest a few times. "*Are* you? Is that why he 'ran into you' in the alleyway?"

Air quotes...really, David?

"No. He said he was working out in the gym." I pause, remembering the man with a dark head of wavy hair and a sweat-glazed bronze back exercising on an elliptical across the room. "*Shit*! David, I think he was the guy we were checking out while we waited for Charlie."

"Damn, you've got yourself one hot friend." He slings a long arm around mine and Charlie's shoulders. "Make that one *more* hot friend. I don't know how many more you can handle."

My eyes roll so hard, I'm surprised their nerves don't snap inside my skull.

"What about me?" Tomas' feigned indignation makes us roar with laughter, and I pull him halfway over the bar to add him to our hug.

The moonlight filters through sheer curtains in my dark bedroom as the three of us huddle under my white duvet, sharing gossip and stories like we're children at a sleepover instead of...well...adults at a sleepover. The pale hardwood and pastel blue walls of my bedroom are a patchwork of darkness and the ethereal light of a clear, star-filled night. Peace finally finds me amongst the mingled voices of our trio, the way it always has since we were young. I rest easy, content to bask in the sound of Char and Dee murmuring about a member of the relay team who's playing three girls.

A crumpled square of paper on the nightstand catches my eye. It's nondescript, covered with ten digits and one powerful sentence written by an elegant hand in cheap black ink. Is Conall still out, merry in the arms of the friends he said he was meeting with tonight? Or is he lying in a bed not so different than mine, staring up at the same lonely sky? It's hard for me to imagine his stoic, closed demeanor disappearing long enough for him to let loose. Maybe he's a different person around the ones he cares for.

Maybe, one day, I'll find out for myself.

My reverie is broken by Charlie gently sliding my phone into my hand. "Text him," he whispers while David rambles on with another story, this one about a girl in his sociology course who's getting married to a professor.

"I don't know what—"

"I can see your brain spinning from here, and I'm assuming it has to do with a certain dark-haired guy from school. So text him. Set up that campus tour you're supposed to be giving him. Nobody thinks you're *actually* dating—you know how David and Tomas love being assholes. Though Conall is definitely easy on the eyes." He chuckles quietly. "Everyone can use another friend. I haven't seen him hanging out with anyone at school. Maybe he's lonely, too. Like you are."

I give a half-assed scoff. "Lonely? How could I be lonely with the two of you hanging off of me like orphaned puppies all the time?"

Charlie's knowing look is clear in the soft light of the moon. "Loneliness has nothing to do with how many people surround you. You can be lonely in a crowded room. We see you, Valorie; we *know* you. And when neither of us is around, we worry about you. Your life is full of people who love you, but Xavier kept you trapped in a glass box of lies for so long...it's okay for you to be a little broken. It doesn't make you weak. It makes you real." His slender finger brushes away a tear that manages to sneak past my eyelid.

My breath catches on a ragged inhale. "What would I do without you two?" I whisper.

"You'd be fine. But we're sure glad you picked us."

Our quiet conversation is interrupted by the crash of a body knocking the wind out of both of us.

"Hey, are you guys listening to me?" David's bright hair obscures my vision as he thrusts his head between us on the pillows.

I screech, shoving him playfully.

"Can't...breathe...suffocating...dead." I feign a dramatic death, complete with vacant stare and lolling tongue. It's pretty spot-on; I should have gone into acting.

As the two wrestle on the other end of the bed, I find myself turning over Charlie's words in my head.

I can't deny this strange compulsion to contact Conall.

Maybe Charlie has a point; maybe instead of avoiding this feeling I should lean into it, extend the hand of friendship to my happenstance savior. Not giving my nerves a chance to talk me out of this, I reach over and grab the paper he gave me.

Me

Hey. Uhm, it's Valorie. From school. So I realized I haven't given you that tour I promised you. How about next Friday? It's the least I can do, since you saved my ass today.

I slide my finger up to the 'send' key and off the message goes, along with all the air in the room. That has to be the most awkward text message written since the advent of the cellular phone.

Did I say "uhm"? Pathetic.

I stuff a pillow over my head to smother my agony and contemplate staying here in the smothering darkness of feathers and cotton until I turn to dust.

The phone's soft chime interrupts my self-loathing.

Conall

Hey, Valorie From School. I've gotta say, didn't expect that to be your full name. It's weird as hell, but you pull it off.

A small snicker escapes. Thankfully, the boys are too engrossed in their own conversation to pay any attention to what's going on behind my screen.

Always a sucker for wordplay, I can't help but form a retort.

Me

It's a famous historical name. Dad picked it out. Mom wanted to name me 'Mitochondria'.

Conall

Good thing your dad was there to save you. I couldn't get a tour from a girl named Mitochondria. I'd be laughing too hard to pay attention.

Oh, someone is clearly very pleased with themselves. I can practically see his self-satisfied smile through the phone. I'd bet it even lasts more than three seconds.

Me

You're a real comedian. So does that mean we're on for Friday?

I wait with bated breath for his reply.

He doesn't keep me waiting for long.

Conall

Sounds like a plan. But, I have a feeling we'll be seeing each other before then…like maybe at lunch Monday. Who knows?

Who knows, indeed. I plug my phone in and set it to vibrate— with the sound on, I'm too tempted to spend all night texting him.

For the first time in a long time, I fall asleep with a smile on my face.

Chapter 10
Friends
- Valorie -

In the week since that fateful night when Charlie nudged me into creating a new friendship, things have changed more than I could have ever expected.

I barely paid attention to David grumbling all Saturday morning about the lack of hot guys at Charlie's track meet, although I made sure to put my phone away and watch Charlie win gold.

David asked who I was texting when my fifth message came through before the first set of field events had finished. When he found out it was Conall, he suddenly became much less absorbed with finding me an athlete and instead busied himself with attempting to read over my shoulder.

After a weekend filled with quips passed through my phone screen, I'll admit I was intrigued by Conall's cryptic promise to see me on Monday. But when I wandered over to the dining hall after my morning lectures and found him sitting at a bistro table on a shaded corner of the lawn, I still assumed he was waiting for someone else. I met his steady stare, ready to say my hellos and move on until Friday, but he simply inclined his head to the empty metal chair across from him. I sat, he filled my plate from the various to-go boxes he had scattered all across the small table, and with one simple act, a new routine was born.

Every day since, he's been waiting for me at that same green iron table, a buffet of food already purchased and set on display for us to enjoy.

The most confusing part, though, is the expression I sometimes spy on his face during days like this one, when I'm able to approach the table unseen. With no one else around, his visage is somehow...sad. As if he's resigned himself to a fate he wishes he could change.

I never have the courage to ask him about it, but I notice. He thinks I only see the small, secret smile he uses to greet me, and not the darkness hiding underneath the grin. I'm familiar with the darkness, I live in it.

I wonder if he's all jumbled bits and pieces inside like I am.

I survey my new friend as I walk towards what has become our table, searching him for any signs of melancholy darkness. Today he's wearing a simple sky blue tee that makes his skin glow. The cotton is fitted closely across lean, defined muscles, the same ones I viewed gleaming with sweat across the crowded gymnasium floor. Dark denim sheathes his long legs that extend out from beneath the table, similar to the jeans I chose to wear this morning.

He's a study in sunlight and brilliance, any remnants of that darkness locked away far beneath his shining surface. An uncomfortable, prickling feeling of inadequacy hits me faster than I can quash it.

"The sunglasses are new," I say with a smile as I sidle up to the table. "Got tired of squinting all day?"

Conall graces me with a grin full of straight, white teeth. I count; it lasts a full three and a half seconds. Progress. "If I get crow's feet you won't want to hang out with me anymore, and then who will I have lunch with?"

"You're right, I could never have a wrinkly friend. What would the tabloids think?" I grab utensils and pile on my own food before he can get to it.

He scowls at my plate as if the plastic disc offends him.

"Don't worry, Conall. If I ever get bored, David will have lunch with you. He's a sucker for a pretty face."

Whoops. I blush, mortified by my accidental word vomit. Conall—as a man in possession of two working eyes—must be aware of his beauty, but I've never pointed it out.

Of course, he doesn't let it go.

"Aw, you think I'm pretty?"

"Don't get used to hearing it," I retort around a huge mouthful of pasta. "Wouldn't want you to get a big head."

He places a respectably-sized forkful of chicken into his mouth, chews, and swallows before replying. "Your concern for my well-being is admirable."

I roll my eyes as I shovel more food into my mouth.

The two of us finish our lunch in companionable silence, accompanied by the soft music of birds and the chatter of students drifting on the warm breeze.

We both gorge ourselves until the table has been picked clean. I stack up our empty containers and manage to successfully weave my way between the obstacle course of tables and chairs on the embossed concrete plaza to drop them into the recycling bin. As I return to our table, I see Conall turned towards me, his mouth downturned and stare unreadable beneath the tint of his sunglasses.

"Ready to head out?" I sling my bag over a shoulder and prop my hand on my hip.

He stands up and holds his arm out to me with a flourish, ever the consummate gentleman.

Laughing, I link my arm through his and affect the most over-the-top British accent I can manage. “Let us promenade, good sir.” Thanks to several *Bridgerton* binge-watching sessions, I’d say it’s a pretty accurate impression. Definitely a seven out of ten, at least.

With that, we’re off, meandering towards our first destination. To begin the tour, I take him through the Science Quarter, with its angular, modernized buildings made of black steel beams and slabs of mirror-like tinted glass. Upon reaching the building that houses the faculty labs, I turn down the side of the mammoth structure and lead him to a side entrance tucked into a shadowed alcove. We climb fifteen flights of stairs to the rooftop observatory that contains the campus’ giant telescope. This hidden platform is one of my favorite sightseeing spots; only the astronomy students come up here. Nobody else wants to brave the climb.

I lean my elbows on the railing and look out over the students milling about like ants far below us.

“A queen surveying her kingdom,” he murmurs behind me.

“Bow before me, peasants!” I shout, bumping my hip against the rail in a fit of giggles.

When I turn to lead him back downstairs and continue our tour, I’m gifted with another of his secret smiles. It lights up my world as brightly as a spotlight.

How have I only known this man for two weeks and I already can’t imagine life without his friendship?

We take a hidden shortcut from the Science Quarter and emerge into the sculpture gardens of the Arts Quarter. Here, the buildings are bedecked in pastel yellow masonry and covered in intricate cornices and arches. I spend five minutes in front of a larger-than-life granite statue of a man reading, telling Conall a story about my childhood.

"This statue is where I hid every time I played hide-and-seek with my father. One time, Dad found me fast asleep in its arms. He left me there for three hours. I was red as a lobster—there were no clouds and it was August. Not a good combination."

The small chuckle he gifts me goes straight into my mental bank of Conall's emotions.

From there, it's a short walk through yet another winding avenue until we arrive in the Technology Quarter. At first glance, this Quarter is the oldest and least impressive, with Romanesque brick faces to their hulking, blocky buildings. I bring Conall into one of the buildings to show him their secret: Beneath their plain exteriors lie floor upon floor of state-of-the-art computer banks and virtual-reality systems. He spends a few minutes perusing the tech hidden away in these windowless rooms before signalling for me to continue playing tour guide.

Around the corner from the Technology Quarter, the Language Quarter looms, filled with columned marble buildings reminiscent of Greece or Rome. Students mill about the area, lounging on the grand staircases or strolling in small groups. Snippets of scenes from student thespians practicing on small outdoor stages or linguists talking in shaded alcoves float to us on the balmy breeze. This Quarter is always boiling over with life and culture.

A preoccupied student crashes into Conall, his head buried in a leather-bound book while mumbling phrases to himself in what sounds to be Latin. He quickly moves to apologize, and Conall straightens him with a murmured "*Bene habet*," patting him on the shoulder and moving us along the trail.

My mouth hangs open. *What the hell?*

"You speak Latin?" I ask incredulously. Nobody speaks Latin anymore unless they're into medicine, theater, or history. I know the barest bit because my parents check off two of those three boxes, but I'm nowhere near fluent.

"I speak twelve languages."

"*Twelve*?"

"It helps with...my job."

Ah, yes, the mysterious private contracting company. Conall never seems to offer any actual information about his work in any of our conversations. All I know is the people he shares his home with also work in the same field. No amount of leading statements or carefully crafted questions have gotten him to reveal more than that.

I continue on, wondering if he can feel me shortening my stride as we slowly near the end of our time together. Once we reach the end of the boulevard, we will have worked our way through all four of the Quarters.

Frankly, I'm not ready for this blissful day to be over.

Sure, I could take him to countless other places on campus and extend this tour for hours longer. There's the conservatory where I work, the amphitheater here in the Arts Quarter, the rec hall, full of games and activities and always some sort of party, the dorms, the dining halls, and the greenhouses. Place after place after place, each less necessary for him to see than the last.

Despite how morose I am at the idea of our time together ending, I doubt Conall would appreciate a thorough exploration of the seven-story Administration building. I can picture the bored-to-tears expression on his face when I wax poetic about the marble bust of our first dean in the atrium.

No, our day of carefree wandering is drawing to a close, no matter how slowly I walk.

Conall angles himself towards a large oak, its branches arching majestically over the end of the path, perfectly framing the slowly setting sun. He leans against it, his back to the rough bark, and crosses his arms as I come to a halt facing him.

I scuff my toe in the dirt, suddenly awkward under his scrutiny. "So..."

"Dinner."

My brain screeches to a halt. "Huh?"

"Dinner. With me."

He looks about as awkward as I feel, his face downcast, hands fidgeting at his waist. Does he think he has to take me out since I helped him with the tour today?

"It's okay, you don't have to do that." I'd love to have dinner with him, if I'm being honest. Today was one of the most peaceful days I've had in a long time. Plus, I'm afraid of what will happen when I'm alone in my room again with only my thoughts for company. But I don't want Conall to think he owes me anything.

"Come on, I know you must be hungry. My treat."

At my hesitation, he softens.

"Please," he adds. "Today has been...fun. I don't usually get to have much fun, and I'd like for it not to end quite yet."

So it's not out of some sense of obligation? Well, in that case... "I accept."

A radiant smile streaks across his face. It's a shooting star, lighting him up. "Then what are we waiting for?"

I think I'm having a heart attack.

A sleek, midnight-blue motorcycle is parked against the curb in front of me, its chrome accents near blinding in the angled beams of fading light. It might as well be a lion crouching on the asphalt with Conall as its master, lounging against the side of it, smug as hell.

"*This* is what you drive?" My voice squeaks out two octaves higher than I mean it to.

"Usually. Cars simply aren't as freeing when you can't feel the wind in your face. Now hop on."

"But..." I wrack my brain, trying to think of a reason not to get on this death trap with him. Not that I don't trust him to keep me safe, but you can only be so safe on a glorified bicycle in DC Metro traffic. "There's only one helmet!"

Yeah, that's a solid reason. Score one for Valorie.

Conall rummages in a leather pack attached to the rear of the seat while I wait. The shiny, black dome of a helmet emerges from its depths. *Damn.* He tosses it to me and I scramble to catch it.

"Get on the bike, wildcat." He smirks. "It won't bite."

My parents have always said I'm too stubborn for my own good. As I squash my curly head into the helmet, I'm starting to think they might be right. There's a glint in Conall's eye—it pushes exactly enough of my buttons to make me sure this is some sort of test of my bravery. Jokes on him, I'm never one to back down from a challenge.

I throw my leg over the bike behind him and fight the urge to scream as he peels off into the balmy evening.

Once I manage to crack my eyelids open, I understand why he chooses to travel this way.

The world flies by us in a blur of colors—greens, silvers, blacks all blend in streaky abstract strokes that make everything surreal. We pull onto the highway and he lets loose on the throttle, ratcheting us up to a speed that would be terrifying if it wasn't so exhilarating. It's like we're flying.

A voice seems to come from inside my brain, causing me to jerk slightly. "I haven't had to stop and resuscitate you, so I'm guessing this wasn't the death trap you expected?"

Smug bastard.

"It's fine, I guess." It's much more than "fine", but he doesn't need the ego boost. I may not be able to see his face, but I can *feel* him smirking. "How can I hear you right now?"

"Speakers and microphones in the helmets," Conall answers. "I can talk to you, play music, answer calls—basically anything you can do with a phone. Or a car," he adds, barely containing his mirth.

"All right, I get it, motorcycle boy. Your cute little bike is *so* cool."

His dark laugh sends a shiver skittering down my spine. "You shouldn't have said that."

He leans us backwards at a frightening angle, cutting off my ability to question his words. I scream as he pops the bike onto its rear wheel in one smooth, entirely too quick motion. If it wasn't for the death grip I've had on Conall since he first revved the engine, I'd be a smear on the concrete.

"Put us down!" I dig my fingernails into the weathered leather of his jacket. "I'm never hanging out with you again!"

The front of the motorcycle smoothly returns to Earth and he speeds off, laughing louder than I've ever heard him. It reverberates through my helmet, giving me a private ticket to his symphony of happiness. The smell of hot asphalt and gasoline mix with his lavender and pine smoke scent in a sinfully wild bouquet. If I could bottle it up and spray it on my pillow every night I would. It's the scent of life.

The trees morph into metropolitan lights flitting by us as the bike slows to a stop in front of a small restaurant. There's a tidy patio with a few sets of tables and chairs, and the aged yet spotless sign over the door names the tiny place Rising Moon. Buttery yellow light filters through the circular window on the door, making the place feel closer to someone's home than a restaurant. As I enter through the door Conall props open, I see my initial impression may be more accurate than I thought.

A wrinkled Chinese woman shorter than my mom stands at the counter in front of a cozy, intimate dining room filled with traditional art. She gasps and runs to us, a smile creasing her weathered skin. A swift stream of Mandarin erupts from her mouth and I try to gently explain that we don't speak the language, but Conall replies first, his accent almost as perfect as hers.

I huff out a breath. *Of course he speaks Mandarin. Probably speaks Martian too. Mister Lexicon.*

She gestures to me, a sneaky smirk on her face that makes it apparent even to me that she's asking if I'm his girlfriend. He slings an arm around my shoulder and says something that makes her laugh and wag a finger in his direction. She leads us to a table by the large windows in the rear of the restaurant, swiping two menus off the hostess' stand on the way.

Conall receives a loving pat on the arm and the woman gives me a warm grin before she retreats into the kitchen.

"So," I say as I slide into my chair, "I guess Mandarin is one of your twelve languages."

"And Cantonese."

"Of course. One simply must be well-rounded," I scoff.

He smirks at my sarcastic response. "I know how much you love Asian food, and this place is the best. I've been coming here for years. There's nothing on the menu that's less than fantastic."

I pull a menu towards me, but don't open it. "She seemed very happy to see you."

"I quite literally ran into Mrs. Huang about eight years ago. I was walking on the sidewalk right out front on the hottest day of the year. My profuse apologies over almost knocking the old woman down were ignored, and instead, she insisted I come inside for some tea and a meal. Ever since then, I've been coming here at least once a week. I don't always stay to eat, but I check on her and her husband and they'll send some food home with me for the house. Their kids live in California, so they're alone here in an apartment above the restaurant, just the two of them."

I'm dumbfounded. It's by far the longest consecutive string of words I've ever heard leave Conall's mouth, and of course the monologue isn't about him. It's about this sweet old lady and her husband, who I can only imagine is as adorable as she is.

He leans over and taps my chin, and it's only then that I realize I'm sitting here like a fool with my mouth literally hanging open. I snap my mouth closed with an audible click, but it falls back open when he reaches over and steals my menu from under my hands.

"Wait, I haven't decided yet," I protest, reaching out to grab the menu back from him.

He moves it barely out of reach. "Do you trust me?"

"Yes." The word slips out before I have a chance to think about it, but it's the truth. For someone I've only known a short time, Conall has become one of my closest friends.

I don't know whether that's adorable or sad.

"Then indulge me with this. I know what you like; let me see if I can pick something out that'll blow your mind. I love a good challenge."

My interest piqued, I motion for him to keep the menu. "Let's see how you do, hot shot."

Half an hour later, I'm ready to have Conall pick out all of my meals for the rest of my life. My stomach is one bite away from bursting, and I have a full Styrofoam container of leftovers ready to go home with me, courtesy of my new best friend, Mrs. Huang.

I don't know what Conall told her I liked when they had their whispered conversation across the table from me. It must translate to "a big plate full of Heaven," because that's what she brought me. Rice noodles smothered in a sweet and spicy sauce, with crispy pieces of chicken and fresh vegetables...I could die happily right here at this table. I might if I eat one more mouthful.

I look up from my empty plate with a pleased hum, but my satisfied grin slips away when I notice Conall. His face is filled with a look of such heartbreaking, soul-crushing helplessness that I can't stop myself from asking, "What's up? Is something going on? Sometimes I look at you and you have such a *sad* look on your face, like the whole world is ending or someone you love is dying." *Sometimes you look as broken as I feel inside.*

I reach out and gently tap the back of his hand that's resting on the small wooden table between us. "Do you want to talk about it?"

He pulls his hand out from under mine, slowly running his thumb over the spot where my finger was. His explanation comes in halting sentences, "I have to do a lot, see a lot, for my job. Things nobody ever should have to deal with, but someone has to or…maybe the world truly would end. Sometimes, when things are quiet, it's a bit overwhelming."

It seems we both have issues with the things that creep up on us in silent spaces.

"What are you, a contract killer?" The joke falls flat, but I'm trying desperately to keep up with his mercurial moods. To bring back the lighthearted fun from earlier. I crave his humor, his happiness. His darkness doesn't scare me, but he belongs in the light.

Conall merely stares at his plate, his vision unseeing.

Shit, is *he?*

"My job keeps people safe. That's all that matters. I shouldn't be complaining, it's unprofessional."

"Everyone has a right to be sad sometimes," I murmur. "It doesn't matter if you're doing 'the right thing'. Professionalism can go to hell. Everyone is allowed to feel, to dream."

Conall abruptly stands, pulling out my chair for me and tossing a fifty onto the table as I grab my bag and shrug it on. At my questioning look, he explains that Mrs. Huang never allows him to pay for a meal. He always leaves the money behind and pretends he doesn't know how it got there when she questions him during his next visit. I know our bill wasn't more than twenty dollars, but I keep my mouth shut about his obvious overpayment. I'm pretty sure this is another way for him to thank them. The meal was so delicious, they deserve every cent.

We make the drive back to campus in silence. The stars are a blur of light and color streaking by in the dark sky overhead. Their frantic pace matches the anxious whirring of my brain.

I should have kept my mouth shut in the restaurant. Clearly, something about my comments at the end of our dinner upset Conall. I was only trying to help. I never should have asked about his work.

I'm such an idiot.

Now, instead of appreciating the otherworldly beauty of the clear night sky at seventy miles per hour, I'm frantically rifling through my brain, looking for a way to salvage the wonderful time we've had.

Conall pulls into my driveway and leaves the bike idling while he retrieves my to-go container from the pack behind the seat, placing it in my sweaty palms. Our carefree day already feels like it happened years ago, and I'm worried my clumsy attempt at getting him to open up may have irrevocably damaged our friendship.

Until he scoops me into a hug when I hold the helmet towards him. He heaves a sigh against the top of my head, releases me, and rubs a hand from his brow to his chin.

"I'm sorry for shutting you out." The words tumble out of him in a whirlwind.

I barely dare to breathe, afraid that any sudden movements will make him stop talking.

"I don't usually talk about myself. People in my...career tend to keep their feelings to themselves. Or at least, I do. I'm not used to someone seeing me." He quirks up a corner of that adorable mouth. It's slight, but I'm still chalking it up as a smile. "Guess I better get used to it, with you around."

Conall swings his leg over the bike with a grace I most certainly did not achieve earlier today. "See you tomorrow, wildcat. Sleep tight." He reverses out of my driveway and races back down the street.

I shake myself and head inside, floating on air.

It's not until I've bid good night to my parents, changed into pajamas, and crawled into my bed that I realize I never once gave Conall my address. Strangely, the idea doesn't frighten me at all.

Chapter 11

Happy Birthday

- Valorie -

David's beer sloshes onto my hand as he clinks his cup against mine, yelling directly into my ear at an entirely unnecessary volume, "Happy birthday, Vally girl!"

I'm finally twenty-one.

To celebrate the momentous occasion, Tomas and his wife closed the bar early and turned Slice of Heaven into my private club for the night. The overhead lights are dimmed as low as they'll go, and colored strobe lights illuminate a makeshift dance floor in the corner where the four-top tables usually sit. Pulsating bass from the maxed-out sound system is so loud, it reverberates in my teeth. My favorite members of the waitstaff are rushing around the black vinyl booths, getting food and drinks for the people who are either not inclined to dance or taking a break in between turns on the floor. I'm partying for free tonight, but the rest of the guests are still paying customers.

David's contribution for tonight was inviting every person I've associated with in the past five years, making the place a comfortable level of crowded just short of a packed house. People mingle around tables and booths, and the polished cherry flooring is gleaming underfoot. I'm sure by the end of the night it'll be splattered with drinks and dropped food.

"Is Conall gonna be joining us tonight?" Tomas is busy lining up a row of shots on the waxed wooden bar top.

Apparently not too busy to ask prying questions about my new best friend, though.

"No, nosy ass."

It's been three weeks since my totally-not-a-date with Conall, and thankfully it seems my screw-up at dinner didn't permanently ruin our friendship. We've seen each other in some form almost every day since then, and he's quickly become a permanent fixture in my life. He's even graduated to spending some time around David and Charlie. Surprisingly, they haven't run him off either. I invited him to come with us tonight, but of course he had to work.

That man is going to work himself into a grave before he hits thirty. Not that I know how old he is, but he doesn't look much older than us. Now I need to know. I fire off a quick text to sate my curiosity.

Me

Hey. How old are you? My mommy says I can't be friends with creepy old men.

I chuckle to myself and take a big swallow of my cider. I can't stand beer, but Tomas bought a full flight of hard cider options for tonight and I'm determined to drink my way through all of them. What's a birthday without a little indulgence?

Speaking of indulgence, a plate of chili cheese fries slides into my field of view, and my mouth waters.

"Thanks, Raul!" I shout over the noise.

The fast-moving server simply waves a hand over his shoulder at me, already on his way back to the kitchen.

Two chestnut hands appear out of nowhere, snatching handfuls of fries off of my plate before I can take a bite of the greasy goodness. David and Tomas laugh as they throw fries into each other's mouths. *My* fries.

"Hey! It's my birthday, get your own fries!" I turn on Tomas, who is now sliding the row of shots our way in an attempt to look innocent. "And you own the place! You can get all the fries you want!"

The boys devolve into hooting laughter at my indignation.

Charlie comes up beside me, leaning against the bar. He swipes a fry through the chili and pops it into his mouth, humming his approval.

"You too, Char? You guys are insufferable!" I complain, trying—and failing—to hold in my snort. We line up along the bar in front of our shots, and I speak up while everyone else eyes their small glasses. "What's in this, Tomas?"

He has a habit of using us as his guinea pigs for new menu items. For better or for worse. Usually, they turn out great, but Tomas is a Curbelo, and they're all sneaky. My stomach roils as I remember the time he asked me to try a new fish sandwich for the lunch menu. He conveniently failed to mention until I took a bite that it was a fish *head* sandwich. I didn't talk to him for a week, and now I always make sure to ask *before* I bite, no matter how delicious the food looks.

"Relax, birthday girl. It's a lemon drop. I wouldn't give you something nasty on your birthday."

I don't believe him one little bit.

We all grab a glass, tap it on the table, and finish the drink in one gulp. I hiss, the tartness of the lemon barely covering the burn of the liquor as it slides down my throat. Between the lemon drop and my mostly empty mug of cider, I'm already slightly buzzed. I need to make sure the rest of my fries make it into my mouth and not my friends', or I'll be sleeping in a corner booth before midnight.

Tomas begins lining up another row of shot glasses as my phone chimes in my pocket.

Conall

By "mommy" do you mean David?

Maybe it's the joke, maybe it's the booze, but either way, I choke, chortling until I've got tears in my eyes.

David looks over at me with a raised brow.

I rein myself in enough to say, "Conall called you my mommy."

Charlie scoffs, leaning in from my other side to chime in, "Please. David isn't mature enough to parent a Tamagotchi. If anyone's the mom here, it's me."

Me

Charlie says he's the mommy. David and I are his unruly children.

Conall

Well, tell Mama Char I'm twenty-four. June birthday. Does that make the cut?

I chuckle again, tapping out a reply.

Me

Ew no. That's like three and a half years older than me. You're practically ancient. Perv.

David plucks my phone from my hand and replaces it with another shot glass. This one is an opaque, murky off-white color, with small brown flecks in it. It's mildly terrifying and reminds me of a bad science experiment. I raise a questioning eyebrow at Tomas.

"Cinnamon toast crunch shot!" he cries.

I squeal, making him crack up. My favorite cereal in alcohol form? Count me in.

The creamy liquid goes down smooth and sweet. I chase it with my final forkful of fries before my boys pull me onto the dance floor.

The next hour passes in a blur of flashing lights and pounding beats. Music has always been a source of relief for me. I lose myself to the mild fuzziness of the alcohol and the off-key singing of Charlie and David beside me. Before long, my feet are aching in my heels and Tomas is ushering us back to the bar to try another mystery concoction.

When I return to my seat, there's a petite, brown-skinned woman perched on the barstool next to mine, her pin-straight black hair falling nearly to her waist. I throw my arms around her and give her a peck on the cheek.

"Karina! When did you get here?"

"About fifteen minutes ago, traffic was terrible. Happy birthday, honey!" She says, turning towards me as I sit.

From behind, you'd never know Tomas' wife is pregnant, but from the front, she's half stomach. Her adorable bump is the first thing to enter the room wherever she goes. Every time I see her, she swears she feels like she ate a beach ball.

"Thanks. How's Peanut?" I gesture at her belly, using the nickname they chose when they first found out they were expecting.

"Feeling more like a whole damn tub of Skippy at this point!" She flags a server to order some food, then tilts her head towards mine. "So what's this I hear about some guy you've added to your posse?"

"Oh, Conall? Your husband has a damned huge mouth," I raise my voice on my last sentence to make sure Tomas hears me over the din in the bar.

The asshole winks at me and goes back to playing mixologist. He's making one too many shots, but I don't bother to correct him. He'll figure it out or drink the extra.

"He's a friend," I reply. "A new one, but a good one. He got me out of a bind about a month ago, and we've been friends ever since."

"Yeah, I heard about your *bind*," she huffs. "Let's just say Xavier and his band of idiots better not show their faces here ever again, or they'll see what happens when you fuck with one of us."

I've known these people since I was little, but being called "one of us" still warms my heart.

"Okay, okay. Calm down, Cujo. Rein it in." Tomas intervenes, placing a Shirley Temple in front of his wife. The ruby red drink fizzes around an iceberg of maraschino cherries taking up almost half the glass.

Karina claps and starts popping cherries into her mouth as fast as she can chew them, cheesing like a kid on Christmas. "So tell me about lover boy," she mumbles around a mouthful of syrupy fruit.

My answer comes out with a scoff, "He's a *friend*, Karina. Like David, and Charlie, and your big-mouthed husband."

"Sure, sure." Her dismissive wave shows exactly how much she believes me.

I roll my eyes again.

Karina laughs. "So tell me about your *friend* then. What's he like? Is he cute? Is he coming tonight?"

Another eye roll, this one with a grumpy sigh. My eyes are in immediate danger of falling out of my head with all the rolling they've done lately.

To appease Karina, I launch into a detailed description of Conall. I detail his clear green eyes, set off by his golden bronze skin and full mouth. Next, his hair: nearly as long and dark as mine, but instead of a wild mass of curls, it falls in sleek waves. I answer questions about his physique—how he's long and lean but muscular in a way Xavier couldn't achieve with a thousand years' worth of workouts. His job may have something to do with that strength, but I can't be sure because he's always so tight-lipped about work.

She segues into an interrogation about his life that puts the Spanish Inquisition to shame. There's a firing squad of questions about his family (nothing to speak of other than his house-mates), his personality (reserved, but kind and funny; I don't mention the occasional darkness that clouds him), and how he treats me (like I'm one of his favorite people, but sometimes like he's afraid I'm going to disappear). By the end of it all, I'm in need of another drink and Karina is grinning from ear to ear.

"So...he's coming tonight, right?"

"No, Kare. He's working." *Unfortunately.*

Her glance slides over my shoulder, and that damned grin ratchets up another watt. "Then who's the guy next to Dee and Char?"

I whip around, squinting through the dim fog of the crowded bar in an attempt to spot Charlie and David. Following the direction of Karina's pointing finger, I spot them leaning against the wall in the corner next to the front door. They're talking to someone who's shielded from my view by their bodies.

I crane my neck until it cramps, cursing my lack of height. I'm seriously wondering if I could get away with standing on my barstool without Karina laughing loud enough to alert the entire bar. Tomas chuckles behind me but I couldn't possibly care about how ridiculous I must look because suddenly David and Charlie are turning towards me. Any second now their companion will be within my view and...there.

My small gasp might as well be the only sound in the bar. Everything else fades.

Conall.

But why? How?

"Thought you said he had to work." It isn't a question, and the mirrored expressions Karina and Tomas are wearing as I spin around are so smug they're probably printed in the dictionary under "smart-ass".

"He said he did. Maybe he got off early?"

I'm graced with a *humph* from Karina. "He got off work early and came all the way here to spend time with a bunch of people he barely knows for your birthday? Must be a good *friend*."

"Shove it up your ass, Karina."

Tomas is howling. His guffaws are so contagious, I find myself joining in, completely ruining the false indignation I was directing towards his wife. Karina lets out a huff and waddles off to the bathroom in the back of the restaurant before I can go back to pretending to be pissed off.

A husky baritone suddenly rolls over my shoulder in a wave of sound, "I guess this is where the cool kids are hanging out?"

A shiver skates across my shoulders, raising goosebumps along my arms. Feigning boredom, I turn around. "Obviously."

"Then you're in the wrong place."

I splutter, completely taken by surprise and left without my usual bevy of sarcastic comebacks. I settle for the obvious since it's the only thing coming to my suddenly empty brain. "It's my birthday! You can't be mean to me on my birthday, that's illegal!"

Conall lets out a quiet chuckle and makes my insides melt a little. "My apologies. I wasn't aware of the law surrounding birthday decorum. Please forgive me, your Highness."

I flutter a regal wave in his direction and receive another tiny laugh in return. He gives me a quick hug and sits in David's vacant stool next to me, placing a red-papered box on the bar top in front of my empty glass.

"For the queen on her birthday."

He got me a gift? Why? He wasn't even supposed to be coming tonight...

Suddenly, my stomach is full of butterflies. Which makes no sense, since David, Charlie, and Tomas have already given me gifts today and none of them made me feel like I had swallowed a mouthful of fluttering insects. Something has my hands shaking as I pull the box towards me. Maybe it's the two pints of cider and shots mixing in my stomach, or maybe it's his tiny smile that's lasted way more than three seconds.

The unassuming crimson wrapping paper crinkles beneath my hands, the exact same shade as the dress I've squeezed myself into tonight. I carefully peel it off, revealing a plain black box underneath. Lifting the lid of the box, my eyes narrow as I peer through the layers of tissue paper at my "gift."

This *ass*...

"You got me a helmet? For your death trap?"

The tiny smile explodes into a full-blown grin. "Take it out."

I comply, and my irritation dissolves into laughter as I turn the helmet so its side faces me. The side of the sleek black dome sports a painting of a lounging lioness wearing a comically large, gem-encrusted, golden crown. A slip of paper covered in elegant script lies alone at the bottom of the now-empty box, surrounded by the crumpled tissue paper.

For the queen of the wildcats to stay safe on her trusty steed. Happy birthday. Here's to many more.

I turn to meet Conall's gaze, confused as to why the world is suddenly blurred and distorted. It's only when he reaches out and brushes a wet spot on my cheek that I realize I have tears slipping down my face. I frantically scrub at the offending damp with the heels of my palms, my skin burning with embarrassment. As a rule, David and Charlie are the only people allowed to see me cry, and never in public. I'm an easy crier, but I have standards.

"S—sorry," I stammer, "I've had a couple drinks, and I didn't expect this, and it's so...sweet!"

He's saved from dealing with my rapidly devolving mental state by Karina returning from the bathroom. She immediately zeroes in on him. The woman is a bloodhound, nearly knocking me off of my stool in her haste to take a seat. Pregnant women shouldn't move faster than lightning; it's not natural.

I take advantage of her return to take a few deep breaths and get my anxiety under control. I am *not* going to have a meltdown over a damn birthday gift. Conall would never understand that I haven't gotten a birthday present from someone other than my parents, Sanderson, or one of the four friends who set this evening up in over a decade. Xavier always said gifts were for children. That rule went out the window when he threw a huge fit the one year I decided not to buy him something for *his* birthday. In hindsight, that should have been a huge red flag. I'm starting to realize his claws dug into me deeper than I thought they did over the years, and those wounds are slow to close.

I grab a fresh mug of cider and drain the entire cup in one gulp. The tart liquid bubbles its way down my throat. That last pint was evidently the limit for my sobriety, because a few minutes later I'm giggling at myself for freaking out over something as small as a few tears.

"Shots! You in, Conall?" Tomas has finally finished his line of mystery drinks, having taken a break to find himself some food and check on the kitchen staff while I was having my mini-crisis.

Dee and Char scamper off the dance floor and settle themselves into our line of bodies. With Conall here, there are exactly enough glasses.

Realization dawns. "Hey!" I giggle; my voice came out higher than I expected. "That's why you had an extra glass! You weren't a screw-up after all!"

"Oh, shit, Vally's finally drunk." David chuckles under his breath.

"Yeah, honey, I've known for about an hour now." Tomas wears a shit-eating grin as he passes out glasses filled with bright green liquid.

I open my mouth to ask what's in this one, but I decide I don't care. The shot goes down in a burst of lime-flavored fizz, and I sigh happily as colors burst behind my eyelids. *When did I close my eyes? Oh, who cares? It's relaxing in here.*

A finger gently taps against the back of my hand, and I know it's Conall without needing to look. Something in my blood recognizes him as a safe place, a calm harbor in the storm of my psyche. The darkness hiding behind his closed-off stare calls to me, a kindred spirit. The bond of the broken soul, something my happy-go-lucky group of friends has tried their best to understand but has never managed to fully comprehend because their brains aren't attacking them all of the time. They don't understand what it's like to *feel* everything, everywhere, all of the time. But I think Conall understands a tiny part of the battle to keep the darkness at bay.

I open my eyes and affix them to his waiting gaze with the bumbling confidence only alcohol can provide. He flashes that small, hidden quirk of the lips, the one only I seem to receive and leans in towards my ear, his breath causing me to shiver. "Dance with me?"

My helmeted head thunks against Conall's as he pulls into my driveway. It's been three hours and four drinks since Conall asked me to dance back at the bar, and I can barely feel my legs. My mind, however, is on cloud nine, and my drunken euphoria has made me bold.

"Conall," I squeal. "Did you see the *stars* on our ride home? They were like a painting! It was *magical.*"

I should be paying less attention to describing the night sky and more attention to my feet. My left foot catches on the seat of the bike as I dismount and I go hurtling face-first towards the pavement.

Conall swoops in, a knight in shining armor, and rescues my face from a date with the driveway. "Jeez," he scolds gently. "You can barely walk. I never should've let you have those last two shots. I was overruled by our friends, but that's no excuse."

He scoops me up into his arms and begins to carry me into my house, ignoring my loud protests.

Our friends. The idea of Conall officially considering himself a part of my small circle of friends has my drunken heart soaring as he walks through my front door.

"Where's your room, wildcat?"

"Upstairs, third door on the"—my mumbled directions are interrupted by a loud yawn, and I snuggle into Conall's hard shoulder—"left."

A soft gasp from the living room can only be one person. Sure enough, I crack open one bleary eye to see my mom hovering in the doorway with a small, welcoming smile on her face but concern in her gaze. Damn. Of course she's still awake.

"She's fine, ma'am. Just a little inebriated. If you don't mind, I'll drop her off upstairs and be out of your hair in a few minutes." Conall's smooth voice is a lullaby.

My heavy lids drift shut as we ascend the stairs. I keep them closed, savoring the comfort and peace until he settles me into my bed and carefully remove my shoes from my aching, tired feet. His fingers brush the swollen, tender skin around my ankles, but where there should be pain, there's only cool, spring waters washing the aches away.

If he were to keep those hands of his drifting further upward, would his cool touch be enough to calm the heat coursing through me? Or would the two of us combust, fire and ice turning to steam?

I sit up suddenly and lurch forward, reaching blindly for his arm in the dark. Spikes of anxiety pierce through my drunken haze. What will happen when I'm alone without sobriety to keep me carefully tethered to reality?

"You know," I slur, "you could stay." My eyelids weigh a million pounds, and I'm losing the battle to keep them open. I flop back onto the pillows and pat the spot on the bed beside me. "You're very pretty, and you're safe. A safe, pretty...pretty man. Who smells like lavender and pine and...man."

Conall's low chuckle reaches me through my sleepy haze, and his lips brush my forehead. Or maybe I'm dreaming.

"Good night, wildcat," he murmurs, but I'm already drifting away.

Chapter 12
Changes
- Conall -

Valorie's hand is warm in mine as I lead her towards the dance floor. The pulsing lights flash against her skin, turning her into something otherworldly and effervescent. Beneath the spinning colors, her titanium irises become a kaleidoscope of blues, pinks, and purples. There's something magical in her gaze, and I'm beginning to think I'm caught in her spell. A part of me worries this is going too far, that I'm losing sight of my end goal, but Valorie stumbles and clutches onto me. Her scent invades my lungs and chases the worry away.

For a moment, I allow myself to forget about the pressing deadline of her death and the fate of this planet. This whole world can go up in flames right now for all I care. There are countless others anyway.

Her friend, the one who owns the bar we're in, set up a smoke machine in the corner of the dance floor. It's turned the area into a hazy mix of pixie dreamland and sultry club. The dark wood flooring is polished to an almost mirrored finish which allows the multicolored strobes to rebound and refract into fragments of color and light. The effect is hypnotic, even to someone completely sober. I haven't had more than the one shot Tomas gave us all, but I'm swept up in the magic of the bar tonight. Or maybe it's the power of the girl following so closely, I can hear her soft breaths.

I pull Valorie towards the back of the dance floor, away from the small crowd of people gyrating near the speakers. Hidden in the fog, we could be the only two people in the whole universe. A private galaxy created only for us. Maybe there, I wouldn't have to be her reaper. I could simply be me.

Her pupils are huge in her heart-shaped face, and her full, red lips part ever so slightly as she looks up at me. I'm inexorably drawn to her, and my heart stutters as she turns around with a devious grin. I'm treated to a view of miles of alabaster skin showing through the chains criss-crossing the length of her backless, scarlet dress. She's Snow White's poison apple, tantalizing and sweet, and I want to taste every forbidden inch of her. Looking this way, she might kill me before I can kill her.

Valorie reaches behind her and grabs my hands, placing them on the curves of her hips, which are several inches higher than usual thanks to the gold stilettos she's wearing. Shoes that high should be some sort of safety hazard, but Valorie's steps are confident. She snakes her hands up and around to clasp behind my neck, drawing a quiet groan from my chest. Her hips roll and swirl, and my wildcat unleashes herself to the sensuous beat of the music.

In this realm we've created, I can pretend she is allowed to be mine.

The song changes to a slower tune, and I slide my arms around Valorie's waist to pull her flush against me, right where I want her the most. My body aches for her in a way I've never experienced. She fits against me like a glove, the warmth of her body and her intoxicating fresh pear scent combine in a heady mix of sensations that shoots straight to my groin.

The more time I spend with her, the murkier my end goal becomes. When did she go from merely a target to this strange mix of best friend and something...more? She's captivating, equal parts stronger than steel and incredibly fragile. I'd give anything to keep her safe, but I can't protect her from me. Not for long, anyway.

She turns her head over her shoulder to look at me, and I drag in a choppy breath. Her lips are mere centimeters from mine, and there's no amount of duty or future betrayal that can keep me from leaning in...

"Wake up, sleepy ass! Are you going to lie there all day?"

I jolt up in bed and yelp when my head smashes into something hard. As I force my sticky eyes open, I notice Finn standing next to the closet door, rubbing at a red lump forming on his forehead. Judging by the soreness between my brows, I have a mark to match.

"That's what you get for hovering over me," I grumble. My dream felt so real. I'm still trying to wrap my brain around the fact that I'm not in Slice of Heaven with Valorie and her friends. *My* friends now. After last night, I'm officially welcomed into the fold.

They won't feel that way for much longer.

"So where were you last night? Gaius wanted to watch this dumb movie and I had to sit through it with him because you ditched. Plus, Gabs was on edge all evening. Were you in trouble?"

"No, I wasn't. Gabby worries too much." I roll out of my bed, trod to the closet, and pull on some jeans and a tee.

Finn trails behind me while I head into the bathroom to freshen up, cracking jokes as usual. "It's not like you to sleep in past sunrise. Have a hot date last night?"

I grumble a denial around a mouthful of toothpaste froth. Despite what happened last night, I would not call anything between Valorie and me a “date.” It wouldn’t be fair to her. A quickly growing part of me wishes we could have met under different circumstances, but facts are facts. Entering into a friendship under false pretenses is one thing, but I would never disrespect her trust by taking it any further.

Finn’s answering scoff is filled with good-natured disbelief. “Then who were you dreaming about until ten a.m.? Judging by the look on your sleepy little face when I came in, it wasn’t a dream about me!” He twists his expression into one of mock disgust. “And if it was, don’t tell me. Please don’t ever tell me I’m the subject of your dirty dreams.”

I toss the tube of toothpaste at him, narrowly missing his already bruising forehead. “It was nothing and no one, Nancy Drew.”

“That sounds about as believable as saying this planet is flat,” he jokes, but his face slowly loses its smirk and I know he’s unfortunately catching on. “Conall,” he moans dramatically, “please tell me it isn’t her. I’m going to close my eyes, and when I open them you’ll tell me it wasn’t a dream about the girl.” He scrunches his lids shut like a child, and when he opens them I’m halfway across the room, staring at my bed as if it holds the secret to figuring out this mess in my brain.

“Con...it’s a dream, bro. It doesn’t mean anything.” He rests a huge hand on my shoulder, and I’m so lost, the gesture manages to comfort me.

“Yeah. A dream.” I take a deep breath and collect myself. Finn is right, it *was* a dream. I’ve probably been overworking myself and it bled into my subconscious. She was the focus simply because we’ve spent so much time together.

We walk out of the room and down the hall towards the large, curving staircase to the foyer. I see Finn glancing at me from the corner of my eye, but I pretend not to notice. He won't stay quiet for long. Silence has never been his strong suit.

Sure enough: "So, are you gonna tell me where you were last night?"

"Out."

"With your new human friends?"

The edge he puts on the last word makes my stomach twist. He's right, though. They're barely my friends at all, and if they knew what I have planned they'd turn on me in a heartbeat.

Finn takes my silence as an affirmative. "Be careful, Con. I know you, and this is something different. You don't get attached to people. Hell, I've barely seen you speak ten words to someone outside of these walls except for the Huangs. Now you've gotta make friends with a bunch of humans only to betray them?" He lets loose a long breath.

Part of me aches to know my family is so worried.

"The girl sounds sweet, she does. You're a healer, which has got to make things worse for you. Just...don't get too attached, okay? We know how this has to end."

If one more person reminds me of "how this has to end" or not to "get too attached" I might explode. Do they think I don't know? That, for a single second, I'm not aware of what I have to do? This is *my* mission. I follow orders and get my tasks done so someday I can return to Avallea. It's what we all do, and I will continue to do so.

Even if it makes me hate who I become.

The daylight streams through the large skylight overhead as we reach the bottom of the staircase, and the room is as empty as I expected. My family spends their weekends on whatever hobby they're currently engrossed in. It's our leisure period, as long as we don't have a job that requires weekend work. If I had to guess, Gaius is probably building something in one of the outbuildings. Domenic and Marguerite are likely playing ping-pong downstairs, and Gabrielle has shut herself in her bedroom with a new record to listen to.

"No greenhouse work today, Finn?" I ask.

Finnegan's talent is green magic, also seen as an innate connection to plants. Our abilities work well together. Both of us are drawn to life and growth, albeit in different forms. Usually, I'd have to drag him out of his massive greenhouse on a pleasant Sunday morning like this one.

"Already finished it while you were upstairs playing dead."

A plan forms in my head, and I decide to invite Finn along for the ride, if only to have a friend to keep me out of my head for a while. I've got to tread carefully, though.

"I'm going to go visit the Huangs and help them out for a bit. I'll have lunch while I'm there. Want to come with?" What I don't say is I'm grabbing lunch for more than myself.

Valorie had a lot to drink last night, and she was heavily intoxicated when I dropped her off at her house. Everyone deserves a hell of a party for their twenty-first birthday, but with her tiny size, I'm sure she's going to be hating life today. A healthy portion of those drunken noodles she loved at Rising Moon will go a long way towards helping her feel less miserable.

I chuckle quietly to myself. Hopefully, the irony of her meal's name is not lost on her.

"Sure," Finn agrees enthusiastically.

He'll do anything for food, and Mrs. Huang loves him almost as much as she loves me. It probably has something to do with the fact he's six-foot-seven and eats everything she puts in front of him.

I laugh at the sight of my giant brother bouncing along like a puppy and lead the way towards the garage where my motorcycle is parked. Straddling the glossy, cobalt bike reminds me of the gift I gave Valorie and the one sparkling tear she shed over it. The memory touches me more than it should. I speed off towards the end of the long driveway with Finn at my back, and it brings to mind a similar journey I made last night with a much smaller set of arms wrapped tightly around me.

Passing the fringes of The Palisades, I spy someone who makes me slam on the breaks, slowing the bike to a crawl.

Xavier Schmitt stands in the driveway of a small house on the very edge of the neighborhood, the hose in his hand spraying a stream of water onto the hood of a silver Toyota Corolla. Logically, I know we're in the middle of a quiet suburban road in broad daylight. However, my mind conjures up images of a darkened alleyway, his perfectly coiffed blond hair dulled by the shadows of looming buildings as he worked to remove Valorie's clothes. I remember the sickening smile on his face, his mocking laughter as he overpowered her and shoved her up against the rough wall. My hand tightens reflexively on the throttle, and the bike lurches forward.

"Conall, what's going on, man?" Finn's voice comes out sharper than usual.

His arms come around my shoulders, giving me a firm shake that snaps me back to reality.

"Xavier," I force out through clenched teeth.

Finn tenses as he processes the name. "*Shi-iit.*" The word is dragged out into two syllables.

As if he somehow heard his name, Xavier looks up from his vehicle and notices me nearly idling by the curb. He raises a hand as if to wave in my direction, but I snap my helmet's visor up and his hand quickly drops. His eyes widen until the whites surrounding his pupils are visible, and he hurries inside, leaving the hose flopping and gushing water into the grass.

Finn snickers and slings curses at the coward, but I don't trust myself to do anything other than force my locked muscles to drive away as quickly as possible.

Mrs. Huang is waiting at the front entrance of Rising Moon when we pull up, a broad grin further creasing her weathered face. Her quiet husband stands behind her, and he greets me with a nod and a firm handshake that means as much as his wife's crushing hug. The Huangs are steady people, the kind who have faced one adversity after another and emerged together through it all. They've been married twice as long as I've been alive, and their love for each other is almost palpable.

Finn and I spend the next several hours helping move heavy boxes of ingredients in the restaurant's storeroom. We take the time to build a new entertainment center in the living room of the Huangs' small, cluttered apartment above Rising Moon. By the time Mrs. Huang calls us for a very late lunch, we're famished. She clucks in disapproval at my loudly growling stomach, places a heaping plate on the table in front of me, and slides an equally large mound of food in front of Finn. We dig in, shoveling food into our mouths with all the speed of a pair of professional eaters.

Mrs. Huang lingers by the end of the table and watches us eat. Apparently satisfied, she gingerly settles herself into one of the empty chairs. "So, boy," she says, looking directly into my reluctant stare.

I loudly swallow my mouthful of dumpling.

"When are you going to bring your sweet girl back around?"

Finn chokes. "You brought Valorie here?"

Shit.

"Of course he did." Mrs. Huang flaps her hand impatiently at Finn to shut him up. "Pretty girl, very polite. I like her. It's about time Conall found himself a nice girl. He can't keep hanging out with you all the time, troublemaker."

I snort out a laugh around my fried rice. Finn may be a gentle giant, but he loves pranks as much as the rest of our family. "Troublemaker" is an accurate description.

"As a matter of fact, I was going to ask you to make her some food. If it's not too much trouble, of course. It was her birthday yesterday, and she may have drank a bit too much." I ignore Finn's stern glare and continue on, "I'll bring it straight to her once we leave, and I'll tell her you miss her."

Mrs. Huang beams. Nothing makes her happier than cooking for someone she cares about, and it seems Valorie has already secured herself a spot on that list. I'm not surprised. Valorie doesn't understand how enjoyable she is to be around. There's an ever-growing group of people I'll be hurting when this is over.

The old woman hustles off to the kitchen, her shock of white hair barely visible over the long counter separating the back preparatory area from the seating portion of the restaurant. She hums to herself as she cooks, her warbling voice occasionally breaking fully into song for a line or two before returning to a quiet hum. I concentrate intently on her tiny head behind the counter, if only to attempt to prevent Finn from launching into what I'm sure will be a well-meaning rant.

I hear him clear his throat beside me.

There it is, right on time.

When I ignore him, he coughs loudly. Another cough follows the first, but my eyes stay glued to the kitchen.

"You should get that checked out, might be contagious," I mutter over another pointed cough from Finn.

"You know damn well I'm not sick. You brought her *here*?"

I bristle, my face growing hot. "Is there a problem?"

Finn sighs, and his next words are much softer, "No, Con. It's...well...you don't bring anyone to meet the Huangs. It took me three years before you invited *me* to come with you."

"It's nothing. I have to keep up appearances; make her think we're close. That's the best way to glean information from her, right? It's what everyone told me to do, so I'm doing it." My fists clench under the table, and I take a deep breath in an attempt to loosen the knot in my chest.

"Don't be upset, man." Finn pats my shoulder and offers up a small smile, but it doesn't quite erase his concerned look. "Gabs says this will all work out one way or the other, so you do what you need to. And if you ever need to talk about how you're feeling..."

"Thanks, Finn. You're right, if Gabs isn't worried, why should we be?" I don't tell him Gabrielle certainly didn't seem comforted by what she saw the last time we discussed my task. He doesn't need to worry more about me than he already does. Finn is by far the most sensitive of our group, and the droop of his shoulders suggests he's already stressed enough over this. Over me.

When did I become the problem child of the group? We usually spend our days worried Gabby will have another vision that scares her so badly she doesn't leave her bed. That, or worrying Gaius will blow something up, either literally while working with his fire magic or when his sharp tongue and lack of filter get him in a bind with the wrong person. Other than the pranking, Finn and I are usually the stalwart ones.

I pull out my phone to check my messages and alerts flash across the screen. Somehow, my ringer was turned off, and I've managed to miss several texts from Valorie throughout the morning. I'm surprised; with all the drinks she had last night, I didn't expect her to be up until well after noon. A glance at the screen tells me it's past three already. That explains things; it's much later than I anticipated.

A rapidly growing part of me itches to answer her right away, but I don't trust Finn not to eavesdrop over my shoulder. For some unexplainable reason, I want to keep my texts with Valorie private, a secret connection between the two of us. I try to rationalize my possessive behavior by telling myself it's for the purposes of screening her messages to make sure the ruse is intact.

In all honesty? I don't believe the lies I'm feeding my family anymore.

A plastic shopping bag is suddenly plopped in front of me with a dense thud, and Mrs. Huang's face peers above its fluttering white handles.

"Here you go, dear. I added tempura cheesecake for her since you said it was her birthday." She manages to catch both Finn and me in a sudden, sharp-eyed glare. "If I find out either of you eats it on the ride over there, that'll be the last food you get from this kitchen."

"Yes, ma'am," we chorus.

She smiles warmly, all seriousness forgotten as she hugs us goodbye. "Then off you go."

Finn is silent as we walk towards the bike. I finally give in once we our helmets and pull out of the parking lot.

"What's going on with you?" I ask.

"Been thinking," Finn answers through the mic in his helmet, the same one Valorie borrowed all those weeks ago.

"About?"

"I think," he pauses, "I'm beginning to see what's going on with all of this."

I let loose a groan. "What does that mean?"

"Can't tell you. But I think I'm going to have a little talk with Gabby and see if we're on the same page."

Another frustrated growl slips free, and I speed off towards Valorie's house.

Chapter 13
Hungover

-Valorie-

I'd say I'm never drinking again, but we all know that would be a lie. I crack open one bleary eye, relieved to find the familiar sights of my bedroom. My worn birch floors and powder-blue walls greet me, bathed in buttery daylight filtering in through the sheer curtains. The white dressers, headboard, and nightstands Mom picked out for me in tenth grade when I said I wanted "grown-up" furniture complete the room's airy, coastal aesthetic. If I didn't know better, I could imagine I was finishing up a weekend away in some Cape Cod bungalow, relaxing by the beach. But this is Sycamore, and I'm spending my Sunday hungover.

Thank goodness it's a Sunday. I can stay holed up at home all day and not have to wear real clothes. Plus, I somehow managed to get a full night's sleep last night.

I can't remember the last time that happened.

Most nights, the nightmares wake me up at least once. I jolt awake, spluttering in the dark from the phantom feel of Xavier's hand around my neck or crying silent tears over shadowy, amorphous tendrils of dread I can't quite place. Today my head pounds like I ran it over with Conall's motorcycle, but at least I'm well rested.

Conall.

Did he actually come to my birthday party last night? I'm almost certain that wasn't a vodka-induced dream. I remember dancing, and drinking, and a birthday gift. A beautiful, thoughtful, hilarious gift. One a cursory glance around my room reveals is...nowhere to be found.

Did I imagine it?

I suck in a deep breath. *Get it together, Val. It was definitely real.*

My cheeks flame with the memory. I honestly thought Karina was screwing with me when she said someone showed up with David and Charlie, but there he was, looking like an Egyptian god in denim and dark cotton. My heart practically exploded onto my stilettos.

Conall doesn't need fancy suits to make him seem powerful. His power lies in the way he stands there like he's my own personal Superman, ready to catch me if I fall off of the ledge of my own brain. It's in the forested depths of his eyes, and the slight quirk of his mouth when he doesn't want me to know he thinks I'm hilarious. It's in the gentle grip of his large, golden hands on my waist when I struggle to get off of the beast he chooses to ride in lieu of a car.

And now, thanks to the brand-new helmet he gave me last night, I've got a beast of my own.

Thinking about Conall and his present brings back hazy memories of the events that brought me into my room last night. I flop back onto my bed, covering my flaming face as my drunken actions come into focus.

I asked Conall to sleep with me.

I sat here in this bed and practically begged him to stay.

How the hell could I do that? He's going to think I'm some pathetic lightweight who can't hold her liquor and whores around, inviting guys to her bed at all hours of the night. What I actually did was finally get the nerve to say the words I've had tumbling around in my messed-up head for weeks. Guess I should thank drunk Valorie. Even if she had absolutely zero tact.

Conall makes something inside of me light up. He excites a part of me I didn't know existed, a soft, gentle part of me Xavier would have destroyed if he ever found out about it. A touch of his hand, a glimpse of those rare smiles that seem to be hand-picked for me, and my day is instantly better. He's seen me beaten and battered, literally, and he's never judged me. To him, I've never been the idiot girl I always see in the mirror, the one too stupid to know she was being used for years by a guy who only wanted a bed-warmer he could boss around. The one too weak to win a battle against her own damn mind. To him, I've simply been his wildcat, and that's a version of myself I think I'm growing to love.

Maybe it's *him* I'm growing to love.

What if he doesn't want to be friends with me after last night?

I drag in a ragged, rattling breath, trying and failing to calm my suddenly racing heart. The walls seem closer than they did a few short minutes ago. Two more shallow inhales do nothing for my oxygen-deprived lungs— they're pressing down on me. I curl up into a ball to avoid the room's crushing weight—maybe save some vital part of my soul from being flattened—but it doesn't work. It never works. The dull roaring in my ears is the sound of a sinister ocean waiting to pull me under. The tears begin to fall and I'm lost to the waves.

Eventually, the tide spits me out. My brain restarts and the world begins to brighten once again. Ragged breathing becomes smooth; tears evaporate into dry, salty tracks on my skin. Shaking turns to tremors, tremors shift to trembling and fade away, until I can stand without fear of toppling over. Steady on my feet, I head straight to the bathroom door across the room, aching for a shower to wash away the sweaty film on my skin.

The clean simplicity of my bathroom is a shock to my senses after the darkness of my anxiety attack. I've always enjoyed the simplicity of this space—pearly white tiles and marble, gold fixtures, with one single snake plant living its best life on the windowsill to prevent the space from feeling sterile. It's soothing, but the light bouncing off of every surface is not helping my hangover at all. I flip the switches back off, allowing the natural light through the window to illuminate the room while I ease myself into the shower and wash my troubles away.

Freshly cleaned and with a new outlook on the day, it occurs to me I can simply text Conall and ask him if things are good between us. At least then I can have closure one way or another. Maybe he'll somehow forgive me if I apologize enough.

Me

Hey...I'm really sorry about last night. I know it's no excuse, but I was super wasted.

Please say you don't hate me.

Or if you do hate me, at least let me know so I don't show up for lunch tomorrow. Thanks.

Three back-to-back messages is probably overkill, but it's too late now. In an attempt to prevent myself from adding to the onslaught of texts I threw Conall's way, I shove my phone into the pocket of my pajama shorts and head downstairs to find something easy for breakfast. Food will help me clear my head and get some energy back into my seriously dwindling reserves.

To my surprise, both of my parents are sitting at the kitchen island, matching his-and-hers coffee mugs resting on the countertop in front of them.

The kitchen is my mother's design brainchild. Pristine white cabinetry with gold pulls is offset by pinkish quartz countertops and custom navy and gold appliances, including a fancy espresso machine in the corner— the focus of my two working brain cells this morning. Walls a shade of such dark gray they're almost black complete the picture of a modern, sleek kitchen that fell out of an HGTV catalog. The two of them may spend most of their time at their offices—or a conference, or some dusty corner of an archive building—but Mom and Dad love having a calming home to come back to.

I move towards the machine and begin grinding fresh coffee beans for a cup. "Hey, guys, I didn't expect you to be around today. No morning plans?" My voice is hoarse from yelling most of the night.

I didn't expect to find them here. They're rarely home, and almost never at the same time. I know they always travel together, so they spend plenty of time as a couple, but I rarely see them more than once or twice a month. Mom and Dad made sure their work stayed close to home when I was younger, but things are more relaxed now that we're all adults. I miss them some nights, but I'm not going to ask them to put their careers on hold for their adult daughter.

Tamping down the ground coffee, I start the machine. The pleasant gurgling and hissing of coffee brewing fills the room. I turn my back on the system to give it some privacy. You can't rush good coffee, it's a cardinal sin.

Mom and Dad are staring at me over the rims of their cups, two identical smirks on their faces. I wait patiently, but they keep staring at me like two annoying, unmoving statues.

"What?" I finally snip, collecting my cup of coffee from the machine and adding some milk and sugar. I take the first sip and sigh happily. Much better.

"Did you have fun last night?" Mom finally asks in a tone that tells me she thinks she knows exactly how much fun I had.

I vaguely remember her standing in the living room entryway when Conall brought me inside, her eyebrows practically hiding in her hairline. So, she's the one heading this inquisition this morning?

I'm going to need another gallon of coffee. Possibly in an IV drip.

"Yes, I did," I answer, dragging a stool around to sit across from them. If this is going to be an interrogation, might as well make it easier to see the prosecutors. "David, Charlie, and Tomas went all out. They practically transformed Slice into a nightclub. David invited everyone I've ever blinked at, and Tomas was making all of these crazy shots. Plus, Karina showed up for a while. It was great." Mentioning Karina or the upcoming baby is usually a surefire way to derail my parents' train of thought, but it seems they're too focused for baby fever to break them.

"That's wonderful, honey," she says dismissively. She's heading towards the question I know she wants to ask. It's brewing like an oncoming storm.

"So, who was that boy, the one who carried you inside?" Mom tilts her head to the left, pretend her question is innocent when we both know it's not.

There it is.

I sigh. "Conall, Mom. He's a friend." Something in the pit of my stomach clenches uncomfortably because calling him a friend doesn't properly describe him. But a friend is all he is, so I push the feeling down until it fades.

It occurs to me it's been at least half an hour, and Conall still hasn't replied to any of my messages. My stomach squeezes again, and I begin to regret drinking my coffee without eating first.

"He certainly seemed...close. He carried you all the way into your room." She says *"into your room"* like she honestly believes something lecherous happened in the five-minute time period when he brought me upstairs.

"Yeah, Conall's protective, and I stumbled in the driveway. He stopped me from falling and apparently feared I would eat pavement if he didn't bring me inside himself. Like I said, protective." I wave a dismissive hand, but my chest tingles. I bite the inside of my cheek to keep a smile from forming.

Her next question shoots my struggling smile dead before it ever has a chance to live. "Does Xavier know about this handsome boy who's oh so *protective* of you?"

My heart sputters and stumbles beneath my sternum, caught somewhere between racing and stopping entirely. I clutch my coffee cup to keep it from slipping out of my suddenly slick hands. "It doesn't matter what Xavier knows or doesn't know." My voice is barely audible, but I manage to keep it steady.

My mother sucks her teeth, not understanding. Her blind love of Xavier is one of her biggest flaws.

"What a terrible thing to say, Valorie. A relationship is a partnership, remember? You need to tell him about this new guy you've been hanging around, or soon it's going to be too late." Her tone is inching towards the one she used when I was five and stole an extra cookie from the jar behind her back.

This instant judgment is out of character for her except for where Xavier is involved. She's always had a soft spot for him, but I'm tired of her thinking he's perfect.

Her ridiculous admonishment pushes me over the edge and I snap, "Oh, he knows about Conall. But I left Xavier two years ago, remember? So his opinion doesn't *fucking* matter."

The silence is as thick as tar and twice as heavy. Mom stares open-mouthed, not noticing she's holding her half-empty cup at an angle, causing it to slowly drip coffee onto the counter.

"And why haven't you taken him back yet? He's such a nice boy, from a good family." Mom's voice is soft, but the question makes my heart ache.

If I told her the truth, would she even believe me? Or is she too blinded by Xavier's facade to ever face reality?

My dad, who has been uncharacteristically silent throughout this entire exchange, now calmly gets up and places a towel under Mom's drizzling latte. He scrubs his hands through his hair and levels me with a stare full of love where I expected anger. The prickle of tears builds under the weight of his gaze.

"It's true, isn't it?"

"What, Daddy?" I croak, struggling to keep the tears contained within my lids.

Dad rounds the counter and stops close enough that our bodies almost touch. I have to crane my head up because his face is over a foot above mine. "A few months ago, I was walking past your door one night when David and Charlie were over. You were in the shower or something—I could hear the water running—and they were sitting around chatting while they waited for you. Probably eating their way through one of my packs of Oreos if I know those boys." He gives me a tiny smile and continues, "I heard David say something to Charlie. Something about Xavier, and freshman year."

A small gasp escapes through my frozen lips, and my hands clench into shaky fists. I know exactly the night he's referring to. Xavier had found me in the library one evening working late on a group project with some guys from one of my Sociology courses, and he wouldn't leave me be. He dragged me off into the stacks and punched and kicked me while I begged him to stop. He wasn't angry enough to break anything, though, so I went home with my friends instead of heading to the emergency room.

I told David and Charlie I fell down the library stairs, but I knew they didn't believe me.

Tears limn my father's gray eyes, so much like my own. "They said he—" he chokes on the words, squeezes his eyelids shut, sucks in a deep breath, and sprints through the rest, "—he hurt you that night, and they were pretty sure it wasn't the first time. I wanted to barge in there and demand they tell me what the hell they were talking about, but then you came out of the bathroom and they switched up so fast I knew you must've already told them off about it. So you tell me right now, Valorie...is it true?"

I freeze, locking stares with Dad. Could I tell him? He'll be crushed. My dad is a protector, a big, burly, boxer-turned-professor who prefers to battle with words only because he spent his twenties throwing punches for a living to put himself through college. He'd do anything for Mom and me.

My unblinking stare stays glued to his, but a single tear rolls down my cheek. The spell is broken; he shoots forward, wrapping his huge arms around me as if I'm a child again.

A second, small set of arms is added to our jumble. A whispered "I'm...I'm so sorry" lets me know Mom has finally broken out of her shock. She's stammering, losing control of herself as she finally comes to terms with what I've been through, with what she's been pushing me to forgive all this time.

I hear her small, hiccuping sobs mixed in with the louder sniffles from my father, but my own tears silently course. Instead of the guilt I expected to feel at burdening them with this pain of mine, there is relief. No more hiding, no more awkward questions about the tormentor I might have loved once upon a time. For the second time in five weeks, another weight sloughs off.

Dad pulls away first, wiping his cheeks. His face is a mask I've rarely seen on him—ruddy skin, flared nostrils, a canyon carved between his narrowed brows. "I'll beat the shit out of him," he grinds out between teeth clenched so hard, a muscle is ticking in his jaw.

I reach up to pat his cheek. "Don't worry, Daddy. Conall already did. Good thing, since you're too pretty for jail." A mischievous smirk crosses my face at the memory of Xavier running from Conall in the alley.

My words have their desired effect; his jaw relaxes and his face begins to return to a normal shade. I spot strained creases near his eyes, but it's a marked improvement.

"Remind me to thank him the next time we see him," Dad says.

Mom interjects, "*Will* we be seeing him again sometime?"

I can't stop the smile from forming this time, and my mom's sharp eyes lock onto it immediately. "Yeah, Mom. I hope so." I clear my throat and put my now-empty coffee cup into the dishwasher. "Now, if you don't mind, I feel like ass. Can you quit the Spanish Inquisition for the day and let me go nurse my hangover in peace?"

They both laugh, all evidence of our earlier conversation seemingly erased. I know them, though; they'll be discussing Xavier as soon as I leave.

"I'm going to go for a walk out back, see if the fresh air can help clear my head a bit. Love you guys." I peck them both on the cheek on my way towards the back door, eager to lose myself for a little while.

Chapter 14
Pleasant Surprises

-Valorie-

I'm determined to spend the rest of the day in the woods, burying my troubles beneath a glowing canopy of greens and golds, and reds. One of the reasons my parents picked our home was the expansive backyard bordered by dense trees on three sides. It's quiet, secluded and perfect for entertaining.

We have the furthest home from the street on our culdesac, with a front yard split in two by the wide driveway Conall saved me from colliding with last night. A saltwater pool takes up a third of the backyard, which my parents had installed when I was ten and they said I could finally swim alone. The rest is blanketed in clover and moss, interspersed with large oaks and various plants my mother has collected. It is an oasis, but my favorite part is the old-growth forest beyond the gate in the back fence.

Growing up, I'd wander out into the woods, lay on a blanket of leaves for hours, and imagine tiny creatures of magic and mystery peering at me through the undergrowth. As a teen, I'd disappear through the gate and spend my days amongst those unchanging trees, belting out songs from my favorite musicals. I'd pretend a handsome fae prince would come to tell me I was meant to be a part of a mythical fantasy world.

Now, as I lay in the grass, the faerie man from my adolescent daydreams is replaced by a face a little closer to home, though no less magical.

Conall's beautiful features fill the blackness behind my lids, and I can't help but smile. His irises are the same hue as the trees around me. That small quirk of a grin I receive from him, the one that always feels like a prize, is there on the corner of his mouth. His jet-black hair fans in gentle waves around the bronzed skin of his cheekbones, and I wish I knew whether it's as silky as it looks. I wonder if his lips are soft as satin, or if he bites them when he's nervous like I do. Those damned butterflies kick up a fuss in my stomach again, wanting to be let free to fly to him, wherever he is.

The buzz of my phone in my pocket shatters my daydream.

I scramble up off of the leaf litter, head swiveling as I take in the changes around me. The sky is much darker than I expected; it's nearly dinner time. I must have dozed off for a few hours, but my head is much calmer after my impromptu afternoon nap.

Another insistent buzz reminds me of why I was woken up in the first place. I fish my phone out of my pocket and my heart balloons into my throat.

Conall

Check your porch :)

Just saw that you texted, didn't have a chance to read them yet. Was working at the Huangs all morning. Mrs. Huang sends her love.

I'll read them when I get home and text you afterwards.

The porch? I'm halfway through the house, tripping over my own feet in my haste to get to the door before my brain fully processes what he said.

He didn't read the texts this morning. He didn't even see them until a few minutes ago. But now he *has* seen them, and he's still talking to me. If my chest gets any lighter, I'll float away into space and never come back.

I throw the door open so hard it bangs against the wall beside me and rush out onto the porch, looking around frantically.

Nobody is here; there's only the faint rumble of an engine in the distance.

My face falls, and I turn to go back inside to ask Conall what was the point of me sprinting a quarter of a mile through the woods to stand on an empty porch. I don't notice the white bag at my feet until my bare toes brush against the warm plastic and I skid to a screeching halt.

Lying on the welcome mat is a packed grocery bag with a twisting line of steam rising from it. The faint aromas of ginger, soy, and peppers waft towards me on the crisp fall breeze. My mouth instantly begins watering. I rush the bag into the kitchen and perch on a stool at the island, ready to unwrap my surprise.

I squeal when I finally tear through to the contents.

Inside is a beautiful slice of tempura cheesecake and a gigantic styrofoam container of the noodles Mrs. Huang had made for me the night Conall and I spent at Rising Moon. A hot pink sticky note on the top has a happy birthday message from Mrs. Huang, and the fact that she lists the bag's contents in detail "in case two boys get grabby hands" makes me snort.

Me

You brought me food? I could kiss you.

I busy myself with getting a fork while I wait for his reply, not bothering with a plate and instead deciding to eat directly from the container. The noodles have the perfect combination of sweetness and spice I remember from that night, and the cheesecake melts in my mouth with creamy decadence. Thirty minutes later, I've eaten half of the noodles and all of the cheesecake. I hide the leftovers in the back of the fridge for another time, although I'm tempted to eat until I burst. My phone chirps on the counter right as I finish pouring myself a large glass of water, and I practically fly across the room to grab it.

Conall

That's all a guy has to do to get a kiss around here? Last night I carried you all the way to your room and all I got was an invite to nap.

My face turns a bright crimson; I clearly wasn't only offering for him to sleep last night, and I know he knows it. I'm grateful for his jokes. They keep me from sinking back into the pit of anxiety always bubbling deep in my gut, waiting to pull me under.

Me

Food is the highest form of currency.

Conall

Well, in that case, I think I'm being robbed. Mrs. Huang's food is top-tier.

Me

gasp How dare you insinuate that my kiss isn't payment enough! I take it back, I'm going to go kiss the noodles instead. Have fun alone!

A healthy dose of banter with Conall never fails to put me in a great mood. Cackling to myself, I head upstairs and decide to run a bath. The noodles have officially chased away the last of my hangover, but my legs still ache from hours of dancing in heels last night. I snag my speaker and my half-finished novel off of the bedside table in my room and perch it next to my phone on the bath tray. A bag of Epsom salt and a few generous pours of my favorite lavender bubble bath turn the near-scalding water into a heavenly potion guaranteed to soothe my muscles. I turn off the lights in the bathroom and slide into the tub, leaving the gentle light of the evening to illuminate the room.

I've barely settled into the final chapter of my book when my new favorite sound echoes through the room.

Conall

So...you want to talk about earlier?

Shit. I was hoping he forgot about this morning's frantic messages. I quickly send him a response saying not to worry about it, crank up my music, and return to reading. By now, I'm squinting in the moonlight that sneaked in to replace the sun while I was lost to the world. Books and music have a tendency to sweep me up into themselves and carry me away to a place where time flows a bit differently. A place where my demons can't find me.

Conall

You sure? You seemed a bit stressed out.

I drag my hands down my face. This once, why couldn't he be dense and self-absorbed? Why does he have to be so damn perceptive all of the time? My nails scratch at the delicate inside of my wrist, turning it red and raw as I fret over how to respond. I don't notice the damage I'm doing until small drops of blood fall onto the milky surface of the water. The sight shocks me back to reality.

Me

I was worried you weren't gonna want to hang out with me anymore. I made an ass of myself last night.

Conall

You didn't make an ass of yourself, you had a good time on your birthday. It's okay to let go around friends, kitten.

Kitten? That's a new one. I might as well make a home for the happy little butterflies in my stomach since they never seem to leave anymore.

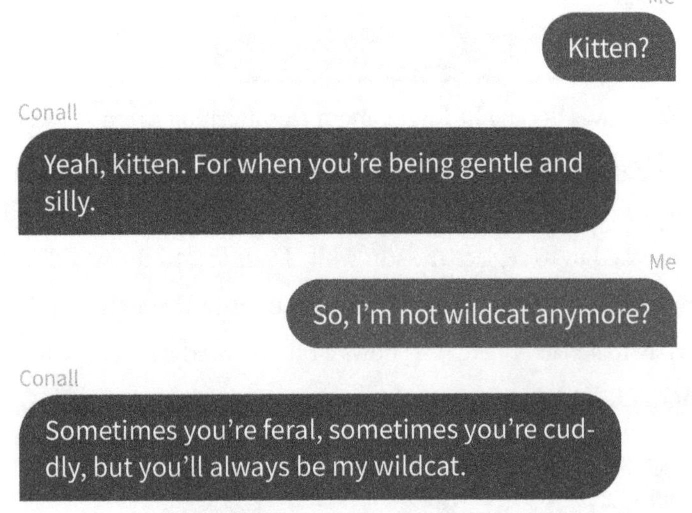

My smile can be seen from orbit, guaranteed. Pretty sure astronauts are up there looking at it right now. I shoot off another apology for inviting him to sleep with me last night. It's understandable, given how amazing he is and how drunk I was, and of course his *looks*, but it was still inappropriate.

Conall

Stop apologizing, it was incredibly flattering.

Flattering? He found my drunken, half-asleep propositioning *flattering*?

A new, burning question consumes me, but I decide to take a breather. No sense in jumping right into the deep end. Once I ask, I can't take it back. I busy myself with getting out of the bathtub, meticulously drying myself, and changing into a tank and sleep shorts. I rush downstairs to get a glass of water and gulp half of it in a failed attempt to calm myself. Finally, I give up and settle into my bed.

Fingers trembling, I take the plunge.

Me

If it was so flattering, why didn't you stay?

I wait with bated breath, but he doesn't make me wait for long. His message has my heart sprinting, galloping out of my chest in an attempt to get to him. The warmth it elicits stays with me long after I drift off to sleep, hugging my phone like a child's stuffed animal.

Conall

Because...if one day I am lucky enough to be the one you choose to be with after everything you've been through, I want us both to be coherent enough to savor every second of it.

Chapter 15
The Fall
- Conall -

The rain lashes my skin on my way towards the dining center, coming down in impenetrable sheets that turn the rest of the world into a gray mass. My enhanced eyesight can barely pierce the gloom. The orange smudges of jack-o'-lanterns are barely visible, hiding from the wet under the covered entrances to every building I pass. The plastic ghosts and witches hanging from the trees have become nothing more than sodden blobs in my periphery, all of them succumbing to the downpour.

Should've brought a car today instead of the bike, I think to myself as I scan the empty pavilion. A car would have been much more practical, given the forecast. When I left this morning on my bike, I had hoped the skies would maintain their murky, yet clear state, but they certainly have not.

My desire to use my motorcycle stems from one simple reason: Valorie is much closer to me when we ride together on the bike. Driving her home is one of my favorite parts of the day, especially with her warm arms around my waist and my nostrils bathed in her pear-fields-and-summer scent. My personal year-round summertime.

My initial hunch proves to be correct—no sign of Valorie outside. Not that I expected her to be waiting at our usual table in this weather, but I never quite know what she'll do. I would not have been surprised to find her huddled under an umbrella, patiently waiting for me to show up for our standing lunchtime arrangement. I'm glad she had enough self-preservation to wait for me inside; I'd feel terrible if she fell ill waiting for me. Humans are so much more fragile than Avalleans.

A smile forms on my lips as I enter the building and peer through the mass of students. I'm on the hunt for a familiar halo of onyx curls. Valorie brings out a freer, lighter side of myself, one I never knew existed. With her, I can be myself.

Occasionally.

If only I could truly be with her, but I cannot. It's becoming more and more difficult to remind myself of that fact, and after last night I fear I may already be too lost to recover my boundaries.

This job may very well kill us both.

She's not in the atrium near the main doors, so I move a bit further into the cafeteria proper. I weave my way through the stragglers at the end of long lunch lines and between the few scattered tables on the fringes of the dining area.

Still no sign of the tiny, spirited woman I've come to long for.

My grin finally slips when I get stuck behind a large crowd of people, forced to wait and watch for a gap in the throng. *Where is she?*

My searching becomes more frantic. I'm unable to quell the sick dread skittering beneath my ribs.

Suddenly, someone mentions her name in a passing conversation, and my head whips towards the sound. When I find the only possible source, the trickle of fear I was trying my hardest to avoid becomes a deluge that rivals the one outside.

Xavier and his equally polished lackeys stand in a shadowed alcove full of vending machines, away from the lunchtime crowd. He's holding court, regaling them with some story that has his arms waving and a cold, bloodthirsty smirk twisting his face. His four companions have expressions ranging from amusement to boredom, but a smaller boy closest to where I stand on the fringes of the crowd catches my eye. He shifts uncomfortably on his feet, eyes darting around the group.

I sidle up to the wall bordering their meeting. Leaning against a large potted plant with a feigned look of apathy, I strain to hear the drivel passing between them. What I hear makes my blood curdle.

"...so she was alone? She didn't have those two fags with her?" someone asks in a nasally voice.

From my position, I can't risk seeing who is speaking, not that it matters. I immediately recognize the slick, supercilious voice that replies.

"Nope." Xavier has the audacity to pop the P like this is some joke to him.

My stomach sours, and I clench my fists. If he doesn't get to the point soon, I won't be able to stay quiet.

He continues, "She was walking all alone, near those stairs that take you below the footbridge to campus."

I don't know whether to be relieved or frightened.

"I knew she'd be there because the dumb bitch always talked about loving to see the 'pretty green plants' or some bullshit."

His high-pitched, mocking impression of Valorie's musical voice has me seeing red. I clutch the lip of the planter to keep myself from slamming my fists into his face. Gleaning information from him is more important than my ever-growing rage.

He continues, "Anyway, there she was, walking along the pathway. Perfect timing, right? It's like she *wanted* me to find her. So I went up to her and asked her how come she wasn't with that fucker she's always drooling after these days. And the bitch had the audacity to act like she didn't know who I meant." He lets loose a sharp, barking laugh. "I told her of course she doesn't know, she's a stupid whore who spreads her legs for anyone now. She probably can't keep track."

His lackeys chortle around him while he crows like an overgrown cockerel.

A gritty substance suddenly appears between my fingers. There are twin crumbling handprints in the cheap terracotta pot I've been gripping as a lifeline.

"And then, and then, this is the best part!"

I don't know if I can take anymore, but something niggles in the back of my head, telling me it's imperative I keep listening.

"I told her the new weirdo will drop her like everyone else, and if she wanted the only person who'd take her stupid shit she needed to get on her knees and beg like a good bitch. But she was too stupid to take what I was nice enough to offer, so I taught her a lesson. Happy Halloween, slut!"

Everything freezes in my mind. There are no people, no crowds, no light or smell or taste. Only a tunnel connecting me directly to Xavier's triumphant posturing and grating laughter.

The timid boy I noticed in his group speaks up, his quiet voice asking the question I need answered, "What do you mean, Xave? Whatcha do to her?"

"Well, the stairs were right there, so...I introduced her to them. Now she won't need to find a costume for next week. Bitch can go as a mummy!"

A roaring sound in my ears drowns out another bout of his preening and cackling. I round the corner, ready to finally kill him, damn the witnesses. I enter Xavier's line of sight, but an image fills my brain and I screech to a halt.

I picture Valorie, broken and drenched in dirty water, lying motionless at the bottom of a staircase while the rain pelts her bruised skin. Has anyone found her yet? How many people are out walking those trails in this weather?

I'm out of the door without Xavier seeing me. He'll never know how close he was to death today. If she's dead, I'm coming back for him. I may be a healer, but for her, I'll become a killer.

I refuse to think about how she's going to make me a killer one way or another.

Thankfully, nobody is on the walking routes out of campus, so I'm able to increase my speed to a level far beyond any typical human. An Olympic sprinter would likely be able to match me, but they wouldn't be able to maintain the pace I'm traveling for long. I can't typically run this fast for extended periods, but my adrenaline gives me strength, and the miles fly by like leaves on the turbulent breeze.

I know the place Xavier was talking about. Valorie showed it to me last week, explaining how her quiet walk to school was often the most peaceful part of her day. I had trouble paying attention to the surroundings, instead entranced by the pattern of light and shadow dappling her creamy skin and the way she sparkled as she spoke of the plants and animals she sometimes saw on her journey. She hummed a quiet tune, dancing around in the green and gold shining upon her. I remember thinking she looked like an angel from one of the antique paintings Domenic has scattered around the Haven.

Today, the journey is cold and drab without her magic to bring it to life. Nature itself seems to hold her breath, waiting for me to reach the spot where Valorie was attacked. I push through the last clump of low-hanging branches in my way and drop to my knees, inhaling in ragged gasps, as tears mix with the rain on my skin.

Red and blue lights flash through the curtain of rain at the other end of three hundred feet of asphalt. A man in a black tracksuit, earbuds around his neck, shuffles his feet near a pair of uniformed officers. Beyond him, two paramedics are loading a gurney into the back of an ambulance. My heart clenches when I see waterlogged curls flopping over the edge of the gurney's thin vinyl pad. I lurch to my feet, putting on one last burst of speed in a desperate attempt to reach her.

As I run, the past eight-and-a-half weeks roll in a silent film through my brain. Valorie smiling tentatively up at me on the day we met, her tired eyes glowing even then. Valorie's hair, riotous as a thundercloud, brushing against my shoulder as we walk by the campus lake on a sunny, warm Wednesday three weeks ago. Valorie smiling at me five days a week from across the table that has become ours, a warm blush tinting her fair skin. Valorie's hands, soft and warm on the back of my neck as we dance under the swirling lights on her birthday. Valorie opening her life up to me, offering me a space in her battered, but unbreakable heart. Valorie always smiling, always trying to push past the things that have hurt her in order to help someone else. Valorie. Valorie. *Valorie.*

Please be alive. I need you to be alive.

The irony doesn't register. She can't die, not anymore. Not my Valorie. Fuck the Web. Fuck the whole world. She's *mine.*

"Please!" I scream, my voice hoarse with exertion. I'll shred every vocal cord I have if it gets them to pause long enough for me to catch up. Every bone, every nerve, fiber and synapse in my body needs to know she's alive.

Somehow, the medics hear me and pause. The one on the left turns toward me, taking in my disheveled state from above an impressively bushy mustache.

"Son, we need to go. What's the hold-up? Do you know this girl?" His gruff voice is strangely soothing, an almost fatherly grumble.

I nod frantically, catching my breath. "She's my..." I scramble for an idea, any false claim I can lay on her that will allow me to stay. "My girlfriend. Please, I came as fast as I could. I can't leave her...please..." my voice gives out by the end, but I think he hears me.

Mustache gives me a once over, and his gaze softens. "We aren't supposed to do this if you aren't family, but frankly we'll need any information we can get when she gets to the hospital." He huffs, his breath fogging in the cold. "All I know about her right now is she's got a guy here, running through the pouring rain to be with her. So...get in, kid."

He calls out to the officers I sprinted past earlier, letting them know we are preparing to head out. One of the cops fixes me with a heavy stare and tells me to stay at the hospital so he can swing by and ask me a few questions. I quickly agree; I'll tell them anything they want to know as soon as I'm sure Valorie will be okay. The mission can wait until tomorrow or next week or never for all I care. For today I'll play whatever role I need to in order to stay with her.

I scramble into the front seat next to the kind medic, and we speed off with my heart in the back of a bright yellow ambulance.

Chapter 16
Brand New

- Conall -

Five hours, forty-three minutes, sixteen seconds. That's how long I've been sitting in a plastic chair, watching blips flash across the monitors connected to Valorie. Every tick is a reminder she's still alive, she's still here with me, even if she doesn't know it. Even if I should be hoping for the beeps to stop instead of anxiously counting every one.

She hasn't woken up since we arrived.

The hours have been achingly slow, but not uneventful. After the longest fifteen-minute ride in a vehicle in my entire life, the ambulance screeched into the emergency bay at Glen County General—the hospital affiliated with Sycamore University's medical program. The knowledge that Valorie was in the hands of one of the nation's highest-rated, state-of-the-art medical facilities didn't ease the frantic pounding in my chest. Especially when the grandmotherly physician kindly directed me to Valorie's private room in the ICU to wait while they ran tests to check for damage. I settled into the beige-patterned armchair, determined to be a model visitor and wait patiently for an update.

That lasted for all of twenty minutes.

I spent the following hour pacing the halls, gnawing on my nails—a habit I have never understood and always found disgusting—and flashing hopeful looks at any nurse or doctor who walked past me.

All of my wordless pleas went unanswered.

I spiraled further into despair, my mind conjuring increasingly darker scenarios with every tick of the large, industrial clock above the desk at the nurses' station. What if she flatlined while trapped inside some archaic machine humans use to scan patients for internal injuries? Logically, I knew there were protocols in place for such an occurrence, and I knew I should be plotting ways to use their fallible technology for my advantage. But, logic escaped me on a muddy trail in the woods this afternoon and never returned.

Then, the quiet squeak of wheels on linoleum reached me. I spun around faster than I should have, startling the nurse wheeling a long, gray hospital bed down the wide hall. She looked up and met my stare, giving me a firm nod, and I almost collapsed there on the hospital floor. I waited quietly in the corner while she arranged Valorie in her room, though I winced every time a monitor or line was attached to her battered skin. Once she was finished, the nurse nodded to me once more and jerked her head towards the door.

"She's stable, but barely," she told me in a low voice once we had reentered the hallway, and my knees wobbled. "The doctors will be back in to talk more with you in a couple hours. The police also have a few questions, I guess they don't know who did this to her?" Her voice lifted at the end, which turned her statement into a question.

I nodded shakily.

She continued, "So they may get here before the doctors do. You be good and answer their questions. Technically you're not supposed to be here, but she needs someone. You can stay in the room with her, but make sure you call her family, okay?" A stern look punctuated her last sentence.

I nodded once more, beginning to feel like the bobblehead doll Finn bought at a baseball game three years ago.

Once she left, I made a quick call to David, the only member of Valorie's inner circle whose number I had saved. Getting his voicemail, I left a message telling him to call me as soon as possible. Afterwards, I settled in to wait.

An hour later, I was joined by the burly officer who spoke to me at the scene, this time without his partner. He spent half an hour asking me to recount any details I could remember about the conversation I overheard at lunch.

In the end, he seemed satisfied with the information I gave him. He cautioned me not to do anything rash. The knowing look he gave me made it clear I was not holding myself together as well as I thought I was. A business card with his name and number, along with the main line for his precinct, was tucked in the palm of his firm handshake on his way out.

Officer Burrows, as his card proclaimed, traded places with two doctors in matching white coats. I'm sure they introduced themselves, but I couldn't find the energy to care enough to retain their names. One of them was the kind-eyed, older doctor from the hallway earlier, still radiating a calm confidence. Her companion was at least half her age, new enough to be torn between nervously shifting on his feet and being eager to prove himself.

The older doctor took the lead, detailing Valorie's extensive injuries in a list that slowly crushed my aching heart into a pulp. One broken rib, contusions along her entire body, deep lacerations on her left extremities from a branch that nearly impaled her as she plummeted, an absolutely shattered left foot, and a barely-there orbital fracture from the impact at the bottom. Plus a sprained ankle which likely occurred during Xavier's initial shove. As they made their goodbyes and promised to return in a couple hours when the results of her brain imaging were in, I swore to myself I would make sure that was the last time Xavier's hands would ever touch her.

It's been three hours and twelve minutes since they left me here, alone with my gauze-wrapped heart and her machines.

I pass the time staring at the girl I reluctantly adore, wishing I was somehow able to help. Everything in me aches to heal her, but there's already a documented record of her extensive injuries, so I'm cursed to wait here and watch her suffer. All because I was too late.

Valorie's face is a mass of small scratches and scraped skin, with a small butterfly bandage above her right eyebrow. Half of her skin is wrapped in gauze and wiring, but the exposed skin I am able to see is mottled and raw. Dried blood has caused mats near her scalp, their flaking clumps almost black in the stark lighting of the gently buzzing commercial bulb overhead. My fingers itch to scrub them away for her.

"Excuse me?" I call, peeking my head out of the door for the first time since I reentered the room all those hours ago.

A round-faced woman looks up from the nurse's station, her lightly lined face creasing into a sympathetic smile. "How can I help, dear?"

"She—" my voice catches embarrassingly, and I cough to clear it. "She has blood in her hair. I need to get it out. She can't lay there with blood in her hair..." I trail off, unsure of exactly what I can do.

"I can get you a sponge and a little bowl, honey. She's not exactly up for a shower right now."

Her kind face reminds me of Marguerite.

I wish I could spirit Valorie away to the Haven and heal her on my own. I'd fill her repaired body with Margie's warm baked goods and her diamond heart with laughter and the chatter of my family. But I wasn't fast enough to save her from this fate. I didn't do enough.

I accept the soft, beige sponge from the nurse and a canary yellow plastic bowl. Returning to Valorie's room, I move towards the sink mounted in the corner and turn the taps, pleased to find the water quickly heats. My face in the mirror over the basin is haggard, lines drawn in the corners and crevasses where there were none this morning. With the full bowl warm in my hands, I return to the bedside and begin gently wiping Valorie's hairline, careful to avoid any cuts or swelling. The water in my bowl slowly turns from pink to red.

"Conall, are you licking my forehead?"

I jerk, blood-tinged water soaking my shirt.

"Wildcat?" My voice is the barest whisper, as if my very lungs are afraid to scare her away. "You're awake?"

"Well, I hurt way too much for this to be a dream, so I guess so. But I don't think you'd be licking me in real life, so maybe I am?" Her words are sluggish from the pain medicine they've pumped her full of, but she still chuckles. It's a tired version of her usual bright laughter, and my heart falters.

"It was a sponge." I wave the offending piece of foam in her direction. "You...I...I was cleaning your hair." I decide to not mention exactly *what* it was I was cleaning out of her hair.

"Oh," she says, "shame." She purses her lips into a pout and a rush of blood heads to a place that doesn't need to be involved in a time like this.

She's injured, Conall. Control your damn self.

I can't resist the jab. "You upset about it, wildcat?"

Her blush takes over her face, and I smile for the first time in what feels like ages.

With her head tilted towards the scratchy blanket in her lap, she mumbles something nearly unintelligible, but I manage to catch the words "control yourself" and "hot mess" mixed in with the garbled string of syllables. I focus on the reddened tips of her ears in an attempt to control my racing heart. Is it possible she could be feeling the same way I do?

A nurse quietly enters the room and brightens when he sees Valorie awake in her bed. He bustles over and begins checking her vitals and asking questions, his voice hushed despite the three of us being the only ones in the room. I can't focus on anything except her slight smile and the lingering blush still radiating through her bruises and cuts. The idea that I could be the one to have made her react this way? It gives me hope.

As quickly as the hope rises in my chest, it is dashed to the floor. My hands start to sweat and my mind races with disjointed, jumbled questions.

Am I truly going to take this girl and make her mine?

Do I have such a reprehensible lack of self-control that I can't bear to keep some sort of barrier around my heart, for both our sakes?

If I take this leap, will I truly be able to look into her eyes in a few months and watch the fire leave them?

How will I possibly be able to end her life and move on like I didn't snuff out what has quickly become the brightest light in my universe?

Bile floods my mouth, and I suddenly realize my answer is already right in front of me. In a choice between the small, battered, incredibly strong woman in front of me and this entire planet, there's no choice to be made.

There never has been.

I don't care that it's selfish. I don't care that this is supposed to be my job. I don't care that I'm sacrificing a planet's potentially lifesaving advancement for the sake of a single human girl. I don't care that I'm betraying Esraa and Amon, who have done nothing but look out for me more than any other Paragons. I don't even care that, although falling in love with a human is technically approved, it means I won't be able to go Home during her lifetime. I. Do. Not. Care. The damned Web can show us another way for humans to advance; Valorie is no longer an option for anyone but me.

The nurse finally leaves the room, and I am once again left alone with the girl who has derailed my world so completely. The barest curve of her lips lifts when her eyes meet mine through her lowered lashes, and my entire face stretches into a beaming grin.

I can't help myself. I have to touch her.

Careful to avoid the intravenous line in the back of her hand, I grasp her fingers lightly between my palms. She looks at our joined hands with blown pupils.

Her head rises to meet my burning gaze, and words tumble thoughtlessly from my lips. "Valorie, I can't do this anymore. I don't want to continue being your friend."

Her face falls and her fingers slip through mine. I desperately clutch them back to me. It's only when her glassy stare wells with tears that I realize my mistake. She tries to look away from me, but I leave her fists in her lap and take her face between my clammy palms, inwardly cringing at the sweat I'm unable to stop.

"Wait!" I scramble up onto the bed beside her, careful not to jostle her or the multitude of wires and wrappings around her. "I'm not finished, Valorie."

"I think you've said quite enough." She sniffles, her gaze cast down.

I'm wide-eyed and begging in front of her. "*Please* let me finish. I promise it's not what you think."

She offers one tiny nod, made smaller by the gentle grip of my hands around her face. She refuses to look at me, but I talk anyway, hoping my raw emotion will be conveyed without her meeting my eyes.

"Valorie, ever since I first saw your face, I've felt pulled towards you. I don't make many friends; my family and my work and a few acquaintances have always been enough for me. That is, until I saw your mussed hair poking out every which way at that garden table five weeks ago. You peeked up at me and I knew then and there I needed to get to know you."

Her gaze finally meets mine, bolstering my confidence enough to keep me pouring out my heart.

"The last eight weeks have consumed me. *You* have consumed me. Your laughter is my air, your smile my is sustenance, your touch is the water that rushes over me and soothes my soul. Day by day I've fallen, despite every intention not to, and now I never want to get back up. I am yours, Valorie, my fierce wildcat, my kitten, my only love. If you'll have me, I'll be yours forever." My lids slip closed, unable to bear looking at her a second longer without touching her. My hands return to my lap and I clench them together until my knuckles pop.

There is a muted rustling in front of me; the curious sound forces my lids open and I find Valorie's mottled face inches from my own. A shuddering gasp whispers through my parted lips as her depthless pewter irises drill into my soul.

And then, she leans in.

Her lips brush mine, damp with her tears, tasting of iron and salt and sunshine. It's a chaste kiss, but it carries a promise of more. I lean in to fully capture her mouth with my own, but she pulls away.

A low groan rumbles out of me, and she chuckles. She rests a single finger against my lips and shushes me, so I breathe her in and wait. Her scent is wrong, the sharp tang of antiseptic overriding the freshness of pears I've come to expect, but she's still there underneath it all.

"I think I've loved you for a while now, Conall." Her damaged, raspy voice is filled with raw emotion, despite her words being a bit slurred.

Tears of my own carve their tracks through my skin, but I can finally breathe.

"Something has called me to you from that very first afternoon. At first, I thought it was grief. I thought it was fear and pain and loneliness. But I'm starting to think maybe, all along...it's been hope." A painful-sounding inhale rattles through her, and it makes my chest hurt in sympathy. "I'm a mess. I'm broken, but trying to fit myself together. Sometimes the days are too much, sometimes the nights are too dark and I fear being left alone with my demons because they eat me up inside. But I'm alive, and I'm fighting. So, if you're okay with a work in progress...I'm all in."

Fireworks explode behind my eyelids as my mouth crashes into hers. My tongue strokes against her bottom lip until she opens for me and curls her tongue around mine. Her teeth nip and tug on my bottom lip, sending waves of heat straight to my cock.

A small, detached part of my brain is flashing a stop sign behind my lids. I know Valorie's hospital bed is not the place for what my body is telling me to do, but pulling away from her is a task I am not strong enough to undertake. Blood thrums in my ears, the frantic beat of my heart mixing with her quiet pants as she tries to get me to take hold of her. I somehow manage to keep my hands firmly fisted in her sheets, afraid of accidentally hurting her while I'm in this state.

A small yawn slips from her swollen mouth when we pause for breath, and that's enough to allow logic to take over. I gently extricate her fingers from my shirt and capture them with my own. Using our intertwined hands, I guide her until she lies against her pillows, a similar position to the one she was in before she awoke and changed my entire life with a few powerful words.

"I'm going to need to hear everything all again once you're sober, kitten, and not drunk on morphine. But that can wait. You've had one hell of an awful day. Sleep now."

She cocks her head towards the empty space next to her and snuggles her head into my lap once I take a seat by her side. "I don't know," she whispers as her eyes flutter closed, "seems like a pretty great day to me." Her breathing slows and she drifts off to sleep, a faint smile still on her plush lips.

I am a changed man.

The gentle, cream-colored walls seem to glow in the soft light of the room. The abstract print on the wall suddenly is a masterpiece reminiscent of Dali or Picasso. I was sitting on a hard hospital bed a few seconds ago, but it has been transformed beneath me into an opulent throne fit for a king. Everything is filled with magical, glittering life I've never seen before. The world has been built anew, or perhaps I'm the one who has been reborn.

Though I loathe to do so, I gradually ease myself out of her grip, careful not to wake her. Crossing to the other side of the room, I grab my phone from the small corner table and step outside into the hall to dial. The small picture of the two of us on my phone screen is overlaid by today's date: October twenty-fifth. Forever to be known as the day my life changed.

David's anxious voice assaults my eardrums before the first ring fades, "What's going on, Conall? I haven't been able to get a hold of Val all day. Neither has Char, and her parents are out of town for some conference until after Halloween, so they're no help. We're freaking out here."

Obviously.

I call his name to redirect his attention. He needs to calm himself or he'll spiral completely when he hears what happened. "David, stop. Take a breath. I'm with her, she's alive. She's at Glen General. That bastard, Xavier...he threw her down a staircase."

The rage in my voice steadily grows as I explain what happened to Valorie earlier today and the conversation I overheard at school. By the end of the call, David tells me he's going to let Charlie know. He says he can't come up tonight, but he will be here first thing tomorrow morning. I reassure him I won't leave Valorie's side until he gets here. Conveniently, I fail to tell him I also won't be going far once he arrives.

He hangs up the phone to go and update Charlie, sounding much less frazzled than he did when he picked up ten minutes ago.

Having her best friends around will help soothe Valorie, although she doesn't seem as upset as I expected.

Does she remember the attack?

In the midst of my epiphany, I completely forgot to explain to her how she ended up in a hospital room. She didn't seem terribly concerned, which should concern *me*. A concussion, maybe? Those doctors never did return with her scan results. Usually no news is good news in hospitals, but I wish they would have given me an update for my own peace of mind.

The second my hand connects with the cold, steel door handle, my phone rings again. I pick it up without checking the screen. "Hey, David, forget something?"

"What did you *do*?"

Fuck. Managing to keep the dread currently clogging my throat from infusing my voice, I feign nonchalance. "Hey, Gabby. What's going on? See anything lately?"

"Conall, I don't know how you did it—and I'm not going to give myself a migraine looking through the Web to find out since it already happened—but remember how I told you weeks ago there might be an option? An unreliable one?"

How could I forget? "Yeah...?"

"Well, you found it. I don't see you killing her anymore."

I can't contain the relieved sigh that bursts out of me like a river flooding a broken dam. Tears fill my eyes, and I let them fall, not bothering to wipe them away or worry about the nurse shooting furtive glances at me over the counter.

"Gabs, you sure?" I ask.

"Yes, I'm sure. You aren't going to kill her. I'm not going to look more into it because I can See you'll tell us all about it later. But, Con," she pauses, "what are you going to do about the task? Did the Underworld give you some kind of change in orders that I missed?"

"I was kind of hoping you had Seen something about that, because I have no clue. But it'll be all right. Esraa and Amon will work with me. They'll have to because I'm not going to let another dehmi get assigned to be her executioner either." The mere notion of it makes my blood boil, forcing me to concentrate on not crushing the fragile phone between my fingers.

"Well, I don't see that either, but there's some kind of...obscurity, like a knot in things. It's preventing me from Seeing anything past the next ten months or so. It's odd, but it could be as simple as you needing to hash things out with the Paragons in order to straighten out the future. Or it could be normal human indecision. Things are harder to see with them, their lives move so quickly and are so unstructured. Plus, I don't focus on them quite as often, and not on such a broad level."

I nod, forgetting she can't see me over the phone.

Gabrielle doesn't spend a lot of time in close human company due to both her otherworldly appearance and her vision-induced migraines. The times she is asked to See the Web around a human's life usually revolve around an established set of parameters and hard boundaries on what exactly she's looking for. She doesn't practice this type of general scrying for unknown threats over a long span of time unless she's connected to the person or event in question. I long for more concrete information, but I stop short of begging her to strain her already-exhausted brain by delving into this "knot" she's Seeing. I'll stick close to my wildcat, and we'll find our own blind way through to the future for now.

"I understand. Thanks, Gab. Can you let Dom know I may not be home for a while? Valorie is in the hospital."

Her quick intake of breath lets me know she didn't See that coming either. She must have been indisposed today. Or desperately trying to give me the privacy to figure my feelings out.

My chest warms with love for my sister and her efforts to make our lives as normal as possible.

"Of course I can, brother. And Con?"

"Yeah?"

"Congratulations. Everyone is going to love her."

Another silent tear rolls and gets caught in my broad smile. "Thanks, Gabby. Love you."

The phone clicks softly as she ends the call.

I tiptoe back into the calm quiet of Valorie's hospital room. She's curled up on her less-injured right side, sleeping soundly. I flick the light off with the switch by the door, leaving only the light of the rising moon from the window to illuminate her delicate features, relaxed in sleep.

Careful to avoid the wires she's hidden beneath her cocoon of thin bedding, I return to the space she had selected for me on her narrow bed. I should try to sleep, but a sudden wave of emotions hits me now that I'm free of distractions. The love and euphoria and stress and terror of the day are all swirling together, a whirlpool of emotions inside my skull. I can do nothing more than rest my head in my hands and cry until the tide finally pulls me under to join her in slumber.

Chapter 17

Visitors

- Valorie -

Drip, drip, drip. The faint plunking of liquid rouses me from an amazing dream. In my sleep, I crafted a world where I was attacked, lying in a hospital bed while Conall gave me a sponge bath and professed his love for me. The details get a bit hazy beyond that point, but I know it was a good dream, despite the whole 'being attacked' issue.

And now this stupid water is waking me up before I can get to the juicy parts.

Wait. Why is there dripping water in my bedroom? Did I leave the sink running and it's overflowing onto the floor? Oh, shit. Mom is going to be *pissed* if there's water damage.

I force my crusty, desiccated eyelids to open and fling myself out of bed. Or at least I try to.

I'm stopped by a painful tugging on my hand.

Looking down, I find a tape-covered port connected by a clear tube to a bag of liquid hanging on a stand next to me. Small, steady droplets of clear fluid are snaking their way through the tubing towards the stake speared through my poor, defenseless vein. I shudder, averting my bewildered consciousness from the IV line before my empty stomach can find some way to stage a protest. I have no issues with needles in theory, but I don't take kindly to waking up and finding them jabbed into my hand in a semi-permanent state.

"Valorie? What are you doing, *chica*? Get back in bed!" David shrieks. His voice is stern, but he settles my shoulders back against the pillows with the reverence he reserves for his mother's ceramic heirloom *Virgen de Guadalupe* she still keeps on their mantle. She's no longer Catholic, but whenever someone points this out she says some habits die hard.

"'Valorie'? Jeez, David. Must be serious if you're full-naming me." I chuckle, a bit loopy from the medication.

"Valorie Catherine Vargas, you had us all worried sick, so you'll keep your ass in bed or I'll glue it there."

I can't help it, snorts of laughter spray out from between my tightly clenched lips. David is the picture of his mother right now—hip cocked out, sour-lemon lips, and a glare capable of cutting glass. But I've known David my whole life, and there's fear behind his grumpy posturing. He must've been worried sick about me.

"Come here, Dee. Fill me in on the gossip, because it seems like I didn't dream the part about me getting shoved down a damn staircase at least." I pat the place on my bed where I dreamed Conall was perched last night. I'm desperately hoping that part was real, too.

David raises his eyebrows while he settles on the thin mattress. "You thought you dreamed it all? Nah, *chica*, the *hijo de puta* pushed you. Conall heard him bragging to his cronies about it and came running. Thank God the boy can sprint like Usain Bolt. He managed to get all the way from the cafeteria to where you were right before they loaded you into the ambulance."

"Conall found me?" My memories are thick and viscous, unwilling to move into an order that allows me to make sense of them.

I remember Xavier's chilling expression of joy at finding me in the rain, then everything flashes forward to the stairs rushing towards my face. There's a sharp crack, the sound of an old stick in autumn, followed by nothing but phantom pain until my hazy dream of Conall and...licking? Fantasies of Conall and his tongue derail the broken train of thought I had begun to assemble, throwing it off of the tracks entirely. I barely manage to rein in my blush. The last thing I need is for David to see it and start interrogating me when my brain isn't working at full capacity.

"Yeah, Vally, he did. He called me yesterday while you were asleep and filled me in, but I was babysitting the twins and couldn't get Mom or Dad to answer the phone until visiting hours were already over."

David's twin sisters are seven, so he'll sometimes take them for a night of fun while his parents go out for a date. The evenings are always the girls' choice—movies, dinner, bowling, whatever they want. They absolutely adore it, and I know David does too. Not that you'd know it by the way he's fuming right now, ranting at the ceiling while I try not to laugh.

"What's the point in having a damn phone if they don't answer it? We have whole-ass computers in our pockets and I'm stuck at home wondering if I should call the restaurant like it's 1997!"

"David, *calmate*. Go back to Conall being here. I didn't dream that either?"

"Nope. He's been here all night, in fact. Got a call about fifteen minutes before you woke up and went downstairs to meet someone. Said he'd be back in a few hours. Plenty of time for you to tell me what the hell has changed between you two." His Cheshire Cat smile is as infectious as it is devious. He mimes holding a bag of popcorn, leaning back and tossing a few imaginary kernels into his mouth.

"Well, it starts with yesterday evening, when I woke up and kind of accused him of licking my face?" Now that I know it wasn't a concoction of my injured, drug-addled brain, it's a bit mortifying.

David's eyebrows waggle like a cheesy movie villain. "Kinky."

"I'd hit you with a pillow if it wouldn't hurt me more than you." I laugh. "Anyways, he was sponging blood out of my hair. Much less kinky." *Unfortunately.*

"Dunno, Vally, a sponge bath from a bronze babe like him? Nurse, I'll take two, please."

We dissolve into childish giggles.

"Wait, that's not the best part. Dee, he said he loves me." I barely breathe the words, afraid uttering them in the light of day might somehow make them lose their magic. "And he kissed me. Which, trust me, was *infinitely* better than the sponge bath."

David slips on his detective's cap, ready to dissect every second of last night on his imaginary notepad. "Tell. Me. Everything."

We spend the next half hour pouring over every detail of my time with Conall, swooning over the wonderful things he said to me and raving about how different he is from the demon of my unfortunate past. Once David has finally had his fill of the play-by-play, he turns serious.

"So...you love him?"

"Dee," I say, "I think I've loved him for longer than either of us could guess. When I'm with him, it's like I'm home. I never thought someone would make me feel like this outside of our little circle and my parents." His comforting loamy eyes and warm chocolate-and-pepper scent give me the strength to voice what terrifies me. "What if I'm too damaged, though? What if Xavier broke me? Is it fair to saddle him with all of my problems?"

"You shut the hell up right now." His voice is a gentle contrast to the fire in his glare. "You are not the sum of the experiences you've been put through. They are a testament to your strength, but they are not the beginning and end of your story. You're all the little things in between the shit that keeps you up at night."

I swallow around the lump in my throat, my eyelids opened wide against the salty brine threatening to spill out of them.

"You're the little kid who scooped up a lonely Charlie on the playground. The girl who fought a boy in middle school who made fun of me for being gay. The woman who spends her days dancing and singing along to stories where people can overcome their adversities with nothing more than a catchy show tune and a little fancy footwork. You're laughter, and a helping hand, and a little pain, sure. But what good is sugar without a little spice?"

I finally lose the battle with my tears, and I do not go gently. David holds me close and shushes me as my turbid emotions wring me dry as a week-old doughnut left out on the counter. He has the decency to not complain when I turn his shirt into a Jackson Pollock painting of tears and snot. When at last I reach a level of exhaustion that prevents the tears from forming and leaves me with only small sniffles, he simply hands me my hospital-issue water jug and tells me to drink. I drain the whole thing, and he refills it from a pitcher on the table beside him.

The fluffy clouds crawl across the sky as David and I gossip in a way only matched by Regency-era ladies at tea or patrons in the hairdryer line at a Southern salon. He tells me how Charlie tried every trick in the book to get his track championships postponed. When his pleas were denied, Charlie almost forfeited so he could be here when I woke up. Thankfully, David eventually told him—correctly, I might add—I'd kill him if I ever found out. He also lets it slip that someone slashed three of Xavier's tires last night, but he won't name any names. I have a feeling I can narrow the list to a select few people, all of them saved in my phone's "favorites" list.

A bouquet of beautiful mixed fall blooms sits in a crystal vase by the window. David explains the gift was dropped off by the runner who found me lying at the bottom of the stairs and called the authorities. I'll have to find a way to thank him somehow. Hopefully, the flowers came with a card, or maybe he left his name with the nurse's station or the cops.

Chatter from the nurses in the hall is punctuated by a boisterous female voice, her muffled words raised in question.

Suddenly, my door swings inward, and in walks David's mother with a covered platter heaped so high it obscures her face. She passes it off to her son and rushes to my side and scooping me into a hug scented with cloves and turbinado sugar.

"Ay, *linda*, how could *el bastardo* do this to you? I'll have his *cojones* for soup!"

Adriana is always a riot of color, and today is no exception. Her light brown curves are wrapped in a figure-hugging silk sheath dress patterned in vibrant primary colors, and her hair falls in sleek, coffee-colored waves over her shoulders. I look up into her eyes—David's eyes—and smile. She's always been a second mother to me, and having her here brings a warmth to the room and makes it less clinical. Anywhere the Wilson-Curbelos end up becomes a home while they're there.

David steps into my field of vision and all of my attention snaps to him. Or more accurately, to the half-eaten treat in his hand.

"*Mami*," I cry, "did you make me *mallorcas*?"

She nods, and I lunge as far across my bed as my tethered hand will allow, reaching for the tray David *conveniently* placed out of my reach. With a swift, loving smack from his mother, David finally hands me one of the fluffy breads. I bite off a huge chunk, the eggy sweetness reminding me of childhood Saturday mornings spent covered in flour in their bright, cluttered kitchen. My empty stomach rejoices, finally receiving real food for the first time in a day.

"Don't worry," Adriana says as she swats a third pastry out of David's clutches and places it back on the teetering mountain she brought with her, "I checked with the nurse and she said if you're hungry you can eat. I said, 'Of course she's hungry!' and I'm always right."

She shoots me a wink and hands me a second *mallorca*.

We sink easily into the kind of conversation you can only have with ones you love. The kind where you talk about everything and nothing all at once, basking in the comfort of knowing each other so well and for so long that actual words are only needed when gestures and shared memories are not enough to get a point across. We would probably sit here talking all night, if not for the tentative knock at the door. The quiet tap has all three of us turning but only stops one heart in the room.

Conall's head peeks through the door Adriana left slightly ajar, and he doesn't look much better than I do. Yet somehow, he's an exhausted angel here in the mute sterility of the hospital, while I'm disheveled and grimy. His gaze meets mine and his face creases into a grin. It spears across the room and lights me up with a million volts straight to my core.

"Hey, you're awake!" He rushes into the room, takes my hands, and looks around as if he only now realizes I'm not alone in the room. "Sorry, I didn't realize you had more company than David. I can leave?" He directs the question to me, but his body curves over the metal bed rail as if he's swallowed a magnet.

David cuts in and introduces Conall to his mom, who says it's about time for them to be heading out anyway. Nobody misses the obvious, exaggerated wink she throws in my direction. Mama Curbelo ushers David to the door. She kisses my cheek and makes me swear to call when I get home...whenever that will be. I'm already tired of the hospital life; my rotating lineup of visitors can't keep the boredom fully at bay.

I'm still looking at the empty doorway, dreaming about busting out of this room for good, when it's suddenly not so empty anymore.

The girl captured in the threshold's clear lighting is nothing short of ethereal. She's at least a head taller than me and Paris-runway slender, all angles and smooth, ripe-plum skin. She affixes me with a curious gaze, her cerise irises at once both innocent and ancient. She's the most beautiful person I've ever seen, and I'm counting Conall.

"Con." Where Conall's voice is all drums and saxophones, hers is piccolos on a soft breeze.

"Gabby, come in and meet Valorie." Confusion must be clear on my face because Conall explains, "Gabrielle is my...adoptive sister. I told you I lived with friends who I consider my family, and she's one of them. Her twin brother, Gaius, also lives with us."

"It's wonderful to see you are well, Valorie," Gabrielle says in a voice that somehow spans time as she glides towards us.

"Call me Val, please," I laugh. "Valorie usually means I'm in trouble."

Her wind-chime laugh is interrupted by the trill of a phone from her pocket.

"Oh, hell," she says, glaring at the screen. "Finn wants me to go pick up some fertilizer for him. He has the *worst* timing. I was hoping I could stay, but it seems we'll have to get to know one another another time, Val." She stands.

Conall gives her a loaded look I can't decipher. "Will you be okay picking up something by yourself, Gab? I could go with you." He winces as if the idea is physically painful.

I don't quite understand what's going on between the lines of their shared, secretive stares and carefully bland conversation. It's as if they're speaking in a code and I don't have the key.

"It's curbside; I pop the trunk and don't speak to anyone. I can handle it. Wouldn't want you to hurt yourself." She winks at me.

Surprisingly, I wish she could stay.

"Text me when you get home," Conall demands.

"Send me Val's number," she calls over her shoulder through the closing door, "we're going to be great pals, I just *know* it."

I hope that's true.

Chapter 18
Temptation

- Valorie -

"Easy, easy!"

"Conall, I'm *fine.* Take, like, several breaths. It's ten feet across flat hardwood to the bed, not a solo trip up Mount Everest." He already insisted on carrying me up the stairs, but I drew the line at being hefted to the bed like an injured calf.

The hospital finally set me free after night had already begun to fall, but not until they cocooned me in a football field's worth of gauze and plaster. I'm on strict instructions to rest as much as possible for the first week of recovery, something Conall is apparently planning on taking to extremes. I'd be more annoyed if his mother-hen act wasn't so damned cute.

I prop myself against the bed's footboard and look longingly at the shower. I'd kill to be clean right now, but I'm not attempting that until Conall leaves. I can only imagine the hyperventilating that would ensue if he saw me trying to maneuver myself towards the tub for the woefully inadequate sponge bathing I have to settle with for the next few days. The doctor said once my rib wrapping comes off I can wrap the cast in cellophane and use a hand-held shower head. Until then, I have to work around my cocoon as best as possible.

"What are you doing, kitten? Get in the bed, please. You look like you're about to fall over." Conall's wide eyes are searchlights darting left and right over his grasping hands. He looks torn between picking me up and tucking me in himself and going into cardiac arrest right here on my bedroom floor.

I grimace at my filthy, worn clothes. David forgot to bring something new for me from the hospital, so I left in the same clothes I arrived in more than thirty-six hours ago. "There's no way in hell I'm getting into my nice clean bed full of funk from the hospital and looking like a walking mud puddle. Nuh-uh. Nope. Not happening." I punctuate each word with a head shake. "So go ahead and head home, I'll text you before I go to sleep." Carefully, I lean forward to brush my lips against his cheek.

He feathers his hands over my face and turns his mouth to meet mine instead. "Kitten," he mumbles against my lips, "I'm not going home. You said it yourself, your parents are away for work and you won't bother them with what you referred to—incorrectly, I might add—as a 'minor issue.'" He pulls his head away enough to fix me with a side eye. "So, I'm staying here with you. The doctor said you need someone with you around the clock, and it was going to take a lot of effort for David to rearrange his whole schedule, so you're stuck with me." His smile falls a bit, and he adds, "Unless you're uncomfortable. I could call Gabby instead? She wouldn't mind, she wants to spend time with you anyway."

I stop his hand halfway to his pocket. "Stay."

I've spent months being too afraid of myself to make a damn move without a liquor shelf's worth of alcohol in me, but now I'm all confidence. Likely due to a combination of the lingering emotional high from our confessions yesterday and an actual high from my painkillers, but I'm rolling with it. David's pep talk earlier may not have completely erased my self-consciousness, but fake it until you make it, right?

I start the water running in the claw-foot tub beneath the bathroom window. A tray of toiletries gets evicted from a stool nearby and I gingerly slide the empty seat to Conall. My ruined clothes get stuck on the cumbersome cast and bandages, and I angrily attempt to rip them at the seams but only succeed in toppling sideways. I teeter, and there's a warm pair of arms under mine to steady me. My hands drift upwards, marveling at the smooth, lean muscles beneath my fingers, until a shuddering breath from behind my ear drags me back to reality.

A sudden flush creeps up my neck. Quickly, I lean my way around Conall's bracketing arms to open the drawer behind him and retrieve a pair of scissors. A few short snips and my clothes are much easier to remove. I motion for him to sit on the stool with his back to me and finish undressing on my own. I may be turning over a new, more self-assured leaf, but I don't think anyone feels their sexiest when they're coated with grime and sheathed in the latest in hospital-issue plaster couture. Only when his vision is safely averted do I perch on the tub's rim and begin to slowly scrub myself clean.

For a while, the only noise in the room is the plinking of water back into the tub and the gentle susurration of the sponge against my stinging skin. I eventually lose myself in the calm of finally being back in my own space. Humming softly to myself, I wash my hair as best as I can, letting my damp curls go wild. There's no way in hell I'm putting myself through a full wash day routine right now. When everything within reach is as clean as it's going to get, I strain to reach the center of my back, but my muscles are too stiff.

Screw it.

"Conall?" My quiet voice breaks the balmy silence, but you'd think I was screaming based on his reaction.

He shoots up, knocking the stool over in his mad scramble to cross the scant three feet of tile between him and my spot on the tub's edge. Chest heaving, he reaches out towards me, stopping short of touching my slick skin. "What's wrong? Are you hurt?"

I hold the sponge over my shoulder and give it a little shake in his direction, trying not to laugh at his overreaction and failing. "I can't reach my back. Can you help me?"

A swath of red spreads across his neck and he takes the sponge from me with his gaze on the floor, dipping it into the water and beginning to scrub small circles along my spine.

"Con, it's only a tub. You didn't have to get so worried. You would've heard if I fell or something."

His movements stutter and quickly resume their journey down my back, skating over my wounds. "Kitten, a day and a half ago I thought I was listening to someone happily recount the story of your murder. When I saw those flashing lights through the rain, saw you getting loaded into that ambulance...I'm going to be protecting you from butterflies for a while before my brain truly grasps the fact that I didn't lose you on a muddy trail in the woods."

"I feel bad for the butterflies," I mutter, hiding my smile behind a tangled section of hair.

"I'll go easy on them if you ask nicely." He plops the sponge into the water and retreats to the other room.

A muffled banging echoes from the hallway. Conall rushes back into the room while I'm still attempting to get my feet under me. A fluffy towel wraps around me, nice and toasty, and I realize the banging sound from earlier must have been the dryer door. The small gesture warms more than my skin.

After spending ten minutes rummaging through my drawers while Conall is showering, I'm cursing my lack of guest-appropriate pajamas. When I'm alone, I sleep in my underwear. On the nights David and Charlie are around, I add a ratty tee that's often more holes than fabric. The coverage doesn't matter much, since they've seen it all over the years.

I never let Xavier stay overnight. It's the one line I was able to keep drawn.

I snatch up my longest tee, the one with the faded Wicked logo screen-printed on the front, and a tiny pair of bike shorts I usually reserve for working outside when summer is ungodly hot. It's not much, but they're comfy and they'll cover the important bits. Sweatpants are too stifling outside of winter, and I'm not sleeping in jeans. They'd be hell to get over my bandages.

"Fuck," I seethe under my breath. It's been five minutes. I've got one leg in the spandex shorts, but I failed to account for the extra girth from the cast wrapped around the other limb.

I twist and turn, nearly tripping over a random blanket stack topped with a pillow on the floor, but no matter how furiously I tug, my efforts are fruitless. These shorts are going to have to go. There's a part of me that's not unhappy about this turn of events, the same single-minded part that catches on fire whenever Conall touches me. Sudden images of his hands delving beneath the mangled hem of my shirt have my pulse pounding, and I focus on carefully checking my bandages in order to calm myself. The last thing I need right now is for Conall to come out and catch me daydreaming about him.

The moonlight lies in bright shafts across the floor of my room, spotlighting some pieces while leaving others in navy shadows. The play of light in dark reminds me of the musicals I love—here we see the chair in bright center stage, there the dresser waiting in the darkened wings. I step from beam to beam, from shadow to shadow, wondering what role I'm set to play. Will I be relegated to backstage, or will I rise and become the lead?

I guess it's all up to me, isn't it?

Conall steps into the room, wreathed in steam and lit from behind by the can lights in the bathroom. He's dressed in only a pair of black cotton pajama pants worn low on his narrow hips. When he looks at me through the gloom, I feel like I own the world.

I decide right here and now: I'm meant for more than a supporting role in my own life. I'm done fitting myself into someone else's mold. What happened with Xavier will never happen again.

This is my life, and I'm going to live it.

I toe the fabric pile responsible for almost taking me out during my shorts struggle. "Did you put this here?"

"Yeah." He scratches the nape of his neck, a blush turning his skin the color of a fiery desert. "I took them out of the hall closet when I got your towel. I'm gonna sleep there, if that's okay."

"Dude..." I shoot him a side eye while thumping my plastered foot on the hardwood a few times, hard enough to make an audible sound. "This isn't exactly a Tempurpedic. There's no way you'll get a good night's sleep on this floor, and you look more exhausted than I am."

"I'll be fine," he replies. "The guest room is too far away. I checked."

He checked? For what? Ghosts?

I take a deep breath. "I wasn't talking about the guest room."

He continues staring at the floor until I might combust from embarrassment. But he lifts his head, and the raw emotion in his stare stops my heart in its tracks.

"Are you sure?"

"Conall," I pause, but not long enough to give him time to respond, "get in the bed."

He walks to the side across from mine and slides in next to me, his bare shoulder brushing the edge of my short sleeve. We talk for hours that pass like minutes, blocking out reality and weaving stories about far-off lands and magical creatures, simply enjoying the sound of our combined voices in the quiet night.

Laying here in the darkness, it may quite possibly be the best night of my life.

I turn towards him, and he mirrors my movement. Suddenly, we're so close our noses practically touch, sharing breaths. His proximity assails my senses, rendering me speechless as I bask in a cloud of his scent—lavender and pine smoke and the last vestiges of his minty toothpaste. I'm completely entranced.

He leans in and presses his lips to mine once, twice, three times, as though I'm a butterfly that might fly away at the slightest movement. My pulse is hammering in my ears; I'm aching for him to give more than these gentle kisses, but his damn self-control is ironclad.

I'll have to do something about that.

On his third featherlight kiss, I capture his bottom lip between my teeth and tug.

His control snaps like a sun-dried rubber band.

Conall turns our kiss into a battleground, nipping and pulling on my lips while his tongue wages war with mine. It sweeps through my mouth, intertwining with my own and sending bolts of heat straight through me, right to my core. All caution for my injuries is thrown out the window behind our heads as I devolve into a mass of colliding sensations. I'd happily kiss him until the world collapses around us.

He rolls over me, bracketing my head on the pillow with his forearms. His mouth abandons mine, leaving me gasping at the ceiling while he presses a line of open-mouthed kisses along my throat. When the edge of my shirt stops his trail, he nibbles on my collarbone and my hips buck upwards into his.

I drive my fingers through his hair, scratching my nails against his scalp as I roll my hips against him, seeking the friction I'm desperately aching for. He's enjoying this as much as I am, judging by how he's straining against his thin pajamas. His hips pin me to the bed, and his low, rumbling moan makes my mind go blank. I couldn't tell you my name if you paid me a million dollars.

"Kitten, you're driving me insane," he breathes. His pupils are blown, an addict high on his supply, and I'm his drug of choice.

Locking eyes with him, I slide my hand slowly down his warm chest, savoring every taut line and trim plane blanketed with the barest hint of softness. When I reach my goal and palm him, running a finger up the length of his cock currently trying to punch through the fabric, he hisses. His reaction makes me feel sexy as hell despite my bandages and bruises, and I repeat my motions with a bit more pressure. I'm rewarded with his jade eyes rolling back slightly, a small moan slipping through his teeth. I'm on fire, alive with lust and love.

I could burn forever with him.

Desperate to have more of my body against his, I arch my back and press up towards him. He slips his hands under the hem of my shirt, then freezes. His face falls, hooded gaze widening, as he pulls my shirt back down to cover me.

What's going on?

A creeping cold washes over me, dousing the molten heat. *What's wrong with me? What did I do?* Much to my embarrassment, tears are prickling at the back of my eyes, looking for a way out. I look away so he doesn't see them, but he pulls my face back to his.

"Shit, wildcat," he murmurs against my lips. "I am *so* sorry."

"Why?" I try to sound nonchalant, but my voice comes out as the tiniest, crackling whisper.

He sits up, bringing me with him to rest against the pillows. "My love, you were *just* in the hospital. You're held together with staples and string, and here I am jumping you when you should be resting. I couldn't be more ashamed, but I can't help myself. You're irresistible."

I should be explaining to him that I'm fine, but all I can focus on is the shape of his mouth when he calls me "my love." How his lips roll in to start it off, open enough for the tip of his pink tongue to curve over the L, and it all ends with the barest flicker of his straight, white teeth against his bottom lip. Absolutely mesmerizing.

"Kitten, are you hearing me? Is something wrong? Where'd you go in that beautiful head of yours?"

I give myself a little shake, snapping back to reality to realize I'm staring off into space with a goofy half-smile on my face. "Everything is fine, Con. I wanted it as much as you did, and I wouldn't have stopped you. I honestly wish you wouldn't have stopped, but I get it."

He tweaks my nose. "When I finally have you, really and truly, it's going to take everything in me to be gentle, to make love to you the way you deserve. I don't know if I'll be able to hold back. I don't want to hurt you." His face sobers again as if what he just said wasn't the hottest damn thing anyone has ever said to me.

I don't understand why he's being so melancholy. I'm fine. I was more 'fine' two minutes ago, but that's because I thought we were getting somewhere.

I jostle his shoulder with my good one, trying to break the tension. "What did I do to the universe to be rewarded with meeting you, huh? How did I get so lucky?"

A shadow crosses over his face, and his smile falters so slightly that I'm not sure if I imagine the blip in his expression. He leans in and brushes another feather-light kiss against my lips, and any unpleasant observations slip right out of my head like sand between my fingers.

"I'm the lucky one, kitten. Trust me."

Looking into the depths of love in his eyes, I can almost believe him.

I can almost forget his look from a moment ago that felt a lot like...guilt?

Chapter 19

Change of Plans

- Conall -

Crack!

The splintered fragments of a number-two pencil fall from Domenic's fist to clatter against the dark, lacquered wood of his massive desk. In the heavy silence, they're loud as gunshots, grating on my fragile self-control. My nerves are already frayed from being this far from Valorie. I left her sound asleep, but I loathe her being alone at all, especially in her current state. It's a necessary evil, however—this conversation has to happen.

I look up at Dom from the pair of leather armchairs he has set up across from his desk for guests to sit in. Or, more often, for one of us to sit in for debriefing or lectures, depending on the situation.

Today it's obviously the latter.

He's on his feet, alternating between tangling his fingers in his perfectly manicured, dark beard and drumming them on the desktop, all the while glaring around the room at the fine art and diplomas hanging on the walls. Dom's office is more polished than any dean's, owing to the near-century-and-a-half he's had on Earth to accumulate the exact pieces he wants. It's a sophisticated mix of art gallery and business headquarters, with a dash of security executive and a tiny pinch of father figure in the framed pictures and knickknacks arrayed around the edges of his desk. His identity is splattered across the room, a three-dimensional Domenic diorama.

Domenic. At once our father, brother, and friend, he's ever the one to keep our ragtag band on the straight and narrow. The head of our multi-limbed being—Marguerite being the heart—he's always here when we need guidance on our jobs or help with our lives. Marguerite might be better with matters of the heart, but Dom loves us in his own way and he's always finding ways to show it. He hides his soft side behind a hard, polished carapace, but he loves jokes, games, and a good party more than any teenager. He took us under his wing when each of us was delivered here as a child, and he's molded us into the best group of dehmi any world has ever had if I do say so myself.

And right now? He's near boiling with fury. It kills me to disappoint him like this.

"Dom, I'm sorry. You have to know I didn't choose this. It was never my intention to shirk my duty."

His gaze snaps to my face, almost like he forgot I was still sitting here. Maybe he did.

"Conall, I'm not angry at you. I'm *worried*." He scratches a hand along his jaw, grumbling. "I don't know what the Paragons will do about this. I'll try to put in a good word, and they know your record is otherwise spotless, but this mission was a big deal for them. I'm concerned about repercussions."

"I will handle their punishment. It's my responsibility, not yours."

"Son, you all will *always* be my responsibility. No matter if you're twenty-four or two hundred." His irises darken, and his face falls. "Conall, you know, whether or not they somehow forgive this...you won't be able to go home to Avallea while you're with her. All your work will be put on hold for an entire human lifetime. Are you truly fine with this?"

"She *is* my home now, Dom. There's nowhere else I want to go."

He turns away from me, swiping at his lids, and my heart sinks like a stone.

Domenic was eligible for an early Homecoming after only a century, something which usually doesn't occur until at least a dehmi's two-hundredth birthday, but he gave it up. He always said he wanted to stay here and run a Haven of his own, and he would follow his charges to Avallea when they made it. We've all tried our best to make sure none of us delay our Homecoming—Dom and Margie deserve to finally get back to Avallea where they belong. And now here I am, choosing to destroy my own chance at an early Homecoming. Unlike him, however, my reasons are purely selfish.

"Dom, I promise I'll keep working. She's got—what—eighty years maybe? I'll be barely past my first century. Plenty of time left to make the cut." The concept of a life beyond Valorie has bile bubbling up into my throat, but I keep my face impassive. It's a simple fact; nothing can be done about our differing lifespans. I'll take whatever time the Web gifts me with her.

His face is soft and sad. "Sure, Con, I'm sure you'll be in the perfect frame of mind to head home after the love of your life is gone."

"Maybe I'll be willing to do anything to leave here once this world isn't full of her anymore."

A dry, brittle laugh rattles out of him. "Boy, you're in too deep, now. Your world will always be full of her, even from worlds away. Even when the emptiness is so suffocating that you would give anything to follow her into the Underworld and never come back."

Dom somehow always knows what we're thinking, and right now I'm dissected, pinned up, and laid bare but his stark words. Merely thinking about a future without Valorie makes my chest hollow.

"I don't know where this all came from. I swear, I was fine. I was gathering intelligence, formulating my methods, doing everything the way it needed to be done. Sure, I never *wanted* to kill her. I hated the idea of killing anyone innocent, but I was fine, I was handling it. It must have been that damned hospital trip. Something about seeing her broken like that changed things."

Dom suddenly throws his head back, guffawing.

What the hell?

"Oh, Conall, you can't be this blind," he wheezes, wiping at his cheeks. "You've been in love with her for weeks now, son, maybe since the very first vision. It's been obvious to everyone, the way you'd glower and bite anyone's head off when they'd mention your task. Remember a few weeks ago when Gaius said it was too bad you had to 'kill a pretty girl?' You practically ripped him to shreds."

I remember.

Three weeks ago, shortly after Valorie's birthday party, we had one of our weekly family meetings around the large mahogany table in the dining room. Since nobody else was occupied with a high-profile job, the bulk of the work-related conversation centered around my progress towards the...conclusion...of mine. I had blustered through the small book of information I'd been compiling on Valorie's lifestyle, relationships, and general schedule. My attempt to hustle the conversation on to other matters so they wouldn't notice my hands, white-knuckled and shaking around the spine of my notebook, was nearly successful.

But, Gaius had to open his big mouth.

Apparently, he had seen Valorie from across the grocery store and realized it was her when David asked her about some meaningless ingredient they needed for empanadas. Gaius has a mental filter about as useful as handlebars on a rocket ship, so when he muttered his quip, I saw red. I was halfway across the room towards him in a flash, and I barely hid my rage by disguising my movements as a trip to get a glass of water—a glass I almost shattered in my hand before I choked the liquid down and returned to my seat.

Or at least, I thought I had disguised my anger. Apparently, my family knew more about my feelings for Valorie than I did. How embarrassing.

"You know what I think?" Dom breaks through my reverie, his face stoic once again. "I think you've been so caught up in trying to be the perfect dehmi, you never took a second to acknowledge you were allowed to have emotions. You've always been about your work. All of your hobbies could be passed off as training. Swimming? Reading? Sparring? Until these past few months, I hadn't seen you sketch in a year. But you need to give yourself space to have a life, Conall. Going home early doesn't mean anything if you never truly live. I don't want an empty life for you, son."

I open my mouth for a rebuttal, but what can I say? He's right, of course. I never allow myself to enjoy much of anything unless it pertains to my work or my family. Reading and drawing are my only real pastimes, and my sketchbook has laid empty for years.

Until Valorie came along.

Now, it's filled with pictures of her. The design on her helmet took me only three days to complete, her light filling me with a desire to create far beyond any previous source of inspiration.

"She's everything to me, Dom. I don't know how it happened, but she's engraved into my skin, my bones, my blood. What the hell am I going to do? I can't kill her."

A quiet knock on the door has us both wheeling around, our mouths falling open at the small group in front of us. Gabrielle stands in the doorway, but the two statuesque Avalleans behind her are the real surprise.

This might be the first time a Paragon has ever left the Sacrarium during a planetary visit. It simply isn't done, but Esraa and Amon don't follow the rules. They make them.

Knuckles still resting on the open door, Gabby's fathomless eyes meet mine. Her quiet words have my heart torn between rocketing through my scalp and crashing through my toes.

"I have Seen."

The five of us have been discussing parameters for two hours now, and those first flutterings of hope I felt when I saw Gabby's face in the office have grown into full-fledged birds within my gut.

After taking half a second to process exactly what she had said, we went straight to the dining room, practically running over plush rugs and down marble staircases. We sat around the Haven's enormous, intricately carved table, bathed in the light of a quickly fading afternoon through the picture windows, while Gabrielle proceeded to flip my whole world on its head.

According to her, there was a way out of my mission. A way, more specifically, for the task to be fulfilled without Valorie's death as the catalyst.

My heart nearly exploded at her proclamation. I was sure she had misread the Web somehow and was leading me astray. Gabrielle is the best Seer we have had in decades, but she'll be the first to tell you the talent is imprecise at best. The Web doesn't line events up nicely like hors d'oeuvres on a platter, but rather throws them against the wall in a splattering of "hows" and "whys" and "maybes" that would drive a lesser being to insanity in a heartbeat. So, I was sure she was simply looking too hard for a solution and was imagining one where none existed, desperately attempting to save me.

But then Amon went and *agreed* with her.

He explained the crux of the matter was not Valorie's death, but merely "the end of her current life." At my confused glare, Esraa took over, and what she had to say left me shattered on the floor.

There is a way to keep Valorie alive, but there's no way to keep her alive and *human*.

And this is what I'm trying to comprehend right now.

"So, you're saying this has been done? We're certain the change can be completed?" I know my tone is harsher than intended, but I've trimmed my emotions as much as possible already. I can't hide my desperation, or my worry at Valorie being subjected to something experimental and untested.

"Once. Maybe more, but we are certain of one instance," Amon replies.

He and Esraa flow through the conversation as if they're two mouthpieces for the same brain, seamlessly picking up at the end of one another's sentences to create a multi-voiced, coherent whole.

"It won't be easy, dear," Esraa breathes.

Amon adds, "There's a reason this is not common knowledge."

"You will have to prove yourself in ways nobody has ever expected of you." Her words are bells on a spring breeze.

His are the call of a herald's trumpet. "There is only one way for it to work, and it relies on you."

"She will need to *choose*." Their combined voices echo in unison, ringing with finality.

"What do you mean, choose?" I've been waiting with bated breath, but all of their words jumble together in my melted brain.

Choose me? She already has, somehow.

Choose to become one of us? How can she choose something she isn't aware exists?

"She must choose to be with you, the *real* you, for the rest of eternity," Esraa explains, "to become one of us, to return to Avallea with you the way any other dehmi returns. She must forgo her humanity and her place on Earth, so that the ramifications of her absence may still come to pass." Her gaze softens, an affectionate expression on her statuesque face. "She must truly want to be with you because she cannot imagine her world without it being intertwined with yours. Not because of an axe over her head."

Amon leans in. "And she must do it of her own free will. You cannot make this known to her, only accept the gift of sharing her life if she offers it to you organically."

The hell? "How can she know what she's offering if she doesn't know what I am?"

"You are allowed to share the details of our world with her on your own time, but you cannot offer her a place with you. She must take the final step on her own, without coercion. Only then will the transformation be successful. The genes *know*, Conall. They will not choose her if this decision was not hers." His stare becomes hard, like frozen fire. "They do not create slaves—no one will be shackled to eternity. Do we make ourselves clear?"

All eyes are on me, four sets spanning a rainbow around the table, but the only color I want to see is stormy pewter.

"Clear as crystal, Amon."

"You have the remainder of the year you were originally assigned to solidify this change of plans. If you do not succeed, we will send another to accomplish what was tasked to you. There will not be a third option for Valorie Vargas," Esraa adds.

My wheels begin turning faster and faster, a race car on a straight track. The deadline gives me until the first day of June, but that's so far from now. So much could go wrong. "If she said yes tomorrow, could this all be finalized before the week is out?"

"No, Conall," Esraa says, "she has the full year. This is not a decision to be made lightly; she must be certain. She has until the end to make her choice...or to rescind it. Whatever her answer is come the first of June, it will be final."

Chapter 20
Naughty List

- Valorie -

"*It's beginning to look a lot like Christmas...everywhere you go...*"

The crackly sound of Christmas music flows out of Dad's old record player in the far corner of the living room. Our house looks like Santa Claus threw up on it, thanks to me and my obsession with decorating for the holidays. I may have gone a bit overboard this year, but I think I deserved it. I missed setting up the majority of the fall decorations thanks to my body being half human, half plaster sculpture at the time.

The initial few weeks back at home were rough. I had a hard time adjusting, and it was made worse by the lack of a true punishment for Xavier. He spent a weekend in jail and I have a shiny new restraining order, but that's all the cops said they could do without hard evidence of him being the one who pushed me. It's all he-said-she-said without any eyewitnesses, according to them. I have a sneaky inkling his dad being the former assistant governor influenced that particular decision. Nothing I can do about it, unfortunately.

Thanksgiving was spent with my cast and splints still on, and although I was able to move around slowly, stretching and bending were not allowed. Conall did his best to help me, fretting all the while like I was going to fall and shatter into a billion tiny pieces if the heater blew on me too hard, but he had no eye for decorating. The poor house was a sad, under-dressed version of its usual vibrant self, so I went all out with the winter decor the second my protective shell was removed.

White lights twinkle on a ten-foot artificial tree in the corner, scattering pinpoints of soft light off of the ornaments and the French doors to the backyard. We still have a little over a week until Christmas, but the tree skirt is already buried under gifts I've accumulated for family and friends. The mantle over the electric fireplace is filled with a carefully staged Department 56 Christmas town. I've been collecting since my grandma gave me my first piece at fifteen, so additional buildings and warmly-lit set pieces spill over onto the bookshelves on either side. Buffalo-checked blankets and cozy, themed throw pillows are overflowing off of the couches and chairs because winter is the perfect season for every surface to become a comfy place to curl up in a nest. Real pine garlands are twined around the banister, filling the house with their crisp scent. There's even an antique silver menorah on the windowsill in the dining room for Charlie.

Bing Crosby is right, it's beginning to look a hell of a lot like Christmas. All I'm missing is the best gift I've ever had, and he texted five minutes ago to let me know he'll be here shortly. Maybe Conall will let me stick a bow on his head and sit him under the tree.

I'd sure like to unwrap *him* on Christmas morning.

My fantasies of exactly what would occur when I unwrapped Conall are interrupted by the quiet creak of the storm door. I turn around, expecting to see him stepping through the front door into the foyer, but I run right into his chest instead. The shock sends me back half a step. He looks amazing, his usual black-jeans-and-a-tee ensemble accentuated by an impeccably tailored navy peacoat and matching winter hat. The pop of color makes his skin smolder and glow, a slice of summer in the middle of winter.

My stomach fizzles like the time I chugged a carton of Pop-Rocks. I think I could be with Conall for a thousand years and not ever get used to the thrill of seeing his face.

"Hey, you. Don't you look adorable?"

"Hello, my..." Conall trails off mid-sentence. "Wildcat," he continues in a low growl. His fiery gaze roves over me from toe to tip. "What are you wearing?"

My brow scrunches as I glance down at myself. I brush past him to the full-length mirror in the foyer to get a better look, but I'm still confused. We're spending the evening outside at a Christmas village Conall found online, so I'm dressed warmly. Fleece-lined black leggings poke out from beneath a snug, cream-colored sweater dress ending at mid-thigh. My knee-high boots and jacket are still by the door, with my favorite beanie like a bright green flag sticking out of a pocket. It's been my favorite for years because the silk lining keeps my curls from frizzing. The fact that it conveniently happens to be the same shade of green as Conall's eyes only adds to its charm.

I spin back towards him and rest a hand on my cocked hip. "I don't get it. What's wrong?"

He prowls towards me, and I resist the urge to pat my dress and check for dirt or specks of dust.

"You look like ice cream," he purrs. "Absolutely mouthwatering. Delectable. If I'm not careful, I'll spoil my appetite before we get to the village."

I hum and tap a finger against my chin, pretending to think as I lean into him. Truthfully, I'm trying to see how far I can push this. I'm aching to make him finally lose his perfect control. "Maybe I should change, then. Wouldn't want you being temp—"

My teasing is cut off by the sudden crush of his mouth on mine. His tongue flicks against my bottom lip, and I open for him. He explores my mouth while his hands trace over my sides and along the curve of my hips to my ass.

Maybe I am ice cream after all, because the heat of his touch has me melting.

Our breaths mingle together as he murmurs against my lips, "You're going to drive me insane, looking like this all night when I won't be able to touch you."

Clenching his fingertips into my hips for control, he grinds against my pelvis, the hard length of him rolling against me. He's impressive enough through his jeans that my brain short-circuits for a second. Liquid heat pools in my core, spurring me on. In the heat of the moment, my leggings somehow both barely there and much too thick for the ideas he's planting in my head.

Another roll of his hips positions him right over my core and my head lolls back to thunk softly against something hard and unyielding. He presses me against cold wood, the flares of heat from his body against my chilled skin causing my body to erupt in goosebumps. I could have sworn we were across the room, but somehow we've ended up against the front door. I don't know how we got here, but I care absolutely zero percent about that right now.

Conall slowly slides his body down mine until he sinks to his knees in front of me. With surprisingly gentle hands, he rolls my leggings past my thighs. My knees are wrapped up in their confines, but my soaked panties are on full display. I move to clench my legs, covering up on instinct, but he eases them back open. The look he gives me is molten chocolate, hot and sweet and utterly sinful.

"Are you incredibly attached to these?" he asks, sliding a finger along the damp center seam.

"No," I breathe. It could be the Hope Diamond; I'd still say no at this point.

A swift yank, a ripping sound, and my ruined underwear slips out from between my trembling legs. I open my hand for them, slack against my side, but he merely chuckles and slips the useless scrap of cotton into his jacket pocket.

A small part of me, the tiny, hated part of me that's been starved for affection to the point where she's barely alive anymore, cringes at being so exposed, so unhinged in front of him. She's embarrassed and afraid. What if I look weird, or smell awful, or make a stupid sound? My thighs start to inch closed again, and I fold in on myself, my confidence faltering under the bright lights of the foyer.

The fire in his stare tempers a bit, soft love filtering through the haze of lust. He patterns a lingering trail of soft kisses over my sensitive inner thighs, each one melting into my skin better than any lotion I've ever used. Bit by bit, my self-consciousness erodes under his ministrations, until all I have left is longing and yearning that almost brings me to my knees.

In a flash, his attention shifts back to where I want him most. One elegant finger trails slowly down, passing over my center with a glancing brush that already has me seeing stars. He reverses the motion, and this time the slick pad of his finger glides over me like water on glass. I groan, seeking the friction he's dangling in front of me. His devilish grin tells me he's enjoying my torture as much as I am.

When he finally replaces that tormenting, demonic fingertip with his tongue, I almost combust.

"Conall," I moan, half plea and half protest.

"Shhh," he rumbles.

The vibrations shoot through me in bolts of lightning.

"It's a long drive to the village. What if there's traffic? Or a line to get in? I could *starve,* kitten. Do you want me to starve?"

"*No.*" It's more whimper than word, but it's the best I can do.

His answering laugh rumbles out of him. He's a thunderstorm, a hurricane, and I'm standing straight in the path of destruction. Curling his long fingers around my hips for leverage, he drags his tongue up the center of me in one long, broad stroke until the tip grazes my clit. Around and around he circles, winding me tighter and tighter until I'm about to snap. As if he can sense I'm close, he switches to light flicks of his tongue, keeping me teetering on the edge of oblivion without allowing me to fall.

"Conall...*please,*" I moan.

I get no response, but a second later he slides one finger into me, pumping slowly without breaking his light, maddening pattern. He finally looks up at me, one eyebrow raised. His feigned innocence doesn't fool me; he knows exactly what he's doing.

"You're *soaked,* wildcat. Is this all for me?"

Another finger joins the first, and I moan, nodding frantically. Release is hovering a hair's breadth out of reach, so intense that it's blurring my vision. I drive my fingers through his hair and pull frantically, grinding my hips against his mouth in desperation. I need him, *now.*

A dark, low chuckle rumbles from where we're connected. "I was right," he murmurs, "absolutely delicious."

Then, he lets loose. His lips suction around me while he adds another finger and increases his pace to a level that would be punishing if it wasn't so heavenly. My back bows off of the door, and only his hand digging into the flesh of my hip keeps me still. Stars and comets and supernovas wheel behind my closed lids as I finally tumble over the edge into the first real orgasm another person has ever given me. I don't know whether to laugh or scream or cry, so my body settles on gasping for air. A drunken smile paints itself onto my face when my lids finally open and meet his, so full of love and adoration I feel ten feet tall and made of diamond.

He gives my ass a light smack, and I can't help but giggle. "Go replace those panties, kitten, but keep the rest on. We've got such a long drive, and I might get hungry again. I do love ice cream."

As I run up the stairs, pushing my newly healed leg to its limit, I seriously contemplate dragging him up with me and skipping the magic of our Christmas plans entirely. Just for a second.

Chapter 21
Winter Wonderland

- Valorie -

Unfortunately for me, Conall does not, in fact, feel the need to stop for a snack on the "long" twenty-minute drive to the Christmas village. It's probably for the best. I do want to get out of the house for a while. Nothing makes the disgustingly cold winter weather enjoyable quite like Christmas. Although, being in a dark car with Conall at the end of a dead-end road might be equally as enjoyable. I don't know for sure, but I'm willing to find out another time.

Who is this new me? I don't know, but I like her.

We squeeze in amongst the cavalcade of vehicles entering the botanical gardens through an archway of giant, lit candy canes. Carols and classic holiday favorites are pumping through hidden outdoor speakers loud enough to be heard over our rolled-up windows and full-blast heater. I'm singing along at full volume because I pride myself on knowing every song that's ever been played on a holiday radio rotation, thank you very much.

A long line of people bundled in their coziest winter wear weaves through the parking lot, heading into a life-sized gingerbread house. I vaguely recall it being the visitor center from the handful of times Charlie brought us to the butterfly gardens in the spring. It was a simple brick building that day, not this sugary holiday masterpiece.

Inside, the line moves surprisingly quickly through a firelit living room made of cookies, frosting, and candies, so detailed they're practically edible. The fluffy marshmallow armchair cushions, white chocolate windowsill, and striped licorice area rug have me practically drooling, and we're not through the line yet. Conall finally hands a crisp bill to the teenage elf manning the graham cracker front counter and we walk away with two red-and-green-striped, all-access lanyards.

The candy-dot trail takes us out through a rear door and into a forest populated by enormous lollipops. Artificial snow drifts slowly around us as we weave through sugary spires, swirls, and spheres in a million different hues, until...

We're finally here. I spin slowly, taking it all in.

If my house looks as if Santa threw up on it, this is what it would be like if he exploded.

The forest spits us out at the edge of the main thoroughfare, right in the heart of the village. Frosted brass street lamps decked in swags of garland and red bows line the avenues and the edges of an immense courtyard designed to replicate a German holiday market. The ethereal ringing of a bell choir echoes from an alcove somewhere out of sight. Groups of people in a riotous rainbow of warm, woolen layers are gathered around various stalls selling everything from hot chocolate and pastries to souvenirs. Buildings bordering the area have their doors open to the elements, their cheery insides displaying shelves and tables full of festive decor and warm clothing. And in the center of it all sits the largest, most ornate Christmas tree I've ever seen outside of Rockefeller Center.

The place is a Christmas card brought to life. It's insane. Conall is going to have to drag me out of here.

"I'll help you find a place to hide from security. We can live here until January if we're clever enough," he chuckles in my ear, and I realize I must have said that last bit out loud. Oops.

"Sounds like a plan. Hope you're sneaky because I never want to leave."

"Oh, I can be very sneaky," he whispers.

The scrape of his teeth on the shell of my ear sends a drop of sweat sliding along my spine, despite the cold temperature.

The enticing prospect of more time alone with Conall can't steal my attention away from the magic for long. An older couple walks by with bread bowls full of steaming stew. It looks and smells heavenly, and I mentally add a bowl to my list of things to try while we're here. I skipped dinner to ensure I'd have plenty of room for food, because eating your way through a festival is the only real way to experience one.

Conall squeezes my hand. "What do you want to start with, love?"

"Oh, man, you're making me choose?" The possibilities are overwhelming.

The sign for Christmas trees swings merrily in the distance. Ours is already up and decorated, of course, but I promised Mr. Sanderson I'd pick one out for his house. He's out of town until December twenty-first, so I'll be setting it up for him.

I point the sign out to Conall. "Let's go there first. They deliver the trees themselves, right? So no reason to wait until we're leaving. All the good trees might be gone by then."

"That would be a tragedy," he says, hand on his heart in a dramatic swoon.

I'm choosing to ignore his sarcasm. "I know, so let's go!"

Forty-five minutes later, we're on standby, watching as a burly lumberjack wraps two Douglas firs in netting and tags them with the address I provided. I found a mammoth evergreen perfect for the vaulted ceilings in Sanderson's dining room, and I also snagged a smaller one for our front porch. You can never have too many trees, and that's a year-round rule.

"Come on, Lorax, let's move." He takes my hand, tracing the pad of his thumb along my knuckles as he leads me into the building to pay for our trees.

It's a comforting gesture, an unconscious need to have some type of contact. A small hint letting me know that maybe, just maybe, he's equally as obsessed with the concept of us as I am.

"I don't know; I think hiring a guy to cut two trees and wrap them in plastic netting is extremely un-Lorax-like behavior," I say.

"At first glance, yes," he replies, "but I know you. If you could, you'd buy every tree they've got on site, have them all transplanted into pots, and turn your bedroom into their new home. Then you'd lose yourself amongst the firs and pines and I'd have to go on an epic journey to rescue you."

"An epic rescue mission, huh? In my bedroom?"

"A convenient setting, isn't it?" The dark gleam in his eye sets a fire in my heart. The heat slinks down and settles itself about eighteen inches lower.

The Norwegian-style "house" they've set up for the tree yard customers is warm and inviting. Golden light spills out from the thick, wavy glass windows, and several pre-wrapped trees are leaned up against the exterior walls for quick purchasing. A plastic reindeer near the entrance holds a wooden sign advertising complimentary cider and cookies inside.

Following Conall through the double doors, I'm assaulted by the smells of pine resin, woodsmoke, and cinnamon. Swags and wreaths line the wall opposite us, while stacks of hand-painted wooden signs for customers to advertise their house as a "*Santa Stop*", "*Christmas Tree Farm*", or "*Snowman Sauna*" are in haphazard rows beside the entrance. I contemplate getting the last one, if only for the *Frozen* reference, but I manage to pull myself away. I'd never get "*Let it Go*" out of my head if I had a sign reminding me every day. A bank of cash registers and several aisles of jams, preserves, and hot chocolate mixes fill in the rest of the chaotic, cheery space.

We peruse the aisles for a few minutes, looking for anything tasty, until our number is called by a grandmotherly figure behind one of the registers. I pay for Sanderson's tree with the cash he gave me, but Conall reaches over and swipes his card when I attempt to purchase my own tree. When he sees me glaring at him, he stands there with his hands in his pockets and whistles, like a cartoon character feigning nonchalance. It's so funny I forget about being angry; not that I was ever actually angry to begin with.

The cashier points out the table full of cider and cookies in the corner of the busy room, and I make a beeline straight for it. The warm, heady blend of apples and cinnamon mixes perfectly with a frosted sugar snowman, sending me to heaven in one mouthful. I prefer cold cider, but a frigid night like tonight is practically begging for this warm, steaming cup.

It's not until I've finished my snowman and moved on to a molasses reindeer that I realize Conall isn't next to me. I don't think he ever made it to the treat table at all. I ask the attendant for a chocolate chip cookie and another cup of cider, then walk off to find him.

There he stands, in the far corner of the room. His back is to me, but it's definitely him talking with two other people dressed much differently—but with the same impeccable attention to design—as him. A pale, chestnut-haired giant stands directly across from him in their alcove, his plaid woolen jacket stretching across his massive muscles as he laughs at something Conall says. Next to him, dwarfed by his size despite her willowy height and dressed in a white (hopefully faux) fur coat, is the otherworldly, magical girl from the hospital. I can't quite remember her name, but her face is nothing like any other person I've ever met. I could never forget it.

I take a step towards them and falter.

What if he doesn't want you there, my poison brain questions, creeping into my consciousness and draining my confidence. *He could have come and got you, but he's over there with his beautiful friends. You don't match them. Xavier never wanted you to speak to his friends either, and he was nowhere near as beautiful as Conall. You're a pastime, expendable and replaceable when you stop being fun.*

Shaking my head violently, I try my best to fight the insidious words, but it's no use. They've seeped in like mud, tainting me, turning me as grimy as they are. The lights lose their sparkle, and the cookies turn to cement in my churning gut, heavy as rocks and twice as hard to move. I flee to a bench outside, where the cold calls to my frozen insides. Conall's goodies take the seat next to me, keeping someone from sitting too close as I shove my head in my hands. Wouldn't want to poison anyone else's night.

"You're mighty hard to find, kitten," a voice drifts to me from outside the dark prison of my head.

It's a voice I'd know anywhere, one I want to hear forever.

"I've been looking for you for twenty minutes, but you disappeared. You almost gave me a heart attack."

"I didn't want to disturb you," I mumble into my palms.

Suddenly, the strings of Edison bulbs around the tree yard laser into my pupils. Conall takes my hands and breathes hot air onto them, warming my frozen fingers, and my frozen heart.

"Disturb me? That's crazy talk, kitten. How could you disturb any part of my life when you *are* my life?"

If anyone else said such a cheesy line, I'd be on the floor laughing. But somehow, it's not so cheesy when it's him.

I return Conall's comforting smile with a shaky one of my own and gesture to the seat next to me. "I brought you cookies and cider. Sorry for running off, the cider's probably cold by now."

He feathers a kiss across my forehead, and all is well in the world again.

Over his shoulder, I notice his two companions from earlier emerge from the building. They look around the yard and the huge one's wandering gaze catches sight of Conall and me on the bench. He drags the girl—I think her name started with a G?—over to us with a brotherly arm around her shoulder.

"I was wondering where you flew off to, Con. You were there one second and gone the next, like a ghost." His voice is surprisingly mellow for someone so large, a smooth chocolate as opposed to the rumbling gravel I expected. "Sometimes I forget you're the fastest out of all of us."

Conall shifts so his body no longer eclipses mine. "I had to go. You were going to blabber on all night, and poor Valorie would've been stuck out here in the cold waiting for me."

It doesn't escape my notice that he fails to mention anything about my anxiety or the reason I was waiting in the cold instead of in the warm building. He's giving me my privacy, and I love him all the more for it.

"Va—huh?" Mammoth man's aquamarine eyes slide past Conall to where I'm sitting, then widen.

It's hard to believe he only now noticed me, but his genuine surprise would be impossible to fake unless he has a secret Broadway career. And I would know if he did; I could probably name every major star on stage in the past two decades.

"Valorie! Like *the* Valorie? Finally!" He's yelling, but he doesn't seem to notice as he bounds over to me and scoops me off of the bench into a bear hug that threatens to crush me.

"Finn, you're going to squish her, and then Conall will be very unhappy when he has to kill you."

"Oh!"

My feet return to Earth, and I heave a breath.

"Sorry, I got excited." My friendly assailant scratches his head and blushes.

"It's okay. Can't complain about a little enthusiasm, right?" *Tell that to my ribs.*

He holds out his calloused, dinner-plate hand, dwarfing my own in a firm shake. "I'm Finnegan, but you can call me Finn. And you're Valorie!"

I find myself smiling and laughing with this strange, teddy bear-man. "Yeah, that's me. It's nice to meet you!" And I mean it. We've only just met, but it's as if I've known him forever. I like him; there's something comforting about his puppyish enthusiasm.

"It's nice to see you again," says the girl.

I'm wracking my brain, but her name is lost in the drugged fog of my hospital days.

She must somehow sense my confusion, because her next words are: "I'm Gabrielle. We met at the hospital, but I don't know how much you remember. You were pretty beaten up, but you're looking much better now." She offers a delicate wince.

I smile gratefully at her. "Thank you. I remember you, but I couldn't quite come up with your name. A lot of details are fuzzy from those days, but now I'm doing well. A little stiff and sore sometimes, but much better than the last time you saw me."

She nods and grins at me. I remember how much I liked her at the hospital, and I'm glad to see it wasn't the medication talking.

"So," Conall says, "what brings you two all the way out here tonight? I would've expected you to be snug at home."

The question seems directed more towards Gabrielle than Finnegan, but he's the one who answers.

"Margie needed some more greenery, and she says this is the place with the best stock. Apparently having half a pine forest on the first floor alone wasn't quite crazy enough."

I don't know who Margie is, but she sounds like a woman after my own heart.

"Of course," Conall chuckles.

"Yeah, she's going crazy getting ready for this weekend." Finn turns and looks in my direction. "You're coming, right? We need some more fun there, and I can tell you're fun. I know these things." He taps his temple and winks at me, his expression glittering with mischief.

I have absolutely no clue what he's talking about. Did I forget something? I turn to Conall, looking for clarification, but he looks as confused as I am.

Finn gasps, aghast. "Con, dude, don't tell me you didn't think to invite Valorie to the festivities! Come *on* man!"

"I wasn't going to go," he answers quietly. "Valorie still has some trouble getting around, plus she's more fun than you guys. I was planning on spending the weekend with her."

"No! No, no, no, you can't deprive me of fun time with my new best friend like that." Finn looks at me with those pleading, puppy-dog eyes. "Will you come without him? I'll pick you up myself. I've been dying to finally meet the girl who made Conall love someone more than his own company."

I snort out a surprised laugh.

"I'm kidding, he loves us all ever so much, we spend every day together braiding each other's hair, blah blah blah. But seriously, I'll pick you up if you need a ride. Whatever it takes for you to come be a part of the family!"

I look back at Conall, only to find him glaring at Finn. Does he not want me to spend time with his family? Or is he jealous Finn and I are hitting it off?

"If you want to go, wildcat, I'd love to take you. I figured you wouldn't want to spend the whole weekend with a bunch of miscreants," he pauses to aim a glare at Finn, who pretends not to notice. "But I would love nothing more than to introduce you to my family."

A blush heats the bridge of my nose. "If everyone is half as fun as these two, I'd love to go."

Finnegan's whoops can probably be heard all the way back at the entrance to the village. I cover my ears and giggle along with him, their simple act of inclusion making me lighter than air.

"Conall," Gabrielle says in a voice that's quiet the way my mother's is quiet. Not in a timid way, but in a demanding way that commands the whole world to listen without needing to be raised much above a whisper.

His head swings towards her, and an entire silent conversation passes between them, ending with a heavy sigh pulled from deep within Conall's chest.

"I'll come with you," she says, "you'll need my help. Finn can take the things back to Marguerite on his own, and the two of you can drop me off later."

"Fine. But I hope you know what you're doing, Gabby."

"You know I do."

Conall extends his hand to me as Finn saunters away, humming to himself and promising to see me soon.

As I take hold of his strangely clammy palm, I have the uncomfortable feeling things are about to change in a way that can never be taken back.

Chapter 22
Avalleans

- Conall -

We make our way back to the village proper and choose one of the foot-paths branching out from the central courtyard like spokes on a wheel. My skittish wildcat keeps sending small, furtive looks my way, attempting to gage why I'm suddenly so closed off. I'm trying not to make her worried, but I think I'm failing. Every muscle in my body is taut as a strung violin, dreading the conversation I'm about to have.

What if she runs away screaming? What if she thinks I'm crazy, or a monster? Or worst of all...what if she finds out the reason we met? The horrid, unforgivable reason lurking behind the greatest thing to ever happen to me? I can't let that happen, not ever. It would tear her apart, and I'd give my entire being to keep her safe and whole. But in order to hopefully spend forever with her, I have to get us over this hurdle first.

Here's hoping Gabby has a plan because I'm completely lost.

The incandescent haze of the iron lamps lining the path gradually fades away, leaving us in near-total darkness. A blue-white glow in the distance lets me know our destination approaches, though it's probably too dim for Valorie's pupils to register quite yet. She'll figure out where we're going soon enough, if she hasn't already. This is the part of the attraction she gushed over the most; I'm praying the environment will make her more receptive to what we're about to tell her.

Meanwhile, Gabrielle is sauntering next to me without a care in the world. She's almost never this relaxed. Her gift is unpredictable and draining by nature, usually leaving her reserved around others. Her carefree attitude should bring me some reassurance, but I cannot seem to stop my hands from shaking. My heartbeat would be more appropriate for the finish line of a marathon or a hostage situation, not a moonlit stroll.

Kitten's quiet gasp lets me know we're finally close enough to the attraction for her to pick up the colorful pinpoints of light in the distance. She hurtles forward, but stops and turns to me with her hand outstretched. The overwhelming love and trust in her warm gaze stakes me straight through the heart. I've never felt anything like this. It's as if the things that make us who we are, those ephemeral pieces, have merged their organs and nerves and systems into one beast with two bodies, inextricably linked forevermore. It is the sweetest and most terrifying experience, and I'm wholly addicted to it.

The Festival of Lights sign overhead is made of the same tiny string lights as everything else in this part of the village. Valorie has been talking about this display all week, ever since I brought up the idea of spending our Thursday night here. If there's anywhere that will give me an edge in the coming conversation, it's this kaleidoscopic trail of lights.

I hope it's enough.

"Get started or you'll lose your nerve," Gabrielle whispers too low for anyone else to overhear.

Thankfully, the winding trail is mostly deserted. The fewer witnesses, the better.

"Make sure to tell her *everything,*" she adds as we walk.

Everything? Absolutely not. I don't care what power Gabby has, I'm not risking it. Simply thinking about it has my pulse racing.

Deep breath. I've faced cold-blooded killers, seen corpses and dying victims, but I've never felt this nervous. How does one girl have the potential to ruin me so completely?

"Valorie, can you come over here, please?"

Can she hear the panic in my voice?

Valorie pauses her inspection of a six-foot-tall bespectacled caterpillar made of blue and gold lights and flits over to me, a large grin stretched across her face. A grin which fades when she registers my strained expression and the fact I called her by her name instead of one of the pet names that never fail to make her blush. I adore that rosy glow; I'm not sure she knows about it, but I soak it in every time. The idea of never seeing it again after tonight has my breathing ticking towards a pant again.

"What's wrong?" Hands twisting nervously, she shifts from foot to foot, like prey readying to run.

In...hold...out. "We need to have a little talk."

Her expression shifts from cautious curiosity to dread in a heartbeat. "That's never a good thing to hear, Conall. Like, ever." Her voice is steady, but the rapid rise and fall of her chest gives away her anxiety.

I hate being the cause of her distress, but I'm too lost in my own fear to figure out a way to alleviate hers.

"Conall, you're scaring her," Gabby murmurs. "It's going to be fine, but it won't be if you keep screwing around and she passes out."

"No, wildcat, not like that. Never. But, there are a few things you need to know, all right?"

She takes a steadying breath and squares her shoulders, a small smile returning to the corner of her mouth. I know her brain is playing every trick in the book to freak her out right now, but she's not letting it win. There's my girl.

"Get to the point then, Conall," Valorie says. "You're interrupting my light display."

Gabrielle snorts beside me, and I shove her without taking my eyes off of Valorie. She doesn't even have the decency to trip.

"Okay." I sigh, busying myself with pretending to admire a fairy-light wolf and her cubs. "Okay. So...the thing is...Gabby, and Finn, and I, and the others you haven't met yet...we aren't exactly..."

"Human."

Thanks, Gabrielle. Way to be gentle about it.

"If you're about to tell me you're a vampire or a werewolf, I'm going to smack you. This isn't 2008."

Is she seriously standing here joking with me? Does she not think we're insane?

"Nobody is a Cullen or a member of any other associated supernatural pop culture team," Gabby laughs.

"But we *are* supernaturals, technically," I continue. Time to rip the bandage off. "Gabby, Finn, Gaius...all of us are part of a group called the dehmi. We come from a place called Avallea. It's another world, one with the sworn duty of watching over the mortal worlds and helping them to advance. That's why we're here."

She drifts away from me, back to that damned caterpillar, and my stomach falls through my soles. This is it. This is where I lose her.

After the longest minute, she returns to where I'm frozen in place. Her face is unreadable, but her voice is strangely calm.

"A dehmi, huh?" She draws the syllables out—*dehm-eye*—as if testing the feel of them on her tongue. "So, you're telling me...you're some kind of space alien cop? Like, for real?"

Gabrielle bursts into tinkling laughter.

I can't help but crack a smile. Leave it to my wildcat to bring levity to this situation.

"Not exactly." I spread my hands in front of me, palms down. "Fighting crime is not usually a part of our duties. We tend to leave criminal justice to the mortal authorities unless something is going incredibly wrong. Same with governing. Our job isn't to become overlords, it's simply to further advancement and help each world become the best it can be. Science, the arts, technology, health-care, those sorts of foci are more typical for us. There is a Paragon concerned with safety and justice, but they work less with the mortal worlds and more with Avalleans on our home world."

"Doesn't seem like this world is the best it can be," she murmurs under her breath.

Honestly, I have to agree.

"This world is still fairly young, and some areas are more...receptive than others. But we still do our duties for all of the worlds under our care, regardless of if the efforts are fruitful."

"I have questions," she says after a pause that has my hands sweating despite the cold.

"I will answer all of them, promise."

She leans against a tree covered in six-inch rainbow butterflies. Their colors turn her alabaster skin into a whirlwind of lights, and I'm momentarily lost in her beauty. "Why?"

That wasn't what I was expecting. "Huh?"

"Why? Why are you guys responsible for other worlds, ones that aren't your own? Don't get me wrong, it seems pretty helpful, but what do you get from it?"

I blink, completely blindsided yet again by her question. Thankfully, Gabrielle sweeps in to rescue me.

Her whisper-thin voice spins a tale even most Avalleans do not know. "Once, a long while ago, our world, too, was young. We had no name, no culture, no identity. Only a rampant need for something to change. We were struggling, failing, and falling in record numbers. Then the first Avallean was born in the mud and filth of our dying, nameless world.

"She was born with eyes capable of seeing the Web, the branching twists of the past and present and future that weave together to rule us all. She was born with a task. She was born to create us, to save our future by remaking us all.

"The first Avallean was shown a way to use the unique atmosphere of our planet to create portals, gateways between our decrepit world and others which were flourishing. The Web directed her, taught her what to say and do. She received plants, devices, *advancements* from their natives. Advancements she brought back and used to remake our world. Gone was the place of blood and dirt and filth where she was born. It became a wonder, a heaven. It became Avallea.

"The First told her people the Web had shown her the price of our salvation. As we were helped, so were we to help others. We were to become stewards, keepers, unseen helpers from the sidelines, never to seek fame, or praise, or to be known to other worlds. And it is a small price to pay for what we were given." Gabrielle's gaze becomes soft and far-seeing, that of someone recalling their favorite dream. One which makes them desperately want to rush home and crawl into bed in hopes of seeing it again.

"Avallea is paradise," she continues. "Here, we have long lives, but we are less than our full selves. On our home world, nobody dies from old age. Illnesses are very few and far between—most are eradicated, or so easily treated they become a minor inconvenience at best. You can choose to return your spirit to the planet if you feel as though you are done with your life, but unexpected death in Avallea is almost unheard of. When it does happen, the whole world mourns.

"Magic abounds, filling us much more than the paltry bit we carry with us to the mortal worlds. There, *everything* is magic. The wind, the trees, the soil, even time itself is changed. Animals are different there, smarter, more sentient than here. Imagine a world where the smallest animals have the intelligence of a monkey or ape from your world. It is a very different place."

A vibrant phoenix glimmers in the distance, drawing Valorie towards it. She speaks with her back turned, steely irises molten with the bird's reflected fire, "So, who's in charge of all of this?"

Gabrielle swoops in with yet another answer. Perhaps her gift has shown her I'm of absolutely no use here. I'm barely standing at this point, so afraid the next answer Valorie seeks will be the one which causes her to run from me forever.

"The Paragons, a group of nine-and-two Avalleans, govern both our world and our dealings with the mortal worlds. They each have a facet of life they focus on, and they come together to solve joint issues as one body. The two additional Paragons beyond the initial nine govern the Underworld, where the spirits of any sentient dead are housed. They are placed above the other nine, the ultimate seats of power in all worlds, living and dead."

"So, why are you guys here? Like, what decides which of you has to leave your magical super-world and come to a mortal world to help out?"

"Every Avallean is raised by their parents until they turn thirteen. On their thirteenth birthday, a party is held in their honor. Afterwards, the Paragons of the Underworld mask their memories of Avallea and everything involved with their former life, then they're shipped off to a Haven for their service as a dehmi. They have no further contact with Avallea until their Homecoming, unless they are being visited by a Paragon."

"Everything...including their parents?" Her face is horrified, tears pooling like sparkling gems in the corners of her lids.

Gabrielle merely nods. "The memories are still there, waiting to be returned to them when they are finished on their assigned world, but until then they are, for all intents and purposes, erased. We make new families, new bonds, during our time away, and *those* memories stay with us when we return to Avallea."

"How long?"

I take this one. "Two hundred years of service is standard prior to returning to Avallea. Some, like our leader, Domenic, are offered an end to their service much earlier. But two hundred is the standard."

"Two...hundred...years," Valorie whispers.

This is it. The one where she flees, taking my heart with her.

She whips around. "Wait, you said magic. Can you do magic now?"

What?

Gabrielle saves me one more time, my brain still struggling to comprehend the emotional whiplash of this conversation.

"To a degree. Every Avallean has an affinity with a certain type of magic, and that magic is lessened, but not depleted, when we leave for our time as a dehmi. So yes, we can do some small magic while we are here, but more when we return home."

"What can you all do?"

"Mine is the gift of the first Avallean, the gift of the Sight. Finnegan has an affinity for green magic, while my twin Gaius is aligned with flame." She turns towards me and simply states, "Conall heals."

"Prove it," Valorie says, staring into my soul, a glint of challenge in her eyes.

Faster than a human could ever react, Gabrielle pulls a small blade from her pocket and slices deep into her palm. Ruby-red blood wells and dribbles over the edge of her hand as she nonchalantly holds the wound in my direction.

Ignoring Valorie's distressed whimper, I grasp Gabby's injured hand between my own and open myself to the well of power that slumbers within my core, coaxing it into action. A brief flash of light is the only outward sign of my ability, but Gabrielle's now-unmarred flesh speaks for itself.

Valorie gasps, an awed expression on her face as she whispers, "You healed me that day, when Xavier...you know. There was a cool, watery feeling, and things weren't so awful. I didn't notice how much I had improved until that evening. I remember..."

"Yes," I answer, "I couldn't stand to see you in pain, even then. I wish I would've gotten to you before the paramedics on the day you went to the hospital, because I would've healed you that time, too. But I was too late." And I will hate myself for it always, but I keep this locked inside.

I cannot bear to watch as she walks away, mumbling something too low for my ears. If Valorie leaves me because I was too slow to save her, that will be understandable. Heartbreaking, but understandable. Who would want a partner they can't count on? One who technically isn't the same species as them? Yes, our bodies are compatible, but it may not be enough for her. And if it isn't, I have to let her go, never being able to tell her what that will mean for her future. For both of our futures.

I wait for what seems like a lifetime, but is probably about fifteen minutes.

Valorie crosses to me and tips my chin towards her. I'm forced to look into her liquid metal eyes for the last time and brace myself for her departure.

I prepare for her to say something cruel or kind or sorrowful, but instead she brushes her lips across mine, soft and sweet. A tear threatens to slip free, but I won't guilt her with my own emotions. I will respect Valorie's choice.

"So, my boyfriend is a super-powered, behind-the-scenes interplanetary helper from a race of magical aliens. Oh, and he's basically immortal. Anything I missed?"

I shake my head, once again dumbfounded. I should be used to this by now. *What is going on?*

"Didn't think so. Super cool, by the way. Don't know if I mentioned that. I'm totally jealous," she says so matter-of-factly, with the same inflection she would use when telling someone she's jealous of their new shoes or a car. While I recover from this casual bombshell she's dropped, Valorie addresses her next question to Gabrielle, who is standing to the side smirking like the cat that caught the canary, "What do I pack for this weekend?"

"Wait!" I'm shouting, but my brain is still moving too slowly to lower my volume. "How does this not freak you out? Why are you not running away, or screaming at me for keeping this from you, or calling us insane?"

Gabby is shaking her head beside me, but my wildcat chuckles and smiles at me as though I've said something hilarious and slightly stupid. "Because, you ridiculous man, I love you. And I already have my proof, so there's no need to request it. You're not very sneaky, you know. I've seen you move way too fast to be normal, you've healed me at least once, and Gabrielle is entirely too beautiful in a very non-human way. It makes sense, weirdly. And I always figured aliens were a logical conclusion. How could it be that out of the millions, billions of planets, we have the only sentient life? Face it, Conall, your revelation isn't very surprising." She punctuates her little speech with a wink before turning back to Gabrielle to pretend she didn't blow my reservations to smithereens with a few sentences.

The girls become lost in the rest of the whirling, flickering light show, happily discussing what is to come this weekend. I should be admiring the artistry with them, but I'm busy getting lost in the idea this might work out in the end.

As long as she never finds out why I came to Sycamore University in the first place.

Chapter 23
The Haven

- Valorie -

Bags packed, check. Toothbrush, check. Cute pajamas, check. My favorite silk headscarf?

Absolutely nowhere to be found.

I've been looking for the damned thing for half an hour now, and I cannot find it anywhere. Now that I think of it, I haven't seen it since before Halloween. If it doesn't show up soon, I'll be forced to wrap my hair in one of my plain, boring scarves for the two nights I'm staying with Conall and his family. I'm sure he wouldn't care if I went to bed wearing a paper bag on my head, but that doesn't stop me from wanting to look cute. I don't plan on seeing anyone other than him while I'm in my pajamas, but it's good to be prepared. Just in case.

Every drawer has been ripped open and rifled through, and my hamper has been completely emptied. The comforter is a lumpy mess on the floor, the sheets are balled up in the center of the bed, and I'm elbow-deep in pillowcases, searching frantically.

A cough from behind me sends me through the roof. I whip around and screech, "Conall, holy shit!"

He chuckles, leaning against the door frame with a grin a mile wide. "Hello dear, lovely to see you too. I must say, that's not the greeting I expected."

"Maybe if you'd make some noise on your way up and didn't scare me half to death, you'd get a better greeting," I try to sound indignant, but it would probably work better if my breathing would return to a normal pace. "I'm gonna make you wear a damn bell."

He hums deep in his throat, leaving the doorway to saunter over to where I'm perched, still halfway buried in the pillows on my destroyed bed. His body looms over me, closing me off from the rest of the room and creating a shell made of warm skin, cool cotton, and denim. My back presses into the mattress as he runs his nose up the column of my throat, inhaling deeply and releasing his breath with a sigh that washes over me. A much shakier sigh drifts from my parted lips.

Another brush up my throat, this time with his mouth. "Wildcat, why are you sitting here like this, all mussed up and rumpled and utterly devastating?"

Lost in the sensation of his body over mine, it takes me a moment to find my voice. When I do, it's tremulous and barely audible. "I was looking for my scarf. The one with the big hibiscus flowers on it that I wear to bed."

His sultry smile turns bashful. A slight blush suddenly colors his cheeks the shade of a desert's summer sunset, warm and captivating. Sitting up, I guide him to his knees in front of me. I put a few inches of safe distance between us so I don't lose my focus and jump him on my bare bed. We have places to be, as soon as I can find my stupid scarf.

"The scarf is at my house," he says, a hand scratching at the back of his neck.

What the hell? "And why, pray tell, is my scarf at your house, a place I have never been to?"

The blush is twice as vibrant as it was seconds ago, and he's scrubbing at his neck like he has a bad case of poison ivy. Bashful Conall may be one of my top five favorite Conalls, I swear.

"Because it smelled like you, and it was soft, and I love you, which apparently turns me into a crazy man who steals things from you to sleep with?" He quirks a corner of his mouth at me. "I took it when you were in the hospital. David brought it in your bag from home, and it was so cute and reminded me of you. Sorry, but not *super* sorry." His tiny smirk turns into a megawatt grin and lights up the whole room brighter than a thousand bulbs.

Gone are the days of counting the measly seconds, hoping for a smile to last more than three. Now, the smiles stick around.

"Where's my phone? I'm calling the cops on you, little thief. You're a menace. Honestly, all women should be warned."

"There's only one woman on my mind, no others need to concern themselves."

I clamber off of the bed. If I don't, one of us is going to make a decision which will lead to us being very late to tonight's party. What exactly is supposed to *happen* at this party is a mystery to me, but Finn and Gabby have both been incredibly kind. I'm hoping I'll get along with the rest of the group too. Conall hasn't told me much about them—every time I've asked he's only said they're "easier to explain in person." I'm going in blind, but hopeful.

My bag is already scooped up and slung over Conall's shoulder—he doesn't give me time to cross the room and try to grab it myself. I scoop up my phone and keys from the bedside table, locking up as we exit the house. He slips my helmet over my head, gives it a tap, and off we speed.

"Holy hell, Conall, do you live in a tent in the woods or something?"

We've been driving through the winding, snow-covered streets of The Palisades for twenty minutes now, going deeper and deeper into the labyrinth of homes. They've become steadily larger, the yards stretching farther and farther between them until there's only a handful on each tree-lined boulevard. And still, he drives on, humming along to the soft rock song piping through the hidden speakers in our helmets.

"Almost there, wildcat," he says. "So eager to get away from me, huh?"

I chuckle, but the truth is I loathe meeting new people. I love parties and get-togethers, but only once the awkward introductions are through. I want us to hurry up and get there so we can get the awkwardness done and over with. The suspense is sending my anxiety sky-high; I'm shivering despite the fact that Conall's body heat is keeping me warm and toasty.

He suddenly turns off of the street and onto a small gravel driveway canopied with more skeletal, leafless limbs. I expect the house to be right around the corner, but we drive and drive for what must be another mile. Finally, I glimpse a break in the thick branches surrounding us.

"Oh. My. God."

Without warning, an explosion of green warmth assaults my senses. A large, manicured front lawn belonging on the front page of a gardening magazine stretches ahead, looping around and out of sight on either side. The massive space is bisected by a circular drive paved with terracotta tiles glowing in sunbeams that are no longer watery and weak. Plants and flowers of every shape and size are flourishing—no empty swaths of winter-brown grass here. Only the obvious, careful intent behind their placing keeps the grounds from looking like the depths of the Amazon. Notes of blooming jasmine, hydrangeas, and lavender float on the breeze. I'm pretty sure none of them should be in season this late in the year. I'm positive not a single species in this yard was present two miles behind us.

While I'm busy gawking, Conall pulls his bike up to the staircase, his front tire nearly touching the bottom stair. The "house" in front of us is a strange mix of modern and ancient that's nothing short of palatial. Several gargantuan, rectangular sections form a three-sided wall around the front staircase, each topped with a combination of peaked roofs and small turrets. Towering walls clad in various shades of cream and tan bricks reach towards the sky, ending in a dark, nearly-black roof. Large decorative windows cut swaths through the walls on all sides; I can only imagine the amount of natural light inside. A carriage-style garage is attached to the house on our left by a small offshoot jutting out from the main building. In the far distance, I can barely see the broad side of a large greenhouse shimmering like cut diamonds.

It's breathtaking. How can people actually live here?

Conall leaps up the stairs and holds out a hand to me.

"Welcome to the Haven, wildcat. Officially, it's known as Haven E-Twenty-Four, but to us, it's simply home."

A little breathless, I join him on the stairs, wondering what I'm about to find on the other end of the antique double doors in front of me.

Hand raised towards the handle, Conall moves to open the left door, but it flies open on its own.

Magic? I think, astonished.

My vision adjusts and Finnegan's mischievous blues glint at me above a large, predatory smile. No magic, then, only a cross between a grizzly and a goof-ball.

"Finn, no," Conall says.

I open my mouth to ask what's going on, but everything becomes a blur of light and earth tones.

Finn throws me over a broad shoulder, knocking the wind out of me, and my legs thump against his muscular chest while he sprints away at full speed. "Sorry, I have orders!"

Judging by his boyish laugh, he isn't sorry at all. Conall shouts as we blaze a track through a foyer, down intersecting halls, and through large rooms that flash by one after the other. At our current speed, it's hard to catch any more than streaky glimpses of open, airy common spaces reminiscent of a cross between a posh museum and a castle. Everything is filled with the natural light I expected upon seeing the exterior, and the multi-story vaulted ceilings make the space seem endless. Finn's bare feet make no noise on the floor, whereas mine would be thundering on the marble beneath us at his pace. Not that I could ever *match* his pace. Charlie couldn't run this fast.

I'm hefted off of Finn's shoulder and deposited, surprisingly gently, into a stool at a bright white counter made of the same marble as the floors. A kitchen fit for royalty stretches around me, complete with blush-enameled appliances large enough to feed a whole army of people. Having been with Conall for a number of meals, I understand the need for super-sized appliances. Tchotchkes and ceramic dishes in every color and pattern imaginable line the walls on warm wooden shelves, keeping the room from becoming too sterile or industrial.

In the midst of it all, a buxom, plump woman bustles around, her back to us as she tends to something on the bottom rack of an oven. She hums a pleasant tune as she works, completely unaware of our presence. Her hair, piled on top of her head in an intricate knot, is a pleasant shade of shining silver despite her not looking much over forty. It's not the gray of old age, but rather a silvery shade that strangely fits her like she's had it her whole life. Maybe she has.

"Margie, I brought her! We have about, oh, ten seconds 'til Conall gets here. I locked a few doors on the way and chucked the keys in random corners, so he'll have to find a workaround," Finn says, nestling himself into a stool beside mine.

When the hell did he manage to lock doors? We practically flew here!

The woman, who I'm assuming is Margie, whips around to face us. Her discerning stare darts from Finn's smiling face to my own, bewildered one, and back again. Quick as lightning, she rolls the tea towel on her shoulder and whips it across Finn's chest.

"You crazy boy, she looks scared half to death! Did you not think to explain to her what was going on as you lumbered down the hall?" She directs her next words to me, her dimpled smile lighting her face up brighter than the milk glass lamps overhead. "Dearie, I'm Marguerite, but please call me Margie. I'm sure this is all very overwhelming, but I only wanted to steal a minute with you before Conall sweeps you away all day. Granted, I didn't think Finnegan would be so literal with the 'steal' part."

"Oh, it's no problem. In fact, it was pretty fun. And Conall is going to flip, which I'm guessing was Finn's goal all along," I say.

Finn shoots me a wink, which answers my question. He doesn't look the least bit bashful about hauling me through his home without even a hello.

A chorus of bangs and thumps sounds in the distance, getting steadily closer. By the cackling coming from the stool next to me and the gentle chuckles from across the kitchen island, I'm guessing Conall is approaching.

The door slams open and in he storms, a thundercloud of emotion spinning in his gaze. His chest heaves under the thin cotton of his tee as he surveys the room, searching for me.

Damn.

I can't help but stare at him; the protectiveness he exudes is so different from anything I've seen. He acts like I'm cherished, important. It's hot as hell.

Our eyes connect and he visibly relaxes, which makes Finn lose his mind. He doubles over, tears of mirth streaming as he howls. Conall pays him no mind, crossing the room to throw his arms around me, his chest to my back. He snuggles into the crook of my neck, inhales, and presses a soft kiss to the junction. Blood bubbles in my veins, hot trails of it shooting straight to my heart with his simple act of love here in front of his family.

We spend hours sitting there, the four of us, sharing stories and laughter. Margie and Finn ask question after question about me—my parents and friends, my studies at Sycamore, and anything else they can think of. They're incredibly easy to talk to. The combination of their friendly openness and Conall's comforting warmth behind me has me spilling more information than I've ever provided to anyone besides David and Charlie.

The kitchen slowly fills up with mouthwatering scents wafting from the various pots and pans bubbling on the stove behind Margie. She's a force here in her element, bustling from one burner to another, to the oven, and back to the island's large chopping board, over and over without breaking a sweat. I offer to help, but she tuts at me and tells me not to worry about her. Instead, they all spend their time teaching me all about their lives as dehmi, what it's like to have magic, and the strange sense of being from a place you know all about but can't remember. I hang on their every word like I'm going to be tested on it later.

They explain the task system, the method of receiving jobs from Paragons who visit them in some type of special meeting room below the Haven. Margie says her task days are over, now that she and Domenic are overseeing this Haven together.

Finn cuts in with a mischief-promising smirk. "Yeah, now you have the best job...you get to hang out with me. One hell of a promotion, Marg, I must say."

I snort a startled laugh as Margie whips a cookie directly at his head. Unfortunately, he catches it in his mouth and we're subjected to a victory dance involving plenty of open-mouthed, exaggerated chewing as Finn gyrates on his stool.

"I, on the other hand, am still toiling away in the dirt. Literally," he adds once his mouth is blessedly free of cookie crumbs.

If I never see that dance again, I'll die a happy woman.

My confusion must be apparent because Conall leans towards me and murmurs, "Finn's affinity is green magic."

"Yeah, okay, because *that* clears everything up. Everyone knows about green magic," I say, rolling my eyes.

I don't want vague explanations, I want details. They're understandably nonchalant about something that's an everyday occurrence in their lives, but this is amazing. I want to soak in every bit of information I can get and lock it inside of me forever.

Finn laughs and takes pity on me, explaining, "Green magic is an affinity for plants, basically. Flowers, trees, vines, anything that comes from the ground falls under my domain. I do a lot of work growing food for the Haven, as well as working with aquaponics and methods for modernizing agriculture. Here, take a look."

He crosses over to the window above the sink and grabs a small pot with the tiniest little green sprout in it. With a flourish, he sets the tiny ceramic vessel in front of me and taps it with a finger, exactly how a magician would use his wand. Brilliant white pansies burst like fireworks from the soil, shooting up and blossoming in record time, like I'm watching a silent movie in fast-forward.

"Ah, so you're a fancy gardener," I tease, trying to hide my amazement.

"A *magical*, fancy gardener, thank you very much!" He cocks his head, and the pansies whip towards me, swatting me across the face. Their soft, fragrant petals caress my skin, doing no damage whatsoever, but Conall growls at Finn until he reels the offending flowers back to their pot.

The three of them take turns explaining their lives while we snack on cookies Margie endlessly pulls out of the oven. She tells me she's aligned with the earth, which is different than Finn's green magic because she's working with the soil and rock itself, as opposed to Finn's plants. She says it's one of the more useless affinities for anyone who isn't a sculptor or mason. Apparently, she doesn't use it too often anymore, unless there's something that needs to be reworked on their grounds. Domenic—who I've yet to meet—controls water, which she says is "a bit more useful."

I think I'd kill for any one of their powers, useful or not. I mean, who doesn't grow up wishing they could do magic? Tiny child Valorie would pee herself if she could see me now, munching on the gooiest chocolate chunk cookie while wrapped in the arms of an alien demigod.

Gaius, the only one of the "kids" I haven't met, is the stealthy, matter-of-fact twin to Gabrielle. According to Finn, they look nothing alike, similar only in their tall, willowy figure. The same goes for their personalities. Gaius has a fire affinity and usually works on technological advancements for a Paragon named Andrew. Margie says his favorites are ones involving explosives. Judging by her scoff, I'm guessing she's been on the cleanup crew once or twice.

Note to self: stay a few feet away from him. I'm pretty sure my hair gel is flammable.

"Oh! Look at the time, dearies," Marguerite says, "it's time to get this food to the dining room! Otherwise, they'll all be a bunch of whining babies, and poor Valorie here will think I've raised you all in a barn and never want to come back over!"

The boys line up next to her and she stacks their arms high with platters, serving bowls, and tureens. Any normal man, even one as fit as the two of them, would be buckling under the weight of all this food. They barely notice it, bumping each other with their hips to try and jostle the other's stack until Margie smacks them with a spatula and tells them to head out. Finn zooms off in a blur, but Conall turns back to me, indecision written across his face.

"Oh, go on. Valorie can walk back here with me and we'll have ourselves a chat on the way. You know I don't like to rush around like you all. We'll be there soon enough," Margie says.

When he continues to hesitate, she raises the weaponized spatula for another round. He wisely decides to make a run for it, but he stops to blow me a quick kiss. I catch it with an exaggerated hand grab.

Margie and I gather up the bread and salad—the only things left after the guys leave—and head out at a much more leisurely pace through the luxurious, yet surprisingly homey, Haven.

Everywhere I look, something new and amazing is waiting to capture my attention. One hall is lined entirely with weapons and suits of antique armor, tiny museum-style plaques telling me they're authentic artifacts from several historic eras. Another has original paintings haphazardly crammed from floor to ceiling as if the world's most insane curator was let loose. They're all priceless, but something about the clutter and warm, plush rugs makes the place homey rather than intimidating.

It doesn't take long for Marguerite to start up a conversation again. Her motherly, hilarious personality has made me feel at home here. My anxiety from earlier is nowhere to be found.

"So, Conall told me about your...trouble with that boy."

I almost drop the salad bowl. Damn, she's going right for the big topics.

"You won't see an ounce of judgment from anyone here. We think you're brave, and Conall is lucky to have you. But, honey, woman to woman, are you okay?"

I open my mouth to give her the same *of course* I say to everyone else, but something about her soft expression stops me. To my embarrassment, moisture pools at the edges of my lids. Words fail me; all I can do is violently shake my head and curse whichever parent gave me the easy-crier genes. Probably Dad.

She drags me into a hug just shy of suffocating in the best way. Truth is, I've beaten myself up so many nights over why the hell I let Xavier walk all over me for so long. I've called myself stupid, pathetic, everything under the sun. But, as she crushes me to her in the hallway of the most beautiful home I've ever seen, all of it melts away.

"I'm pretty lucky to have him, too," I croak, wiping the back of my hand across my cheeks.

"Of course, dear. I'm no Seer like Gabby, but I foresee a long, Bonded life for you two."

"Bonded?" I ask as we resume our walk.

"Conall hasn't explained it? Hmmm...how to put it," she says. "In Avallea, we are effectively immortal. So, there's a *lot* of time for relationships. Many people will enter into recognized unions for a number of years, then eventually decide to end those unions in order to experience a portion of life with someone else. All completely amicably.

"But Bonding is different. When two decide to enter into a Bond, they pair themselves forever. They become fiercely protective of one another, essentially two halves of the same being. It's incredibly serious and rarely done, because Bonds are only broken by death, and the remaining partner tends to follow their lost love into the Underworld. You almost never find a Bonded individual existing beyond their partner's death."

"Wow. An eternal pairing, literally. That's heavy."

“Yes,” she says, “it is. But for some, it’s everything.” And with that revelation, she stops in front of a set of double doors, the smaller twin to the ones at the entrance. Using her hip, Margie bumps the door open and sashays into the crowded room. “It’s time to party!”

Chapter 24
Party Time

- Valorie -

"That makes three games in a row! Best team ever!" Finn gives me a fist bump and sticks his tongue out at Conall and Gaius across the beer pong table as if he's five years old.

I can't help but laugh. We've been on a roll since the party left the dining room and moved downstairs to their massive games room a few hours ago. Gabrielle and Marguerite played a few matches against Finn and Domenic until the other three players bowed out and Finn recruited us to continue playing. He claimed me as his partner, much to Conall's chagrin, and we've been winning ever since.

Gaius twirls a lick of flame between his fingers absentmindedly while we break for bathroom trips and refills. The drinks have slowly added up over hours of playing. I have a buzz despite our team being undefeated. That little snake of fire twisting and twirling, never burning him, has me captivated. I saw Finn grow a whole plant from almost nothing earlier, but something about this casual display drives home that I'm in a room full of people who can do genuine magic on a whim.

Gaius must notice my staring because he locks eyes with me, smiles, and blows gently on his hand. The flame spreads into a wave of dandelion-seed sparks carried towards me on a small draft. I stiffen and yelp, expecting them to burn, but they settle over my skin like fireflies, twinkling merrily in the windowless room.

"You look like a Christmas tree," he says. His pupils reflect the sparking wisps, making them seem filled with the fire he commands so well.

The warning from earlier rings true: Gaius is definitely a trickster. Since we've been downstairs, I've watched him swap sugar for salt twice, jump out and scare Marguerite, and switch Conall's Maker's and Coke for soy sauce.

Could I have ratted him out? Yes. Did I? Nope. He's a hellion, a twelve-year-old kid in an adult body. It's hilarious to watch him skitter around, leaving good-natured chaos in his wake.

"I'm getting a drink, Sparkles, you want anything?" he asks.

Guess I've earned myself a new nickname.

"Sure, whatever you're having."

He chuckles darkly, and I instantly know I made a mistake giving him free rein over my drink. I'm not at all worried he'll hurt me; I'm only hoping he brings me something drinkable.

He reappears in front of me with twin glasses in hand, faster than I can change my mind and ask for something sealed and safe.

"To having fun, Sparkles," he says, handing me a cup of murky copper liquid.

I clink mine against his and echo, "To having fun." Then I scrunch my lids closed, brace myself, and take a large gulp.

A symphony of flavors washes over my tongue. Sweet apple comes in first, followed by a hint of citrus and spice. The burn of strong liquor lurks underneath it all, tempered by the fruity mix.

"It's delicious," I exclaim.

Gaius nods, taking a swig from his own glass. "My special recipe. It's a kicker, be careful. Let me know if you want another one when that's done. It's not like you're driving tonight." He walks over to where Finn and Gabrielle are dancing in the corner near the vintage jukebox Gaius rigged to play music off of his phone.

Conall and Marguerite are nowhere to be seen. Neither is Joran, a visiting dehmi I was introduced to earlier.

"I trust my family has been welcoming?"

I whip around to find the member of the household I've interacted with the least leaning against the wall behind me. Domenic may be twice the average life expectancy of an American male, but he has the looks of a well-kept, middle-aged man. His irises are a darker shade than either Gaius' ice-blue or Finn's cerulean, and his dark brown, close-cropped hair and beard add to his severe visage. Only the subtle twinkle in those navy blues give a hint as to how fun he can be. I know for a fact he was the one who purposely distracted Conall with a nonsensical conversation about birds so Gaius could swap out his drink earlier.

I raise my cocktail and smile. "I don't know. I have the distinct impression everyone is trying to get me drunk so I can't escape."

"We lock the doors in" — he checks his bare wrist, where there is quite obviously *not* a watch — "five minutes. Then we all turn into monsters and prey on any humans left in our clutches. But, I'm sure Conall explained that to you."

"Oh, of course. Well, it would be rude of me to leave now," I say.

He lets out a boisterous laugh, and I join him. Everyone here seems so happy. From what I've learned about the Avalleans and their dehmi, I would have expected a bunch of burly, brooding soldier types, all rigid and unyielding. But they seem to be all fun and games. They're a more tight-knit family than most of the biological ones I've seen.

"My son seems to have finally found someone who brings out the best in him. Took him long enough."

My gut churns at the sudden image of Conall going through dozens of other beautiful, talented dehmi girls in his quest to find that "someone". I know I shouldn't, but I can't help myself. I ask, "Has he brought a lot of girls around?"

By the way Domenic cracks up, I've told the funniest joke of the night.

"No, my dear," he says, "quite the opposite, in fact."

We chat for a while, more like old friends than two people who met today. He tells me about the ins and outs of running a Haven, and I hear more about how he gave up his early ticket back to Avallea to be here. In return, I explain my job maintaining the exhibits at the campus conservatory, which interests him more than I expected. Surprisingly, we both have a love of animals and musicals, although his favorite show is Cats, which I despise.

"It makes no sense. I've watched it a dozen times, but I can't stand it," I say.

"Well, can we at least both agree the stage play is better than the movie?"

"One-hundred percent," I agree solemnly. I may be firmly in drunk territory, thanks to finishing the last of Gaius' magical drink, but the recent Cats movie was atrocious. No amount of alcohol could change that fact.

"Did you get a chance to speak with Joran? I hope he wasn't too unpleasant."

I don't know how to answer his question. My earlier meeting with the scruffy, older dehmi amounted to little more than a stiff handshake and a few sentences, but I had the intense impression the short interaction was enough for me to somehow be judged and found lacking. Joran was gruff, yet friendly, with Conall and the others, but he cooled off considerably when Conall introduced us.

I settle for keeping my response polite, but vague. "Yes, we met. He was...reserved."

"He's utterly devoted to Avallea, but has never been one for niceties. I hope he didn't color your opinion of our little band," Domenic says with an apologetic wince.

"No, not at all," I say.

Domenic looks over my head and gives me a fatherly pat on the shoulder. "Looks like my time with you is up for the evening. I think Marguerite is looking for me. See you tomorrow, Valorie. And hopefully many more days afterwards."

I bid him a good night, promising to invite him to tour the conservatory soon. One refill from Gaius later, and I'm totally, blissfully drunk. I spy Conall lounging against the back wall, sipping from a longneck beer bottle. My drunken brain becomes laser-focused on those slim shoulders and hips, that firm jaw with a side of softness, and the secret smile waiting for me in the right corner of his full mouth.

"Looks like things are winding down," he says when I weave my way to him.

I didn't notice until right now, but the room is markedly emptier than it was an hour ago. Everyone appears to have drifted off to their own devices. Marguerite and Domenic left after our conversation ended, while Joran never showed up for games. Not that you'll catch me complaining. Gabrielle is finishing gathering some dishes in the corner of the room while Finn snores in one of the plush leather chairs near the home theater. Gaius is suspiciously absent, and I'm praying he's nowhere near my bags stashed inside Conall's room.

Conall tips a finger under my chin, tilting my head up to more easily brush his lips across mine. My body blazes with a heady combination of lust, love, and whiskey, and I melt into his arms like candle wax, soft and dripping with emotion.

"Do you want to go upstairs the leisurely way or the fast way, kitten?" he asks.

"Dealer's choice."

He chuckles, holding out his arms to me. "Hold on tight, then."

I fold myself into his arms and take a deep breath. A flashing blur of colors mixes with the distinct, stomach-plummeting feeling of climbing upwards, and we're already stopping outside of his door. He unlocks it with an old-fashioned key and leads the way into the moonlit space. I spy the arched windows across from us and rush over, entranced by the view.

Conall's room is at the very top of the Haven, facing towards their expansive rear yard. Silvery in the midnight glow, the acres of trees and greenery seem to stretch for miles towards the dark line of the forest beyond. From this angle, I can see the greenhouse I glimpsed during our arrival, as well as a jam-packed, yet manicured garden with winding walking trails. An open dirt rectangle is sectioned off halfway down one of them, ringed with small sheds around its perimeter.

"The training yard," Conall says softly behind me, noticing the direction of my gaze. "Come on. Let's get you into bed, kitten."

He leads me over to where my bags are placed next to his dresser, and I snort. The errant scarf that caused me to completely wreck my room is draped over them, taunting me with its bold print. I yank out my pajamas, but Conall chuckles and returns them to the bag, placing one of his shirts on top of my handful of toiletries instead. The small display makes me smile. I nod, zip the bag closed, and head into his attached bathroom. The clean lines, soft linens and black-and-white neutral scheme reminds me of an upscale hotel, not the bathroom of a single man in his twenties. Sober Val would love its simplicity, but not-so-sober Val thinks it's entirely too bright for her swirling, mushy brain.

When I emerge, washed and dressed in his well-worn black tee, he devours me with his look alone. The threadbare shirt hits me at mid-thigh, but the way he's looking at me from his perch on the bed makes me feel like I'm wearing nothing at all. Suddenly, a wave of crushing arousal washes over me, and I have to stop myself from running across the room to him. The floor is tilting a bit, so running would probably end up with me on my ass anyway.

With careful, measured steps, I manage to reach the edge of the bed without stumbling. He moves over, pulling me down until I'm half on top of him, my hip thrown over his and my arm across his chest. The position causes his shirt to ride up almost to my waist, but I don't move to readjust it. The cool air is heavenly on my flushed skin. Conall's hand coasts a hot line up the back of my leg to my hip, branding me with his touch.

I'm on fire and he hasn't kissed me yet. I search for his mouth in the dim light, desperate to taste him, but he releases another of those low, infernal laughs of his and rolls me over next to him. Finally, I receive a kiss, but it's a chaste one, far from the bruising battle of lips and tongue I'm craving.

“Go to sleep, wildcat,” he whispers.

“Why?” I groan. “We’re finally alone, here in your bed for the first time, and you want to sleep?”

He presses his lips to my forehead, his cool touch a balm to my buzzing, lust-fevered skin. “Because you’re drunk on some concoction of Gaius’, and the first time I make love to you in my bed I want you to remember every second of it for the rest of forever. So, go to sleep, and dream of the long future we have together. There will be endless nights where we can ravage each other beneath the stars, but tonight is for holding you in my arms and wondering how I could ever be so lucky.”

His beautiful, heartfelt words bring tears once again and I let them fall, not the least bit embarrassed to show him how much they mean to me. How could I argue with him? I curl up against his chest, and his strong arms envelop me in a cocoon of warm skin and his unique blend of lavender and pine and something purely Conall.

“I love you,” I whisper into the dark.

“Love is much too small to explain what I feel for you. But until we find a word capable of encompassing endless, unfathomable adoration and need, it’ll have to suffice. So, until that day, I love you too, kitten.”

Chapter 25
Destruction
- Conall -

Waking up with Valorie curled around me in my bed is a level of heaven I was unaware existed until today. Her milky skin is covered in small pink lines from pressing against the pillow and sheets, and her face is scrunched up slightly against the weak pre-dawn light. I've never experienced something so purely adorable.

I press my hand to her forehead and push a bit of my healing magic into her skin. She had at least one drink made by Gaius last night, possibly two. Plus a fair amount of beer during our games, despite her and Finn sweeping the pong tournament. Without my help, she'll be in no state to spend any time out of this room today. That would be tempting, if it wasn't for the fact she'd likely be lying on my bathroom tiles and vomiting instead of in my bed with me.

Satisfied she's going to be in a much better state when she eventually wakes, I remove my hand and carefully extricate myself from her grasp without waking her. I pad over to the window and pull the curtains closed.

Valorie grabs my pillow and snuggles against it to fill the space where I was lying in the rumpled bed without becoming fully conscious, and I take a minute to watch her sleep before I snap back into action. I scribble a quick note and stick it on the side table by her phone. In my closet, I find a pair of joggers and a workout tee in a shade of deep hunter green I know my wildcat loves.

Pausing on my way out of the door, I can't help but turn back to take one last look at her. Her face is smooth and calm; no signs of discomfort or pain. No anxiety can touch her here in the safety of my room. Our home is a haven in more ways than one.

I drink in her peace, letting it fill me up before I ease the heavy, oak door shut with a barely audible click.

I hurry through the halls, eager finish my morning training and get back in time to be ready when Valorie wakes up. I don't pass another soul, and I'm hoping this means they're all still in bed. Logically, I know this is the safest possible place for her, but something in the back of my head is still uneasy. I flash back to last night, and Gabrielle's demand that I tell Valorie the circumstances behind our meeting seeps into me like cold sludge. It drips through my brain and I shiver despite the roaring fire I pass in the living room.

How could I ever possibly tell her that I was originally tasked with meeting her so I could kill her? Despite knowing I was practically forced to do so by fate itself—and that her death was meant to bring about a medical marvel—it doesn't matter. There's no way I could risk losing her over something which doesn't factor into our lives anymore. Gabrielle's gift is not foolproof; she must be wrong in this.

She has to be.

Sliding out the side entrance, I make my way along one of the gravel footpaths Finn and Gabrielle have woven through the crowded shrubbery and flowers. Morning dew soaks into my clothing as I brush past the dense greenery. It's lush and full in the dead of winter, all thanks to Finn's affinity. A pear tree near the entrance to the training yard is still laden with ripe fruit, so I twist off a low-hanging pear and bite deeply. This is instantly a huge mistake. The fruit's heady, luscious flesh reminds me of the foyer of the Vargas' home and a very different delicacy I sampled there.

I finish off my pear while concentrating on the specifics of the workout I have planned, trying to keep my mind from wandering down that wonderful memory lane any further. It wouldn't do to walk into the training yard at full mast, only to find it inhabited by someone else trying to get in an early workout.

Thankfully, I find I'm the only one here this morning. My bare feet leave soft imprints in the damp earthen floor of the yard as I settle into the opening movements of my routine. By noon it will become a dusty tan expanse, but this early in the morning it is still moist and chocolate brown.

This has always been my favorite time of day—when the world is new and fresh and the events of the day have not yet tainted it with noise and struggles. The evening is almost as nice, but there's something special about the first light of a new day. Full of hope, like I've become lately.

"At this rate, you'll shrivel into a raisin before you get back to Valorie," says a voice from behind me.

I lower my dumbbells, sweat running in rivulets, and turn around to find Gabrielle spreading her yoga mat on the dirt. We have an indoor gym off of the game room, but she enjoys the fresh air as much as I do. Gabby and I run on similar wavelengths. We often work out together in comfortable silence, not needing to fill the space between us with conversation.

I catch the towel she throws me and wipe off, throwing the sweat-soaked cloth around the back of my neck. "What time is it? I left my phone inside."

"Almost noon. She's been up for hours now, by the way." A pause as she moves from *bitilasana* to *bhujangasana*. "You never told her, did you? About the first task."

Not this again. "No, Gabby, I didn't. I don't think it's a smart move. It's only going to hurt her, and if I lose her it's all over. For both of us. It's too risky."

She sighs. "You're making the wrong choice, but it's your choice to make, I guess. Remember, Valorie spent years of her life being lied to by someone who claimed they loved her. How will she feel when she finds out you kept this from her?"

Her frank words rattle me. Is this the right move? Would it be better if I told her after all? I run my hands through my hair and shake off the sudden worry I'm making the wrong choice.

"I can't risk it right now, Gabby. I'll tell her in the future, okay? When she's more comfortable with our life. You have a good point, I'll give you that. But it's not happening today."

She looks away and moves smoothly into her next pose. "I still think you're not giving her enough credit, but okay, Con. If this is your choice, you might want to go find her. She's hanging out with the guys, and I think they assume you've already told her. I know Marguerite and Domenic think you have. Never know what could slip out. Things have been...murky today."

I'm off like a shot, out of the yard while she's still speaking. I don't know why I'm so worried—Valorie spent all day yesterday talking to my family with no issues—but there's a sinking in my gut I can't shake. The

Web doesn't allow me to See it the way Gabrielle does, but something about our conversation feels like a premonition. And it isn't a good one.

Why the hell did I forget my phone this morning? I was so focused on not waking the angel sleeping peacefully in my bed, I did the bare minimum and ran, eager to be out and back as quickly as possible. Now I have to rely on my senses to find them in time to prevent whatever is driving my intuition insane. No phone also means no way to warn my brothers not to mention the task to Valorie, and they love to talk. If I only had a way to contact them, I wouldn't be sprinting frantically through the undergrowth, sweat and dust clinging to my skin.

I continue to run through the twists and turns, cursing their lack of straight directions, all the while straining for any sign of voices hidden amongst the garden.

There!

I finally hear the faint sound of Finnegan's laughter. Thanking the Web my brother laughs louder than a foghorn, I race towards the fire pit situated in the shadow of the main house as fast as my legs can take me.

My stride slows about twenty yards from their chairs and I listen as I approach, not wanting to seem crazy by rushing into their conversation covered in grime and panting. Instead, I creep quietly through the brush, same as any completely normal person.

Finn is asking innocent questions about her life. Right now they're talking about Xavier and how he wouldn't leave her alone. The mere mention of his name sets my blood to boil.

"So you broke up with this guy two years ago, but he still hung around?"

I'm glad to hear he sounds as disgusted as I did when I learned about Xavier. She feeds him some self-deprecating remark about how she should have been more firm with him and how she never thought he would get to this point. It's all nonsense. She has no fault in this; all the blame lies at Xavier's feet.

"Well, I'm extra glad Conall managed to convince you he wasn't a crazy, murdering stalker, then."

My blood runs cold.

"What do you mean?" she asks.

I'm rushing now, trampling Finn's precious flowers under my feet in my haste to get there and stop him from clarifying. It's no use; he's already started his sentence by the time I arrive at the edge of the clearing where they're lounging. I'm forced to wait in the shadows of the fruit trees and pray Finn will look up and read my rapidly moving lips.

"Well, you know, the whole task thing."

She shakes her head at him, uncomprehending. Maybe he'll let it go...or maybe not.

I can't take the risk.

I move into the sparse fringe of bushes at the edge of the clearing, staring daggers at my brother.

"Finn, no." It emerges from my throat as a growl, a warning.

Unfortunately for me, my wildcat can growl as well.

"Finn," she says with all the eerie calm of an approaching hurricane, "what do you mean?"

He stammers, a gazelle caught between us. Doomed either way.

She draws herself up, every word a scathing sentence. "*What. Do. You. Mean.*"

I would be awed if I wasn't so terrified.

"Nothing! Just, y'know, the whole I-have-to-kill-you-but-I-don't-want-to thing. But that's old news now, you know? It all worked out."

The entire world stops, holding its breath as she slowly turns in my direction.

If looks could kill, I'd be ash on the pavement. Maybe she would be too, because this look she's fixed me with is pure agony, all sharp and jagged shards of glass.

"You...I...what?" Her voice is small, but each word spears right through me.

I'm riddled with holes; my words flood out through the punctures. Maybe enough of them will pool together to create a river and float her back into my arms. "It was my original job. I was sent to learn about you, to find out the best way to—"

"To *kill* me," she says.

"It was supposed to be painless, merciful. And the Paragons—they gave me a real reason, one that would help humanity in a big way. We all hated the idea, yet it had to be done. That's our job. But, once I met you, I didn't care. I wouldn't—couldn't do it. I've loved you from the day I saw you in my meeting. You called to something inside of me. So I refused, and the Web gifted us with another way." That's the closest I can get without openly telling her of the circumstances surrounding my new deadline. At this point, only the threat of her death is keeping that from rushing out, too.

As my eyes frantically search her face, I can tell my words fall short. My breath burns in my lungs, ignited by her fiery expression.

"And yet, you never told me. You let me live a lie because you didn't trust me enough to give me the full truth! You hid this from me, made me look like a fool, like I was too delicate and simple to be trusted entirely. I was never allowed to make my own decision, never given the full picture. A pretty face, good enough to warm your bed, but not to be confided in."

"No, no that isn't—"

"Oh, it most certainly is," she seethes, but her anger isn't enough to hide the pain pooling behind her steely glare. She's standing less than two feet away, yet suddenly she's miles from me, drifting out of reach.

"I'm so, so sorry. Please don't leave me, Valorie. I love you. You are my whole life, my salvation, my absolution. My everything."

"Love isn't enough, Conall! You have to show it, *mean* it! Love is an *action*, not a statement. And I can't waste more years of my life being hurt the way I was in the past. Even if it kills me, I can't go back to the lies and the pain. I *won't*. I would rather die."

She looks me dead in the eyes, and something softens. Not like forgiveness—no, nothing so blessed. This looks like resignation, and it's terrifying.

"I would have understood if you had come out and told me," she whispers. "It wasn't your fault, you didn't make the rules. But you didn't care enough to try and let me in. I was always on the outside, always a joke. The silly, clueless girl."

"I'm not him, Valorie, you know me. I love you, *please!*" The flood of tears drowning my face mirrors her own, two halves of a tragedy that could have been, *should* have been ecstasy.

"I know," she chokes out, "that's what makes it hurt more."

And she turns and walks away, trailing my heart behind her on a string.

I don't know if I'll ever move again.

Roots will sprout beneath me and tether me to this spot where I had her, then lost her. I'll be a monument to poor decisions, visited only by ravens and crows and the ghosts of my own hubris. It's all I deserve.

Finn crosses my field of view, his face a mask of tears that matches mine. I know he blames himself, but this is my cross to bear. She was right; how could I expect her to pick me when I never told her the whole truth? I never should have doubted Gabrielle. I was a coward, and now I'm alone.

"Con, I am so, so sorry. I—I didn't know. I swear."

I should reach out and hug him.

I should tell him I don't blame him, because I don't.

But I can't find the energy to do more than whisper, "She's gone."

And then the world fades into a special shade of black, one that matches the hole where my heart used to sit and beat a rhythm orchestrated for her.

Chapter 26
Fragments

– Valorie – – Conall –

Wake up.
Choke down breakfast.
Four classes today.
Feed the animals in the conservatory.
Eat dinner.
Sleep.

Wake up.
Avoid the backyard.
Work out until I collapse.
Help Finnegan with the front shrubs.
Force down a meal.
Sleep.

Wake up.
Cereal this time, Honey Combs.
Only two more classes left.
Dinner with my parents.
Stare at the shower wall.
Sleep.

Wake up.
Pretend to read a book.
Lunch with Gabrielle staring at me.
Wander the halls.
Skip dinner.
Sleep.

Another day.
Manage to finish finals.
Drift through the conservatory.
Push my food around.
Sit and stare at the moon.
Sleep.

Decide to get out of bed.
Barely.
It's been two weeks.
No food today, please.
I can't stomach it.
Nightmares.

David drags me out of bed.
Or is it Charlie?
Only *his* gifts are left under the tree.
Manage a bath, no shower.
Standing is too much effort.
Fall back into sleep.

Please don't wake me.
I only see her in my dreams.
I'm so sorry.
Is she okay?
I miss her.

I'm all alone.
But he will never leave me.
I wish I could see him.
I never want to see him again.
I miss him.

Chapter 27
Waking Up
- Valorie -

"She's been practically bed bound for three freaking weeks. Yeah, well, I don't give a damn! Uh-huh, you better. Okay, bye."

David thinks I can't hear him through the closed door, but I can. What I can't figure out is who exactly is on the other end of his heated phone call. Not that I can muster up the energy to care. I don't care about much at all these days. It's pathetic, but guess what. I don't care about *that,* either. Everything falls just short of being worth the effort.

Has it truly been three weeks?

My mind is still stuck back in that dappled clearing, watching the man I thought would be my forever crush my heart in his fist. Has the planet managed to turn twenty-one times since I lost him?

Maybe David is exaggerating. It's a frequent occurrence.

Where have I been? Cowering here when I was the one who did nothing wrong? Screw this. The world should be mine to live in. *He* can go hide.

I sit up in my bed, suddenly prepared to get up and begin my life anew. My eyes flit across the room, trying to find some sign that the world has experienced the same irrevocable change I have. There are none, because nothing has been altered except for me. Instead, my gaze lands on a plain black shirt draped across my dresser near the door.

A shirt that is not mine.

A shirt that, were I to go and grab it, I know would smell of pine forests and lavender fields.

A shirt that is also a bomb, destroying the feeble spine I was relying on to start the day. To restart my life.

I crawl back under the blankets, hiding from a world where nothing is changed and yet shirts are now explosives. Maybe tomorrow I will be strong enough. Tomorrow my spine will be steel. Tomorrow, my anger will become armor.

Tomorrow I will try again.

The blooms are a myriad of blues and pinks, purples and yellows, and every shade in between. They blanket the ground so thickly, there's no telling what is beneath them. Maybe there's nothing below. Maybe the whole world is a flower, powder-soft beneath my bare feet as I run under a clear blue sky.

I blink, and the blossoms distort. The poppies become redwoods, the peonies become oaks. Birches, willows, and elms reach up, up, up, until the air is dark and clogged with leaves and branches that poke and prod and scrape. Beautiful, even as they cause me pain. Like someone I know but will never hear from again. Like a name I'll never say.

"Get up." The voice echoes through the forest, strangely clear.

Why would I need to get up? I'm already standing.

"Get *up*!"

The branches shift and roll, tossing me this to and fro. They no longer poke; now, they tumble like boulders, threatening to crush me.

"Valorie, get the hell up!"

David's face is inches from mine as I open my eyes, blinking away the last vestiges of sleep.

"Jeez, *chica*, you sleep like the dead," he says as he moves back so I can sit up. "I was about to go get some water to throw on you, like they do in the movies."

I rub my itchy eyes, torn between being angry he woke me and grateful to escape the strange nightmare. I don't usually have vivid dreams, and I hope this isn't the start of a new trend. Sleep is the one place where my anxiety doesn't find me, and I desperately need it to stay that way. Especially now.

"What time is it?" I grumble while trying to hide my head back under my pillow.

I should've known it would never work. David rips the blankets off of me and snags my pillow. Smart move—if I can reach it, I can smack him with it. The boy is too fast for his own good. He should join Charlie on the track—he'd win the gold if he applied himself to do more than ogle his man. Or maybe I'm extra slow because I've been nearly comatose for three weeks. I'm pretty sure muscle starts to atrophy after two.

"It's five o'clock. And before you ask, yes, five in the evening. On Sunday. And we have no more classes until February, so we shouldn't be sitting here."

I already know where this is going, but I let David build up to his grand finish. In the meantime, I drag myself out of bed to remove the fuzzy carpet from my teeth. Victorious in the battle against halitosis, I begin a losing battle with my reflection while I wait for David's crescendo. Sure enough, after another three minutes of beating around the bush, he finally gets to the point.

We're going out tonight. Non-negotiable.

David is already in my closet when I return from the bathroom, having reduced my zombie-like appearance by half and wrestled my hair into an up-do that looks somewhat presentable. He's chucking clothes onto my bed like the Crown Jewels are hidden somewhere behind a dress or pair of pants.

His muffled voice drifts out from the depths of the closet as the mountain of fabric grows. "Charlie is meeting us at Slice in thirty. Here." He emerges with a scarlet slip of fabric draped over a shoulder and holds it out to me. "Put this on. You'll look hot as hell."

"I don't need to look hot, I'm not trying to bring anyone home," I say.

He shrugs and waves me off. "Doesn't matter. Confidence is key, Vally. You've gotta take care of yourself."

Sensible David is the worst. He has this knack for being annoyingly correct and he won't let anyone forget it. There's no point in arguing with him because one, he'll win and two, by the end of the night you'll realize he was right all along. Might as well save myself the trouble.

Sighing, I take the dress.

Sensible David strikes again. I'm not looking for company outside of my friends, but I do feel close to a million bucks with my subtle curves wrapped in snug red cotton. A pair of my favorite black ankle boots puts me a few inches above my usual height, though I'm still below eye level for both of the guys. The boots look like they'd be at home on a motorcycle, all buckles and straps and thick heels.

I try not to notice the resemblance.

I'm trying not to notice any of the resemblances.

A man in the back booth has hair only a shade lighter. The girl four stools from the door has as fake tan which tries but fails to capture *his* natural sun-kissed bronze. A half-full bottle of Tanqueray above Tomas' head is the same brilliant clear jade shade of *his* irises but holds none of their sparkle.

I'm a ship unmoored, looking for guiding stars where there are none. My sky is perpetually gray and roiling with clouds, the heavens obscured. Now, I need to learn to guide myself with something beyond the celestial. I made my choice, even if part of my heart wishes I hadn't.

A cold glass bumps against the back of my hand where it's resting on the bar top. Tomas winks at me, swirling a black straw in the fresh mug of cider in front of me.

Black, like chin-length waves I'll never run my fingers through again.

Hollow like me.

Tomas breaks through my spiraling. "Someone is awfully quiet for her first single night out on the town in a while."

"Why is there a straw in my cup?"

He chuckles and takes the straw out. It becomes a magic wand; he taps me on the nose with a flourish made for a sideshow stage. I dab a foamy droplet of cider off of my face, glaring at him.

"You're awfully moody for someone who kicked their man to the curb. You should be singing Beyoncé and dancing on a table somewhere." He flicks his hand back and forth as he struts around in a circle.

"I didn't *want* to leave him!" The words explode out of me.

David, Charlie, and Tomas blink at me, for once all stunned silent.

Tomas recovers first. "Well if you didn't want to leave him then why did you?"

"How could I stay with someone who lied to me? Again! What will everyone think? I'll look like some idiotic, lovestruck pushover!"

It's obvious, how could they not see it? I had no choice. Sure, he apologized, but other people wouldn't know that. They'd only know I let him get away with a lie because he claims he was trying to protect me.

Now David starts in on me. "Valorie, who would know other than us and his family? I'm going to come right out and say this, so don't be mad. You're letting your anxiety get the best of you. Who the hell cares if you forgive him? It's not like you have to broadcast how he screwed up!"

"But—"

"I'm not finished," he says. "You're sitting here saying the whole reason you're staying away from the only guy I've ever seen treat you well is not because you think you could never trust him again, but because you're worried about what strangers would think if they ever found out he lied. And that's stupid and shallow. You're throwing your happiness away over nothing."

I'm stunned. I don't know how to begin to respond. Am I being shallow?

"I think what David means," Charlie says gently, "is we love you, and we see how happy you and Conall have been together. Is this thing he lied about something he regrets? Do you think he'll do it again?"

I shake my head slowly. If I'm being honest, I think Conall would rather die than do this to me again. I may be too dense to see what was so apparent to my friends, but I'm not blind. Conall was as destroyed as I was when I left.

Charlie nods. "If that's the case, I think you should at least consider seeing him. One time, at least, so you can see how you feel when he's there in front of you. Then you can make a decision for yourself, not for anyone else."

That seems...reasonable. I don't know if I can bear to see him again and find out it was easier for him to move on than it has been for me. But the boys are right; if I don't speak to him one more time, I'll never know for sure.

I heave a sigh. "Okay."

"Okay?"

The three of them should join a choir with their ability to speak in unison. Or maybe an army would be better suited.

"I'll see him again, if he wants. I'll give him one more chance to set things right. Not right now, but sometime soon. I'm still angry, you know?"

Charlie smiles and holds up his drink. David, Tomas, and I follow suit, clinking our glasses together as the weight begins to fall off of my chest for the first time in three weeks.

"Then let's drink and whine about things until you get it all out, so you can face tomorrow with a clean slate."

Chapter 28
Found

-Valorie-

I stumble out into the halo of light beyond the bar's front entrance the instant the clock over the bar strikes midnight, needing a bit of fresh air. When we arrived, the bar was empty except for a few small groups having Sunday dinner, but things started to pick up around eight when the night life began. Now, Slice of Heaven is teeming with people out enjoying their evening.

Once the heavy wood and glass door clicks shut behind me and the din of the crowd is reduced to a dull roar, I can finally take a breather. I'm definitely drunk, but who cares? I don't have work or class tomorrow, and I'm not driving. Time to live a little. I'll be facing my fears soon enough—a little liquid courage can't hurt.

Raul saw me heading out on his way back to the kitchen. I told him I'd be back, I needed a quick break from the heat and press of people inside. But the truth is I need a break from *seeing* for a minute. David and Charlie moved to the dance floor after our third shot, and the sight of them twined around each other turned the back of my throat into sandpaper. I turned away to give them their privacy, but Karina showed up shortly afterwards with the baby. Watching Tomas' eyes melt into puddles while she talked about their infant asleep in the bucket seat next to them was too much to bear.

So here I am, hiding from the happiness of my closest friends on a dark bench at the edge of a parking lot in January. At least it isn't snowing. It's freezing outside, but the winter night has a harsh type of beauty to it, more angular than the soft days of summer. The sky is a deep, clear navy with a smattering of stars. A few wisps of cloud drift across the moon and dissipate in the crisp breeze winding through the dense copse in front of me.

Do I have the guts to go back to Conall's and ask him to talk? His family probably hates me at this point. They invited me into their home for the party and I ran out. The second day wasn't half-over when I made my escape. I had a perfectly good reason to do so, but the Avalleans may not see it that way. They may take Conall's side. After all, he is their family. I'm only a human who made his life difficult.

Lost in my own mind, I hear the rustling a split second before his silhouette breaks through the trees.

White-blond hair gleams in the faint corona of the overhead lights, but the rest of his terrifyingly familiar face is still painted in the shadows of the tree line. Until he takes one more step out of my nightmares and into reality.

Out of the past and into the present.

"You aren't supposed to be here," I breathe. Adrenaline shoots through me, burning away my drunken haze.

Xavier takes another step towards me, all cocky bravado. "Then call the police. Oh, wait. I don't think you can."

He smirks at my trembling hands, and I curse myself for leaving my phone beside Karina at the bar. I have no pockets and didn't want to be distracted out here. Now I'm probably going to die, all in the pursuit of some damned peace and quiet.

"You've fucked up my life, Valorie."

Yet another step has me scrambling to my feet.

"You didn't seriously think those charges were going to stick, did you?"

Step.

"But still," he continues, "it has made quite the problem for me. I lost my internship with the school, and you know I'm too busy to turn in assignments. Not without my little *helper*."

Step.

He reaches towards my face, his hand twisting in a mockery of a caress. I know if he manages to make contact with me, he'll never let go. Only one of us will leave here alive, and I'm only now realizing how careless I've been with my survival. Why did I never take David up on his offer to sign up for those Krav Maga classes with me?

Another backwards shuffle towards the safety of the bar...

...and my back hits the icy bumper of a brown SUV, still halfway across the lot from my destination.

Shit.

Xavier is a panther, circling his prey. Now that he's succeeded in boxing me in, he's got time to play. One more foot of flat pavement and his hand will be within reach of my throat.

I'll be finished.

"I'd suggest you think very carefully about your next move if you enjoy your pathetic life."

The cold, almost bored voice comes from somewhere to my left, but I don't dare turn to look. Xavier does, though, and one second is all I need to skid around to the other side of the vehicle. Feeling slightly safer with half a ton of steel between us, I swing a glance towards the shadowy figure who rescued me.

If this car wasn't already supporting most of my weight, I'd be flat on the ground.

Finnegan stands in the buzzing light of a street lamp, shooting a look of pure fury towards Xavier. The dichotomy of stark light and murky darkness make him look larger than his already formidable size, a mammoth with a glare promising slaughter. He may have green magic, but his glare is all furious flames.

"Hey, man, mind your business. I'm talking to my girl, it's all cool," Xavier says with a dismissive flick of his hand.

Wrong move, asshole.

In an instant, Finn stands nose-to-nose with Xavier. He moves entirely too fast to pass as human, but I'm not going to tell anyone. Xavier doesn't seem to notice, which is good because I know he would say something if he saw anything weird. He's never been one for subtlety.

"From what I hear, she hasn't been your girl for an awfully long time, *man*," Finn sneers. "Take the hint. Desperation doesn't look good on anyone."

I can't contain my short burst of laughter. It rockets out of me and echoes off of the blacktop like a thunderclap. Finn is unmoved, but Xavier's stare is magnetized. His glare snaps to me, my laughter a lodestone for his wrath. How dare I find his humiliation amusing?

I wither under the heat of his rage, a plant facing a lava flow. A shark's toothy smile spreads across his face. It's a look promising retribution. One that says he's going to hurt me for my slip-up, wait and see. The restraining order is supposed to keep me safe, but I know Xavier better than anyone. If he ignored it to show up here tonight, it's meaningless to him. He will always do what he wants, consequences be damned. Were the law ever to come for him, he'd hide behind the long arm of his father's political connections.

Crack!

Xavier's head rocks on his shoulders. Without Finn's death grip on his shirt, he'd be a pile of khaki slacks, white Lacoste, and pasty flesh on the dirty pavement.

Finn looks at Xavier as though he's an overly large speck of dirt with the audacity to be on his shoe. "I thought I made myself clear: *leave her alone*. Don't look at her, don't talk to her, don't think about her. Now, run along like a good boy, or else I'll get *really* angry."

His hands shift from clutching to shoving. Xavier sprawls on the ground, dazed. A breathless second passes before he clambers to his feet and runs off.

I catch a glimpse of Xavier's face as he retreats out of sight, and my blood curdles. It's only a fleeting look, the barest of flashes, but it boils with revenge. When he can't find a way to get to Finn, he'll come back for me.

"You're coming over tomorrow so I can start to teach you how to fight."

The moan of wind through the bare branches is the only sound that follows Finn's ridiculous statement. Finn can't expect me to go back to the place where *he* lives and traipse around unaffected.

I finally break the silence with a resounding, "Uh, no." *Hell no, actually.*

"Uh, yes," he counters. "I know you don't want to see Conall, but I don't want to see you dead. I like you, Valorie, whether you're with my brother or not. He screwed up, but that doesn't mean you should miss out on training that could save your life. If he was smart like me he would've been training you already." He puffs his chest out in an over-the-top pose that has me laughing despite my best efforts to seem unyielding.

He does have a point. I already know I haven't seen the last of Xavier and his friends. I should be prepared. I can't expect to have a supernatural bodyguard hanging out in every shadowy corner.

Which reminds me...

"Finn," I say, "not that I'm not grateful for your prescience, but why are you loitering out in the parking lot of the bar I happen to be at?"

He has the decency to look slightly sheepish, but only slightly.

"He asked me to keep an eye out. Which, apparently, was necessary! Jeesh, Val, was that the same guy who put you in the hospital? And he's freely running around in the world, waiting for a chance to jump you at midnight?"

I manage a detached sort of nod. My head is starting to spin from an overwhelming combination of my fading adrenaline rush and the aftereffects of downing half a bottle of alcohol not long ago. I need a place to sit, but you could not pay me to sit on the parking lot asphalt. There's a desiccated glob of chewing gum next to my foot and three shriveled cigarette butts within five feet of where I'm standing. My skin crawls from picturing my ass anywhere near that mess.

An arm gently wraps around my shoulders, and I jump before realizing it's Finn's. He meets my terrified eyes with a comforting, soft smile. "You look like you could use a ride home. Come on, Val. I drove here, just in case. Seems like I'm on a roll tonight, huh? I'm making all the right decisions, and I didn't even have to ask Gabby for help."

I stop him before he can shoot us off towards wherever he parked, letting him know about my friends and phone still safe and clueless inside the bar. Two breaths later he deposits me at the front door, promising to wait right here for a grand total of three minutes until he comes in to check on me.

Cheeky grin aside, I know he's deadly serious. I also know he'll make a hilarious, yet embarrassing scene if I make him come in to find me. It would be an overreaction if I hadn't been accosted in plain sight ten minutes earlier.

I open the front door to the bar and I'm swiftly struck by a queasy sense of otherness. Here's a room packed with people, including some of the ones I love most, dancing and drinking without any idea of what happened right outside. The heavy, warm atmosphere and thick scent of alcohol and pizza hit me with a hammer blow, completely different from the thin bite of the night air at my back. It's as if I'm caught between two worlds.

I guess, in a way, I am. Now that I know the secret of the man standing behind me, the hidden lives of his family and their magical, mystical world behind the scenes.

The secret of the man I still love, whether or not things are possibly ruined between us.

If I had the choice, would I choose them over this? A fresh start, where I could be of use?

Carlos, the bouncer, looks at me and coughs, reminding me I'm holding the door open at midnight in the dead of winter. I throw an "I'll be right back" over my shoulder and run to grab my phone.

Tomas is slinging shakers filled with something cherry scented behind the crowded bar. When I tell him I'm heading out, he promises to let David and Charlie know where I've gone.

"Two minutes and forty-seven seconds," Finn says with a glance at his watch when the door swings shut behind me once again. "You cut it close. Now, hold on to Papa Finn."

I laugh and step into his outstretched arms. He's almost twice as brawny as *him*, but somehow his snug, muscular embrace still feels like home. I don't know whether to smile or cry as we jet off into the night.

We lurch to a stop beside a white Dodge with tires half my height. Finn's truck is as massive as he is; I need a boost to scramble into the shadowy interior of the cabin. For a man drafted into a group of hyper-advanced immortals, his ride is surprisingly fuel-inefficient.

I point this out to him, and he tells me it's for hauling supplies. He also says it's a hybrid, and finishes up with a "mind your own business."

"So, how do you know my address?" I ask when it's clear that his truck's built-in GPS display is staying turned off for this trip.

"I came with Con when he dropped off Chinese for you, the day after your birthday thing. Thanks for the invite, by the way."

"I didn't even know you!" I shout.

I glare at him and realize he's snickering.

A swat on the back of his head has him breaking out into full-on cackles without ever taking his eyes off of the dark streets.

The dark shapes of trees and homes fly by beyond my window as we lapse into silence. Finn has the radio turned off, but the quiet is strangely comforting instead of unnerving.

It's only when we round the corner into the entrance to my neighborhood that Finn decides to ask what's likely been on his mind the entire night.

"Do you think you'll ever forgive him?" The question is quiet, hesitant.

"Honestly? I think part of me already has."

Finn's relieved sigh holds a thousand words. "I know he messed up, I promise I do. He was going to tell you, but he was afraid it would make you hate him. He panicked when we all told him he needed to hurry up and fill you in before, well, something like this happened. He made the wrong choice, and I can't say it's because he's only human since he's...well...not, but you get the point.

"I've never seen him smile like he does with you. It's like you've cracked the code, opened the vault that held the real him. You freed him. He loves you so damn much, Valorie."

"I want to give him another chance...soon. But I'm still afraid," I whisper.

We turn the corner and my house comes into view, a single light on by the front door. A light I know I forgot to turn on when we left the house this afternoon.

"Well, I hope 'soon' means super duper soon. Like, in about thirty seconds."

Because Conall is sitting in the rocking chair under the porch light, waiting for me.

Chapter 29
Forgiveness

- Conall -

I have never been one for dramatics. Among the eclectic members of my family, I am the one who tends to get the most emotionally difficult tasks. All dehmi are expected to show restraint and professionalism when dealing with mortals, but healers tend to take their stoicism more seriously than most. I'm known for being adept at keeping myself dispassionate in unpleasant situations, at least to the outside observer. Inside, I can sort through everything without anyone ever knowing.

Ironically, that aloofness is what earned me the task that led me to *her*.

But now, watching Valorie step out of Finn's Ram into the glow of the solitary street lamp at half past midnight, no amount of practice can stop my hands from trembling. Eleven years of daily training barely keeps my muscles locked in this chair instead of sprinting along the drive. I bide my time, drinking in the sight of her in case this is the last time I'm graced by her presence.

If she sends me away, I will have to go.

Even if it kills us both.

She is beautiful to a distracting degree, all soft lines and curves. The shine in her depthless gaze is brighter than the moon and gentler than a summer breeze as she turns towards me and begins her ascent towards my perch. Whether this seat becomes a throne or an electric chair will all depend on her.

With every careful step Valorie takes, another memory of our time together scrolls across my retinas. Looking into her sleepy, slate eyes on that first, fateful day on campus. Her valiant fight in the alley and the gentle admiration that slipped from both of us in the aftermath. Lunches spent devouring facts about each other. Lazy afternoons watching her study in her favorite moss-cushioned patch in the forest, or dancing along to show tunes in her kitchen on cozy evenings. Warm thighs and a cream sweater dress with Bing Crosby serenading us as she fell apart. An alabaster back and soapy water, and jokes about dangerous butterflies.

A battered, beautiful face whispering that she loved me.

That same face fracturing as I ruined everything.

And then she's suddenly in front of me, and the past peels away to make room for the present.

I stand a safe, agonizing two feet away, gaping. No words make their way past the clog of emotions in my throat. Twelve languages are carefully organized in my internal Rolodex, each one brilliant and expressive. Yet none of them have the right combination to express how sorry I am for hurting her.

"Hi," she whispers into the frigid night. Her shallow breaths puff tiny clouds of fog into the space between us, as though they want to erase the distance as much as I do.

A single crystalline tear caught in her lashes shreds every fraying mental rope I used to bind myself to this spot. My body rebels against my brain and quickly wins the war. All composure broken, I lurch forwards and envelop her in my arms, cradling her head against my chest as our sobs ricochet off one another in a broken symphony.

My splintered heart may be shattering completely or reforging itself, I cannot tell. All I know is I will never leave her side again.

If she lets me stay.

"I'm sorry, I'm sorry, I'm sorry," I say on every shaky exhale. Every breath is a prayer that my goddess will allow me to stay beside her. I breathe in, savoring the gentle scent of sun-drenched pears for what could be the last time as I struggle to compose myself.

I hope it's not too late.

Her trembling chin tilts up towards mine, and I seize the only chance I'm going to get.

"Wildcat," I plead, taking her upturned face in my hands, "I love you with every atom of my being. Mountains will crumble, seas will rise, planetary axes will shift, but I will never stop being completely consumed by you every second of every day. I would cast aside the universe and all of its infinite eternity for the chance to spend a finite number of days at your side. I'll be your hero, your villain, whatever you need me to be. Because my world has no meaning anymore without you in it. I'll be anything, *anything* you want, even if you want me to be gone. But if I get the chance to choose, I want to be your everything."

She remains unmoved beneath my hands, her quiet hiccups and small convulsions the only signs that she is still here with me.

I have lost her.

I'm too late.

I start to rebind my muscles in their scraps of twine, preparing for when I will have to let her go for a final time. The worst part is: I have damned us completely. She cannot survive past our deadline, and I cannot survive without her.

I have doomed us both with my idiocy.

Gabrielle was right, but I was too blind to see it.

The smallest of movements interrupts my silent lamentation. Her chilled body balances against me as she stretches up onto her toes. She should not be out here without a jacket; I'm surprised Finn didn't offer her one. Maybe he expected she would seek out my body heat instead, and that would help my case somehow. He's always been an optimist.

A gentle, feather-light brush of her lips eviscerates every racing thought in my head.

Stars and comets whirl in front of my eyes. I'm too stunned to close them, too afraid this may be another frantic, desperate dream.

Is this another beginning for us, or is it our swan song?

She slowly pulls away, but she doesn't go far. Can she sense that I need her closeness? Does she know I am completely terrified she will evaporate if I dare to blink? Or is this merely a reprieve before she tells me she never wants to see my face again?

I have never been so hopeful or terrified. My heart gallops towards her while the rest of me is frozen.

"Kitten, I don't understand," I whisper. *Please, help me understand.*

She leans gracefully past me and unlocks the door, leaving me in stunned silence as she walks over the threshold and toes off her boots. My frantic stare darts between her face and the dark doorway. I'm searching for clues, anything to help me put the pieces together.

Everything grinds to a halt, and the whole world begins anew with one phrase:

"Come on."

"You're sure?" Inwardly, I curse myself for asking, but I need to hear her say it.

She nods, damp skin creasing with a supernova smile. "Positive."

I dart inside and scoop her up, not wanting her to have a chance to rethink anything. Maybe it's wrong of me to capitalize on the situation, but I'm not taking any chances.

She's *mine.*

I bury my face in her hair, relishing the tickle of soft spirals against my skin. "I thought I had lost you forever," I say.

She chuckles quietly. "For a minute there, you almost did. Good thing I'm so madly in love with you, or you'd have to find someone else's hair to hide in."

"Never," I grumble, clutching her to me until she lets out a small squeak of protest. Rationally, I know she's joking, but I can't find the humor in the situation. Not when it was so nearly my reality.

"Conall," she says, "you're shaking."

I look at my limbs where they're banded around her body. They are, in fact, vibrating strangely.

She slides her hands down to cover my own and tugs gently. "Put me down."

"I can't." There's a desperate crack in my voice. She's the only thing keeping me together. If I let her go, I may crumble into dust.

"You can," she says, more firmly this time.

It takes every ounce of my willpower to set her gently on her feet. I hope she doesn't ask me to move further away than this, because I don't think I can. I'm still clutching her hands to my chest as though she may disappear if I'm not touching her in some form.

"Come on," she says again with a tug on our joined hands.

I follow her as she walks backwards, content to observe until she trips slightly over her own feet. One small stumble is all it takes for my no-longer-ironclad self-control to snap again, and we're sprinting up the stairs in a rush of air and breathless laughter. We reach the door at the end of the hall and I let us in without stopping, finally coming to a halt in the center of the room. The door falls shut behind us, ensconcing us in smooth blackness.

I know Valorie can't see a thing, but every heightened sense I possess is dialed in on her—her rapid breathing, her heady scent, the faint glow of the alarm clock's numbers against her dress.

That dress...I barely noticed it in my earlier panic, but now it's driving me to distraction. Skintight red cotton coasts over each of her curves in a sensual waterfall, coming to an end midway between her hip and knee. A triangle of creamy skin is bared by the low neckline, accentuating two perfect half-moons. Whoever designed this wonderful bit of fabric created a piece of art.

Which is a shame, seeing as how all I want to do is tear it apart.

"How attached are you to this lovely, terrible thing?" I ask, running my hands over her waist to her hips and pulling her flush against me.

She chuckles, a low, enticing sound that cuts straight through me. "The dress or what's under it?"

"Don't toy with me, kitten."

"Aw," she coos, "but it's so fun."

Valorie drags my head to her level and captures my bottom lip between her teeth, stopping my demand for an answer. Her fingers dance along the nape of my neck. She runs her tongue lightly along my lip and releases it with a soft pop.

"I couldn't give half a damn about the dress right now, Conall," she says, "but David might kill you if you ruin it."

Jackpot. "I'll take my chances."

Her small gasp is almost inaudible over the sharp hiss of ripping fabric. I gently untangle her arms from the sides of her ruined dress and let it slide to the floor. The matching scraps she mistook for underwear when she dressed herself are now all that obstructs my view of her, but I'll let them stay. For now.

"Well, that was hot," she says breathlessly. "Unnecessary, but hot."

"I think the outfit is much improved." I glide my hands down her body again, mapping every curve and plane until I come to a stop against her hips. "Black lace. A good choice, though I hope you weren't planning on letting someone else see these when you picked them out today. You belong to me, kitten. And I belong to you."

"Of course I wasn't. Don't be silly." She pauses, and her arms come up to wrap around her body, shielding it from my view. "Wait! You can see everything in the dark, can't you? I forgot!"

She's panicking, but I don't know why. "Of course I can, kitten. I can see every beautiful inch of you. You're my favorite view." I scramble to find some way to comfort her, anything to stop her shrinking into herself like she is.

All at once, it hits me. The reason behind her being embarrassed when all I see is magic beyond any gift an Avallean can control.

"It's him, isn't it?"

"Please don't be angry," she whispers.

The quiet plea cleaves me in two.

"Oh, I'm furious. But never with you, love." I want so badly to hold her, but I don't know if I'm allowed. Will it make things better, or worse?

She sucks in a deep breath. Ever so slowly, without ever looking away, she lowers her arms. The fists balled at her sides don't escape my notice, and I could destroy Xavier for those alone. One day, I will.

But now is not the time for vengeance.

"Do you want to stop and go to bed, kitten? Because we can." It may cause me to combust, but I'll do anything she needs.

One by one, she undoes the buttons of my shirt and sloughs it off of me with excruciating slowness. There's a new fire in her movements now, smoldering and deep. When her hand reaches my waistband, she runs a maddening fingertip around the bare skin above, the touch as dangerous as a knife's edge. A shiver rolls across my flesh as she says, "I want to go to bed, but I don't want to stop."

Thank the Fates.

I barely pause to yank my jeans off and throw them onto the growing pile of clothes in the center of the room before I have her on the bed in a blink. I reach out and graze my knuckles over her cheekbone, then trace the slender column of her throat with my fingers until I hit the scalloped edge of her bra. She sucks in a breath as I slide a finger under the cup and roll it around her tight nipple.

"This has to go," I murmur, snaking my free hand behind her back to try and unhook it, but I can't find the latch along the lacy straps.

"It's in the front."

Her tiny giggle morphs into a moan as I finally remove the damned thing and replace my finger with my mouth, swirling my tongue in small circles. I ghost my hand up and down her spine, lost in the intoxicating softness of her skin. Goosebumps follow in my wake. If I had the time, I'd map every one of them, a glorious Braille meant only for me. I'll spend forever learning every line.

Her small moans and grumbles increase as she writhes beneath me, searching for something more than my teasing. She's caught between frustration and pleasure, and it's driving me as crazy as it is her. In the darkness, she can't see how hard she's making me, but I'm positive she can feel the evidence straining against my boxers where I'm pressed against her.

"Conall, please," she begs, "I need you."

Holding a gun to my head wouldn't make me deny her.

She reaches between us and eases my boxers off of my hips as much as she can, freeing my cock. It springs forward against my stomach with a glistening bead at the tip. I finish what she started. Once my clothes hit the floor, I peel her panties down her legs to join them.

I line myself up at her entrance, rubbing my broad head through her arousal. "You're drenched, kitten. All for me." It comes out as a growl.

Suddenly, something occurs to me that stops me cold.

"Shit—I don't have any protection. I didn't think you'd forgive me; this was the last thing on my mind."

I could punch myself. We're finally here, and I'm not prepared.

"It's all right, I'm on the pill. And I haven't been with anyone in years. Not since, you know." Her blush is adorable, the pink haze mixing with the flush of desire already painted on her face. "And I'm going to go out on a limb and say the guy with the healing magic is clean."

"The guy with the healing magic has never done this at all, so he's clean."

She pushes herself up abruptly, almost smashing her forehead into my nose. "You're a virgin? But you're so...so..."

"Glad to see my inexperience isn't readily apparent," I say. "I've never had anyone I wanted to get close to. Not until you. You're it for me." I plant a small kiss on the tip of her nose, unable to keep from touching her.

Love and lust blend in her gaze, an irresistible cocktail. "I'm honored."

"So am I."

I capture her lips in a lingering kiss, intending to be romantic, but quickly lose focus as I rock my hips forward and ease inside her, inch by decadent inch. By the time I am finally seated completely, sheathed to the hilt, I'm panting against her open mouth.

"Conall," she gasps. "Full. So full." Her blown pupils meet mine, glazed and glassy with need.

"Are you okay, kitten?" I groan. "Can I?" It's taking everything in me *not* to move. I don't know if I'll be able to be gentle; she's too exquisite.

At her frantic nod, I give an experimental roll of my hips and almost explode. I don't know if I'll be able to last.

I don't know if I'll ever be able to leave this bed.

Another slow slide has me seeing stars, and my wildcat rewards me with a long, low moan as I repeat the motion again and again, slowly increasing the pace. My mind scrambles for anything—flowers, star systems, an exhaustive list of the pranks Gaius has pulled in the last six months—anything to slow the waves of heat already threatening to barrel along my spine.

"*Harder*," she cries.

She circles my waist with her hands and lifts her hips to meet my thrust, plunging me in until I bottom out against her.

There's my wildcat.

I grip her hips and pull out to the tip, then drive back into her, hard and fast. Her back arches off of the bed as she claws at my back with every thrust. The pleasure-pain drives me out of my mind. I'll wear the brands of her ecstasy for days to come, even if it means fighting my magic to keep them there.

The slick sounds of damp skin and rough kisses mix with our moans and fill the room. My movements grow sloppy; I can't hold back any longer. I reach between us and rub her clit in tiny circles until she's manic beneath me. She's scrabbling at the sheets and crying out my name like a prayer.

Her velvet warmth pulses around me as she comes undone, and I follow her over the edge. I manage to roll onto my side as I collapse onto the bed so she isn't crushed beneath me. She nestles into my arms, spent and sated.

That was...indescribable.

A small sniffle disturbs the replay running through my head. To my horror, I look down and find quiet tears raining onto my chest.

"Kitten? What's wrong? Did I hurt you? Valorie!" I knew I should have been gentler, but I couldn't stop.

If she's hurt, I'll never forgive myself.

"I'm fine, Conall," she says with a watery chuckle. "You can stop trying to heal me."

Huh? Where our bodies meet, my hands glow faintly in the darkness, pouring my magic into her. I pull back the wave of power, locking it away inside of my chest. I can't think of a time when I've lost control of my ability.

"You promise you're all right?" I can't help but ask again.

"Yes, I promise. Everything is wonderful. I love you so much." Another sniffle, and a small sob. "I wish you were the only one I'd ever been with." And then, barely audible: "I wish I wasn't so ruined."

“Don’t you dare,” I say, scooping her into my arms. Neither of us has managed to retrieve clothes, but there’s nothing sexual about our embrace now. There’s only comfort.

I don’t expect an explanation, but the words pour out of her in a flood. “He broke me, bit by bit, all while making me think I was never worth more than the crumbs of affection he let me scrape off of the floor beneath him. He left me twisted up inside, confusing love and pain and fear, and it’s taking a while to untie the knots. Can you heal that, magic man?”

“I promise you I can, but not by magic. Give me some time, and I’ll fix it all. You only have to believe,” I vow.

She moves to rise, but I sprint to the bathroom and come back with a damp rag before she can leave the bed. Despite her protests, she relaxes further into the nest of pillows with each pass of the warm cloth.

I’ll take care of her like this every night if she’ll let me. It would be the most important task I’ve ever been assigned.

Afterwards, when she’s snug and clean in my arms beneath sheets and starlight, I hear her whisper, clear as the dawn, “I believe in you.”

Chapter 30
The Conservatory

- Valorie -

The air outside of the conservatory is damp and quiet. This far from the center of campus, the raucous parties in the dorms fade away to little more than a gentle thrum of bass through crackling speakers. You wouldn't think ten a.m. would be a prime party hour, but any time is party time during spring break at Sycamore. The comparatively tame front yard barbecues will transition to much rowdier house parties once evening falls. I plan to be far from here by then, and hopefully elbow-deep in takeout and drinks on Charlie's couch.

I push through the twin sets of double doors into the atrium and the morning's calm is replaced with angry squawks and chittering echoing through the branching hallways. The animals here are spoiled rotten. If I'm not on time, they make sure to let me know they're pissed about it. I'm a whole five minutes late today, which means they're practically starving.

Adorable little brats.

"I'm coming, I'm coming!" I shout into the deserted rotunda.

The food preparation room is right off of the center area, which sounds great in theory. In actuality, it means a lot of trips back and forth with a heavily laden feed cart. I'm trying to convince Sanderson to let me install a separate prep room in each hall, but he's not seeing the purpose.

Of course not, because I'm the one doing the feeding. He's wonderful, but sometimes the man is a bit clueless. I should do it and ask for forgiveness later. If he even notices.

Shutting myself into the cramped prep room blocks out the worst of the noise. The occasional hoot or yip still reaches me from the crack under the door, but at least it's quiet enough for me to start cataloging today's meals. I grab some of the labeled jars, cartons, and baskets overflowing the shelves on the wall beside me. These get joined on the steel worktable by the fresh meats, plants, and fishes I pull from an industrial fridge on the opposite wall. Thankfully, the whole carcasses for the larger predators are kept in a separate walk-in freezer—there's no way I'd have the space to store those in here.

Half of the chopped veggies and proteins get sorted and stacked in the fridge for Dane, the graduate zoology student who feeds the animals on my off days. Technically, he's supposed to feed them every day as part of his independent study, but this is second nature to me at this point. I grew up tailing Sanderson and his associates up and down these halls; these animals have known me their entire lives at Sycamore. They're used to me, while Dane only transferred to our campus last year.

"Something told me I'd find you here."

I'd know that voice from beyond the grave.

"Was it the schedule I know you copied off of my fridge, stalker boy?" I ask with a wink.

"You know, I think it might have been. What a smart girl you are," Conall says, wrapping his arms around me from behind.

He rests his head on my shoulder while I finish the last of my prep work. Conall helps me load up today's meals onto the gray cart by the door, piling them much neater than I do when I'm alone. I go to push the heavily-laden cart out of the room, but he stops me.

"Let me push that, kitten," he says.

I swat playfully at his hands, giggling. "Back off, magic man. I may not have your alien super-strength, but I like pushing the cart."

He gives in with an overly dramatic sigh and follows me.

"They're all awfully grumpy today," he remarks when we stop in front of the large aquarium housing Larry, Mo, and Curly.

The three axolotls press against the glass, eagerly searching for food. Their chubby pink bodies tumble over each other amidst the swaying plants.

"They're a bunch of babies, whining for their breakfast." I toss the blackworms into the water and move down the line.

Conall watches me feed every species in the building like I'm his favorite TV show. He asks questions about each animal we pass, which is great for me because I love talking about everyone here.

"Tina only eats her meals if you hide them next to this rock," I say while I clamber into the Eastern box turtle habitat, carefully avoiding the small clutch of eggs.

We've been attempting to breed Tina and Tony for years. This is their first successful mating—those eggs are precious. I'd rather break an ankle than crush them by taking the easier route through the rocks.

When he questions why we skip the large Burmese python enclosure at the end of the hall, I answer, "Noodles only eats once or twice a month. He's probably sleeping right now, so we'll leave him be."

On and on we roam, up and down the winding rows of animals while I entertain Conall with tales about them. From the pygmy hedgehogs we took in when the county police raided an animal hoarder, to the brightly colored poison dart frogs rescued from a busted drug ring. The idiots attempted to lick them for hallucinogenics. Every animal here has a story, and most of them are unpleasant ones. Maybe that's why I relate to them so much.

"Training with Finn is going well, I hear," he says while he helps me fill up the cart for the last time.

This bunch of food is the heaviest. It's for our larger animals in the outdoor enclosures.

"Surprisingly well. He says I'm a fast learner."

The added muscle from our training sessions is coming in handy this morning. Hopefully, Finn won't want to fit in a session today. I'll be exhausted after finishing up the rest of the feedings.

Conall pushes his bottom lip out in an adorable pout, holding the door open for me and the overloaded cart that I still won't let him push.

"I still don't understand why I can't train you. Why does Finn get all the fun?"

"I told you, if you're there in the yard I'll spend all my time staring at you shirtless and never learn a thing."

"I don't have to be shirtless, kitten."

I wave my hand towards his body in an all-encompassing gesture. "When you look like *that* you do."

His pleased snicker follows me all the way to the private exit to the outdoor enclosures, and I find myself laughing along with him. I've always enjoyed my mornings with the animals, but having Conall by my side has been infinitely nicer than my usual solitude. Everything is brighter with him around; he's my personal sunshine. I want to spend every day like this, lost in laughter and finding the fun in mundane tasks together when we're old and gray.

A sudden, horrible realization pierces through my brain. My steps falter, and Conall looks at me with concern. I'm too stricken to worry about answering the question that's written in his expression.

There won't be any growing old and gray. Not for him, anyway.

It'll be me, here on my own when Conall inevitably gets sent off on some mission far from here or goes back to his own world without me. Or worse, he'll stay at his Haven and remain young and beautiful one neighborhood away while I waste away through the years. We'll cross paths in thirty years and he'll still be the man I love, but he'll see me and be disgusted.

How could I possibly stand that?

A pair of strong arms and the scent of pine and lavender envelop me, holding the panic at bay enough for me to return to reality. I drag in a ragged breath.

"We have an expiration date, don't we?" The words are muffled against his chest, but I know he can hear me perfectly.

The hand rubbing soothing circles on my back stills. "What do you mean?" he asks, pulling back so he can see my face.

"You won't be here forever," I say. "Or maybe the more important fact is *I* won't be here forever. I'll get old and frail and you just...won't. It's not feasible to expect this to last when we're so different. I wish I was born an Avallean, or you were born a human, or I could become like you or something. Why couldn't that be possible? Why do we have to end? I don't want us to end..." my rambling trails off into dejected sniffles, and I turn away.

I'm halfway to the enclosure filled with white-cheeked gibbons when it occurs to me: Conall isn't glued to my heels like he's been all day. When I turn around, he's standing where I left him, staring into space like he's concentrating on something I can't see.

"Conall?" I call.

He looks up at me, his expression unreadable. "What if it was possible?"

I open my mouth to ask him what the hell he's talking about, but the creaky wheels of my brain slowly begin to turn.

Is he saying what I think he's saying?

Could I truly become an Avallean?

What would that even entail? You can't up and change your actual *species* on a whim...can you? I can't exactly say I've ever tried to, unless you count attempting to become a mermaid when I was seven. I expect becoming an Avallean would involve swallowing a lot less pool water.

He jogs up to where I'm waiting, and I admit, "I'm gonna need some explanation."

As we walk, Conall tells me there is a ceremony the Paragons can do to turn me into an Avallean. He says it's almost never done, as dehmi rarely become so close with humans while on assignment, but they've already said they would make an exception in this case. All I have to do is ask.

A huge grin spreads across my face. This is a perfect solution to our problem. I'm practically skipping behind my supply cart, envisioning an eternity of fun and happiness with Conall and his family.

Conall doesn't share my enthusiasm. His brows are downcast over the compressed line of his mouth. Is it because he doesn't want me to be like them? But why would he have mentioned the ceremony if that were the case?

I swing open the gate behind the gibbon house and place their basket of food at the bottom of the large tree they congregate in. Five little faces peer out at me from the branches, eagerly waiting for me to leave so they can pounce on their meal.

When I return to the cart, leaving the shrill clamoring of happy primates behind me, he's still pensive and quiet. "I'd appreciate it if you told me why you look so upset. I'm about to freak out," I tell him honestly. "This seems like a great idea, so what's the problem?"

He sighs. "It's not as easy as it seems. There are...stipulations."

A catch.

Of course, there's a catch.

Several catches, from the sound of it.

I wheel my way towards the musical din of the aviary, head tipped up towards the cloudless sky. I need to keep moving so I don't freak out, and the gentle touch of the spring breeze on my face is helping me stay calm.

These "stipulations" can't be anything too terrible. It's probably something simple he thinks will upset me. Conall worries too much where I'm concerned. Maybe I have to go live in the Haven with them, or I have to start completing jobs like they do. Whatever it is, it can't be dangerous. Conall wouldn't put me in harm's way.

I wish he would hurry up and tell me. I'm starting to spiral over here.

We make it all the way to the sleeping barn owls at the very end of the hall by the time he finally starts talking. By this point, I'm a nervous wreck, despite repeatedly telling myself everything will be fine.

He sits with his head in his hands on the low wall outside of the aviary exit. I perch anxiously next to him in the lukewarm midday light, flightier than the birds happily munching on their meal. My foot taps a nervous beat against the rear wheel of the cart, waiting for the bomb to drop.

"If we complete the ceremony, we have to leave."

A small bit of my anxiety fades away. Okay, so I do have to go live in the Haven. That's nothing. Of course he would think I'd be worried about moving, but it's not the end of the world. I barely see my parents at home, anyway.

"That's fine," I assure him, "I like the Haven. I won't have any issues living there, as long as your family doesn't mind."

He's already shaking his head before I finish speaking.

"No, Valorie." His voice is low and cautious, a tone one would use on a cornered animal. "We would have to go to Avallea."

"*Oookay*," I say slowly," and when would we come back?"

"You would not be able to leave our world for what amounts to thirteen years here."

Screech.

The jerk of my foot sends the supply cart careening away in front of us.

Stay calm, Val, stay calm. "I'm sorry, *what*?"

Way to go, not.

My focus is spotty at best, but I manage to grasp the gist of what he's saying. According to Conall, in order to become an Avallean, my entire body would be converted from human genetic material to an Avallean's genetics. Avalleans apparently have a strange, mixed form of DNA containing minuscule bits and pieces of material from all of the worlds they watch over. This allows them to send dehmi wherever they're needed without acclimating them to the planet beforehand. It's also what allows them to smoothly return home once their time on a mortal world has been served.

However, this pieced-together quilt of a genome means all Avalleans have to spend their first thirteen years of life solely within the confines of their home world. Their body needs this time to stabilize before they are able to leave, otherwise, they risk having their very genes become unstable. Conall says that would result in their immune systems attacking their own cells, not unlike autoimmune diseases here. In this case, there is no treatment or cure. The affected Avallean simply dies a horribly painful, slow death over a matter of weeks.

Thick silence blankets the yard when he's finished. I start heading back towards the main building in hopes the motion will once again help me stay calm while I work through another new pile of information. Conall follows silently behind, giving me space to think.

Icy anxiety slinks its way through my body, doing its best to freeze me solid while my legs continue to move. I either have to give up the man I love, or lose contact with my entire known world for over a decade. By the time we came back, I'd be thirty-four. What the hell kind of choice is that?

I peer over my shoulder at him as we reenter the main hall. He's bathed half in the shadow of the building and half in the bright light of day, and I have to catch my breath. The dark lines of his face, gleaming forest eyes, and the gilded oil slick of his wavy hair combine to paint a portrait that's half angel, half demon, and all mine.

"What would I do in Avallea?" My mind is not cut out to sit around barefoot and pregnant, so he better not say that or I'm out. I need some type of work to do to ease the cacophony constantly swirling inside of my skull. Here I've got my work at the conservatory, but what will I have in an entirely new world?

"Whatever you want," he replies with a wistful sigh. A glint of hopeful longing is shining deep within his irises. "It's not draining like the intense capitalism you find here. In Avallea, everyone picks something they enjoy to spend their time doing as a profession. Everything is useful in some way, and the Paragons ensure everything functions smoothly without hampering the joy of life. There is peace there; nobody needs to fight or struggle to eat or stay warm. The magic of the world itself provides for its inhabitants."

Magic. How could I forget that they have magic in Avallea? *Wait...*

"Would I have magic?"

His grin is lightning, bright and intense. "Yes, wildcat, you would."

That might settle it. There's no way I could pass up the opportunity to have magical powers. Ten-year-old, fairy-obsessed Valorie would come back and haunt me if I did.

"And in thirteen years we could come back? To visit, at least?"

He kisses the top of my head.

Conall knows how much I love my little group of people here. He knows what's running through my head right now, holding me back from jumping at this chance. There's no need to say all of it out loud.

"It's not common because it's taxing to move between the worlds frequently, but yes. I'll make it happen whenever you wish."

In thirteen years, everyone would be fine. David and Charlie are spending the next five or more years in Europe for Charlie's research position, so I wouldn't be seeing them much anyway. My parents would still be young enough that I wouldn't have to worry about them not being here when we come back. I don't see them much these days either if I'm being honest. Some physical distance may be good for all of us.

Back in the dim halls of the main exhibit building, I lock the cart inside the preparation room and lean heavily against the cold door. This day has become more tiring than I expected, but I've made my decision.

"Okay, I'm in. I'll become a magic-slinging alien freak for you." He laughs at my exaggerated wink and sweeps me up in a kiss.

I can feel the tension leaving his body right here under the dim hallway lights.

"Thank goodness that's over," I sigh against his shoulder. "I'm exhausted."

He takes a small step back and grimaces. "There's also the matter of *how* the ceremony is completed."

Here we go again.

I sigh. "What's the problem this time?" What could be so bad that he picks this as the second shoe he's going to drop? What's worse than telling me I literally need to leave my entire world behind?

Suddenly, Conall finds his interlocked hands incredibly interesting, the way he always does when he's nervous. Guess I'm not the only one experiencing the stress of today's conversations.

"In order to give your body the material it needs to complete the change, you and I would have to exchange pieces of our souls. We would be inextricably linked, forever. You would never be free from me. We would be one, in life and in death."

That's all?

Relief floods me in a wave. He says this as if it should scare me, and I guess logically it should, but it doesn't. Not at all. The whole reason I wanted this in the first place was to ensure Conall and I could stay together. It's only slightly terrifying to hear we would be tied to one another by our very souls. 'Til death do us part, literally.

I'm less worried about me, and more about him.

"Would that be a problem for you?" I ask, afraid to look him in the eye. "Would you regret it down the line, being stuck with a mess like me?"

Will he grow to hate our tether in a hundred years, or a thousand? A shiver runs through me at the idea I could be alive a millennium from now. Immortality is much scarier than being soul-bound to Conall. In fact, I don't think I'd be comfortable with living indefinitely if I wasn't going in with the assurance that I'd have a teammate for the long haul.

Forever is a long time to be alone.

"Never," he snarls, his ferocity as alarming as it is comforting. He grabs my shoulders and pulls me into his chest in a rough embrace, as though he thinks I'll disappear if I'm not crushed against him. "No matter where I go, if you are not there it is no place for me. I want nothing to do with the riches and wonder of the cosmos without you by my side. You are my eternity, my immortality. Without you, there is no life for me."

The tears finally fall. I try to stop them, but it's no use. I soak his shirt with years of pain and loneliness. Years of worrying David and Charlie would always be the only people to understand me. Years of fear that one day they'd move on with their lives together and I'd always be the annoying tag-along. It all flows out in a deluge of emotion, and I'm left with a heart that's a thousand pounds lighter.

For once, the devil inside my brain can't take away my peace.

Chapter 31

New Beginnings

- Valorie -

"Valorie! We're going to be late!"

I spare a second in the frantic destruction of my closet to look over at the clock. *Shit*. It's already eleven? Where did the hours go?

"Valorie!"

"Hold on a second, Mom! Chill!" I aim my shout in the general direction of the door, not caring enough to get up. They'll hear me. Mom is probably halfway up the staircase at this point, anyhow.

I should have taken Charlie up on his offer to let me ride with his family this morning. Things would have been much less stressful; the Rothschilds are the calm antithesis to David's wild clan. Spending time with them is always soothing. But no, my parents wanted us all to ride to graduation together, and I'm trying to spend whatever time I can with them while I still can.

The end of the month is sneaking up on us. Only two weeks left before everything changes.

Aha! Buried under bags full of, well, more bags, a single gold heel struggles to escape the wreckage of the closet floor. I heroically rescue the poor shoe and slip it onto my foot, where it can live out the next few hours in the company of its friend before probably ending up right back where it started. It might make it into a moving box this time, but I don't have high hopes.

I navigate the maze of cardboard boxes and duffel bags strewn about my bedroom floor. The official story is I'm moving in with Conall, so everything I own is getting packed and taken to the Haven's cavernous storage room. Since we can't take much of anything with us to Avallea, I already gave Gabrielle full reign over everything I'm leaving behind.

I thunder down the stairs as fast as I can without toppling over. "I'm here! You can quit having a complex."

Dad chuckles under his breath from his spot by the open front door, but mom doesn't find me funny. She's the if-you-aren't-early-you're-late type, and my repeated attempts to explain we don't need to arrive an hour beforehand since they both have designated professor parking and floor seats have fallen on deaf ears. I'm surprised she isn't already in the car with her elbow mashed into the horn.

Since I value my life, I shoot a wink at dad and follow them out of the house and into the back seat of their Durango without riling her up any further. We pass the short ride to the college's stadium in companionable silence. It strikes me as we pass through the campus gates—this may be the last time I'm in a car with my parents, and they don't know it. They think I'm moving to a place within a ten minute drive, not a whole world away. It's a sobering thought, but I know they'll be fine. They haven't needed me in a long time.

We pull up at the college, and from that point on everything seems to roll by in spurts, like an old, moth-nibbled roll of film stuck in fast-forward.

David, Charlie, and I find our spots in the back half of the line of graduates winding through the stadium's main entry tunnel.

A brush of air and invisible press of lips to my forehead lets me know Conall has arrived just as the ceremony starts. Two seconds later, he pops up in the crowd, beaming next to the waving bunch of dehmi I've come to love over the past weeks.

Sweat beads on my neck and rolls down to get caught in my collar. I silently curse the staff member who chose navy blue for our regalia.

Speeches blend and blur into a faceless whirlwind of jumbled words and applause.

The press of bodies shuffles forward in time with a loudspeaker's roll call.

One diploma, two handshakes, three posed pictures, four families cheering for me in the crowd.

Then, it's all over. Goodbye, Sycamore. Next stop, Avallea.

Someone plops into the Adirondack chair next to mine, their body haloed by the slowly setting sun. I know who it is without him needing to speak—that gigantic frame can only belong to one person.

"Are you nervous?" Finn asks, his ever-present smile becoming soft and comforting.

"Honestly? A little. I'm used to nervousness, though." Nervousness, nausea, clammy hands, chest pains—anxiety leads to a ton of fun experiences, and I've collected the whole set over the years.

He leans over and pats my arm with a giant, yet strangely delicate hand, calluses scraping gently against my skin. Sometimes it feels like Finn and I have known each other for years instead of a handful of months. We spend almost every day together, between our frequent training sessions and slightly less frequent, but much more enjoyable, hang-outs. He's quickly become one of my best friends, and I'll miss him when we leave.

If I could, I'd bring Conall's whole family to Avallea with us. Hell, I'd bring our whole mismatched crew.

We look out over the bustling graduation party in my backyard. Our families and friends are mixing together in the twilight, the line between ordinary and extraordinary smudged away for one night of celebration. Domenic and my father stand with Sanderson and David's dad, Marland, chatting animatedly about something that has them all laughing. All of the moms have taken it upon themselves to teach Margie how to play cornhole on the opposite side of the yard, while Conall and Gabrielle have their heads together, deep in conversation with David and Charlie by the tree-line. Of course Gaius has decided to help Charlie's dad with lighting a tiki torch perimeter around the gathering. He's trying to be covert, but I watch him sneak a few lazy flicks of flame out towards far away torches when he thinks nobody is looking.

Everyone I love is encapsulated in this small slice of forever. I soak it in, begging my memory to brand itself with the pure happiness in front of me. The smell of the charcoal grill and honeysuckle, the friendly chatter and the cicadas droning in the background—I implant it all into my brain while I have the chance. It's achingly bittersweet, somehow both wonderful and melancholy, and I find myself fighting back tears at the sight.

Conall hugs the boys and heads over to where most of the dads have gathered. I expect him to turn to Domenic, but instead he taps my father on his shoulder and begins talking. He tilts his chin towards his fidgeting hands, avoiding eye contact.

I ask Finn, "What's going on down there? Why's Conall nervous? He's doing that hand thing he always does when he can't find his words."

"Hmm, dunno." Finn shrugs, suddenly finding the wood grain beneath his fingers very interesting.

Normally his secrecy would set my heart racing, but I chuckle and punch him in the arm. "You're a terrible liar. You know exactly what's going on, don't you?"

He sports an overly agonized face, rubbing his arm and pointing. "No clue what you're talking about, but he doesn't look too nervous anymore. Maybe he was worried your dad would murder him for stealing your virtue or something."

"You're such an ass," I laugh.

Across the lawn, my father and Conall are embracing in that awkward way men do, complete with lots of back pats and swinging arms. *What the hell is going on?*

My confusion only grows when Conall begins to head towards our spot on the deck. He's followed closely by David, Charlie, and Gabrielle. Even Gaius peels away and joins their procession as they reach the bottom of the stairs and begin to climb.

"Kitten," Conall calls softly when they arrive in front of our chairs, "can you please come over here for a second?"

Everyone is staring at us and wearing Cheshire cat grins from ear to ear, but I'm still bewildered. I move to stand in front of him, but it isn't until he lowers himself to the ground that I begin to grasp what's going on here.

Conall's voice is all sultry moonlit nights and summer breezes, and his gaze overflows with emotion as he says, "Valorie Catherine Vargas, I'll keep this short because I know you don't like people staring."

He's absolutely right, and all eyes are on us right now, but I can't focus on anything other than what he's saying right this second.

"You came into my life like a meteor, obliterating everything I was and remaking my entire world into a new and beautiful place. I cannot imagine another second without you by my side. Would you please do me the honor of being my wife for the rest of eternity?"

I gasp as he pulls out a small blue box from behind his back and presents it with a flourish. Nestled inside is the most perfect ring, an oval shaped emerald accompanied by tiny sparkling diamonds in a white gold band.

All I can do is nod through the elated tears pouring down my face. I collapse into his arms as our family cheers around us.

Conall whispers, "I wanted to do this the human way for your family, so they know exactly how cherished you are. And the stones are all lab created, so nobody was hurt and there wasn't any mining involved. I know sustainability is important to you, with your work and the animals."

I breathe in the bright lavender and smoky pine that's uniquely Conall, and it smells like forever. How did I ever manage to find someone who fits me so perfectly?

Who knows, but I'm never letting him go.

A trio of face-splitting smiles surrounds me as my parents and Sanderson appear at the top of the stairs. I'm forced to let go of Conall to allow us to talk with our families. We're both passed through a sea of smiling faces and well-wishers until I end up deposited in front of my two oldest friends. One look at Charlie and David and I burst into happy tears again, flinging myself at the two of them so hard they rock backwards.

"Congratulations, Vally, you deserve every bit of happiness," David says softly into my left ear.

Charlie murmurs his agreement on my right.

My ribs creak and my nose twitches as it's tickled by a blend of honey-brown curls and silky dyed strands—cherry-blossom-pink this month—but I wouldn't change a thing. I've spent so much of my life sandwiched right here between the two of them, and now we're going our separate ways for a long while. It's exhilarating and terrifying, but I manage to shove my devil back into its cage.

I won't let anxiety taint this. My demons have no place here.

They pull back in unison, thrusting their arms in front of me. "And look, we're going to be triplets, like always!"

Shocked laughter pours out of me at the sight of the matching diamond bands on their left hands. Of course the three of us would embark on this next phase of our lives together. We've always been in sync. I won't be around to witness it, but I'm so happy the two of them are going off to start their lives together.

"Listen, you two," I keep my voice low so the other revelers around us don't hear. I'm not giving much of an explanation for my upcoming absence to anyone else, but the three of us do everything together. They deserve some type of warning. "Conall's work is going to be taking us to some pretty remote places for a few years. I may not be around for a while, or have cell service, but I promise I'll come back eventually, 'kay?"

The two of them look like they're gearing up for a round of questioning, so I shake my head and pull them into another hug. Any more talking about our ticking clock and I'll crack.

A voice drifts through our huddle. "Mind if I cut in, boys?"

Margie hovers next to us, smiling as we untangle our mass of limbs and hair. Charlie ruffles the top of my head, David plants a smacking kiss on my cheek, and the two of them head over to congratulate Conall. Seeing them together, I realize what they must have been conspiring about while Finn and I were people-watching.

Margie's arms are open and waiting for a hug. I fall into them, eager to soak up every bit of her motherly charm. We bonded on that first day in the kitchen at the Haven, and I spent many days by her side while I was recovering from my hospital stay last fall. Thanks to her, I'll always associate chilly autumn afternoons with fresh pumpkin bread and raunchy jokes inside a warm kitchen.

Thud. Thud-thud.

Three bodies barrel into us at high speed, and I'm quickly crushed under a dog-pile of dehmi. They're all laughing and shouting over one another to try and be the first to officially welcome me to the family. All I can see are jostling arms and mismatched bits of clothing. Even waifish Gabrielle is a foot taller than I am.

"It was so hard not to tell you! You almost made me spill the beans!" Finn yells as he squeezes his head under Margie's arm to find me.

Gaius pokes in next, shoving Finn back out in an impressive feat of strength. "Welcome to the club, sis." He gives a roguish wink.

I'm hoping he doesn't know which bedroom upstairs is mine.

"I knew it would work out if Conall could only stop being such an idiot. Congratulations," Gabrielle says. She somehow manages to look completely unruffled in all this chaos. There's suddenly a far-off, puzzled look on her face, laced with a fear that's out of place here, but she ducks out. I miss my chance to ask her if she needs help.

To my surprise, Domenic wades into the throng. He looks around at his family's antics and says, "You'll fit in just fine if you can survive all this nonsense." A quirked grin and a nod, then he disappears.

Conall finally reappears and his family envelops him, pressing him against me in the center of the storm. He catches my eye and shrugs, his indulgent expression saying *What can you do?* I lean in and kiss him inside our tent of bodies while the party rages around us.

It's the most wonderful insanity I've ever experienced.

Chapter 32
Preparations

- Conall -

The rapid rustling of leaves is my only warning. A small, yet surprisingly spear-like oak branch crashes to the ground six inches from my head. A sneeze-inducing puff of pollen explodes out on impact, coating me in green dust.

"That one almost hit me!"

A chuckle from high above is her reply.

I'll admit that, when I brought Valorie to this untouched glen on the edge of the Haven grounds, lying alone on the warm grass while she climbed trees wasn't exactly what I had in mind. I've always known she enjoyed the call of nature, but I didn't think she would want to experience it quite so directly. I expected us to spend a lazy Tuesday tangled up together, picking bits of grass and leaves off of each other's bodies after shedding our clothes.

She immediately decided to climb, however, and I can never resist her excitement. Now I have a rock under my back instead of my girl in my lap while she scales a massive, knotted oak.

I move away from the annoyingly sharp stone and onto a softer patch of grass. "Are you coming down soon, wildcat?"

"You know," she calls, "you could come up here. It's beautiful!"

"I quite like my view from here, thanks." She has on a short, lime green dress today, and this angle affords me a few choice glimpses as she climbs.

"Perv," she laughs.

Another leafy branch hits the ground where I was seated a moment ago.

I watch her for a few more minutes until she disappears from view around the bole of the tree. Having her out of my sight makes my skin crawl, and the gilded clearing is much less exciting with only the robin's egg sky for company. It's time to get up and join her.

The limbs shift and sway as I slink up to find my wildcat nestled in the crook of a wide bough nearly twenty feet up. She's oblivious to my presence until I crouch behind her and aim a careful puff of air directly into hcr lcft car.

"Shit!" Her arms windmill around as she lists dangerously to one side, her eyes like saucers.

I can't help but laugh while I help her return to safety, only this time I lean back along the rough bark and flatten her against me, chest to chest.

Her smile is radiant, brighter than the rays beating down from the almost-summer sky. Here amidst the shadows of the canopy, she's other-worldly, an elven maiden I've stumbled upon in her forest home. Valorie once asked me if fairies exist, and I told her nothing of the sort lived on this particular planet. Seeing her now, dappled in shades of green as if she's part of the leaves themselves, I may need to rescind my statement. Were a human from ages past able to see her now, how could they not believe in magic?

Her shallow, excited breaths draw me in. My thoughts narrow until all I can think about is her full lips on mine and the rival sensations of soft skin and craggy bark. I sweep my lips against the seam of her mouth and she opens for me, twining her tongue against mine. She breathes out a soft sigh that settles in my core, and I need more of them. I can never resist her sounds, her scent, the way her body softens at my touch. She drives me to the brink of insanity and hurls me over the edge every time.

My hands go to her hips, grinding her into my lap as she sucks my lower lip into her mouth. Her small nibbles send shockwaves through me, and I know she can feel precisely how much I want her. I should have brought her to the forest floor first, but I couldn't bear to wait another second. If my brothers knew how every bit of my training and composure flies out the window around Valorie, they'd find a way to use her to gain the upper hand in sparring with me. Now I'm torn between continuing to kiss her here in the trees, or having to let go of her mouth long enough to get us both to the ground.

She pauses her attack on my lips to trail a line of wet kisses across my jaw and down to my collarbone. I arch my neck to give her better access, but she doesn't take advantage of it.

"Kitten?"

All I get in response is a quiet "Shhh."

Her delicate fingers grasp my cock through the fabric of my pants, forcing a gasp from my lungs. One firm squeeze and I'm already so turned on it's almost painful. She's barely touched me and I'm panting up into the rustling treetops, trying not to explode like a teenage boy with his first crush.

Valorie unzips my jeans and frees her prize without pausing her nibbling on my collarbone, a confident move that's hotter than the Sahara. I fist my hand in her hair and drag her face up to mine as she swirls beads of arousal around the swollen head. Bliss rolls over me with her first teasing stroke, but I force my lids to stay open. She is a vision far beyond anything that could exist behind my closed lids; I don't want to miss any part of this experience.

Her grip tightens as she reaches the base. She slowly pulls her hand back up to the tip and gives a decadent twist of her wrist. I'm seeing entire galaxies, gasping into the open air as she increases her pace. She's an angel, a demon, a wild creature made only for me. Every plunge of her hand pushes me closer to the edge, and I'm ready to take the leap.

"Con? Val?"

Oh, *fuck.* Why the hell is Gabrielle here? I love my sister, but in this instant I could kill her with a smile on my face.

One glance upwards and she will find me in a very compromising position. Delicious, but compromising.

A hand slaps over my mouth in time to muffle my next moan. "Gabrielle," Valorie calls in a voice so nonchalant I would think she was caught in some monumentally boring task if it wasn't for her slick hand running up and down my shaft, "I'll give you ten bucks if you come back in, oh, five minutes or so?"

Five minutes? She expects me to last another five minutes? She'll be lucky to get a single one.

"See you in five, then. We need to discuss tomorrow." Gabrielle's gentle voice drifts off as she moves away.

Tomorrow. Tomorrow is important, but it's for the best she comes back later. Currently, I wouldn't be much of an asset to any conversation. I'm not positive I could tell you the date. All I know is I might die right here in this tree if my wildcat takes her hands off of me. I nip at her hand, lick her palm. Anything to touch her, caress her, taste her as she rocks my world.

Release is already burning its way down my spine. I'm a train off the rails, barreling towards the point of no return with each slide of her damp palm, every twist of her wrist over my dripping head. My hips move of their own accord, thrusting upwards as she pumps.

I'm so close.

"Kitten," I choke out, "I—I...I can't stop..."

A devilish smile is my only warning. Her hot mouth closes around my cock and she hums low in her throat.

I am undone.

When I'm finally spent, I pull her up, nestling her against me while I catch my breath. She smiles and pecks me innocently on the chin like she didn't flip my entire world upside-down on an oak branch two stories in the air.

"You're indescribable," I breathe into her hair. She smells like summer fruit, and sweat, and *me*. I can't get enough.

"Can I come back now, or are you guys still doing naughty things to that poor tree?"

Our laughter leads the way as we descend to meet up with Gabrielle in the clearing. There's an overly large picnic set up on one of Margie's old quilts in the middle of the grassy circle, sandwiches and salads piled high in a wicker basket. Gabby is busy pouring a red liquid which—judging by the tangy smell—is cranberry juice into fluted plastic glasses while we settle ourselves onto the blanket across from her.

"So, here's the plan," she says once we've made our plates. Her head turns to Valorie on my left. "Thursday morning, Finn and I will come get you at five, while Conall is here prepping the Sacrarium." It's my turn to meet her gaze as she says, "Esraa and Amon will get here on time, so don't be late. We'll start at six thirty on the dot. That's enough time for her to get bathed and dressed and all of us to conquer those two hundred stairs without breaking our necks."

It's nowhere near two hundred, but my sister loves dramatics as much as the rest of the family.

A certain small facet of her plan buzzes around in my brain. My brows furrow, and I grumble, "Finn stays *outside* while you help her get ready, Gabby." I love my brother, but I won't be able to focus on my part of the preparations if I know he's far above me in the bowels of the Haven, sharing a room with the naked woman I love.

A dismissive wave. "Sure, sure."

It occurs to me the third member of this picnic has been awfully quiet lately, and I'd bet Gaius his very own key to my room that I can guess why. Sure enough, her hands are fisted in her lap, an untouched chicken salad sandwich on the plate at her feet. As if she can sense my gaze on her, she looks up and meets my concerned look with pupils blown wide and unseeing. That plump lower lip tucks in under her top teeth, and I reach out to rescue it from her anxious self-mutilation.

"Penny for your thoughts?" I murmur, rubbing soothing circles on her thigh.

She leans into my touch, a small action which never fails to send a flood of warmth through me. Her trust in me, despite everything I've done, is a miracle.

Her voice is almost a whisper, though it would never stop Gabby or myself from being able to hear her perfectly. "Just nervous. What if I screw something up?"

"There's nothing for you to screw up," Gabrielle cuts in, her expression gentle as she leans in towards our side of the quilt. "You show up, and they work their magic. I know you can manage standing next to lover boy over there. You two are nearly surgically attached to one another as it is."

Her terrible joke earns a small laugh, and I shoot a grateful tilt of the head at my wonderful sister.

With the tension broken, the rest of the afternoon passes in a collage of jokes and stories and enough food to feed a small army. The balmy air is cut by a breeze full of the sweet headiness of honeysuckle which keeps the worst of the heat off of us while we eat and talk the day away. We tear through a plate of cookies hidden at the bottom of the picnic basket until none of us can manage another bite. Stuffed and sated, we lie on the pink and white quilt and I play with Valorie's hair while Gabrielle tells us tales of visions she's had that never came to pass.

"And there was this one" — she gasps, barely containing her fits of laughter — "I swear it was so real, where Gaius and Domenic were dancing this ridiculous jig at the holiday party. Complete with costumes and a song. I spent all day trying to See what liquor made them that crazed, but I could never quite sharpen the picture enough." With a sigh so large and aggrieved you would think the world was ending, she says, "Oh, well, there's always next year."

Valorie is near tears, practically convulsing against my chest from laughing so hard. She'd be on the ground if my arms weren't firmly around her to hold her up. Lids screwed shut in her mirth, she doesn't notice the look of pure horror that crashes in a wave across Gabrielle's face. A cyclone of fear barrels through the twilit glen, wiping away any traces of levity.

"Gabs, what is it?" I ask.

Her stare is darting wildly around the clearing as she scrambles to her feet. "It's nothing. I've got to go."

"What the hell did you See, Gabrielle?" I bolt to my feet, barely managing to keep Valorie from falling over. I don't know if I'm yelling or not at this point. I need to know what made her look like someone was dying. Like someone is *going* to die.

She faces us, but her gaze is lost halfway in another time. "Don't worry about it, Con. I just need sleep. I'll be there bright and early Thursday, Val. Don't make us late."

And she's gone, silvery hair whipping behind her like a spectral harbinger as she flees her own vision.

"Gabrielle!" My shout ricochets off of the evening gloom.

She doesn't reappear.

Chapter 33
Last Hurrah

- Valorie -

The sun is almost below the horizon by the time I pull into David's driveway for our so-called engagement sleepover. I had planned to get here two hours ago, but moving all of my belongings into storage at the Haven took longer than I expected, even with Finn's help. And I may have loitered around the grounds for a bit once we were finished. I was hoping to catch a glimpse of Conall while I was there, but he was busy with Dom and Margie setting up the space for tomorrow's ceremony. It's held in some type of underground chamber I've never seen. Finn said it's only used for meeting with Paragons, like a inter-dimensional conference room.

Sounds fancy. And intimidating.

Gabrielle hasn't left her room since she fled our picnic yesterday evening. Finn says she won't speak to anyone, not even Gaius. She keeps mumbling something about "It can't happen" and "Need to fix it." It's pretty terrifying, and I can tell the whole Haven is on edge.

For once, I was relieved to leave the mansion. If I can't get an answer as to what's bothering her, I need a distraction. Otherwise, I'll be up all night long worrying about the worst-case scenario, and I absolutely do not want to show up tomorrow morning with exhaustion written all over my face. There will be enough anxiety ricocheting through my brain without adding sleeplessness to the mix.

I race up the patio steps and into the muggy depths of the Wilson-Curbelo's small covered porch. It's barely dusk, but moths have already congregated around the wrought-iron sconce next to the door. I grab the knob and open it without knocking, slipping in through the slimmest crack in an attempt to keep the bugs outside where they belong.

"*Ay Dios mio,*" David's mother tuts when I slam the door behind me. "Those bugs are driving me crazy, and it's not summer yet." She waves me through the kitchen and into the cozy dining room decorated in turquoise and gold.

"Cozy" describes the house perfectly. It's slightly smaller than ours, but in a comforting way, like the whole house is hugging you. Our house is all smooth surfaces and crisp lines, but Adriana and Marland have their home decked in colors and embroidery, everything covered with some memento or representation of their two cultures. Like the flowered chair cushions David's grandmother made for their mismatched dining chairs, or the traditional wedding outfits in a shadow box halfway up the staircase.

As a kid, this house always felt like one big party to me, all vibrant hues and lively music. Now that I'm older, I can appreciate the calm of my own home—or I guess my parents' home—but something about David's house still brings me back to our innocent days of childhood fun.

Thinking about David summons him from the top of the stairs, and he motions for me to follow him, likely rescuing me from a long conversation with his well-meaning but loquacious parents.

“Escape, escape,” he stage-whispers dramatically as we tumble into his room like we’re twelve again.

Charlie slams the door and we collapse into a pile of giggles on the floor.

All of the lights in David’s small bedroom are off, but strings of fairy lights across the ceiling give off a dim glow. A giant mound of every soft thing the boys could find takes up the entire floor. The television has been moved off of the dresser and onto an orange crate next to the pile to create what David has dubbed “the optimal viewing experience.” Currently, it’s more like the optimal hysterical laughter experience. I doubt any of us can see the Netflix menu that’s waiting patiently for us to stop acting like fools.

When we’ve wiped our cheeks and collected ourselves, Charlie asks, “No Conall tonight?”

I shake my head, giving the party line: he’s busy with work. I wish he could be here, but part of me cherishes spending last night of my humanity with the two guys who have had my back since the beginning.

Oh, how I wish I could tell them the truth. It kills me to know tomorrow they’re going to try to text me like they’ve done every day, and Gabrielle will have to pretend to be me. It’s her job to keep up appearances until people get used to the idea of not contacting me. She’ll feed everyone a story about a trip to a remote area of Japan where I won’t have consistent cell service. Hopefully, people will buy it. The lie hurts, but it’s the only way. With Dee and Char, I already planted the seeds in their heads the other night, so hopefully it won’t seem too suspicious.

But for tonight, I’m going to forget everything and celebrate with my best friends.

"Drink up, bitch!" David's voice reaches a decibel level usually reserved for jet engines as the Jenga tower tumbles to the floor for the fifth time tonight.

I groan. "All right, all right, but this is my last one. For real this time." The tequila goes down smoothly, sloshing around with its siblings and nearly half of a pepperoni lover's pizza in my stomach. "I've got an early flight tomorrow, remember?"

"Nobody wants an airport hangover." Charlie nods sagely, his irises twin pools of deep blue staring straight into my soul.

I stiffen, sure that he's suspected something is up with my story, but he only laughs.

"David is going to be completely cut off the day before our flight to London. I'm giving all the liquor to Tomas and hiding his keys."

"You act like I'm some kind of alcoholic," David complains, hand on his chest in mock affront.

"No, honey," Charlie soothes, "you just love any excuse for a good party."

I snag another slice of pizza, gooey cheese slopping halfway onto my plate. A large scoop of chow mein joins it, nearly buckling the cheap paper already soaked with grease and sauce as I lean in for more food. Pizza and Chinese food, our go-to party spread since we were first trusted with the take-out menus in sixth grade.

David's face is wrinkled in disgust. His eye twitches as he looks at my plate like it's physically hurting him to be in the same room as my masterpiece. "What is that monstrosity?"

"What? It's delicious. Sweet, spicy, savory, all mixed together!" I finish putting the last chunk of General Tso's chicken onto my pizza slice and take a large bite. I don't care what David says, it's the perfect combination.

"You're one to talk, Dee," Charlie says from where he's lounging in our makeshift floor nest of pillows and throw blankets, "you eat your fries dipped in peanut butter."

"Now *that's* good eating." David laughs maniacally.

Char and I pretend to gag.

I'm going to miss this so much.

David and Charlie leave for Europe ten days from now, so they wouldn't be here if I chose to stay. That doesn't lessen the sting of knowing this is our last night together for more than a decade.

"Hey, Vally," Dee calls.

He's standing beside his computer desk, adjusting the volume of our playlist. Anything to avoid his mom comes up here threatening us all with a *chancla*. David swipes his hand across the desk and holds something out to me. It's my phone, complete with a tiny flashing red light at the top.

"Your phone keeps going off. I think someone called you."

I have no clue who would be calling me this late at night. Both of my parents left after dinner for a conference in Atlanta, and Conall wouldn't interrupt my last night with Dee and Char unless it was an emergency. If it was a true emergency, he'd probably be calling all three of us on repeat until he reached me.

Maybe it's Finn wanting to touch base? No, that makes no sense. We already hashed out the details when we were moving my things earlier. They'll meet me on the corner by David's house early in the morning and run me to the Haven to get ready.

I told David I was getting an Uber to the airport.

Maybe it's Conall after all. Maybe they finally figured out what was freaking Gabrielle out so badly. Maybe someone is hurt. Maybe, maybe, maybe.

Shut up, I tell myself, refusing to let my anxiety take over. It's probably nothing. There's no reason for my clammy hands or the heartbeat pounding in my temples. Everything is fine, I'm sure.

If I say it enough times, I'll believe it.

Right?

I slap a tense smile on my face and hold my hand out to him. "Hand it over, loser."

David gives me an odd look when he drops my phone into my hand and I know he saw right through my fake nonchalance. He's probably wondering why I'm freaking out over a phone call. The two of them always know when I'm anxious; I can never hide it from them. The truth about Conall's family is the first big secret I've ever kept from David and Charlie, and I'm surprised it's held up to their scrutiny for this long.

Heading out into the hallway for some privacy, I check my missed calls list.

Unknown number.

Great. Now I have to call some stranger and have them awkwardly tell me I have the wrong number when *they* called *me.* And they'll yell at me for inconveniencing them, conveniently forgetting again I'm only returning their call. Happens every time.

I'm tempted to erase the notification and continue on with the night, but I know if I leave it I'll be wondering if it was actually something important for the rest of the night. It'll needle at me until I can't focus on anything else. I might as well bite the bullet.

One ring turns into two, then three, then four.

I'm about to hang up and try again later when a gruff voice grumbles, "Hello?"

"Uhm, hi, yeah," I stammer, twisting my free hand into my hair. "You called my phone, but I think you had the wrong number?"

"Valorie? Valorie Vargas?"

The fact that he knows my name makes my stomach fall through the floor. "Yes?"

"It's Joran. We met at the Haven in December."

Well, at least it isn't a stalker.

Still, why in the world would Joran, someone I probably said three sentences to, be calling me? How did he get my number? I didn't know he was back in town. He wasn't around earlier today when I was moving.

His voice grates, "Conall asked me to give you a call. Apparently, the boy dropped his phone down some stairs. He said Finnegan is coming to get you in about fifteen minutes." Joran gives me an explanation, but it leaves me with more questions than answers.

I start pacing the hallway, the movement keeping me from freaking out too much. I'm trying not to be rude, since Joran is honestly a bit scary, but I don't understand what's going on. "Why is he coming to get me? I'm a bit busy."

He sounds annoyed as he replies, "Something about preparing for tomorrow."

"But we already prepped for tomorrow. Finn said he and Gabby will be here in the mor—"

"I'm only the messenger, girl, not a psychic. Get to the damn trees before somebody sees you. It's too early for them to run in plain sight."

The phone goes dead, and I'm left with a dull headache. Oh, and the annoying task of getting to the patch of woods at the end of David's street without him and Charlie asking a billion questions.

I pace a few more laps in the hall while I formulate a plan, the quiet scuff of my socked feet against the red carpeting barely audible over our muffled music.

I could say Conall wanted to bring something by for us?

No, they'd be suspicious when I come back empty-handed. And I can't tell them it's my parents, because they know Mom and Dad are on a plane to Georgia by now. I'll have to tell them Conall wanted to swing by and see me, and let them make fun of me for not being able to go one night without him. I can handle their jokes.

Creaking open the bedroom door, I peek in at the happy couple cuddling in the pillow nest. David is attempting to braid Charlie's short hair while his man looks for a movie for us to watch. Neither of them pays much attention as I tell them I'll be right back, and I duck back out into the hall.

Night has truly fallen, the star-filled sky radiant above me while I quietly leave David's house. Nobody is on the sidewalks except for me, and only a couple of cars enter and leave driveways near the entrance to the street. They're too far away to notice me in the dark, but their headlights make me nervous. I duck hastily into the copse of trees and look around.

Without the glow of the stars and the full moon, it's pitch black beneath the trees. Dry grass crunching and rustling beneath my feet, I turn slowly in a circle, looking for my friend.

"Finn?" I call in a whisper, barely loud enough to be heard. There's no reason to be quiet—I could yell and nobody would hear me—but instinct keeps me secretive. My hands start to sweat again, and I wipe them on my pajama pants, waiting for someone to show up.

Branches creak and crack behind me, and I turn towards Finn.

"Finally, I was getting anxious..." My sentence fades into a gasp.

I immediately recognize the person behind me.

It isn't Finn.

Chapter 34

The Knot in the Web

- Valorie -

"Well, well, well, if it isn't a little lost girl all alone in the woods."

Xavier emerges from the bushes, his taunts oozing ahead of him in the gloom. It's enough to make my blood run cold, but I can't let him see any reaction. He thrives off of the high he gets from lording over others, and I won't give him that satisfaction tonight.

I draw myself up to my full height, desperately wishing I was wearing something more intimidating than *The Lion King* pajama pants and a threadbare tee from last year's Broadway production of *Grease*.

"Go away, Xavier. I'm waiting for someone." My flippant wave fakes a confidence I'm not managing to find inside.

"Out here in the dark?" He chuckles.

The menacing sound drips like cold oil along my spine.

"Looks to me like you're waiting for trouble, Valorie. And trouble came to find you."

I tuck my shaking hands behind my back where he can't see them and pray I can keep up this disinterested facade. The cloud of anxiety that followed me around has dissipated these past few months, but seeing Xavier drags me back to that dark, sad place I lived in for so long. How I ever confused the fear he filled me with for love is beyond me, but I won't ever make that mistake again. I'm not helpless anymore. I only have to stay calm until I can make my escape.

Where the hell is Finn?

He must still be on his way to get me. Until he shows up, I'll have to fend for myself. I face Xavier head-on, prepared to listen to his self-absorbed rambling for a while. The quicker I get this over with, the quicker he'll leave. Maybe if I act like I don't care what he thinks, he'll get bored and go away.

A girl can dream.

I huff, hands on my hips. "What is it? Let's get this over with."

Immediately, I know it's the wrong move.

"What the hell did you say to me?" Xavier's eyes bug out and his fists clench, warning me with not a second to spare.

My fists fly up into the defensive stance Finn has drilled into my head over weeks of training. Still, I manage to barely block his blow. I throw a perfectly formed fist and whoop when it connects with Xavier's nose. The look of utter shock on his face is priceless. I wish I could frame it and hang it around my neck.

He takes a split second to process then goes berserk, flinging punches and kicks at me like a toddler throwing a tantrum. It's the exact method Finn taught me *not* to use, as poorly formed moves are typically easier to dodge or block. Unfortunately, I don't account for the slick undergrowth or the fact that Xavier weighs twice as much as I do and isn't pulling punches for training purposes. All of my sessions with Finn took place on the flat, dry dirt of the training yard—a far cry from this damp forest floor. My feet are planted on a springy patch of clover, and it quickly becomes apparent I'm woefully unprepared for my first taste of actual combat. I guard my face but lose my footing, skidding along the grass until a rock sends me hurtling into the slick ground.

Out of nowhere, something hard slams into my side once, twice, a third time. Sharp, hot pain radiates through my ribcage with each blow. Wheezing, I sit up in time to catch Xavier's foot before it can break something. I may be downed, but I'm not going out without a fight. If I can hold on until Finn arrives, everything will be fine.

Starting tomorrow, I'm doubling my training time.

"You want to know why I'm here?" Xavier shouts from where he stands, far above me.

Another kick punctuates his question. This time, he catches my shin. My scream spikes in tandem with the *snap* under my skin. I start dragging myself along the ground, dirt grinding itself under my fingernails as I scrabble for purchase. There's no way for me to escape him, though. Not with a broken leg.

There's nowhere to run this time.

Finn, please hurry.

"I'm here because you're out running around with some loser, making me look like a fool when you're supposed to be on my arm like a good trophy. I *earned* you, you stupid bitch." His heel lowers almost gently onto my left hand, but he keeps slowly adding pressure until my bones are grinding together beneath his muddy leather loafers.

Only Xavier would stalk someone into the woods in Cole Haan shoes and a navy sports coat, so assured he would get his way without dirtying his expensive clothes. Well, wasn't he wrong. He's completely disheveled, covered in blood and grime from his gushing nose. It would be laughable if I wasn't fighting for my life.

"I'm here because you've forced me to fail half of my classes without you doing your job and making sure my assignments are complete! I'm here because you made me look like a fool! I'm here because you *belong to me*!"

Antagonizing him is undoubtedly a stupid move, but I can't handle him walking over me anymore. I sit up, directing my swollen visage straight at his feral grimace, and roar, "I belong to *no one*!"

His fist connects perfectly with my cheekbone, a direct hit. It hurts, but not as much as the sickening crack I hear when the back of my head hits something hard on the ground. My free hand reaches around to poke at the mushy, wet mass beneath my hair.

A rock. The stabbing piece of shrapnel at the base of my skull must be a rock.

My mouth is filled with thick, ferrous liquid, too much to breathe around. I try to expel it, but only manage a series of weak coughs that send a spatter across the grass in front of me.

I stare at it, vision going in and out. Finally, I realize why my spit is a muted crimson against the shadowy ground.

It's blood.

"Oh, shit," Xavier whispers. He's backing slowly away from me, torn between staring at his bloody hands and my battered body in the grass. "Shit, shit, *shit*! Look what you did! Why couldn't you shut up?"

A wet, exhausted laugh gurgles up from deep within me as he panics. Something about him freaking out, blood glazing the brown leather of his precious, stupid shoes, has my body laughing until I'm convulsing. I'm so tired, but I can't stop. Everything smells like dirt and iron and broken blades of grass, and the whole world is a mess of throbbing pain.

"Fuck this. I'm not sticking around here waiting for someone to show up. You're all ruined now anyway. He'll get rid of you, too."

The coward turns and flees towards the street.

Somewhere above me, an owl hoots into the stars. I'm guessing there are still stars, but I can't see them, or much of anything else. My vision blurs and refocuses over and over, until I'm finally able to see another shadowy figure step through the brush in front of me. It's not Finn, and it isn't Xavier either. From this angle, my view isn't much more than a pair of denim-clad legs.

That won't do; I can't have a conversation with a pair of jeans.

I roll my head upwards until I can see his face. My hysterics have finally sputtered out, replaced by a dull fog. Distantly, I am aware the squelch of my skull against the ground should hurt, but I don't feel much of anything right now. Colors, sights, smells, sounds—everything is muted.

It takes a long second for me to piece together the features of the man in front of me, but when I do, a detached sense of relief throbs behind my forehead. "Joran," I garble.

I think I smile at him. It might be my imagination.

He crouches next to my head. "Miss Vargas, so good to see you like this."

Well, that's a weird way to say "I'm here to rescue you." I'll take it, though. I'm too tired to argue.

"Can you...Conall?" The bubbles are back in my throat, making their red journey out of my lips and onto the grass once again. I need a healer, but that's a sentence far beyond my capacity right now. Hopefully, Joran will put two and two together, and quickly.

"He's not here right now, Miss Vargas." A strange, cold smile forms on his stubbled face.

Ugh. I know he's not here, which is why I'm trying to ask for him. Come on, Joran, I need you to work with me here.

I'll have to try a different tactic.

"Finn?" I ask in my new, broken English. Finn is good, he'll know what to do. Let's get Finn here, please.

He shakes his head slowly.

My vision stretches and dims, forming a tunnel that makes me strain to see his expression. It doesn't look like pity. He looks...happy.

I manage to dig deep and find the strength for one more word, though I'm beginning to think it's the last thing he's offering me. "Help?" Energy spent, I roll onto my back and look up at the far-off, blurry leaves.

"Oh, I am helping, you silly girl. I'm helping Conall, and Domenic, and all of Avallea. One day, they'll thank me for this."

My battered, aching heart turns to ash in my gut.

There's no help to be found here. This isn't a rescue.

It's an assassination.

Words are beyond me at this point, so I keep my stare on the branches waving hello far above me and pray Finn makes it in time.

Making the most of his captive audience, Joran continues, "For too long, Avalleans have been slaves to the mortal races. Races and worlds far, far beneath us. Why should we be the ones to toil thanklessly for them, when we could be gods?"

His hand slices through the air in my direction. "And you! It's disgusting that a dehmi with as much promise as Conall Raoult would fall for the ploys of some stupid, human chit. He should have killed you when he had the chance, soft-hearted boy. But no, he fashions himself in *love* with *you*! How absurd! And for those idiots in the Underworld to waste their powers making a *mortal* into one of us? For them to treat you as if you could possibly ever be equal to an Avallean? It made us all sick when we found out."

"Us"? He definitely said "us". Are there others who think this way? Conall said the Avalleans are peaceful. He said they're thankful for their time as dehmi, because it pays for their lifestyle and security back home.

Apparently, not everyone subscribes to their ideology.

His voice turns low and sinister, losing the fervor from his speech. "They wanted to send a younger dehmi from our brotherhood to deal with you, but I asked for the pleasure. Little did I know Conall would tell me your little sob story about Xavier during my visit. I barely had to get my hands dirty. All I did was make sure Xavier knew you would be alone in the woods tonight, and now" — he looms over me, twisted, pursed lips filled with scorn, feet inches from my nose — "it looks like it's only a matter of time."

I want so badly for him to be wrong, but somehow I know he hasn't lied to me once tonight. I try to move away from him, but it's no use. My blood has turned the churned dirt into mud beneath me, coating my back and sucking me in. It's as if the ground doesn't want to lose its hold on me.

Not that I would be able to attempt an escape even if I could roll. I barely have the energy to extend my twisted fingers and tear a dangling strip of fabric from the edge of his fraying pants. Hopefully, someone will know what it means when they find me.

They *are* going to find me, right?

A flash of light in the forest could be a shooting star or a god's wink telling me everything is fine. But no, it happens again, and it's only Joran photographing the mangled remains of my body, presumably for his brotherhood buddies. I'm sure they're waiting back at whatever secret lair they use to hatch their plans to kill innocent women in the woods.

My vision fades again, and I see myself from far above. Then back through my own eyes. Away, and back, over and over until I would be nauseous if I still had that level of control over my body. The pain comes rushing back for one more blistering round and drifts off into the night. This time, it does not return.

Finn, where are you?

David...Charlie...anyone?

Conall...

I'm sorry.

My heart thumps and sputters in the silence, a drum beat for a dirge.

It heaves and stutters.

Gallops and stumbles.

And then...

It stops.

Epilogue

- Conall -

Finally.

Today is the day.

I spent most of the night tossing and turning in my tangled sheets, unable to sleep without Valorie's soft warmth in my arms. The idea that this morning will be the beginning of our eternity kept my blood racing until I seriously contemplated going to David's house and crawling into the burrow the three of them made to sleep in on his bedroom floor. I know that's what happened, since I received a picture last night of the three of them piled atop a mound of bedclothes, laughing and smiling for the camera with the glow of several strings of white lights around them.

I couldn't interrupt her last night with her best friends, even if it meant a largely sleepless night for me. Instead, I sketched her profile by moonlight, creating a thousand different Valories until I finally plunged into slumber, hand still curled around the pencil currently jabbing me in the cheek.

Part of me aches with the knowledge that I'm stealing her from everyone and everything she's ever known, but it's a small part. Valorie made her decision, and I have to respect her wishes. She spent too long under someone else's thumb; I won't take her agency from her. Selfishly,

I wouldn't want to convince her to stay here, not that she could choose that option and live. I'll simply make sure to keep her as happy and safe as possible for the next thirteen years until we can return here to her family.

I hope she loves Avallea. I know I will. It's in my blood. It's my home.

Not much is told to the dehmi about our home world—things are purposely kept vague to keep us focused on our tasks—but I know it's a world of endless peace and prosperity, where magic flows like oxygen. How can an ethereal, magnificent creature like Valorie not thrive in a place so mystical?

The quiet klaxon of my alarm clock on the nightstand lets me know it's time to begin. Clothes and the few personal items I'm allowed to bring to Avallea are laid out on the chair in the corner, ready and waiting. I shrug into the bright blue shirt Valorie bought me for Christmas, remembering her jokes about how my wardrobe needed some life, some color.

She's become so confident in her own skin lately, such a change from the anxious girl I met all those months ago. I constantly try not to recall the awful day when I almost lost her forever, but it crops up in my memories when I least expect it. Through the terror, a part of me was so infinitely proud of the fact she was able to stand up for herself.

She's changed so much in these past few months. No longer does she bow to other people's whims without a care for herself. She's willing to start a fight and, thanks to Finn's teachings, she knows how to finish one. I know her anxiety will never truly leave her be, but she has come such a long way, and I cannot wait to see her flourish in a new world where she can be herself. I'll be by her side every step of the way, starting with this morning's ceremony.

Which I will certainly miss if I don't hurry.

I purposely left myself next to no time to get to the Sacrarium. I knew any extra minutes would be spent trying to convince myself not to go check on Valorie in the chamber where she's preparing with Finn and Gabby. I was hoping for some type of message from one of them, maybe a picture of my smiling family readying for this morning, but my phone has been silent all night. Now, it's no longer needed. Gabby will be in charge of both my and Valorie's phones for the foreseeable future. I grab mine off of the dresser to bring to her and head towards the door.

Well, this explains the lack of correspondence. The battery is dead. There's no time to charge it now, so I'll tell Gabrielle to make sure to plug it in when we leave.

Sprinting out of the bedroom, I stop and almost lock my door, but decide against it. Gaius has no reason to come in here if I am not around to fall for his pranks. The door squeaks slightly in a quiet goodbye as I close it for the last time.

I thunder through the hallway, taking the steps two at a time. Nobody is around to complain about the noise this morning; everyone is already downstairs. I will be the last to arrive at this rate, which means Valorie will already be there. She will be waiting for me, surrounded by my loved ones and the Paragons of the Underworld. The image sets my heart to racing faster than my feet fly across the plush, red carpet.

Down and around I go, through the hallway I got stuck in when Finn stole Valorie the first day I brought her to our home. Over the small burn mark in the foyer floor where Gaius lost control of a flame he was playing with when we were fifteen. I master the rough, freezing stone stairs leading to the place where this all began with a vision of my mercury-eyed girl one year ago.

The door to the Sacrarium is shut tight in front of me, ice-crusted steel glinting faintly in the blue-white light of a single, glowing crystal embedded in the jagged wall. A few deep breaths help to calm the gallop of my heart, but not by much. Small fizzles of electricity seem to have replaced my blood, and I bounce from one foot to the other in a vain attempt to settle myself.

So much for stoic, unflappable Conall. I feel like a newly assigned dehmi on his first set of practical exams, jittery and nervous. One more breath and I give up on trying to calm myself and seem unaffected. Let my family make their jokes; I will suffer through them forever if it means I get to have Valorie by my side.

With a wide, unbreakable grin across my face, I shove open the heavy doors. Lost in my euphoria, I barely notice the icy surface pulling at my hands, leeching their warmth and sticking slightly when I remove them. Every atom in my body is focused entirely on making its way to Valorie's side as quickly as possible.

A quick scan of the room confirms all five members of my immortal family are here, congregated around Esraa and Amon at the front of the room. The Paragons stare intently at something between them, but my view is blocked by a phalanx of stiff backs. The ensorcelled chandelier shines shafts of pure moonlight onto seven heads, gilding them with silver light, but the star of this morning's ceremony is conspicuously absent. My head swivels, trying to find her in some nonexistent corner of the sparsely-decorated room.

It's no use. Valorie's not here.

"Where is she?" I ask, trying to keep my tone light. I don't think it works, but it doesn't seem to matter, since nobody pays me any mind.

"Finn?"

No response.

"Gabrielle?" I am inaudible, a ghost.

All pretense of calm gone, I begin yelling as I rush towards them, "Where is she? Somebody talk to me!"

Gabrielle turns, and all of my momentum screeches to a halt at the sight of her tears.

She chokes and hiccups as she says, "Con, we tried to call you—tried to get you to open your door."

"You didn't answer," Gaius speaks now, his mask of grief making him match his twin sister for the first time.

No. That can't be true. I would have heard something...would have felt *something.*

My knees threaten to buckle beneath me and send me to the hard floor. Only sheer will and paralyzing terror hold me upright and rigid. My frantic eyes examine my family's faces in the cold light, searching for a reason behind their pain on what should be the happiest day of my life.

Domenic, the unflappable bastion of our family, shakes as he faces me. The sight of his trembling sends another spear into my heart. "Finnegan and Gabrielle were worried when Valorie did not meet them at the assigned location this morning. They went to search for her."

"And what?" I cry. "They couldn't find her? She's missing?"

Why aren't they out looking for her? Why is everyone *standing here*?

Gabby, sweet, caring Gabrielle, burdened with Seeing all of us, drops to the floor and wails. When Finn moves to pick her up, I finally see what the Paragons have been so focused on all this time.

There she is.

Not missing at all.

I make no conscious movements and yet, somehow, I'm at her side in a blink. For a brief moment, my fallible retinas trick my brain into thinking she's merely asleep in her crusted, dirt-stained pajamas. My brain believes it when my nose says the tang of iron is from the metals in the room, and not from the sticky mat of curls and broken flesh at the base of her skull. My skin processes her cold, lifeless texture and claims it's from the frigid air. The silence of her heartbeat? My ears assure me it's only because my own is pounding too loudly, covering her sweet melody.

But it's all a lie. A sweet, glorious lie, when the truth is right in front of me.

My knees finally collapse, slicing open against the stone table she's resting on. I pull her into my lap and cradle the only person to ever truly understand me. Hands blazing with all the healing power I can pour out into her body, I rock back and forth, torn between silence and screaming. Finn and Domenic attempt to peel my hands off her, shouting that I'll burn myself up for nothing, but they're wrong.

I'll burn myself to ash if it brings her back.

My nose buried in her hair, I inhale, searching for her. Beneath the musty taint of mud and gore, the faint whiff of pears and warm spring days is a ghostly wrecking ball, smashing through the twisted horror of this morning and filling me with her. Each deep breath tears me apart, but that sweet thread sews me together enough to stand again. I brush her mangled curls away and wish I could look into her bright, thunder-cloud eyes one more time, hear her laugh in the loud way she tried to hide from the world, see the smile that rebuilt my whole world despite my best efforts to ignore her. She didn't need to become an Avallean; she was magical from the very start.

And now I've lost her.

"*How*!?" I rage, whirling around at my family without letting go.

I'd carry her forever if I could, but eventually, I'll have to leave her. The idea is horrifying, world-ending.

"How?" Sobs drown out the rest of my questions as they whirl themselves into a vortex inside my skull.

Who was it?

Did she die alone in the dirt, like an animal?

Was anyone there to hold her hand and tell her not to worry?

Did she think we abandoned her?

Did she think I *abandoned her?*

My blurred vision focuses on Gabrielle's broken figure in front of me. Through the mangled remains of my brain, wisps of memory tease their way to the forefront. Gabby running from the clearing on that bright, wonderful afternoon. Her forced solitude in her room, ignoring everyone. The muttering, whispering tracks she would wend through the grounds, avoiding the questions we would pepper her with.

"You *knew.*" The hiss emerging from my ragged throat is inhuman, a demon's rage-filled rasp. "You knew this was going to happen. You *Saw* it, with that damned talent of yours, and you hid it from all of us! Did the Paragons put you up to this? Turn you against us, against your family, so they could ensure Justine makes her damn discovery? Were you hiding this the entire time?"

She reaches for me, but I whirl away from her grasp, desperate for answers. "Con...no, I swear, I—I would never do that! I Saw something vague in the clearing—a shadow, a murky spot—but it never cleared up, so I was trying to get details before I came to you. I didn't know...I couldn't See.... "

"Then *why*?" The last word is a broken wail, a call to the void, to anyone who could possibly bring her back.

Finn steps in front of me and holds out a small scrap of dark material. "We found this in her hand. It smells like—"

"Joran." His scent is all over it, unmistakable.

He's worn one style of jeans as long as I've known him, never listening when Margie tried to convince him to modernize over the years. He should have taken her advice; it might have made him harder to track.

"I don't understand why he would betray our family." Of course Domenic is disturbed. He and Joran have been close for decades. But I don't need to know why. Joran's bullshit reasoning doesn't matter at all, frankly. All I care about is how my father's old friend has signed his death warrant. A warrant I'll be more than happy to fulfill.

Taking one last gulping breath into her hair, I lift my face towards my family. I know what needs to be done. "Form up; we've got a hunt to begin."

"My son," a voice like the wind itself calls from behind me, stopping all of my turbulent, half-made plans.

I have no choice but to face Esraa and Amon's kind, sad faces, covered in crystalline tears. Two sets of glowing stares bear down on me, at once both inquisitive and comforting.

A small spark of hope flickers, adrift in my sea of grief. They control the Underworld itself...

As if she can hear my desperate pleas, Esraa gently places her hand on Valorie's silent heart and says, "There is a way."

"A way—a way to save her?" I choke. "You can bring her back?"

Amon shakes his head and my hopes are capsized until he says, "No. But you can."

Someone behind me gasps, possibly Margie, but I'm stunned into silence. My family might as well not exist. I'm hanging off of the words of the Paragons in front of me, waiting for them to explain.

The smile Esraa wears is tiny and fragile as glass, but I cling to it almost as fiercely as I cling to Valorie's cold shell, still wrapped safely in my arms as though holding her now can make up for not protecting her when she needed me most.

Esraa's hand glows with a gentle white light as she declares, "I have sent one of our own to locate her spirit and journey with her to a safe place deep within the Underworld. There, she will be protected by our sacred stewards. If she and her guardian can make it to this location, we can complete the ceremony so unfairly postponed today."

Postponed.

"Postponed" is a good word, a temporary state. Postponed means they think I have a real chance at saving her. It means they think one day, she'll be alive in my arms again. With that to bolster me, I can do whatever it takes to get her back.

Shoulders square, head back, trembling hands forever wrapped around Valorie, I ask, "Where do I come in?"

"Ah," Amon sighs, "you must complete a journey of your own through the Underworld. And, as one of the living, you will not have a guide like your lost love. Use your strengths and your wit, my son, and claim what you have lost."

"If you accept, we will send you to the very entrance of the Underworld. There exists a quiet settlement of souls who refuse to move on. Find the mapmaker, Sorail, within its walls. Inform him your goal is The Crystal Forest." He reaches out to clasp my shoulder. "Be swift, my son, and we will find you when the time is right. If you make it, that is."

I lay the body that housed my heart and soul gently back onto the stones, promising I will find her, wherever she is. "I'm ready. Let's begin."

"Well, give us a second to get some traveling clothes, won't you?" Finn drawls at my back.

In the rear of the room, my four siblings stand in various states of undress. A pile of durable canvas and leather clothing is haphazardly stacked in front of them, with Dom shoving more into our pre-made packs in one of the plush armchairs. Margie must have disappeared sometime during my conversation with the Paragons, but I can smell the aroma of baked goods drifting on the chill air, so she's somewhere close by.

My brows nearly reach my hairline. "What are you doing?"

"Going with you, of course," Gaius grunts, shoving his leg into a pair of green hiking pants. "Margie went to get us some goods for the road."

Here she comes, stumbling back down the slippery stairs with her arms filled with the bulging sacks of shelf-stable travel rations we keep on-hand in case of emergencies. Thrown over her shoulder is a plastic sack full of produce and fresh breads, the latter responsible for the scent which preceded her arrival. Dom finishes adding food to the heavy-duty backpacks and zips them shut, a rolled sleeping bag tied to the top flap of each kit.

I don't bother arguing; I know it wouldn't work. My family is as stubborn as they come.

We pile together in the middle of the room, exchanging farewells and good lucks as we hug goodbye. Marguerite's soft hair tickles everyone's noses and Domenic's beard is scratchier than ever, but for once, nobody complains. As much as I wish they could travel with us, I know Dom and Margie need to stay here to run the Haven and search for Joran. They both promise to make Valorie's revenge their top priority, and I believe them. She is loved by everyone here almost as much as I love her.

I hope she knows this.

I'll tell her when we meet again.

Another swift kiss and fierce hug from the parents who gave up their early tickets home to Avallea so they could raise us instead, and we're finally ready to go. The past twenty minutes have felt like an eternity, but now no loose ends are left untied.

I face the newly formed portal, my family at my back. A swirling vortex of light fills the six-foot-tall oval, obscuring the world beyond. On the other side is a realm filled with unknowns; one where no living person beyond the Paragons of Death themselves is permitted to travel. All of our information on it comes from fables and hearsay, none of it proven to be fact and possibly all fiction. Am I prepared to jump in and risk everything, including my siblings, all for a chance to rescue the woman I love?

Absolutely.

The Playlist

Please enjoy a sampling of the amazing music that inspired Strands in the Web. For the full playlist, visit my website or social media, or search Strands in the Web on Spotify. All songs are property of their respective artists.

Same Boat – Lizzy McAlpine
I Don't Miss You At All – FINNEAS
Daydreams – We Three
Kiss Me Slowly – Parachute
Flares – The Script
Fashion Forward – The Home Team
Find A Way – SafetySuit
How Do I Tell You? – Lizzy McAlpine
Air I Breathe – Mat Kearney
See These Bones – Nada Surf
Valiant – The Spill Canvas
New Girl – FINNEAS
Same Way Too – We Three
Pancakes For Dinner – Lizzy McAlpine
Body Fat Percentage – We Three

Timeless – We Three

Fortress – Mat Kearney

When The Day Met The Night – Panic! At The Disco

Staplegunned – The Spill Canvas

Catch You – Dashboard Confessional

You're Dead Wrong – Mayday Parade

Airplane Mode – Hayd

Kerosene – Anson Seabra

Hold Onto Me – Mayday Parade

I Won't Give Up – Jason Mraz

Claudia – FINNEAS

Immortals – Fall Out Boy

Die Alone – FINNEAS

Connect The Dots – The Spill Canvas

Not An Angel – City Sleeps

Sunsets and Car Crashes – The Spill Canvas

Chasing Cars – Snow Patrol

Stolen – Dashboard Confessional

This Is Me – Keala Settle, Missy Elliott, Kesha

i wanna love somebody – We Three

doomsday – Lizzy McAlpine

hate to be lame – Lizzy McAlpine feat. FINNEAS

Till Forever Falls Apart – Ashe, FINNEAS

Body – Sleeping At Last

Crossfire – Brandon Flowers

hill that i'll die on – Jonah Kagan

Architecture – The Spill Canvas

Sky is the Limit – Mark Ambor

Acknowledgements

This book could have never happened without the help of way too many people to name here, but let's give it a shot.

First off, to my husband and daughter: I love you both endlessly, despite the fact that this book would have been finished way faster without you two constantly being up my ass every second of the day. Niko, thank you for always supporting me, even though you'll probably never actually read this book. You were the first person to tell me to be an author, and you're the devil on my shoulder telling me that a little more money spent is never an issue when it comes to publishing.

To Mom, Jeff, John, Justin, Uncle Roger, and the rest of my (very large) extended family: Thanks for reacting with absolutely zero shock when I said, "I think I'm finally going to write a novel." In fact, I'm pretty sure most of you asked what took me so long. Your complete confidence that I would be great has been so helpful. I love you all.

To Chris, who immediately insisted that my book would be so famous I'd forget all the little people and need wheelbarrows for all my money: Words will never express how grateful I am for your friendship. Your hilarious jokes, awesome merch ideas, and insistence that I'll need to preemptively pick a cast for my movie deal never fail to make me smile. Here's to the crazy curly-hair gang.

To my beta readers, Amanda, Katiria, Dakota, Melissa, and Devon: Thank you for politely tearing into my poor, defenseless little book baby, and helping me make it better than it ever would have been on my own. You were the first ones other than me to fall in love with Valorie and

Conall, and your mildly threatening comments and messages will live forever in my heart (and my docs folder).

A huge thank you to Mara for being the best admin/not-an-actual-PA/Internet bestie a girl could've ever hoped to find. Love you, girl. You'll move over here some day.

Thank you to my street and ARC teams, who continue to take time out of their busy lives to sing the praises of Valorie and Conall's story on their pages and in reviews.

To my Book Beasties, who went from random women I found in a bookstagram chat to some of my best friends: You are all amazing. Every day that I get to spend talking about smut and joking around with you all is filled with so much love, laughter, and camaraderie...and farm jokes. I never would have been able to navigate this journey without you girls. Love you more than Jana loves chickens.

And to you, the person who took a chance on this book, who decided to pick it up and immerse yourself in this world I've poured my sweat and blood and tears into: You freaking rock. I may not know you, but I love you. Stay awesome, and I hope to see you around for the next one.

About the Author

K.T. Host has been writing in some shape or form since she could hold a pencil. From poems, to stories, to scientific papers and professional statements—if you can create it with words, she's probably done it at least once. She has a bachelor's degree in biological sciences, which gives her unique insight into the inner workings of world-building and character design and helps her flesh out her stories. K.T. lives with her husband and daughter in a secret cavern in the deepest recesses of the cosmos, where she beans her books directly to you via a complex linked system of teleporters closely guarded by various international police agencies.

Follow K.T. on Instagram @k.t.hostauthor, on Facebook at K.T. Host, or on TikTok @kthostauthor to stay up-to-date on her latest shenanigans. Head over to https://kthostauthor.wixsite.com/kthost to sign up for her newsletter for even more sneak peeks and insider information.

www.ingramcontent.com/pod-product-compliance
Lightning Source LLC
Chambersburg PA
CBHW070612310726
48982CB00001B/62
9798990860919